Moira Forsyth is an author and editor. She has two grown-up children and lives in the Highlands of Scotland.

Also by Moira Forsyth

A MESSAGE
from the
OTHER SIDE

Moira Forsyth

SANDSTONEPRESS
HIGHLAND | SCOTLAND

First published in Great Britain by
Sandstone Press Ltd
Dochcarty Road
Dingwall
Ross-shire
IV15 9UG
Scotland

www.sandstonepress.com

The publisher acknowledges subsidy from Creative Scotland towards publication of
this volume.

ISBN: 978-1-910985-73-1
ISBNe: 978-1-910985-74-8

Cover design by Antigone Konstantinidou
Typeset by Iolaire Typography Ltd, Newtonmore
Printed and bound by Totem, Poland

For Rob

Acknowledgements

Grateful thanks to my sister Dorothy, always my first reader, to the Sandstone team and to Ruth Killick and Lucy Ramsay for their support.

Contents

Family Ties
2014

1

The dead are everywhere.

It began to dismay Catherine, how often and in how many places she saw the faces of those who had died. Sometimes their dying was so recent she had scarcely had time to get used to it, and once or twice took a few seconds to remember – oh, it *can't* be him. With some it was mildly dismaying; with others a plunge of shock.

She saw them in the street, on trains, at airports, in restaurants and bars, often when she was just waiting. Sometimes she felt she spent most of her life standing in a queue. On either side of her, people were poking and peering at smartphones, texting or checking something on the internet. She alone stood blankly doing nothing but shift her bag occasionally from one sore shoulder to the other. Then a face would catch her attention and she would say to herself that's – then the name, coming to her seconds later, would remind her: no, he's dead. Most of the dead were men. She did once fancy she saw Rose, but that was wishful thinking. She had had no news of Rose for years. She was probably still wreaking havoc in whatever pocket of London she now inhabited.

Of course, she acknowledged it was a stranger she saw, though uncannily like the person she had known. If they were far away, at the end of a train compartment as she was getting off, there and gone again, she sometimes went on believing – or wishing – she had seen him. The dead were everywhere, and had, perhaps, a message for her. What that message could be, she had no idea. At any rate, in all these faces, lined and worn or calm and thoughtful, usually grave but occasionally with the enigmatic smile of those who have escaped us, she saw something she wanted more of. Her memory tugged, making her think she was missing something.

It was not this disturbing idea, or the brief visions, that really unsettled her. It was that not one of them was the person she most wanted to see. The person who was, in a sense, the most dead of them all. That was the one person with a message she wanted to receive, but as the years dwindled past, she had given up hope.

A woman in the office had gone to what she called a séance, but which seemed to have been a spiritualist meeting. She was someone who so completely inhabited her office cubbyhole with its family photographs and small fluffy animals, her sign saying 'You don't have to be mad to work here, but it helps!' it was hard to imagine her away from work.

'I didn't sleep all night after,' she said. 'Not a wink. I says to Billy, it upset me, the idea of it.' She seemed more excited than upset, that the dead might communicate with the living. The medium was a silver-haired man called Gerald. 'A lovely suit and tie, he must make a fortune, we paid a tenner to get in.'

'So did you get a message then, from the other side?' Colin asked, leaning in the doorway, apparently on his way out, but still listening to the women talking. Colin was as reluctant to return to work as the rest of them, for all he kept saying he had to get back to his photocopying.

Catherine, having made her mug of tea, did not usually linger more than the few minutes necessary to show she didn't think herself too good for them. This time she waited, to hear what Irene would say.

'Yes, if you could call it a message. It was from my mother.'

'When did your mother pass away?' Colin said, his voice hushed with respect.

'That's the funny thing, well, not funny, but you know what I mean. Ten years to the day. When I went there, I'd forgotten, then when he said, does anyone know somebody called Isobel, Isobel has a message for you, I thought, it's the 30th of April, it's the very day she passed.'

Catherine was ready to pass herself, if only out of the door and downstairs to her office. Enough from the other side for one day.

Later, crossing the almost empty car park, she saw Dougie the janitor talking to someone by the gateway, and the someone was Hugh. She knew it was Hugh by the turn of his head, the way it angled when he was listening, his silvery hair that had always been fair, his tall thin frame, the slight stoop acquired as he got older. It was Hugh. She almost called his name.

The man turned and walked away and Dougie began tipping rubbish from the office waste baskets into the recycling bin, humming to himself. The man did not walk like Hugh, it was a cheaper sort of gait, not Hugh's graceful loping stride.

It had been close, this time.

She wanted to say to Dougie, what was that man saying to you, but when Dougie smiled and said, 'That you off then, last out again?' she only said, 'Yes, time I was home,' and fired her key at the car so that the lights blinked their welcome and she could drive away.

Of all of them, it was Hugh she missed most. He was her sister

Helen's first husband, married to her when she was only twenty, pretty and blonde in satin and lace, flanked by bridesmaids in blue, and smiling but doubtful parents. She was too young, they said, and he was too old for her. Catherine thought of him as a kind of brother, not that she had any idea what that might be like. It was a gap in their lives, having no brother, and perhaps that was why they had both married young. Yet neither of those marriages had lasted. After he and Helen had divorced, what was Hugh to Catherine but a friend, communicating no more than an annual note on a Christmas card. Then, of course, she had moved north, and all that had changed. Her life was quite different, because of Hugh. He had saved her when she needed saving.

She had been indoors all day, at lunchtime eating a sandwich at her desk, so she scarcely realised the sun had come out in the afternoon and the evening was fine, the sky clear and rosy. Soon the term would end, and she could take her long summer break. Flora was in Canada and not due home for several weeks, so she could work in the garden, have Helen to visit, go south, perhaps even have some kind of holiday. Without enthusiasm, she made vague plans.

What passed for rush hour in this part of the world was long over, the roads quiet at half past six on Friday. Once she was home, Catherine sat in the car for a few minutes, gathering up bag and briefcase and the groceries she had bought at lunchtime, listening to the end of the news on Radio 4, an item about a well-known author who had just died. *Am I going to start seeing her now?* she wondered. She was still troubled, though what Hugh might have wanted to tell her, she could not fathom. They had had an undemanding relationship, even at the end when they had so much needed each other.

Of course, going into her house, this house, she always thought of him.

The phone was ringing as she put her key in the door but she did not hurry; it would be one of those unwanted sales calls, someone from a far continent mispronouncing her name. After a moment her answerphone cut in and it went quiet. No message from that side, at any rate. She put the groceries away, and her briefcase. Then the telephone began again, seeming more urgent this time.

'Catherine Sinclair,' she said. Silence. Another automated call, and yet she had the sense there was someone on the line. There was – very faintly – breathing. 'Hello?' she said sharply. She was about to hang up when there was something more than breathing, a kind of reply.

'It's me.'

There are so few voices you know at once, from two syllables. This time, it could *not* be, she must be wrong. '*Gil?*'

What she expected was that the other person would say 'What? It's—' then the name would come, a stranger, so that she could say he had the wrong number and put the receiver, thankfully, down. The pause, a fraction too long for this, made her draw in her breath.

'Gilbert Sinclair,' she said firmly, not a question. There might be another Gil, not another Gilbert Sinclair. Later, she thought, how peculiar of me, why didn't I just say, 'Who is this?'

'I was,' he said. 'That's who I was.'

2

I killed a man in Reno, once.

Kenneth had never forgotten this line, though he could not remember the film, or the actor who spoke it. All he remembered was a man sitting across a table from another, turning a cigarette packet over and over in his hand. A Western, he thought, a saloon bar. He could see the thin brown hand and worn shirt cuff, the cigarette packet on its end, on its side, on its end.

Kenneth wasn't even sure where Reno was. Could it have been Humphrey Bogart? Not in a Western, surely. Steve McQueen, then. Or – no – he was sure now: it was Paul Newman, speaking to a woman. If it was a Western, a saloon bar, the woman was wearing a garish dress, her hair piled up with ribbons, her wide-mouthed lipsticked laugh husky with tobacco. For a moment, he yearned for a woman like that, imagining how simple such a relationship would be, at least at first – these things have a way of becoming complicated. No, it was a man, speaking to another man, someone so unmemorable he couldn't picture him at all. Not that he could see Paul Newman clearly, all these years later – or possibly Steve McQueen. All he remembered was the line, and the cigarette packet turning on the table, end, side, end, side. 'I killed a man in Reno, once.'

It was the casual way he said it, with a tiny ambiguous pause before the word 'once', putting a doubt in your mind. Perhaps he had killed many people, if not in Reno, then elsewhere.

The point was, the man had a past. It glimmered for a moment, mysterious, even threatening. Here was a man with a story he could tell, if he chose to, a story that might explain, or at least illuminate, the whole film. Someone had once given Kenneth the idea that everyone had a line that explained them, and if you knew that line, you could understand the person. He had adopted this theory so long ago he almost thought of it as his own.

Even when he discovered that the line about Reno did not come from a film at all, but a song, he stuck to it as a defining statement, because by then he had learned what his own line was.

In the small corner shop where he bought his newspaper every morning two women were leaning close over their baskets, one with a litre of milk and the *Daily Express*, the other with a packet of cornflakes and a tin of beans. He was fascinated, since he had lived on his own, by other people's shopping, and always looked at what they were buying. One woman was young but stout, and despite the warmth of the summer morning, wearing a padded jacket that made her barrel-shaped; below it her plump legs bulged in unsuitable leggings. The other was older and smarter, heavily made up and with rings on most of her fingers. They took up the whole of the narrow aisle, and the one who was speaking as he murmured 'excuse me' and tried to reach the till with his paper and a single pint of milk for the working day, barely moved to let him go by.

'That's her all over, I says to him, what did you expect?'

'He should never have got married in the first place,' said the second woman. They nodded, agreeing.

At the till he smiled at Mr Patel's surly teenage son as he always did, but the boy gave nothing back but his change. In the car, it occurred to him that some unfortunate man, so neatly summed up by the women, might be tagged forever with this line: he should never have got married. That might have been his line too, at one time.

He was not first to arrive at work, though for years he had been. Derek and Jimmy had opened up at half past seven and were taking the van out to pick up the Polish workers from the B&B, so that they'd be on site by eight. He nodded at them as he went past and opened the door to his office. 'Not a bad day.'

The sun had come out, the enclosed yard capturing its warmth on concrete. It glittered on the windows of the low breeze block building next to the old hangar where they kept machinery and vehicles.

'Aye, if it stays dry.' Derek heaved himself up into the driver's seat. Jimmy dropped the stub of his roll-up and ground it into the tarmac. Then he too got into the van and they drove out of the yard, leaving the gates open for the delivery that was expected later that morning.

The office smelled stale, as it always did, but familiar, of dust and the dregs of many cups of tea and coffee left standing as he drank one after another from different mugs that Kelly gathered up at the end of the day and put in the sink in the little kitchen space on the other side of the corridor. The cleaner washed up when she was there, but leaving late one Friday he had seen her use the same cleaning fluid she used for the floors, so now he washed each mug before he filled it. Kelly had her own pink flowery mug, and washed and dried it herself, keeping it in a drawer in the outer office that was really hers, though the men hung hard hats and yellow hi-vis jackets there.

He hooked his jacket over the back of the chair and switched on the computer. Kelly would bring the post when she came in, so he put the kettle on while the computer was warming up.

The telephone began ringing as he scooped a dripping teabag from his mug. He hoped it wasn't anything to do with the job they were on. Smaller contractors had gone on getting work, so the recession hadn't affected them much, but twice now a whole housing development had stopped before it really got going. No one was buying the houses. They had to put the services in first though, so he'd scored that way.

He left the mug on the draining board and went to pick up the phone. He didn't even want the tea, but habit made him go through the ritual every morning.

'Sinclair,' he said.

'It's Catherine.'

He was so taken aback that for a moment he had to say to himself, Catherine? He could not remember the last time she had voluntarily got in touch – years.

'Well,' he said. 'This is a surprise.'

'I've had a bigger surprise, a shock, actually.'

Her cool voice brought back the ache of guilt and resentment she had engendered in him for so long, that and the twinge of anger. She had left him, after all.

'Is something wrong?' Perhaps her mother had died at last. No, there would be no shock in that, since the woman – whose name he had forgotten – must be getting on for ninety. No reason Catherine would tell him anyway.

'I had a phone call,' she said, 'from somebody who said he was Gilbert. I thought you should know.'

When a few seconds had passed, and he realised he had not

drawn a breath, he said, 'What on earth do you mean – someone who says he's Gilbert?'

'He said that's who he was.'

'Did it sound like Gil – when was this?'

'Last night.' She paused. 'Yes, it did. I thought it was him.'

'And now you don't?'

'I'm not sure.'

'What did he say?' He tugged at his shirt collar. It felt tight, though he had the top button undone already.

'Just that it was Gil, or no—' She sighed. 'I said something like, is that Gilbert Sinclair, and he said, yes, that's who I was.'

'It's a joke,' he said. 'Some crank.'

'It didn't seem all that funny,' she retorted, but mildly. She must know how strange it sounded, to allege she had heard from his brother, years after he had vanished from their lives.

'What then – did he say anything else?'

'I said what do you mean? He sort of laughed, then the line went dead.'

He thought she sighed, or perhaps shivered – a slight quaver in her voice. 'It wasn't him. He wouldn't know where you live now, for one thing.'

'He might have found out,' she said. 'Or – he might have thought he was calling Hugh. He might not know.'

'Did you check the number?'

'Withheld. Anyway, I thought I'd better tell you. Just in case.'

In case what? Did she think whoever it was would try *him* next? 'Don't worry about it.'

'Even if it was some crank, who on earth could it be, and why would they call me? Or Hugh? I wondered if it was – I don't know – one of his friends.'

'No point in worrying about it,' he repeated, but the blood had risen to his face and he was sweating.

'I suppose not.'

'How are you, apart from this?'

'Oh, I'm fine. I'm well.'

'Good.'

There was another short silence, that should have been filled by Catherine saying, 'And you?'

Listening to her silence, he thought she was rattled. There was something else required of him, something he had not said. There was of course, nothing he *could* say. Not after all this time.

'Well,' he suggested, wanting to end the conversation, 'call me if it happens again.'

'Then what?' she asked. 'You'll trace the call?'

'I just meant – if you're worried—' He stopped. He had been going to say 'I'll come round,' but he didn't want to do that.

'Don't bother about it,' she said, as if he had actually made the offer. 'I'm all right. If there's another, and it's in any way … threatening, I'll call the police.'

She had gone. He sat holding the dead phone, gazing out of the window at the yard, where Kelly was now parking her little silver hatchback carefully into the space next to his four-wheel drive. In a moment she would appear, tripping across the yard in high heels.

Damn Catherine, disrupting his morning with her story about Gil. She'd got het up about nothing. They were all the same, women, melodramatic. She must have changed then, said another, mocking voice in his head.

When Kelly came in he was glad to see her, looking fresh and young, with her immaculate and (in his view) unnecessary make-up. He spoke to her briefly about the need to get the yard tidied before the Health and Safety visit next week, then signed a birthday card she'd bought for Jimmy.

At eleven, she said, 'Will I make your coffee?' but he got up and unhooking his jacket, said, 'No, I'm going out.'

'You've no appointments,' she said anxiously, wanting to be sure she hadn't missed putting something in the diary. 'Are you going up to the site now? I thought you were doing that in the afternoon?'

'That's still the plan.'

As he went out, she called after him, 'If Mr Robinson phones—'

'I'll be back in an hour. He can wait.'

Kenneth drove out of the open gates, passing Novar's delivery lorry as it turned into the access road. Kelly would deal with it if Donny wasn't around. He frowned, unable to recall seeing Donny this morning. Something would have to be said soon; the other men were getting restive. Donny took liberties, Derek had reported, though Kenneth wasn't sure being an alcoholic meant you were actually taking advantage.

On the road, Radio 3 turned up loud (Vivaldi, but never mind, it would do), he drummed the business out of his head, pushing aside yet again the feeling he'd had for months, that he didn't want to go on. What choice did he have? Other people's livelihoods depended on him.

In twenty minutes he was in the hills; in this part of the world it didn't take long to go beyond houses and traffic. It was summer so there were one or two caravans, easily overtaken on the long straights, all of which he knew to the inch. He was a fast, confident driver.

Just over the brow of the hill you could see the turning for the cottage. The lane ahead was narrow and rougher than he remembered after the tarmac ended at the Forresters' farm. He hadn't been here for a year or more. In the past Jim Forrester had kept an eye on it; even now, Maureen would probably notice if anyone was there. Did he really, after all this time, mean to let it out one day? He should have put someone in to clear the place and get it on the market. But he knew why it hadn't happened.

It could not be Gilbert who had called Catherine. If he allowed himself to think that, he was off his head. Yet he had felt compelled to come. He engaged four-wheel drive on the steep part, past the Scotch pines and the burn on the right, then the five-barred gate, and the house itself.

There was no outward sign anyone was there, or had been there, for years. The weather had been dry for weeks; there was no fresh imprint of tyres on the track. The grass was long and a sheep had found its way through a breach in the drystone dyke. When he pulled the gate open it reared its head and scampered off.

He stood on the front path, narrowed by encroaching weeds, and gazed at the house. Front door in the centre, window either side, two windows set in the roof: a small grey croft house like thousands of others across the Highlands. As he stood in the quiet, hearing nothing but the wind sighing in the Scots pines and the low gurgle of the burn, something trickled down his back like fear and he believed for a moment, against all sense, that the cottage was not empty after all.

He made himself go up to the door. The key was kept beneath the stone, so he reached his hand down, but felt underneath only earth, damp and cold. He stood up and kicked the stone away, annoyed. It must be here. Yet the stone had moved easily, so someone had been here before him. He had another key at home but he no longer kept it on his ring. The Forresters had one. For some reason he didn't want to go down and ask them for it. It occurred to him to try the door. The handle turned easily in his grasp, but the door held, still locked. He went round to the back, pushing through nettles and cow parsley, all of it so overgrown it leaned across the path. Time he did something about it – a disgrace to leave it empty, and people without homes.

Through the dusty windows of the little lean-to porch he could see a couple of pairs of wellingtons, one fallen on its side, a watering can, an old waterproof hanging behind the door and a tin bucket they had used to bring in coal. The door opened a little stiffly, but it was never locked. The porch smelled warm and musty, of earth and dust. The door into the kitchen, the back door proper, would be bolted of course. The house looked empty and shut up, but the missing key, the queer sense he had that there was someone else around, made him steel himself, though he was a man who had only once felt fear. He put his hand on the knob and turned it.

The door creaked, but it opened.

He went into the kitchen of the house he had left in anger and fear more than thirteen years ago, a house he had come back to only to shut it up, to close it off to Gilbert and Rose who would never come back. The old feeling rose, that sick frustrated anger, that he could never just let out, since the one time he had it had all gone so wrong. Did he imagine it, or was that sweetish musky scent still here, from the dope smoked so long ago? The kitchen was cool; the front of the house got the sun. He turned slowly, looking around. On his left, on the draining board by the sink under the window, were an open pack of cheap tea bags, a half-full carton of milk and a packet of chocolate digestives, also opened, a few gone.

Someone was here, but he was no longer afraid. A squatter, a vagrant, what? Not Gilbert, at any rate, not with those groceries. Grimly, he smiled. I'll soon sort you out.

The key he had failed to find under the stone was lying on the small Formica-covered table along with a box of matches. He picked up the key, and went to inspect the rest of the house.

I'll soon sort you out.

3

That guy is just a waste of space.

It was one of the things Joe said. When he left, Catherine told Helen she should be glad, he had been a walking cliché. That's a cliché too, Helen protested. Catherine was angry on Helen's behalf, but Helen herself had not thought of these sayings of Joe's as cliché, perhaps taking them too literally. She used to picture the 'waste of space' guy being hustled out of the space he occupied because he was wasting it, and hadn't earned the right to continue to occupy a tiny patch within a tiny part of a tiny universe. What would they put in his place – a biscuit tin perhaps, a lawn mower, something enjoyed or useful, the space more profitably occupied than by the man. She wondered where he might go, displaced like that. Perhaps he would die, so that he no longer occupied any literal space. She knew as she drifted on like this, standing by the hedge at the bottom of the garden, not weeding, that it was all nonsense, yet her mind persisted with it.

She hadn't particularly been thinking of Joe – or no more than usual. It was because of Catherine.

'The oddest thing,' Catherine had said on the phone last night, 'I thought I saw Hugh, speaking to our janitor.'

18

'Did your janitor know Hugh?' Helen had asked, surprised, then realised this was not the right question.

'I wasn't sure whether to tell you.'

'Did you think I'd be upset that Hugh had come back? Or wasn't really dead?'

'Oh, Helen, stop it. Of course it wasn't Hugh – I just imagined him. He must have been in my mind. I'm sorry.'

Helen wasn't sorry, as it was quite an interesting start to a conversation, much more so than the usual call with Catherine.

'How odd if it was.'

'Odd? Impossible.'

'I suppose so.'

'It's strange,' Catherine said. 'He's not the only one I've seen like that. When it couldn't be them.'

'Who else?'

'Well, Alan. James, my old boss. Dad.' Catherine paused. 'Hugh quite often, actually.'

'Maybe it's their ghosts, trying to tell you something.'

'It's a trick of the imagination – but I must work out why I see them. *Think* I see them.'

Standing by the hedge with the wooden handle of a garden fork warm in her hand, Helen took the idea further than the conversation had. Catherine had soon changed the subject. Perhaps Hugh had come to fill the space vacated by a waste of space person, slipped into it while it was warm, to make use of it. Helen's eyes filled with tears. Dear Hugh. She was sure Catherine still missed him. Twenty years ago, when she moved to the Highlands, Catherine had said anxiously, 'Do you mind my seeing Hugh? We're just friends of course, but he's very good to me.'

Strange that Hugh, inoffensive and kind, without guile or ill will, was the one who introduced Catherine to Gilbert Sinclair, and then Kenneth.

Conscious of the fork and the unweeded border, Helen dropped to her knees and dug about for a while conscientiously, uprooting dandelions (though they were far tougher and more persistent than she or Patrick would ever be) and easing up buttercups. She soon had a full bucket beside her, and feeling virtuous, got slowly to her feet, gasping at the pins and needles in her calves.

'Helen?'

'I'm here!'

'Where's here?'

'At the bottom—' She went up the path so that Patrick, standing by the back door, could see her.

'Phone!'

He handed it over as she reached him.

'Who is it?'

'Some guy.'

'You should ask,' she mouthed, but smiling.

Patrick strolled down the garden, but not to weed, she was sure, just to fill in the minutes while she was on the phone. Helen sat on the bench by the back door.

'Hello?' There was a noise in the background, traffic, then a siren, so she could barely make out the soft voice. 'Sorry, who is it?'

'It's me,' the voice said. Helen's mind went to Joe, as it always did when something unexpected happened. One day he would call, then where would she be? Her heart lurched. 'Or used to be,' the voice went on.

It was familiar, but it wasn't Joe. She would not be disappointed, she would *not*.

'I can hardly hear you,' she said. 'Would you speak up?'

There was a laugh, cut short. She listened to silence, her heart beating fast, then put the phone down on the bench and got up to look for Patrick. He was mooning about by the apple tree, whistling softly. For once she was irritated. Look at him, she thought, he has to be prodded into every single thing. He was supposed to be completing his tax return. If he wasn't going to get that done, why couldn't he come out and help her, and do something useful? She heard her mother's voice in her head. Shut up, Helen, she told herself. He's a lovely man. You can't have him different.

'Who was it?' he asked. He rested his arms on her shoulders and kissed her. He didn't care who it was; that was another good thing about him.

'I don't know – some weirdo. He wouldn't say.'

Patrick frowned. 'He asked for you, though.'

She rested her head on his chest and Patrick put his arms round her. 'Is that all?'

'Is Helen *Guthrie* there. So I guess it's somebody who's not been in touch for a while.'

Helen pulled back and looked up at him. 'What? I've not been Helen Guthrie for years. How would someone like that get our number?'

'Strange,' Patrick agreed, but she could see he was not even curious. 'You and your boyfriends. What's for dinner?'

They walked up the garden with his arm on her shoulders, hers round his waist. They would go to bed now, since that was what they did when he was at a loose end. I must remember the bucket of weeds, she thought, I must empty it in case it rains later. There were clouds massing on the horizon beyond the fields next to the cottage, gunmetal grey against the blue of the rest of the sky.

21

Is that Helen Guthrie?

The first rumble of thunder sounded far off, still on the horizon, as she pulled off her tee shirt and jeans and Patrick came through from the bathroom undressed already. 'Right then, ma'am,' he said, cheering up now that the dull day had a purpose, and pulling back the quilt for her.

Outside, the clouds began to heave themselves across the paling blue of six o'clock. It wasn't until afterwards, as Patrick dozed and she lay listening for the next thunder clap in the heavy air, that it came back to her.

It's me.

She could call the number back if it wasn't withheld. She thought of Catherine seeing the dead, fooled into thinking they had really appeared. It was like that. Gilbert might as well have been dead for ten years. She did not want Catherine to have to start worrying about him all over again.

She lay thinking she must get up and cook supper, but could not bring herself to do it. She turned to Patrick, sniffing the faint trace of his morning aftershave, the sweat of the hot day they had had, the musky scent of his hair. It was thinning at the temples, but she would not say anything, for he was sensitive about his appearance.

'Patrick,' she said.

'Mmm?'

'I'd better get some supper, eh?'

'Mmhm.'

'The phone call – I think I know who it was.'

He grunted softly, tugging her close. She wanted to tell him, wanted to tell someone who would think it unimportant, but advise her what to do. Why she thought he could provide this reassurance she didn't know.

She disengaged herself from his arm. 'I have to get up if you want anything to eat.'

Downstairs, the kitchen was darkened by the heavy cloud, so she switched on the light. A jar of marmalade sat on the table, left since breakfast time, and the sink was full of unwashed dishes. Helen turned her back on them and went to find the phone. Eventually she remembered it was still on the bench. Spots of rain peppered the window panes and the air outside was cool. The bucket of weeds was in plain sight, down at the end of the path. By the time she had rescued the phone and disposed of the weeds the rain was becoming heavy and Patrick had got up. She could hear the television as he watched the news. She ran hot water into the sink, and began to tackle the dishes.

By the time she remembered she hadn't checked the number of the unknown caller, they were in the middle of dinner. Patrick ate fast so that he could get off to the pub for the weekly darts match. When people – women – said how terrific to have a younger man, Helen laughed. Patrick was middle-aged already, liking the pub and his mates, Sunday lunch, wearing the same old clothes all the time and living every week just as he had the one before.

When he had gone, she called Catherine.

'Are you all right? We spoke just last night.'

'I thought I'd tell you,' Helen said, 'I've had a strange phone call.'

'What?'

'Patrick answered. Whoever it was asked for Helen Guthrie – that was the first strange thing. Then when I picked it up there was a male voice, I *think* it was male, just saying "it's me". Then there was a lot of noise in the background and I said to speak up or something. Anyway he sort of laughed and hung up. If he hadn't asked for me by name, my *old* name, I'd have thought it was a crank or a wrong number. When I checked the number that called, it came up withheld.' She paused, expecting Catherine to say this was not worth bothering about. 'Cathy? Are you still there?'

'Sorry. Just "it's me" – that's all he said?'

'I know this is weird but I thought it might be—'

'Gilbert Sinclair,' Catherine said.

Helen took a deep breath. 'Have you heard from him too?'

'The same thing happened to me, yesterday, just after I got home.'

'Before or after you saw Hugh?'

'I didn't see Hugh, that has nothing to do with it.'

'You don't know that.'

Catherine gave a 'pfft' of impatience. 'Yes I do. The phone call was real, there was someone there, and it did sound like Gilbert. That doesn't mean it was him, though. Somebody is up to something.'

'I was worried, when I thought it was him.'

Catherine's tone softened. 'Were you? It's all right, that's finished, in the past. But I did call Kenneth and tell him.'

Helen was taken aback. 'I thought you never spoke to him.'

'We live in different worlds. I never have any reason to speak to him.'

'It was a bit spooky,' Helen said. 'Did Kenneth think it was him?'

'I'm sure it wasn't Gilbert,' Catherine said firmly, and changed the subject.

Afterwards, Helen poured herself another glass of wine from the bottle they had opened at supper time, and pondered how people could have such different views of the same person. She had met Gilbert only once or twice, and thought he was weird.

Yet Hugh had got on with him and Hugh was the most conventional of men. Then there was Joe who – strangely, she thought – had taken a shine to him at Catherine and Kenneth's wedding. Joe had been in good spirits, that day.

Kenneth, of course, had hated Gilbert.

The rain had cleared, leaving the air fresh and cool, and there was still light in the sky when Patrick came home. If he was surprised at her unusually warm welcome, given the amount he'd had to drink in the Saddler's Arms, he did not say so. He knew enough simply to be grateful.

In the night, Helen woke with a start, heart pumping. What was that noise? She lay listening to nothing, just more rain, pattering steadily through the leaves, trickling down the windows. At her back, Patrick was in the deep sleep of the carefree and slightly drunk, snoring a little, his arms tightly round her, his breath coming in puffs of cool air on her neck. She snuggled closer to him. If it was the phone that had wakened her, she wasn't going to get up to see who it was, especially if it was Gilbert Sinclair.

As she began to drift into the dreaming state that has visions, but is not yet unconsciousness, she saw Hugh's house, his lovely house, but on the driveway half hidden by daffodils (it must be spring), that old van of Gil's, growing in her mind softer, as if it were melting, a dissolving blur. She gave a little cry, and Patrick tightened his hold, as if in fear himself, though she wanted it to be reassurance.

Creative Space
1994

1

It was Hugh Guthrie who introduced Catherine to Gilbert Sinclair. Hugh took her to The Factory.

'You have to see this,' he said. 'It's an astonishing place.'

It had been a corset factory, erected by a millionaire philanthropist early in the twentieth century, an attempt to bring industry and employment to the poverty and rural remoteness of the region. He had run a bus around the villages, collecting and then dropping off his mainly female workers at the beginning and end of each long day. The factory had shut down more than eighty years ago, and the place was for a time used as Council storage, then lay empty, a 'To Lease' sign erected and the building closed up. At the end of the drive the original factory sign was faded and overgrown, a once famous name now obsolete and almost a joke. Gilbert had made no attempt to tidy the exterior and the drive had a thick growth of grass and dandelions along the centre.

The building was L shaped and the longer side was still unused; it was boarded up and fenced off with red danger signs at the padlocked gates. Gilbert leased the short side, which in itself was two spacious floors with tall, many-paned windows.

'It's a sort of antiques warehouse then?' Catherine asked as they drove up to the entrance. It was impressive; the sunlight glittering on hundreds of window panes did not reveal that several were broken.

Through the open front doors, they went into a panelled entrance hall with a marble fireplace and a broad staircase leading to the first floor. There was no one about. Hugh nodded towards double doors beyond the staircase. 'That's where most of the furniture is. Let's go upstairs first.'

The top floor was one enormous space. At the far end were several rows of fixed shelves crammed with books whose spines at this distance were palest fawn and green, the colour leached out of them over time by sunlight filtering through the tall windows, hazy with dust motes, lending a glow to the place. About half of the remaining space was scattered with smaller pieces of furniture: occasional tables, ladies' writing desks and standard lamps, and the rest with long tables crowded with china, mainly tea sets and dinner services, many chipped and incomplete. Once, she learned from Hugh, women had sat at these tables, stitching corsets by hand, or using manual sewing machines. Between the last table and the bookcases there was an empty space with dents in the floorboards showing where other tables had once stood, and smaller scuffed marks from chairs the women had sat in, day after day, stitching. This empty expanse shimmered in the afternoon light, as if they might have to cross a misty river to reach the books.

There were no gaps in the shelves. Perhaps nobody ever bought a book. Catherine imagined that if you took one away, surprised by the depth of colour on the rest of the cover or the dust jacket (and there were some surprising dust jackets), the others would sigh and ease themselves along to fill the space.

'I've found a few treasures here,' Hugh said as Catherine stood with her head on one side, reading titles and authors.

'Are they in some sort of order?'

'I doubt it, knowing Gil.'

'Is he the owner?' Catherine asked. She glanced around. 'It's so quiet – where is he? I could be stealing all the first editions.'

'You'd have to find them first,' Hugh said with a smile. He drew out a slim hardback and opened it. '*A High Wind in Jamaica*. Have you read it?'

'Yes,' Catherine said. 'It's a terrifying story. Makes *Lord of the Flies* look tame.'

'Really?' Hugh looked at it with renewed but temporary interest. 'Fancy that.' He pushed the book back into place.

'Gil?' Catherine asked. 'His name's Gil?'

'Gilbert Sinclair.' Hugh turned away from the books. 'Do you want to browse a while? I'll see if he's downstairs.'

'All right.'

Someone who rented an old Factory and filled it with second-hand furniture was an unlikely friend for Hugh, Catherine thought, listening to his shoes clattering softly on the bare boards as he ran downstairs. This Gilbert Sinclair was probably a friend of a friend.

She drifted away from the books and began looking amongst the china and oddments on the long tables. A shaft of sunlight caught a crystal bowl, glinted on a heap of Indian tree side plates, and a blue glass vase. It was a junk shop: there was no sort of method, and probably nothing was antique, just old or unwanted. Still, there might be something good to be found. Since her divorce, she had been gradually replacing things she had left with Alan. She had left in too much of a hurry, abandoning china and pictures and glass he was only going to put in storage when he went to Saudi Arabia. Sometimes in the middle of the night, she mourned the blue-glazed bowl they had bought

31

in Perpignan, the little water colour of the beach at Swanage. They're only *things*, she told herself sternly.

In this silent space, the sun warm on her face and hands as she turned over a china plate to see the maker's name, she felt peaceful. Underneath, there was a tug of excitement: change was coming. She looked up, hearing footsteps on the stairs, quick and leaping as if the climber were taking them two or three at a time.

A thin untidy man came across the great space towards her. For a moment he was a dusty blur of a person, then he moved out of a patch of sun and so did she, and she could see him. He had an eager, anxious face and brown curling hair that grew long over the collar of his blue shirt. His sleeves were rolled up as if for action.

'Hello,' he said. 'Catherine?'

'Yes.'

'We're making tea – come down and join us? Hugh's washing my cups. He thinks they're dirty.'

She laughed. 'That sounds like Hugh. Are they?'

'What – dirty? Probably, but they're very nice cups. Crown Derby.'

'This is your place?'

He swept his arms out. 'All mine. Do you like it?'

'It's lovely, very peaceful.'

His face fell. 'Oh, you would mind then, if I put a café in – over there?' He indicated a wide empty space near the windows. 'I thought a little café – good coffee and tea and home baking. People might come for that and then buy things. I *want* people to buy things.'

She went down the broad stairs by his side while he talked about how difficult it was to let something go, if he happened to have become fond of it. She liked how he simply went on talking, as if she had replied, even when she hadn't. It was restful; she did not have to make an effort. He led her to the main room on the ground floor, which was similar to upstairs, but with less light, perhaps because it was so crowded. It was packed with sofas and chairs and heavy furniture: ugly sideboards too big for any house smaller than a mansion, and mahogany wardrobes that had once housed evening dresses and fur coats. It was all so dusty she suspected nothing had been brought here, or sold, for a long time. It was a smaller space than upstairs because some of it had been partitioned off for offices, lavatories and a small kitchen, where they found Hugh wiping gold and green rimmed cups with a clean handkerchief.

'Now,' Gilbert Sinclair said, 'what kind of tea do you like?'

'Oh, anything.'

Gilbert looked at her hard. 'You don't mean that, I hope.'

'Earl Grey – but Hugh doesn't like it.' She was thinking, two different tea bags, that would do, but there were three tins on the none-too-clean worktop and she suspected they all had leaves in them, not bags.

'First flush Darjeeling? Assam? Oolong?'

'Don't tease her,' Hugh said. 'Just get out your PG Tips.'

'We'll have Darjeeling.'

Catherine did not like Darjeeling, but now could not say so.

They took their fragile cups of tea out to the area that was full of sofas. There were plenty of seats, but none of the furniture was arranged so that they could face each other sociably. Gilbert set down his cup and saucer on a chest of drawers and heaved a sofa round to face two armchairs.

'Let's be comfy,' he said.

When Catherine sat down a small puff of dust rose around her from the cushions, and she worried a little about her clothes.

She balanced the cup and saucer carefully on her knees. The tea, when she sipped it, was light, faintly perfumed, and much nicer than expected. She found herself facing both men and was slightly disconcerted by the intensity of Gilbert's gaze.

'Hugh's told me about you,' he said.

She was up to that and did not give him the answer she thought he expected: 'Nothing bad, I hope'. Anyway, what was there to say except that she was an old friend of Hugh's because he had been married to Helen?

'He hasn't told me about you,' she returned. 'Till today – bringing me here.'

Gilbert smiled. 'Did you find a book you wanted?'

'Not yet.'

'You'll come back though?'

She would come back now she knew how to find the place. She thought of the warm space upstairs, that was probably icy in winter, the rows of books, the china and glass, and a little table she liked, wondering if the scratch could be polished out.

A door closed and there were voices and footsteps on the flag-stoned floor of the reception hall. Two women and a man came in, then paused, taken aback perhaps by the cosy trio drinking tea. Gil leaned forward mouthing 'customers' at Catherine, then stood up and waved the people in. 'Hello – do feel free to look around. Lots more upstairs.'

The three of them began to wander amongst the furniture.

'Do you sell much?' Catherine could not help asking.

'He discourages it,' Hugh said. 'He's a hopeless salesman.'

'But how do you make a living, Gilbert?'

'He doesn't.'

'Gil. I always think Gilbert sounds Edwardian, like somebody in a frock coat.'

Catherine laughed, having a sudden vision of him in this frock coat, and carrying a top hat. Hugh got up and drifted off, cup and saucer in hand, amongst the sofas. Gil set his tea down on the floor next to his feet.

'Is your sister anything like you?' he asked. 'I can see *you* married to Hugh.'

'No,' Catherine said. 'We're quite unlike each other. Though it was hard to—' She looked up guiltily, but Hugh was out of earshot. 'Hugh's so nice, and Helen—'

'Not nice?'

'Oh yes, but very *different*.'

'I'm completely unlike my brother,' Gil said. 'He's an engineer. But it was reassuring for my parents that one of us played rugby and got a useful degree, and could live in the real world. The *allegedly* real world.'

'Whereas you—'

'This isn't what people call a proper job, is it?' he said with a faint smile.

She had the sense that comes rarely, of meeting a new person and knowing them as you know someone you have been with all your life. Gil seemed far easier and more open than Hugh. He would retain an air of being enigmatic, yet she felt already she could say anything to him, they could be friends for ever.

Afterwards, driving home, Hugh said, 'I knew the two of you would get on.'

'He's very easy to talk to.'

'He's a hopeless case, but a nice fellow, harmless.'

'He has a brother who's an engineer,' Catherine said. 'You can't see it, can you? Strange how brothers and sisters can be so unlike.'

She was thinking of herself and Helen, but Hugh said,

'Kenneth – yes, I know Kenneth well. That's how I met Gil and heard about his – warehouse? It's hardly a business.'

It was the engineer Hugh was friendly with; that made more sense.

'I'll have them both round, and some other people,' Hugh said. 'A wee party, to welcome you to the Highlands. Would next Saturday be all right?'

'You're so kind to me.'

He would not come in for more tea. 'I'll be in touch about Saturday.'

She had nothing else planned; her new life lay before her like an uncharted sea. Now a few ripples had appeared, as if something was moving beneath the surface. She waved him off, closing the gate at the end of her garden path.

Indoors, she went upstairs as she always did, coming back into this new house, not just to use the bathroom, tidy her hair or change her clothes, but to stand on the threshold of what would be Flora's room. She worried it might not be right, that Flora would dislike it, she would have missed some obvious reason why it was unsuitable. You could not tell with Flora.

Soon she would be here. Alan would be travelling to the Middle East, to take up his new job. He had let her off the hook, leaving the country. Now she was free to move away herself, though not of course abroad. She had made much of Flora being able to keep her friends, stay at the school she was used to. Then, like a traitor, she had upped sticks and come to Scotland. It had been hard to persuade Flora, indeed impossible.

'I have to have a job that keeps us both now,' Catherine had explained. 'I can't turn down such a good opportunity. 'Besides, you love Scotland, you love visiting Granny and Grandpa, don't you?'

'I visit them *now*.'

'It's near Hugh,' Catherine said in desperation, since Flora had met Hugh only twice in her life.

'You can't marry *him*,' Flora said. 'He's Auntie Helen's husband.'

'Not any more. But I don't want to marry anyone.'

This was true. One marriage was enough; what she needed was a career.

Leaning on the door jamb of Flora's untested bedroom, she sighed, and turning her back on this unhappy last conversation with her daughter, went downstairs to make supper. In a week, Alan would be leaving and her mother would bring Flora here. Time enough to worry about it then.

As she ate, she flicked the pages of the newspaper, a local one bought to familiarise herself with this new place, but of course it only made her feel even more a stranger. Her thoughts drifted to the afternoon, and The Factory. She would go back and buy that little table. It would sit nicely in her new hallway, with a bowl of flowers to hide the scratch if it couldn't be polished out. If she wasn't careful she'd end up like Helen, thinking the house was more important than anything else.

'How can you bear to leave it?' Helen asked when Catherine told her the house in London had to be sold, so that she could have her half of the equity, and Alan his.

'It's only a house.'

'It's your *home*.' To Helen, all houses must be homes.

'I don't like it that much,' Catherine told her. 'I don't mind.'

'You must find a place you love then, this time,' Helen said.

How she had wept, leaving Hugh, because she had to leave his house as well. Perhaps she had always loved Rowanbank more than she had loved him. She had argued with Hugh that she must be entitled to stay, but that was a lost cause; Rowanbank had been a Guthrie house for generations and Helen's contributions had been entirely to do with soft furnishings and what she thought of as suitable 'pieces'. That meant large lumps of driftwood Hugh tripped over regularly at the turn of the stair or in the hall, and elaborate wrought-iron candle holders which, if the candles were lit, would surely have been a fire hazard. Remembering this, Catherine thought she might not after all buy the table. Still, she would go back; she did need a jug to hold flowers. Getting up to make tea, she thought of Hugh and Gil on the armchairs in The Factory, the thin china cup and saucer, delicate in her hands, and with a warm ache of happiness she leaned on the worktop, unable for a moment to move. How good of Hugh to think of having a party for her. He was such an old woman, wiping the cups with his clean handkerchief, but remembering the state of the crumpled tea towel she had glimpsed by the sink, she was grateful. Gil was still a mystery to her, but she was certain he was not looked after by a woman – or indeed anyone.

She telephoned Alan at quarter to eight, to speak to Flora before she went to bed. Her daughter's imperious voice both amused and alarmed her. She was *seven*. A lifetime of coping with Flora alone was a daunting prospect.

'Goodnight, Mummy,' Flora said, suddenly as she always did, having had enough of the phone call.

'I'll see you in a week.'

But Flora had hung up already, so she was at least spared any final words with Alan.

Later, she might phone Helen, who would be amused by The Factory and of course Gil. For the moment though, she longed just to sit in her living room, bare and still uncurtained, to stretch her legs out on the sofa and lean back on cushions, reading. A little while on her own, something she had not yet got used to.

2

'Can I bring anything?'

'Of course not. Nothing needed.'

'Some food?'

'There are people bringing food,' Hugh said. 'They're local caterers: the *Hungry Bunch*. Silly name, but they're reliable.'

'I'll bring wine.'

'That will be nice,' Hugh said, so politely Catherine thought perhaps he had ordered that too from the Hungry Bunch. She would buy something good that Hugh could keep for himself later.

Catherine was unable to imagine who his guests might be, apart from herself and Gilbert Sinclair. Though he had a wide acquaintance through work – he was a partner in a local solicitors' office in Dingwall – Hugh always seemed solitary. Perhaps all the guests would be people he knew through business. Or hillwalking? She knew he spent many of his weekends on the hills, but had not supposed that a very sociable pastime.

Going up the long drive, where rhododendrons, whose deep red and pink blooms were just fading, pressed close on either side, she thought of Helen. No wonder she had not wanted to leave Rowanbank. It was a stone house amid alder and birch, a rowan close by the wall, all in new leaf, lushly green. In spring daffodils and bluebells grew in great drifts under the trees. Close to the house was a closely mown stretch of lawn glistening with recent rain. The double doors stood open and on the broad gravel area in front of the house several cars were parked already.

Catherine, drawing up beside a red Jaguar, hoped she had selected a space where no one could block her exit. She liked to know she could leave at any time. She was not fond of parties, but there was no question of slipping away early, since it was in her honour. She felt for a moment intimidated, then decided the Jaguar, and the Range Rover on the other side, must belong to Hugh's partners. Hugh's old Volvo was nowhere to be seen but there were former stables behind the house, used as garage and outhouses. His elderly Labrador bitch was sitting on the front step, and she rose, waving her tail, when she recognised Catherine. She petted the dog for longer than she needed to. Should she just walk in? The door was ajar and she could hear voices. She could also hear another car coming up the drive. She took a deep breath and headed inside, the dog trotting at her heels.

The downstairs rooms were large and square. The double doors between the sitting room and dining room behind it were standing open so that she could glimpse the food laid out on a table, though the platters were all wrapped in cling film, and the only person in the farther room was a girl in white T-shirt, black trousers and an apron. She was putting jugs on the table, mayonnaise or cream, Catherine guessed, taken up by this for too long a moment. Hugh found her before she saw him.

They leaned towards each other and their cheeks almost touched. Hugh did not go in for kissing, but neither did she.

'Let me introduce you to everyone.'

First was a woman she'd last seen behind the reception desk at

Macallum & Forbes. By the time they had exchanged awkward words, Catherine had forgotten her name. Then came George Macallum and his wife, very county in shades of green, a woman who appeared to be only temporarily without a dog or horse. Next Ronald Johnson, shy and unmarried.

Catherine was taken up with answering questions and explaining herself, while also holding a glass of warming wine in one hand, trying not to drink it fast because she was nervous. She had forgotten about Gilbert Sinclair until he appeared at her side and took her arm.

'Here you are!'

'Oh, Gil, hello – I'm so glad to see someone I know.'

'My dear, come and *talk* to me.'

There were more people now, the room becoming crowded, so they moved to a corner near the double doors and stood gazing at the food.

'I'm starving,' he said. 'Are you?'

There was no sign of the caterers so perhaps they had abandoned the buffet to its fate.

'I think we'd better not unwrap anything.'

'Impossible without a hacksaw or an electric drill, I should think,' Gil said, poking at the cling film covering a tray of tiny tartlets.

'Oh don't – you'll damage them!'

'I'm rebuked,' he said. 'Let's have more to drink instead. What's that in your glass?'

'White wine.'

'Not a good enough description. What do you like?' He was by the table of bottles now, and picked out at once the wine Catherine had brought. Unable to give it to Hugh in the way she had planned, she had left there on her arrival.

'I brought that one.'

'I knew you were a wonderful person. We'll open it. Leave that nasty stuff – I fear it's Chardonnay – and have a clean glass.'

They went on talking, the clean fruity wine going straight to her head, so that she did not mind Gil's questions. With everyone else it was 'So what's brought you to the Highlands?' or 'How do you know Hugh?' or 'And what do you do?' – the kind of thing you could answer without revealing a thing. No chance of this with Gil, whose questions were direct and personal, and yet she was not offended, and had no sense he was anything but childlike in his curiosity.

She told him about Alan and Flora, what she thought about her new job, her house, coming to the party knowing no one...

'You know *me*!' he cried.

'So I do.' She smiled. 'But only a couple of weeks ago I didn't, and we've only met twice.'

'What has that got to do with it? We're kindred souls.'

She laughed. 'I would never, in a million years, be the kind of person who bought an old factory and filled it with furniture and books.'

'You'd like to be, though,' he said, gazing at her.

She looked away. 'I need security. I have Flora to think about.'

'We both think life is absurd, don't we?' he said, laying a gentle hand on her arm. She had not thought so, but now she did. Life had been serious so far; did that mean it was also absurd? She was a little fogged by the wine, but for a moment she felt wildly that she was free, and might do anything.

'My sister has a theory,' she said, 'that everyone has a line, a few words that define them. Something in their life that tells you the one important thing. Oh dear, I'm not describing it well. Once you know this line, you *understand* the other person, but if you get the line wrong, you never will.'

'Your line,' Gilbert said with confidence, 'is that you are the oldest in your family.'

'I am,' Catherine said. 'My sister is younger. Though I don't know – anyway, it's her theory.'

'Your sister sounds remarkable. I need to meet her too.' He put his head on one side. 'Guess my line.'

'Oh – you're the younger son?'

His mouth tightened a little. 'Close,' he said.

'I don't think you ever know your *own* line.'

'Right next to the drink and the food,' a voice said. 'I might have known.'

Gil's face clouded. 'You made your way here pretty fast too, I see,' he said, in quite a different voice. Catherine looked round. How rude, she thought, interrupting like this. Though of course, at parties that's what you were supposed to do.

This man looking at her had the same intent gaze as Gil.

'This is my brother Kenneth.'

Catherine held out her hand. 'How do you do?'

'Better every minute,' Kenneth said, taking her hand in a firm grasp.

'This is Catherine. Hugh brought her to The Factory.'

'Oh God, that place.'

'I like it,' Catherine said. 'It has such a peaceful atmosphere.'

'No wonder – it's always empty.' He was taunting Gil. He was good-looking, sturdy and muscular, his hair dark and springy. She guessed he was the older brother, but Gil had a worn appearance, and was thinner in every way.

She had wanted to go on standing in the corner, listening to Gil, feeling comfortable and a little drunk, though of course she must stop now, or how on earth was she to get home?

'More wine?' Kenneth asked.

'Oh, no, I mustn't, I have to drive. I was hoping,' she added, a half-laugh escaping, embarrassed, 'Hugh would suggest we start eating soon.'

'Hugh?' Kenneth grinned, making his way towards the table. 'No point waiting for him.'

Gil stood back with a faint sneer. Try it if you like, he seemed to imply. He was right – Kenneth's ham-fisted attempts to penetrate the plastic food covering wrecked half a dozen savouries before he had made any headway. Really laughing now, Catherine stepped in and used her nails to pick apart the seal underneath.

'Ah, the woman's touch.'

Afterwards, she could not think how it was she did not recoil from his clichés, return at once to Gil and go on talking to him. She blamed the wine, not the heat of the man next to her, a heat he gave off like a scent, so that she went on being by his side, forgot Gil, listened to him, talked to him, found herself in a corner balancing a plate of food she was suddenly ravenous to eat. He wolfed his down, gulped a glass of red wine and went on talking, his whole attention focused on her.

Later, standing outside the house, cooling down in fresh air, the sky still pearly, the horizon streaked with pink, he said, 'I can't risk driving now – would you give me a lift home?'

'Where do you live?' Did he want to go already, she was wondering, since for once she was content to stay late, having envisaged a long chat with Hugh when everyone else had gone. That might be hours away; she knew in any case she would say yes. She did not want him gone. Pull yourself together, she scolded this new Catherine.

Kenneth lived in Strathpeffer, a village on the road west. She wondered where Gil lived, unable to imagine him anywhere other than The Factory. Where *was* Gil? She felt guilty about abandoning him for his brother.

'No rush,' Kenneth said. 'I don't want to drag you away.'

She glanced at her watch: ten o'clock. 'In an hour or so? I feel I've not really spoken to Hugh – or any of the other people he invited so I could meet them.'

'They're all bores anyway, you're better off with me.'

The arrogance of it. 'Well – I'll just—'

'We could slip away?'

He was joking, surely. 'I don't think so,' she said. 'An hour then?'

He watched her go with his faint smile, rocking on his heels, the glass of red wine in his hand almost empty again. You'll be back soon enough, the smile seemed to say.

'Have you seen Hugh?' Catherine asked a woman in the hallway, momentarily on her own, her husband probably fetching another drink. Catherine had the instinct of the separated woman for the securely married with their barrage of rings halfway up the finger, their comfortable references to 'Jack' or 'Bill' or 'Donald', the men who made them complete.

'He's in the piano room, I think,' the woman said.

'I'm Catherine Harrigan.' She decided not to add, this party's in my honour, by the way, it was intended to introduce me to people like you. But it's ok, I don't mind, I've already met the only two people I'm likely to be interested in.

'Lynne,' said the woman, 'Lynne Macdonald.' A portly man came up with two glasses of wine. 'This is my husband – Conor, this is Catherine – sorry – Harridan?'

I feel like it sometimes, she wanted to say. 'Harrigan. Hello, Conor.' She flashed him a smile, shook his hand firmly, then turned and went through the doorway across the hall, hoping she was right, and this was the room where she would find Hugh.

He was in one of the leather armchairs that flanked the empty grate, Gil in the other. They were drinking whisky. The dog lay between them, and thumped her tail twice, but did not get up.

'He's escaped from his own party,' Gil said.

'I'm sorry – I've not spoken to either of you properly. I've been a really bad guest,' Catherine said, hovering, since the room was set up to allow only two people to sit and talk, or perhaps listen to someone playing the grand piano over by the window.

'We don't like parties,' Gil said.

Hugh smiled. 'They're all quite happy without me.'

'You'd be better off here with us,' Gil said. 'Stay.'

'I said I'd give your brother a lift home.'

'Ah.'

'*Ah* – what does that mean?'

'See, we're friends,' Gil said to Hugh, as if confidentially, leaning towards him. 'She's quarrelling with me already.'

Catherine laughed. 'You're impossible to quarrel with.'

'I've played my part,' Hugh nodded, 'bringing you together.'

He was slightly drunk, she thought, sleepy drunk, content to sit here with Gil, hidden from everyone else.

'You've done her a much worse turn than that,' Gil said.

'What's that?'

'Let my brother find her.'

'Catherine's a sensible young woman,' Hugh said. 'She knows how to take care of herself.'

'Well, I hope so.'

They seemed to have forgotten she was there.

'Well, goodbye then.' She hesitated by the door. 'Thank you – it's a lovely party.'

46

Neither of them answered, but they watched her go. She had missed something, she thought, it was not all joking.

She should leave now. Hugh wouldn't mind as he was not even at the party himself. She could see Gilbert any time, now she knew where The Factory was.

When she found him again, Kenneth was with two women and George Macallum. George was flushed and ribald, one of the women in the circle of his arm, leaning on him. The other woman was focused on Kenneth.

'Do you want to stay a bit longer?' Catherine said it so coolly, he raised his eyebrows. Then, abruptly, he seemed to make up his mind.

'Let's go,' he said, turning, his hand under her elbow. 'Night all.'

Her car was nose to tail now with two others. Damn, she thought, and must have muttered it aloud, for Kenneth said, 'I'll guide you out.'

She did not want to rely on this, given how much he must have had to drink, but he was competent, and saw her safely onto the drive. He got in.

'Thanks for this,' he said.

'What about your own car?'

'Somebody from the works will pick me up in the morning and take me through later to get it.'

'The works?'

'The business. Where I work.'

'Someone told me you're an engineer. Who do you work for?'

'Myself,' he said.

'Oh.' Glancing sideways, she saw him afresh, a man with employees, responsibility, even power.

'We usually subcontract, he added. 'For the bigger boys.'

47

Not having any idea what this meant, or who the 'bigger boys' might be, Catherine drove out onto the main road, not answering.

'Anyway,' he said, sounding bored, 'work. No need to talk about that.'

The road was empty so late at night, the sky pale violet, a full moon translucent and high.

'How late the light stays here, when the summer begins,' Catherine said.

'You're from the south of England?'

'Hertfordshire – but London for years now. What about you – you're a Highlander?'

'Yes. But I graduated at Aberdeen, and worked down south for ten years. Then came back – gave in, you could say, and joined the family firm.'

Before he could ask her another question, she said, 'You and Gilbert – you're not at all alike.'

He laughed. 'That's the understatement of the year!'

When they reached his village, she slowed. 'You'd better give me directions.'

Up a steep hill they drove past Victorian houses with long driveways, half hidden by trees as old as they were. He must have money, she thought, living here. After this there were fields on both sides, then on the crest, several modern houses, looking raw and barely finished, but large, on substantial plots of land.

'It's the one furthest along on the left,' Kenneth said. Only the moon lit the sky now and she could not see the house, only that there was a veranda in front and huge windows. The house was split level, garage and basement below the level of the approach, built into the side of the hill.

'You must have a wonderful view,' Catherine said. Below, the fields had vanished in darkness but she had a sense of open space facing the house, with perhaps fields or hills rising on the far side of the distant road.

The engine was running softly. Kenneth leaned over and turned the key. Silence. Something shot through her like electricity, his hand on her knee briefly, his voice that she was to come to know too well. 'Come in and see it,' he said. 'It's a bit basic yet – I only took possession a week ago.' He unbuckled his seat belt and opened his door. 'You're right about the view. You'll have to come back and see it in daylight.'

She felt reckless as she got out of the car. The air was soft and cool on her face. Kenneth went up two steps onto the veranda and opened the double front doors.

Inside, he switched on lights. The hall was large and square, floored in oak. The smells of new paint and new wood permeated; everything was fresh and unused. She followed him into one room after another, each leading to the next, open half-empty spaces waiting for furniture, curtains, rugs, to make them seem like someone's home. Even now, beneath bare electric bulbs, she sensed how much natural light would wash through the house.

'It's beautiful,' she said.

'It's my present to myself.' They were in the kitchen, a long room running the depth of the house on one side, probably overlooking the backs of the old houses, muffled with mature trees. She guessed the living rooms at the front would have the best view.

Water drummed in the kettle. 'Sorry,' he said, 'there's nowhere to sit – my table and chairs arrive next week. We'll take this through to the front room.'

'Could I have tea?' Catherine asked, forestalling him with the cafetière. 'I won't sleep if I have coffee this late.'

'I won't sleep anyway.' He grinned at her. 'I can't get used to being here. But I'll have tea too.'

When they were seated at either end of the long leather sofa in the room at the front, Catherine asked:

'What did you mean, the house is a present to yourself?'

'It's a place of my own again.' He shrugged. 'My marriage broke up two years ago. I was living in a cottage that belonged to my folks, my grandfather's place. Then Gil turned up after being in London for about five years, so I went back to the family home, just west of here, to let him have the cottage. It wasn't a great arrangement, but better than letting Gil live with my parents. '

'You couldn't have shared the cottage with him?' She knew the answer to that already. 'I couldn't live with my sister,' she went on. 'I mean, I love her, but—'

'We don't automatically love people who happen to be in the same family.'

'Well, usually...' She hesitated. 'It's the shared history, isn't it, belonging together?'

'Not in our case.'

She thought he was probably the one difficult to live with. 'I'd better go.'

He watched her for a moment. Embarrassed, she got up.

He rose too and held out his hand for the mug. 'Let me take that.'

'Thank you. And thank you for showing me your beautiful house.'

'You haven't been upstairs yet.'

'No.'

'Another time?'

Was he teasing her?

At the door, the outside light came on, illuminating the veranda, some scrubby bushes, and her car in the broad turning area, still unsurfaced. It lit up their faces too, as she turned to say goodbye. He was not smiling, but there was an amusement in his expression she did not trust.

He went on standing there as she drove away. In her rear mirror her last glimpse outlined him in the doorway, a dark figure.

To have a house like that, she thought, I begin to see what Helen means. Though for Helen they must have draughty bedrooms and original fireplaces and cornices you can't dust.

She kept her mind on the house, all the way back to her own, dissatisfied now and restless. She had hardly drunk the tea, but would not sleep anyway.

3

'Thank you,' Catherine said to Hugh on the telephone next morning. 'It was a lovely party.'

'It was a party, at any rate,' he said gloomily. 'The house is not looking its best.'

'I'll come and help you clear up,' she said

'Don't worry, it's all done.'

He looked round his drawing room, as he insisted on calling it. What other name was fitting? He had cleared up broken glass, one piece smeared with blood because someone had too carelessly pushed it under the edge of the curtain. Yet these were, he considered, his friends. You never knew. He had opened windows; collected dishes and unbroken glasses; wiped surfaces; rubbed a little Brasso into a white ring left by a wine bottle on his bureau; vacuumed, set the furniture straight and eventually begun on the kitchen. Yet his house did not look quite itself: it seemed bruised and forlorn, much as he felt.

'Come and have coffee anyway,' he said. 'If you'd like to.'

'I would. Last day of freedom before Flora arrives.'

The house looked as it usually did to Catherine, who said so.

'I like coming here. It's restful.'

'You're welcome at any time,' he told her, meaning it, since she was restful too. The old awkwardness that had arisen as he and Helen separated, was gone. Helen's moving on to much less suitable men had made it possible for them to go on being friends. Besides, Helen was in the South of England and Catherine was here.

The kitchen became fragrant with coffee. On a brass tray were bone china cups and saucers, a jug of warm milk and a plate of thin golden biscuits.

'Right,' he said. 'We can take this through to the piano room. It's sunny in there.'

The dog followed him as he carried the tray through, claws tapping on the polished wood floor.

In the mornings the sun shone in the east window on the fireplace end of the room, but by the afternoon the curtains had to be drawn to protect the piano sitting in front of the French windows that opened onto the garden. Almost, Catherine could still see Helen rattling the curtains open with an impatient sweeping back of velvet folds, letting bright daylight in. 'It's a piano!' she had cried. 'I'm not playing in the *dark!*' Hugh's face tightening, his silence.

They settled in the chairs she had found him in last night with Gilbert Sinclair.

'You belong here so beautifully,' Catherine said. It was his grandmother's house, Helen had told her, when she came here to live with him. She was giving up everything to be with Hugh in the wonderful wilds of Scotland. Not that wild, in this part of Ross-shire, as it turned out. Catherine had made only one visit during their marriage, and even then, only a few months after the wedding, there was some strain.

'You know I didn't grow up here,' he said. He still had the

accents of his childhood, English public school. 'But I was a student in Edinburgh – and – I liked hills.'

He was thinking of his student years, weekends with the hill-walking club, or heading for the Campsies when the afternoon lecture was over, having the long summer evening ahead, a hill he could climb and be back before dark.

'My father wasn't happy about my coming to Scotland.'

'Scots law,' Catherine said, realising. 'It must have meant you were stuck here for good, for your career.'

'That was the point,' Hugh said, 'and it worked out well. When my grandmother died, this house was here for me, and I applied for a job with George. Then I got a partnership.'

'You must have missed your family,' Catherine said, though she knew he had not. His father still sounded like a Scot, but his mother was from Surrey. They were cheerful pleasant people, who lived in St Albans not far from the Harrigans. Helen thought them boring and made no attempt to be a daughter-in-law. Of course, she had been only nineteen. She had met Hugh when he was visiting his parents, at one of her own parents' drinks parties. She had come with a broken heart (another boyfriend gone) to find Hugh, kind and steady, a man who would never let her down. His Highland home, she may have thought, would provide enough romance.

'What did you think of Kenneth?' Hugh said, to change the subject. 'Did he show you his house?'

'Yes. It's lovely.'

He laughed, taking her slightly frosty tone to relate to the house, not Kenneth himself. 'Are you being polite? Was it not your style? You prefer this—'He glanced round his own mellow room.

There seemed no polite answer. 'I wondered how you came to meet Kenneth,' she said instead. 'Are you his solicitor?'

'Yes, but it was hillwalking at first. James Heslop, who's in the medical practice in Strathpeffer, introduced us – he's a keen hillwalker. These days the business takes most of Kenneth's time.'

'Why is that?'

'His father, Iain, had a heart attack last year. He's all right, but he gave up work to please Kenneth's mother as much as anything. He plays a lot of golf.'

Catherine thought of her own parents, but all that sort of thing seemed too far off to worry about, since they were so robust and energetic. She wondered what Kenneth thought about his father – had they got on well, working in the same business?

'Well enough,' Hugh said. He poured more coffee into her cup. 'So you think you'll go back to The Factory?'

'I liked Gilbert. And The Factory is an amazing place. Perhaps I could take Flora, she'd like all the junk upstairs.' She blushed. 'Sorry that sounds rude. Bric-a-brac.'

'Junk,' Hugh said cheerfully.

'They don't get on – Gil and Kenneth?'

'They do not. It's hardly surprising – they're utterly different and Kenneth was always the favourite, Gil the outsider. At least with their father. Though not Mary, surprisingly.'

'Mary's their mother? Why is it surprising?'

'She's a Sabbatarian. Free Church.'

He saw he would have to explain this to her, and did. 'A woman of stern principles. Gilbert is her only soft spot.'

'Not Kenneth?'

'Not noticeably.'

They fell silent, Catherine absorbing the new information. The sun had been slipping slowly into the room and shone across the rug in front of the fireplace, where the dog slept, twitching her tail, whimpering in a dream. Catherine was conscious of birdsong in the trees beyond the French windows at the back of the room, of a car going by faintly on the main road, of the dog's wheezy breathing, the tick of the carriage clock.

'When is Flora coming?' Hugh asked, startling her.

'Oh – I was dreaming. Sorry. Tomorrow.'

'Is Alan bringing her?'

'No, my mother.' She sighed. 'She's going to stay a few days, till Flora is settled in school. But it will soon be the summer holidays, so she'll hardly have a chance to make new friends. It's bad timing, but there was the job and I have to have a job. At the end of term she'll go to Alan's parents for a couple of weeks, then mine. I've arranged some leave in August.'

She was justifying herself to her mother, not Hugh, and smiled at him, with a wave of dismissal, to change the subject.

'Parents and children,' he said. 'Ah well.'

'Yes,' she said, suddenly ashamed, remembering Oliver. On that impulse, she could not help asking, 'Are you all right, Hugh?'

'Me? Of course.' He smiled, but it was a sad smile, she realised, always sad now. *Helen,* she thought, embarrassed.

He rose, and took up the tray. 'I'll just take these through.'

Even with Hugh, there were things you had better not mention.

4

'What do they make there?'

'They don't make anything. It's a sort of sale room.'

'You said it was a *factory*.'

'It used to be. They made corsets once, hundreds of women using sewing machines.'

'What's a *corset*?'

'Long ago, women wore corsets under their dresses, to ... hold their tummies in and make them look slim.'

'Why didn't they just go on a diet? Your friend Gilbert doesn't make corsets?'

'No, silly, he sells furniture.'

'You're muddling me,' Flora said. She leaned back in the front passenger seat, that she was so newly allowed to sit in, and folded her arms, frowning.

It was almost the end of the summer holidays. Her grandparents had brought Flora home from her holiday with them, and she was sulking now they'd gone. She still misses her friends, Catherine's mother had said, stirring a pot even Flora had been leaving undisturbed lately.

'I've been saying to your father, we must have gone wrong

somewhere.' This to Catherine after Flora was in bed. Behind his newspaper, her father grunted and rustled the sports page.

'Why?'

'You and Helen both divorced. I can't understand it. You need to work at marriage, to make it stick.'

'Neither of us fancied being stuck,' Catherine said, turning the subject away from what failures she and Helen seemed to be. 'Anyway, I don't see why it would mean you and Dad had done anything wrong.'

'I can't think of a single thing. We did our best, brought you up to—'

Helen and she were alike in one thing, Catherine thought. Neither of them listened to a word their mother said. Helen didn't care but it still pricked Catherine that her mother could get under her skin. Tomorrow Mr and Mrs Harrigan would get on the train and go home; Catherine and Flora would take up in earnest their new life here. To mark it, she decided to introduce Flora to The Factory.

'Wow,' said Flora as The Factory came into view and Catherine turned onto the approach road. 'It's huge!'

'Gilbert has about half of it – the rest is derelict. Not in use.'

Flora considered, trying out the new word. 'Der-e-lict.'

Gil had seen them arrive. He was at the entrance and stepped forward as Catherine and Flora got out of the car.

'This is Flora.'

Gil took Flora's hand, shaking it and bowing. 'I'm thrilled to meet you, Miss Flora.'

Flora stared, then drew her hand away. 'Are you Gilbert?'

'Gilbert Sinclair, at your service.' He ushered them into the foyer. 'But you can call me Gil. Would you like the guided tour? Fourpence, but for you – twopence.'

Flora said nothing; she was sizing him up. Make her like him, Catherine thought.

'This way—' Gil led them into the ground floor area, opening the double doors with a flourish.

'You have lots of sofas.'

'I do. And wardrobes and sideboards and tables and chairs – lots of everything. Would you like to buy some furniture?'

'I haven't any money. I spent it on an ice cream when I was out with Granny.'

'I'm sure your mother will kindly lend you some.'

Flora tugged Catherine's arm. 'Can I buy something?'

'Perhaps – there are smaller things upstairs.'

'I'd like a sofa,' Flora said firmly. She looked up at Gil. 'Which is your favourite?'

'Come on – I'll show you.'

Flora followed him across the floor, weaving between tables and chairs, until he stopped at a long sofa of cracked brown hide, much worn, but soft and slippery.

'Stand here,' Gil instructed. They stood side by side with their backs to the sofa.

'Sit!'

They sat, and with their landing a puff of dust rose on either side, making Flora sneeze.

'What do you think? Comfy?'

'It's a bit dirty,' Flora observed.

'We'll get a duster and some beeswax in a minute. But first – what's your verdict?'

She looked up at him. 'Do you mean do I like it?'

'Yes.'

'*Quite.*'

Gil got up. 'What about this one?'

They moved further off, leaving Catherine behind, trying one after another, getting more and more dusty. Gilbert looked back once, smiling, lifting a shoulder as if in apology.

'Will I put the kettle on?' Catherine called.

'Yes, please.'

He and Flora had reached a chaise longue, and were trying that out.

'Hard,' was Flora's opinion.

Catherine cleaned up the little kitchen as best she could; it did not appear to have been tidied since her visit with Hugh. There were dirty cups crowded on the draining board, and the sink was grimy in the corners with hardened shreds of food.

As the kettle boiled Flora came running, as only someone small could run through the lumber of furniture, and the narrow spaces between.

'I found one!'

'Found what?'

'A sofa I want.'

'Good for you.'

'Can we get it then? Gil says it's quite cheap at the price.'

'It doesn't matter how cheap it is, I don't have space for another sofa.'

'It could go in my room.'

'No, it—'

Flora's expression stopped her. Not now, she thought, not a row so soon, when I'm in the bad books anyway.

'We'll see,' she said.

Flora turned away in disgust, knowing what *that* meant.

'Now, my dears, let's see what lovely biscuits we have to tempt Miss Flora.' Gilbert touched Catherine's elbow as he came into the kitchen. 'Don't worry,' his expression said, and despite herself, she was reassured. Flora, at any rate, had succumbed, and willingly helped him set out cups and saucers, and put chocolate biscuits on a plate.

'You choose where we're going to sit,' Gil said when tea was ready, and he carried the tray after her as she wove her way towards the sofa she was determined to have.

It was not quite as bad as Catherine had feared: a small wicker sofa with cushions that looked quite new and clean, in brown corded velvet.

'Very cosy,' Gilbert said, and Catherine laughed, agreeing, as they all squeezed on to it, the tea tray on a low table in front of them.

'I don't take up much room.' Flora balanced her fragile cup and saucer on her knees. 'I don't usually drink tea,' she informed Gilbert, 'but just this once, I'm going to have it.'

It was Lapsang, to which Catherine had added milk, and Flora set her cup down after one sip. 'I think I'll have a biscuit to take the taste away.'

Catherine, catching Gilbert's eye over Flora's head, had a pang of loss so severe she could not for a moment think what it meant.

How long ago it was since she and Alan had been able to look at each other, as parents do all the time, smiling about their children, aching with love and pride. She had thought you could not do that with anyone but your children's father, and yet here was Gil, and it was as if he loved Flora already.

'We might actually be able to fit this into your bedroom,' she conceded, full of gratitude, 'if you don't mind not having as much floor space to play.'

'And it's cheap at the price!' Flora exclaimed, taken with this phrase, so that Catherine was obliged to pause and say:

'I wonder what the price actually *is?*'

'Twenty quid to you,' Gil said promptly.

'Oh – that is quite cheap.' Taken aback, Catherine thought she should have made a closer inspection – could wicker furniture get woodworm?

'I got it thrown in with some wardrobes,' Gilbert said. 'Twenty quid will cover my costs, and I can bring it in the van.'

'Have you got a *van?*' Flora asked, impressed.

'I do.'

She tugged Catherine's arm. 'Let's look at *more*. We could put other things in his van.'

'All right,' Catherine said, rising too. 'I'm looking for a wee table for the hall and I saw one last time – '

They went upstairs, Flora leading the way.

'This is a huge success,' Catherine murmured to Gil. 'She's been so cross with me, taking her away from all her London friends.'

'It's a success with me too, I assure you.' He drew her hand through his arm, confidential, but like a woman, she thought; there was no hint of flirtation in the gesture. 'I've not sold a thing for weeks, so you're my best customers.'

'How do you manage? Are you making any money at all?' She blushed – it was not the sort of question you asked people. But he did not mind.

'Not much. Still, live in hope, eh?'

He was off, expertly negotiating the long tables in pursuit of Flora, picking up small items as he went, to show her. Thin as a broomstick, he was like a character from Dickens, perhaps, or a Gothic novel, something faunlike about him, flourishing a dented copper warming pan in one hand and a feather duster in the other. Herbert Pocket, perhaps? You would not be surprised to find him roaming the corridors of Gormenghast, or huddled over a brazier in a London street in *Oliver Twist*. You could almost not take him seriously – and yet she did. He is kind, she thought, he is a kind man.

At home, while Flora arranged her new collection of chipped china rabbits (I won't take a penny for them, Gil had said. Good riddance, I'm afraid) Catherine began preparing supper. Her hands were sticky when the phone rang, so it was a minute or two before she reached it, Flora yelling helpfully from upstairs, 'Telephone, Mummy! Answer it!'

'It's Kenneth.'

At first, her head full of the strangeness of the afternoon, she could not think who it was. Then she did.

'Oh, hello – what a coincidence, we're just back from Gil's place.'

'Why is that a coincidence?'

'Well, he's your brother and—' She stopped, feeling foolish. 'I'm getting supper ready,' she said, regaining ground, 'so what did you want?' Now she sounded rude.

'I wondered if you'd like to come and have dinner with me. At the house. My kitchen is kitted out now and I even have two armchairs and a second sofa.'

'Oh, we have a new sofa,' Catherine said, to give herself time to think. 'From Gil's place, from The Factory. It's very nice – he's going to deliver it next week.'

'That flea-ridden junk shop! I hope you're getting it fumigated.'

'It's perfectly fine,' Catherine said, but panicking. Fleas? 'Quite new,' she added firmly.

'I think I can do better than that,' he said, 'so what about it?'

'I'm afraid not. Flora's here, my daughter, and I can't leave her to go out at night. We don't have a babysitter yet, and anyway it's too soon.'

'When will it not be too soon?'

'I don't know,' she said, flustered. 'I suppose – well, I don't know.'

'I'll call you in a fortnight,' he said, and put the phone down.

Catherine stared at the receiver in astonishment. What a – a – *boor*, she thought, dredging this word up from some literary memory. As if I'd dream of going to dinner with him in his fancy house!

'Who was that?'

Flora leaned over the banister preparatory to sliding, feet hovering above the stairs, long hair hanging down the other side.

'Don't do that,' Catherine said, 'the rail's too – not in this house.' She heard it creak as Flora came down.

'Who *was* it, I said!'

'Gil's brother.'

'He's got a brother? My goodness, is he funny too?'

'You could say that.'

Flora went demurely to bed, full of her triumph in acquiring a sofa, four china rabbits and three books. Gilbert Sinclair was easily the best grown-up she had ever met.

The evening seemed long and empty to Catherine, sitting in her sparse and tidy living room. She tried television but found it wanting, fetched her book but was quickly bored – another wrong buy. She seemed unable to make good decisions – the house was wrong, she felt that already, shoddy somehow, thin at the edges. The sofa – what had possessed her to agree to that? And the book, turning out differently from the way she had expected, reading the enticing blurb. Nothing was as good as it seemed at first. Except perhaps Gil. Not Kenneth. Not that she had been sure of him that first time, something about him setting her on edge.

At least her mother had gone home.

For a moment or two she was almost tearful, unable to explain to herself why she had come so far, to the other end of the country, to live and work. She could have got a job anywhere, what she did so generic it hardly mattered where she did it. Now she was hundreds of miles from Helen, something that had seemed a good idea, but in practice – she saw with bleak honesty – making things difficult for both of them.

Thinking of Helen she remembered Hugh, and comforted herself with his kindness, his willingness to help. Perhaps it would be all right, in time. She could call him, or Helen, to tell them about Gil's success with Flora and make a funny story of it. She need not be alone.

The Theory of One Line
1994–6

1

There were times when Helen was tired of being herself, and longed to be a different woman, who did not show her feelings, or indeed *have* those feelings which so troubled her, always shifting. A woman who never had pink patches of freckled sunburn on unguarded shoulders, or broken fingernails; whose career progressed with decision and elevation. Who had in fact, a career. This mythical woman, hardly human, took on vaguely the appearance of her sister Catherine. Perhaps, she wondered, surprised one morning by this thought, I want to be like Catherine. Yet how critical they were of one another, affecting sympathy while underneath there was only impatience.

'Helen and her *men*,' she guessed Catherine thought, even said, though to whom she might say it, Helen could not imagine. Hugh, or perhaps this Gilbert she was always going on about. Catherine was close to Hugh, but Helen did not mind. He was a good man, and had deserved better. The other woman, the one Helen was not, would have had the sense not to marry him in the first place, or having done so, would have made the marriage a success.

'Why can't you girls *stick* to your husbands?' their mother had asked, meaning Helen, for she had admired Hugh, while never caring for Alan. Helen had peeled herself away from Hugh, from marriage.

'I was so bored,' she said aloud, standing at the kitchen sink, looking out of the window at the garden belonging to Mrs Harcourt in the bottom flat. At her bird table sparrows fought over the food cages as they flew back and forth, indignant and greedy.

Perhaps it was only Hugh's grand piano had kept her with him through six years and Oliver's birth. If she had played – say – the fiddle, she could have left much sooner: picked up the violin in its stiff black case, packed a few things and gone. You cannot take a piano with you, and on her own, in this rented flat, she was lucky to have a second-hand upright. I wanted to marry him because of the piano, she thought, seeing again the lovely room with its faded Turkish rugs on floorboards darkened by the sun to the colour of rosewood. All afternoon the sun had come in the big windows at the back, lighting the gold and white jug of flowers on the table by the door. What hours I spent in that room, she thought, till Oliver was born.

She had the familiar wrench of loss and sorrow. That was why I left, she thought, not just boredom. I could have put up with that, for the piano, for being safe. She was not safe now, nothing was safe after Oliver. Almost always since then she had wakened with a sense of dread, as if some terrible thing had happened and she would remember it soon. Then she did.

She saw and felt again the softness and coldness of him, the white blanket, his stillness in the wooden crib Hugh had made. How often she had bent down to check he was still breathing, in those first anxious weeks. Then, when she thought it was all right and he would indeed survive her amateur mothering, he stopped breathing.

It was dark in her mind, that time, and in that darkness she had been unable to stay with Hugh, who had become a distant stranger. Do *not* think of it, she told herself. This was the trouble with an empty day. There was no Catherine to call on or meet for lunch. Why had she moved so far away?

Do you fancy Hugh after all, she had asked Catherine that last Saturday, when they met in the National Gallery as they so often had while Flora was at Alan's.

'Of course not.' Catherine had dismissed this. 'He's a good friend, and he said he'd make sure I met people.'

'I can't think why you're going,' Helen grumbled. 'You'll miss London, you know you will. And I'll miss *you*,' she added, for she was not so sure Catherine would miss her.

'You can come and visit, and anyway, I'll be home every time Alan is on leave, so that he can see Flora.'

'He doesn't want to take Flora to Saudi?'

'Certainly not. I wouldn't allow it if he did.'

'You might not have the choice.'

'That wouldn't happen.'

Helen thought: I was right – she never loved him.

They walked round the Rubens room in perfunctory fashion after lunch, not looking at the paintings, so wallpaper would have done as well.

'I must go in a minute,' Catherine said at last. 'I have things to buy for Flora. It's strange, being without a job – the new one doesn't start for a month.'

'Why did you give up your old one so early?'

'Time to pack and to be around more for Flora. I didn't like it much anyway.'

'I hope you like the new one.'

'It's a job, it looks secure and it's a step up.'

Helen was on the verge of saying, you never like your jobs, you didn't like your husband, you don't care about your house. What do you love, Catherine? The answer she would have liked – you, Helen – would not have come, and as they were to part it was best to keep the peace between them.

'Sit down a minute,' she said. 'You'll be gone soon and we won't be able to talk to each other except on the phone.'

'All right. But not here.'

They moved to the eighteenth century, and sat down in front of a Gainsborough, a portrait of an aristocratic family formally posed against a backdrop of country mansion and green fields and woods. Neither of them warmed to the family, given their own circumstances, but it was better than Rubens.

'Why don't you come too, come to Scotland with me,' Catherine said. 'I'll put you up till you get some teaching. I'll be working for the Council, remember, so I can find the right contacts.'

'You don't want *me* living with you!'

'You'd soon find your feet.'

'Why would I go back to the Highlands?'

'I know you were unhappy. But you loved it, you always said how beautiful it was, what a great place to live.'

'I said it was a great place to bring up children.' Seeing Catherine's expression change, Helen regretted this, and went on hastily, 'It's nice of you, thank you, but now I'm back in London – well, I love it *here*, I always did.'

'What is there to keep you here, though? Not being close to Mum and Dad?'

Helen could not resist saying, 'I've met somebody.'

'Who is it?' Catherine sounded surprised, as if she meant, if it's important, why didn't you say – if not, why bother me now?

'His name's Joe. He's lovely.'

Catherine looked sceptical. 'Well, that's nice, but if it – doesn't go anywhere ...'

'It will. I'm sure it will.' She glanced at her sister. 'I know you see me as someone who isn't good at relationships, but I know now what's been wrong.'

'Tell me.'

She still looked more amused than interested. Helen sighed, feeling annoyed. 'I've got this theory,' she said, 'that there's something about everyone you have to know, before you *know* them.'

'What on earth does that mean?'

'There's a central truth – everyone has this central truth about themselves. Like – they would always rather be alone, or they're an orphan, or they did something terrible when they were only sixteen. Like murder someone. Or let someone die.'

'Surely that's true of only a very small number of—'

'Oh, I know, I'm dramatizing,' Helen interrupted. 'To let you see the *idea*.'

'Well, I don't.'

'If you know the one central truth about someone, you understand them. You see them in the light of this truth.'

'So – how do you find out?'

'Often you don't, so these people always remain a mystery. I think Hugh was a mystery to me because I never understood. I didn't have the one line that would have unlocked him. I mean, I even explained my theory to him in the hope ... but he didn't get it.'

'So,' Catherine said, 'you think you know this – this *truth* about what's his name – Joe?'

'No,' Helen admitted. 'But now I'm at least aware I have to find it.'

'I see.' Catherine did not sound convinced, but she put her hand on Helen's arm and gave it a gentle squeeze. 'Now I really do have to go.'

As they came out of the Gallery into the sunshine and crowds, Catherine said, 'Hugh is easy – he has no dark secrets and you know at once what kind of man he is. Alan too. I should have known about Alan.'

'What was his one line?'

Catherine shrugged. 'Oh, he was sociable.'

'Isn't that a good thing?' In the sunshine, pausing on the steps with London before them, teeming and noisy, Helen took courage and asked, 'Why did you *marry* him? I always wondered.' She held her breath, since Catherine might take offence.

'He was funny,' Catherine said, sounding almost surprised. 'He made me laugh and he was so friendly and open. I thought I might become more – I don't know – relaxed. Light-hearted. If I was with him.'

'But—' Helen wasn't sure she could say the obvious thing here, but Catherine answered it anyway.

'What that turned out to mean was a lot of sitting around in pubs saying nothing to people you didn't even like much. He could stay there for hours – it was what he liked doing. Talking about football, drinking beer.' She shrugged. 'My own fault – you should make sure you know about people, before you marry them. More than I did.'

'So you were bored too,' Helen said.

As they parted with a brief hug, Helen felt herself becoming tearful, as if her sister was going to the other side of the world instead of a short flight away.

When she was on the tube, crammed into the remaining seat in the carriage, she thought again about this conversation. She had quite liked Alan, but Hugh had been nicer. Much. He had also been solitary and orderly and methodical: things she was not.

Still, if all went well, she would not have empty Saturdays any more, and she would be with someone who suited her much better. Whatever Joe's faults – not that she had discovered them yet – he was never boring.

2

You could not rely on Joe. Years later, Helen thought how different her whole relationship with him might have been had it happened twenty years later and they both had mobile phones. She could have kept track of him, and he might have told her what he was doing, or given her more warning if he wasn't going to be around. As it was, Joe was one of the first people she knew to get a mobile phone, when many of her friends still scorned them. He saw the advantages.

There were times when Joe's unreliability worked in her favour. He appeared out of the blue, probably letting someone else down, with a new car – or once, alarmingly, a huge motorbike – ready to take her out. He wanted her to drop everything, the moment he was back. Mostly she did, since being with Joe was much more exciting than being with anyone else.

'Right – where do you fancy tonight?'

'I've not had supper – do you want something to eat?'

'We'll eat up in town. Little place in Soho I fancy trying – my pal Bernie runs it. All right?'

'I'm not dressed for that.'

He was in her tiny hallway and she was in his arms. 'Bed first? You lovely girl – come on then.'

It was ten o'clock before they were eating in Bernie's cramped restaurant, full of people who knew each other.

'You're ruining my digestion,' she told Joe. 'I never eat so late.'

'Try this,' he said, pouring the rioja.

What was Bernie going to do when his friends stopped coming for dinner? It was such a small restaurant she didn't see how he made any money, since everyone stayed for hours and he never got the tables cleared for another sitting.

Sometimes they were not back in her flat before three or four in the morning, taking expensive taxis home. He always had cash and rarely used his American Express card. He was not a man who liked paperwork. He took a roll of notes out of the inside pocket of his leather jacket, peeled off what he wanted, gave a generous tip, and was off and up the stairs before Helen.

'Come on, girl, get your key out.'

'Hush, you'll wake the neighbours.'

'Give them something to talk about.'

'You've already done that, with a new car every other week and that motorbike!'

As soon as they were indoors his hands were all over her.

'I wouldn't like to get in a fight with you,' she gasped, feeling the hardness of muscle as he gripped her. 'How tough you feel.'

'Women think they can fight men off,' he shrugged, 'but they don't stand a chance. Men are always stronger.'

She wasn't going to get in a fight with him, so what did it matter? His strength was good; she felt protected. He had old-fashioned ideas about the frailty of women.

He smoked but, in deference to her, not in bed. He sometimes got up again after sex, pulled on his jeans and a jersey and sat in an armchair with another cigarette. In those early days she rose too, giving up the night since it would soon be morning.

During that first summer when Catherine went to Scotland, it grew light while they were sitting there, the grey London dawn coming bleakly into her little sitting room. 'I'm exhausted. I don't know how you do this.'

He shrugged. 'It's the weekend. Party while you can.'

'If it was just the weekend – but I'll soon have work to go to, even if you don't.'

'I've got work.'

'What?'

'I'm my own boss. I suit myself when I start and finish.'

'What kind of business is it?'

They had been seeing each other for two months. The school holidays were nearly over and she still had little idea of how he spent his time when they were apart. They'd gone all the way to Brighton on the back of that motorbike, and walked over Hampstead Heath one morning he was full of energy he needed to work off. Once when he was driving a Jaguar, they had gone to Cambridge to meet someone who was keen to buy the car. She assumed he was some kind of car dealer, but he shrugged off questions about his business.

'Ask no questions, you'll be told no lies.'

She hated this answer. Seeing him lounging in her Windsor chair, dropping cigarette ash on the carpet, filling her room with smoke, she wondered if she even liked him. He wasn't her sort. He said he had grown up in Glasgow then left at eighteen to find work in London. He had never gone to university, though he admitted to being 'at college' for a while, but she was no wiser about that than when she had first met him.

'You know all about *me*,' she said. 'What's the secrecy for?'

'No secrets,' he said. 'I have a few things going, that's all.'

'Selling cars?'

He stubbed out his cigarette in the ashtray she'd put by the chair. 'Furniture, antiques, that kind of thing. We got a warehouse just outside Watford.'

'We? You have a partner?'

'Two. You met them. Charlie and Brian.'

She could not remember which was which, or even if Brian was the man she was thinking of, that they'd met one night at a club, and whose wife had said to her as they occupied adjacent cubicles in the Ladies, 'Joe says you're a teacher, right?'

Unused to carrying on a conversation while she peed, Helen said only 'yes' until they were out and washing their hands. In the mirror their eyes met, Gaynor's heavy with make-up. She was older than Helen, glamorous in a showy way, with heavy jewellery and short skirts.

'I'm a music teacher. I work in primary schools and I have a couple of private pupils too.'

'You're not his usual sort,' Gaynor said, amused, 'but he's smitten right enough.'

She watched him now in the cold early light, the white sky outside revealing nothing about what kind of day was coming, though the flat was stuffy from yesterday's heat.

'It's just that school starts next week. You could come here in the evening, and I'll still have weekends, except I've taken on a couple of Saturday morning pupils, so—'

'Will I move in?'

'What?'

'Would it make it easier for you if I move in?'

She had not reached that stage. Where, anyway, was *his* home? In bad moments she wondered if he had a wife somewhere. There had been a speculative look in Gaynor's eye when she questioned her that night in the club. So you're his bit on the side this time, she might have been thinking.

If he offered to move in, there was clearly not a wife. Relieved, she said, 'Would you like to? What about your own place?'

'I've been kipping at Brian and Gaynor's when I'm not here, to be honest. I gave up my place weeks ago.'

Perhaps the wife had thrown him out. Perhaps Gaynor had had enough of putting him up.

'We could see how it went...'

'Just say if you'd rather not.' His smile was rueful. 'Sorry, didn't mean to put you on the spot.'

'No, no it's fine, it would be lovely.'

'Tell you what, I'll give up the fags. You'd like that?'

Laughing, she went to sit on his welcoming lap, and put her arms round him. 'I would.'

Afterwards, she began to panic. She knew so little about him, and there was a dangerous edge to Joe, with his secrets. Too late: he was moving in before school began.

She expected him to come and go mysteriously as he always had, out of contact for a few days, reappearing without warning. For the first few weeks, it was not like that at all; it was a kind of honeymoon. When she came home from school he was there, cooking the evening meal. He went outside for a cigarette when he couldn't do without one, and he filled the only vase she had with flowers, then brought her a jug that looked old and valuable. Perhaps it was true about the antiques, for the next week he brought home a round mahogany table. Her kitchen was a galley, so she had no dining table and was tired of eating from a tray on her lap. The wood was burnished, the bow legs intricately carved. It took up most of the middle of the sitting room.

'Pity you've got that piano,' he said as they edged round the table on their way out one day. 'Takes up a lot of space.'

'Not as much as your table!'

'I thought you liked it?'

'I do. It's beautiful.' She kissed him. 'But I need the piano.'

'Got to get a bigger flat then,' he said as they went downstairs to the street door.

'I can't afford a bigger one.'

'Don't you worry about that.'

He opened the passenger door and she got in. He made sure she was settled in the car before he got in himself. He always did this, just as he always walked on the outside of the pavement when they were together. In some ways, he was what her mother would call a gentleman. Not that her parents had met Joe and she was in no hurry for that to happen. They lived in the house where she and Catherine had grown up, in a leafy road of 1930s half-timbered houses, her father growing tomatoes and playing golf in his spare time, her mother a stalwart of the WI.

Joe took her to an exhibition preview at a small gallery in Highgate. Another surprising thing was how wide his acquaintance was, how catholic his interests. He knew the gallery owner, not the artist, but he said they should buy something as this was a painter whose work would increase in value.

'What if you don't like the pictures?' Helen teased.

'We don't have to put the bleeding thing on the wall, girl. I'll keep it in the lock-up, wait a bit, then in another year or two, sell it on.'

'That seems a waste. I'd rather buy something I liked and have it to look at.'

'If you like one of them,' he said, 'I'll get it, and you can hang it on the wall in our new place.'

As they reached the gallery he said, 'What about Highgate then? D'you fancy a place here?'

'Can we afford it?'

He put his arm round her waist and squeezed. 'Course we can. Come on then, this is it.'

There was no missing the gallery, since on this warm summer evening the preview guests had spilled out onto the pavement with their glasses of wine. She felt the buzz of excitement that went with all Joe's excursions.

Joe introduced her to the gallery owner, a little man in an embroidered waistcoat waving a cigarette in an ebony holder. His laugh was hoarse with years of smoke inhalation and he had a Glasgow accent many times thicker than Joe's, whose veered between Govan and North London depending on his mood and who he was talking to. Helen thought Frankie a bit of a poser, but he made her laugh and seemed such a friend within five minutes she felt she could ask him, when Joe drifted off to speak to other people, 'Which one is the artist? I can't imagine, looking at the paintings. Everyone looks too civilised to produce one of *them*.'

'Over the top, eh?' Frankie said with a wink. 'They sell though. I don't see him in this crowd. He'll be outside having a fag, pontificating aboot his art.' He reached out and caught a girl by the arm. 'Never mind, here's Rose, she'll tell you about the paintings. Won't you sweetheart?'

'Oh, hi, Frankie,' the girl said. She looked Helen up and down.

'I'm Helen Guthrie.'

'She's with Joe,' Frankie said, grinning, so that Helen worried this meant more to Rose than mere information. Not that Rose would attract Joe. She was stocky, with no looks, and dressed in dusty black. She also seemed, as Helen shook her hand, a bit grubby, her dyed red hair unbrushed and lank.

'Right,' Rose said. 'How long's that been then?'

'That I've been with Joe? Oh, not so long. A couple of months.'

Rose raised her eyebrows. 'You're doing well.'

Catherine had a gift for chilling you with a look. It was a gift Helen longed for sometimes.

Later, she said to Joe, 'Who was that girl, Rose something? Is she Will's girlfriend? The artist.'

Joe stopped outside an Italian restaurant. 'This do? I'm starving after all that cheap wine. Frankie's commission's about ninety per cent and he still buys antifreeze.' He pushed the door open. 'Ok?'

'Rose?'

'Oh, give it a rest. I've known Rose for years. She's always hanging round some guy's neck. It could be Will now, for all I know. Piss, his pictures anyway – I wouldn't waste my money.'

'So you didn't buy one?' She wouldn't have minded Will's painting being consigned to a lock-up in Camden.

'Too right. Frankie's losing his touch.'

They went into the restaurant, where it turned out he knew the waiter and there was a long conversation about football before they even ordered their food.

Rose. They had barely spoken before Gaynor appeared, and Gaynor by contrast seemed quite a pal, so she had gone round the exhibition with her. Gaynor had drunk several glasses of the cheap wine, and was able to tell her a lot about Frankie and the artist and several other people, that Helen found illuminating. Joe's world opened up a little more.

Gaynor said nothing about Rose, except, 'That cow.' Then with a squeeze of Helen's arm, 'You keep away darlin', she's not the kind you want to get friendly with.'

There was no need to worry about Rose – or anything else. In a fortnight Joe had found them a three-bedroomed flat in a 1930s block in Highgate, close to Hampstead Heath. He arranged it so that Helen got out of the lease of her own flat without a penalty, and he took her to Heal's to buy furniture, since the new flat was largely unfurnished. She did not see whether he counted out several thousand pounds to pay for all that, since she had wandered off to look at lamps and coffee tables while he arranged delivery.

Go back to the Highlands and live with her sister? She was glad she hadn't even considered it.

Three months after they moved into the new flat, Helen realised she was pregnant.

3

'What does Joe say?'

'I've not told him yet.'

'Why on earth not? Do you think he'll throw you out? Honestly, Helen, I wish I'd met him. Is he reliable?'

'Will he make an honest woman of me?'

'You know what I mean. Will he take care of you?'

Helen bit back, 'I can take care of myself', since it looked as if that was not the case. She was still angry with herself. They had been careless.

'Oh dear.' Catherine's voice softened. 'I'm sorry, it can't be easy.'

'What if this baby dies too?'

'Oh, Helen, that won't happen – it *won't.*'

'I wish you'd not gone to bloody Scotland.'

'It's done now.'

'Are you sorry? Are you not happy there?' She might come back, Helen thought, I could do with her here. She would stand up to Joe.

'I'm fine. Flora has a new best friend, so that's a help, and she likes her teacher.'

'Yes, but you?'

'Never mind me, you're the one who needs—'

'What?'

'You must tell Joe.'

'Yes.'

'Call me tomorrow, after you've spoken to him.'

Joe was late home. He was often late. She should eat supper now and not wait for him, but she felt queasy. She had not actually been sick, but that hadn't happened last time.

She was so afraid of having another baby she had wondered whether to tell Joe at all. Telling Catherine had been a way of ensuring she wouldn't just see a doctor and get an abortion arranged as soon as possible. Could you hide that from a man you were living with? If she could have planned it for one of his absences, his 'buying trips' as he called them, then perhaps. The trouble was, she never knew when he'd go off or when he'd come back. The unpredictability of his behaviour was less exciting now they were living together.

She was standing in the kitchen doing nothing when she heard his key in the door. Usually, when he came to kiss her, putting his arms tight round her waist, nuzzling her neck – you lovely girl, missed you – she could smell drink and his mouth might have tell-tale commas of red wine in the corners. Tonight he was fired up with some other stimulus.

'Hey – Helen – you there?'

He was standing in the hall, his black overcoat dripping water. It had been raining all day. His hair was even blacker because wet, plastered to his head like a cap.

'Fucking weather,' he said, grinning.

'You're dripping water everywhere!'

'Never mind – I'm going out—'

'You're just in, you can't—'

She would not have said that a few weeks ago. She'd have gone out with him. Now, weary with teaching and the fatigue of early pregnancy, she could not be bothered. Why sit in a bar talking above noisy music to people she didn't even like much, when she could be here in their beautiful flat, reading and listening to the music she chose herself. He liked something *with a beat.*

'Wait – back in a mo. The guys are bringing it up and I need to give them a hand.'

'Bringing what up?'

'I've got a present for you, haven't I? Fucking weight though. Jesus, you ever tried moving one of them?' He was hugely pleased with himself, almost dancing with it, a dog that's just brought back a rabbit, tail wagging wildly.

'What present?'

He was off downstairs, leaving the door open. She followed him, pausing at the top of the stairs. Their flat was on the second floor, so she could hear but not see the commotion at the main door, as three men began bringing something in. Joe looked up from the landing below, where he was directing operations, and saw her.

'Get back inside, you! It's a surprise. Go in the lounge, right?'

She sat on the new leather sofa, waiting. Whatever they were bringing upstairs was cumbersome: progress was slow, and there was a good deal of swearing. Sweating too: she could smell it on them, as the men, breathing heavily, eventually brought it in and lifted off the covers they had used to protect it from the stairway walls.

He had brought her a grand piano. A baby grand, but still, a piano, a Hoffman in walnut, polished and cared for, not a scratch on its surface.

Breathless, Joe presented it with a wide sweep of his arms. 'Ta-ra!'

'*Joe!*'

'Guy says it needs tuning, but what d'you think? Nice, eh?'

They stood round her looking exhausted and sweaty and pleased. She could have hugged them all, but in the end hugged only Joe, in tears.

Now she had to tell him about the baby.

For a few days, she had no opportunity to call Catherine. Joe stayed at home, cooking for her, making her put her feet up, more pleased with himself – and her – than she had ever seen him. She should have realised pregnancy would be something he approved of.

She was teaching him to play the piano.

'See,' he said, 'I'm not blaming my mum and dad, no way, but there was things I missed as a kid. Never learned to play the piano, never had a bike.'

'Really? I thought all boys had bikes.'

'Not in Govan,' he said. Glimpses of his past, that he guarded so carefully, gleamed now and again.

'So you can't ride a bike?' she teased.

'We'll start with doh ray me,' he said. 'Leave out the bike for now.'

He had no patience to learn, wanting to play Chopsticks right away, so the lessons deteriorated into laughter and needing a drink. *She* was not to have a drink; she had to be careful.

'Another thing,' he said, dishing up spaghetti for them one night she was late home from school because of the Christmas concert.

'What?'

'You got to give up that job.'

'I will nearer the birth, now they've improved maternity pay,' she conceded. 'I can't do it yet.'

'Why not? We don't need the money – I can take care of things.'

'It's not just the money. I have to be sure I can go back to work after the baby.'

He wasn't having that. She would be at home, taking care of their son. He was sure it was a son. She had told him about Oliver, in the tender aftermath of love-making, the night the piano arrived. He had been all warmth and reassurance. He'll be right next to our bed, no fear, I won't let you go through that again, don't you worry. It was clear he blamed Hugh in some way. She let him do that, shamefully, not wanting him to blame her.

'I have to have a job,' she said. 'What if I lost it, and – and it doesn't work out somehow between us – where would I be then?'

'We'll get married,' he said, briskly mixing Bolognese sauce into his pasta. Then, to her further astonishment, he flushed. 'Got a few things to sort out first, but – yeah. Before he's born.'

Next day, when he had gone out, perhaps to deal with these unspecified few things, Helen was filled with uncertainty. It was a Saturday, almost Christmas, so she had no pupils, and the day was supposed to be for shopping, only she was so tired she could not be bothered. I'll go to Foyle's, she thought, and buy book tokens for everyone. That will do, this year.

There was too much to think about. Because he had asked her, did not mean she had to marry him. It hadn't been much of a proposal.

She must phone Catherine, then – oh God – her mother. If she told her parents, she would have to introduce Joe to them, and her mother would think, where did she pick him up? Not our sort.

Mine though, she thought defiantly, my sort. The lovemaking, the excitement, the piano, his instant acceptance of the baby, that he seemed to long for, filled with pride already – with all that, what was there to be afraid of?

4

Catherine was sure she wanted no more children herself. It had been hard enough the first time, so soon after Oliver's death. She could not face that anxiety again.

Alan had made little effort to keep in touch with Flora; his new life in Saudi claimed him. His mother, calling her from Gatehouse-of-Fleet, complained he was not even coming home for Christmas.

'He wants us to go out there. Dad says maybe we should, but I'm not keen.'

'You could take Flora,' Catherine suggested, being generous. Flora had been particularly difficult that week, having fallen out with the new best friend.

'Oh, I don't think I'd want to take a child to that place. But you could come here with Flora at Christmas. We'd like that.' Alan's mother treated Catherine as if she were still her daughter-in-law. She seemed to think it would all work out, once Alan was home again.

'I'm not sure yet what's happening—' Catherine hedged.

All the way to the Borders, an awkward journey, for too much rich food and Flora being utterly spoiled. Something to be avoided.

Helen was calling more often these days, usually just as Catherine got in from work. Having collected Flora from the childminder, she would be starting to cook when the phone rang. She noticed Helen never called when Joe was with her. The glow of the day when the piano arrived seemed to have dimmed. Helen had begun asking about Christmas, and eventually Catherine agreed she would come south with Flora.

When the phone rang at six the next evening, she assumed it was Helen.

'Don't worry, I've done it, we got flights,' she said.

There was a pause, then, 'Catherine?'

'Sorry – I thought it was my sister.'

'It's Kenneth Sinclair.'

'I know.'

'How are the babysitting arrangements?'

'What?'

'Are you free for dinner yet?'

Flora was having a sleepover with a new friend on Saturday night. Left without an excuse, Catherine agreed. Kenneth had been at the back of her mind, a problem unresolved. He had said he would call in a fortnight, she remembered, but it was the end of November. Months had gone by.

She told herself she was curious to see his house again, but she could also ask about Gilbert, whom she'd not seen since the last time she had visited The Factory in October. She had decided to ration further visits, since Flora could not leave without buying something and there was a limit to her tolerance of china knick-knacks.

'Can I bring anything?' she asked.

'No. Just yourself.'

This Friday in the office, when everyone was saying *what's doing at the weekend*, she would have an answer. *Nothing much* wasn't good enough, after nearly six months of living here, listening to everyone else talking about their garden, the hills they would climb, and their nights out.

Then she changed her mind. In this part of the Highlands, she had discovered, everyone knew everyone else. She did not want to advertise a visit to Kenneth Sinclair just yet.

5

'What have you done with your daughter?' he asked, taking her coat, and when she told him, said, 'No rush to get home then?'

'Not unless it starts snowing – I think it might.'

She had brought flowers and wine, and he put the wine near the fire to warm it. There was a bottle there already, a glassful drunk. Later she saw the flowers still lying on a chair in the hall, as if he didn't know what to do with them. From the kitchen came a warm smell of tomato and garlic.

'It's lasagne, is that ok?'

'It smells lovely.'

'It should be ready in about twenty minutes, I reckon. Want to look and see if you think so?'

He opened the oven door and they inspected the lasagne, not quite bubbling yet.

'Glass of wine?'

'I'm driving, so better not.'

'One glass can't do any harm. By the time you've eaten, it'll have worn off, won't it?'

'Half a glass.' She was tempted by the fire, the comfortable sofa, the earthy scent of the wine as he refilled his own glass. She had been too hard on him; he was making an effort to be a good host.

'So what do you think?' he asked, sweeping an arm out. 'My new furniture?'

'Beautiful. Your house isn't full of clutter, the way most people's are.'

'You mean it's too bare?'

'No. Elegant.'

He laughed. 'Nobody's ever accused me of that before. I think I need a few bits and pieces ... Women know about these things.'

'Pay a visit to your brother,' she said. 'You'll find plenty of bits and pieces in The Factory.'

'You're kidding.'

'Flora loves it. My house is filling up with—' She stopped, not wanting to say 'junk'. 'Anyway, he does have some nice things.'

'I'll have to meet this young lady, and put her right about my brother,' he said lightly.

'Why would you do that? She loves Gil.'

'As long as none of his London pals turn up.' He leaned from his armchair to the fire, to pick up the wine bottle and refill his glass. The firelight glowed on his arm and face, red lights glinting in his hair. He was so unlike Gilbert she could scarcely believe they were related.

'What London pals?'

'They appear from time to time. He was in London for years. He only came home because he was skint.'

'I worked in London, and my sister lives in Highgate.'

'I've no idea where he lived. It didn't interest me. I was just glad he was out of our hair.'

'You really don't like him.'

This was quite different from the mild irritation she and Helen induced in each other. In trouble, that vanished. She shook her head when he held out the bottle, on her guard again, distanced by the scorn in his voice.

He got up. 'Better check the dinner.'

As she listened to him moving about the kitchen, she wondered about his family. Gil had come home when he needed help, so perhaps his parents felt differently.

Kenneth reappeared. 'Ready, I think. I made a salad – is that ok, do you think?'

'It sounds perfect.' She went through to the kitchen where he was setting out the meal. Everything looked new – table, chairs and china. She thought again of all she had left with Alan, but pointlessly, since he was in Saudi, his house rented out. She kept finding she lacked some essentials and still looked for dishes or books that were no longer in her possession.

She waited till Kenneth had dished up before she ventured, 'Everything seems so new. Did you leave everything with your wife, when you left?' She wondered if this was a step too far, but he gave a bark of laughter.

'I left in a hurry, glad to get out. She was welcome to her pots and pans. I left a lot of my music though.' His face darkened. 'I might get that some day. When I can face it.'

Face *her*, she thought. It must have been bad. 'I left a lot too. I don't miss anything much, though I thought I would. It's inconvenient and I'm not as well off as you. I couldn't just buy a whole lot of new stuff.'

'It's news to me that the woman doesn't come off best,' he said. 'What about your ex? How's he doing?'

'Every case is different, isn't it?' Defensive, she laid down her fork, looking straight at him, then disconcerted by his intense gaze, glanced away. She would not speak to him about Alan.

They ate in silence for a few moments. Whether it was the

food (it wasn't bad; he could at least cook) or the effect of her half glass of wine, she relaxed at last in a wash of tiredness, the week behind her. What did it matter if they didn't get on – she needn't see him again.

Before he gathered up their empty plates, he rolled up the sleeves of the fawn shirt, revealing muscular forearms. He was a hairy man, going by the curled hair on his arms and the dark v revealed by the open collar. She reached out to help and his hand brushed hers as he picked up her plate. She withdrew as sharply as if she'd had a shock.

'I've got cheese,' he said. 'Oatcakes? I haven't mastered desserts yet.'

'I don't usually eat them. I only make pudding for Flora.'

'All women like pudding,' he said.

She laughed. 'Don't you ever believe what you're told?'

He stood with plates in either hand, challenging her. 'I bet you eat chocolate.'

'Oh. Chocolate. Occasionally.'

He raised his eyebrows, not believing this either, and went to make coffee. They took it to the living room and laid it on the coffee table. The cheese was indifferent and the oatcakes dry, but the coffee was strong and good.

Kenneth began building up the fire again.

'Help yourself,' he said. 'I wish you'd have another glass of wine.'

'I won't risk it. I'm driving into the city, remember, and the weather didn't look too promising. I'd better check it's not snowing.'

He had no curtains yet, so she went to the far end of the room, to the window looking downhill over the village, as if she could see out into the darkness. The two lamps lit were near the fire. As she stood peering, he switched them off.

'Better?' he asked, but it was all she could do not to gasp at the sudden darkness. What was she afraid of? He was annoying, even antagonistic, but not dangerous.

Through the double-glazed windows she was aware of whirling whiteness, obscuring everything beyond more thoroughly than darkness could.

'You can put the lamps on,' she said, turning into the room again. 'It is snowing.'

He was very close to her in the dark. He had only come to look out of the window, but there was that prickle again, a nervousness, in her sense of him, giving off heat like scent, alien and yet already too familiar. He moved away without speaking and switched on the lamp nearest the sofa. Now he could see her, but she could see him only in the glow from the fire, burnishing his skin and hair.

She hesitated. 'I think I'd better go,' she said. 'It's quite a drive home.'

'I'll get your coat.'

Perversely, now she wished she had not said she would go.

'You'll come again.' He held out her long winter coat that was cold from hanging on a stand by the front door. The silky lining chilled her neck as she fastened the buttons. 'Bring your Flora with you. Maybe Sunday lunch?'

'We don't usually bother with a big Sunday lunch.'

'Good God, what sensual pleasures *do* you allow yourself?'

'What?'

He was laughing at her. 'You're a hard woman, Catherine Harrigan,' he said. 'What do I have to do to get you to like me? You don't, do you?'

'Maybe you could try being rather more *courteous*,' she said, offended. 'Do you realise how rude you are?'

'Safe journey.' He opened the door and for a few seconds his hand rested on her back, then she stepped out. 'Call me when you're home – got the number? Then I'll know you're ok. The main roads should still be fine if you leave now.'

The exterior light coming on illuminated the snow drifting towards them, landing softly on the broad front step and on her boots. She turned up her collar and fished car keys from her bag, her fingers clumsy in gloves.

'It was a lovely meal and I didn't mean to be ungrateful. You *annoy* me.'

'I know,' he said, grinning. 'But you'll be back, won't you?'

She gave him a wave, not answering, glad she had turned her car when she arrived, so that it was easy to drive away. The headlights swept the whitened drive in front of her, the wipers doing no good as the flakes seemed scarcely to land on the windscreen, but whirled in front of the car. She drove cautiously onto the empty road, heading home.

6

'Have you met this Joe?' Catherine's mother asked.

'No, but I will tomorrow when I go up to London. Why don't you come with me?'

'I can't leave your father with Flora.'

'Why ever not?

'We want to make the most of having her here, now you're so far away.'

Rebuked, Catherine gave up. It would in any case be easier to see Helen on her own, meeting Joe for the first time.

'What do you think, he's not Jewish, is he?' Barbara Harrigan asked.

Flora was with her grandfather upstairs in the big loft, where his model train set, rarely touched these days, was running for her. Faintly, they could hear its whirr and beep and Flora's excited voice as she changed a signal for Grandpa or rearranged the model people on a platform.

'Joe? No, whatever gave you that idea?'

'Maybe he's really Joshua or something.'

'Joseph, I should think,' Catherine said, intending to reassure, but her mother's mouth tightened.

'Catholic, then. She said he was from Glasgow.'

'Did she?' Catherine had imagined a Cockney wide boy, when Helen referred to his 'deals' with cars and antiques. She rearranged her mental picture of Joe. 'It doesn't matter, does it? As long as he makes Helen happy.'

She had been suspicious of Helen's happiness. New man, new flat, expensive presents and nights out, a social life Catherine had tried not to envy, though she'd hardly have wanted it herself. Then the pregnancy. It was all too much, too fast, and there was something in the way Helen spoke about Joe that worried her. She was, however, prepared to defend him to her mother.

'At least he's doing the decent thing,' Mrs Harrigan said.

'What?'

'They're getting married.'

Helen had not told her *that*. Of course, she was trying to keep her mother happy. Marriage would make it all right. Catherine hoped it was true. She thought she hoped so.

Christmas week had been one long imprisonment. Catherine's mind was in Scotland, and if it hadn't been for Flora, she would simply have stayed there. After the snowfall at the beginning of December the weather had turned mild, so she could have taken Flora walking on Rosemarkie beach, she could have had Christmas dinner with Hugh, invited Gilbert over for a meal, and gone to the lunch party her colleague Susan had invited her to. Susan had girls a little older than Flora, so that would have been another connection made.

At least she would see Helen.

Helen had said, 'Northern line to Highgate – we're only a ten-minute walk from there.'

The first thing that struck Catherine when her sister opened the door was how pretty she looked, her hair loose instead of pinned up in an untidy knot, her clothes much smarter than her usual layers of long skirts and tops, and revealing the first swelling of pregnancy. Her cheeks were pink, but that may have been the heat in the flat. How efficient their central heating must be, or how high the electricity bills.

'Where's Flora?'

'With Mum and Dad – sorry, they're clinging on to every moment with her. You know. Bad Catherine, removing their grandchild to the wilds of Scotland.' She followed Helen into the flat. Given Joe's business, she had expected old furniture, even antique, but everything was modern and functional, as impersonal and co-ordinated as a show house. If Helen had had an impact on it, this wasn't obvious, but perhaps she had tidied for Catherine's visit. It would be the first time.

'I brought you flowers,' Catherine said, laying them on the work surface in the kitchen. Here, there was evidence of daily life: unwashed dishes in the sink and an opened packet of biscuits on the table.

Helen was hunting in the depths of a cupboard; she emerged with a glass vase. 'They're lovely – I'll put them in this.' She set it down, hesitant. 'Would you like coffee? I've gone off it, like I did with … before, but you have some.'

'I'd rather have tea.'

'Ok, we'll have tea.'

She made no move, as if she wanted to say something. Catherine, guessing, said, 'Mum told me you're getting married.'

'Oh, yes. Probably …'

'She seemed quite sure.'

'I thought it would reassure her, make her like him.'

'So it's not true?'

'I didn't say that.'

It wasn't like Helen to be evasive. Perhaps it had been her idea and Joe was not so keen.

'Are you keeping well?' she asked instead.

'Fine.'

'Will I put the kettle on?'

Helen seemed to give herself a shake. 'No, you go and look at my piano – I've been dying to show you. I'll make tea.'

The piano was at the end of the living room opposite the window. Helen, having filled the kettle, followed Catherine through and lit the lamp that was nearest. The wood gleamed in the soft light.

'It's lovely.' Catherine touched the keys. 'In tune too!'

'It was way out, but I found a man – he came just before Christmas, thank goodness, so I've been able to play. When I get time.'

'So – when is your wedding?'

'In the spring. Probably.'

'Right.'

'I'll let you know.' She closed the piano lid.

When they were seated with their tea, Helen said, 'I've been feeling awfully sick. It'll pass, it did before. I've definitely got a bump now, though.' She patted her stomach. 'Tell me about you, tell me more about the job and what you're doing and everything. Phone calls aren't good enough, are they?'

Catherine did not have much to say about work, but there was The Factory, a place she thought Helen would love.

'I like the sound of Gilbert,' Helen said. 'Is he married?'

'You're a bit transparent. No, and not likely to be.'

'Why not – oh.'

'Well, I don't know of course, but I somehow don't think he's interested in women. Or, actually, men. He's a bit fey.'

'But nice.'

'Oh yes. Unlike—' She hesitated. It was better not to mention Kenneth.

'So,' Helen said, 'there's someone else on the horizon?' She never missed.

Before Catherine could say a word, she was rescued by the sound in the hallway of someone coming in, and Helen leapt up.

'It's Joe,' she said. 'Oh good, I told him you were coming.' She was flushed and bright.

Catherine rose and turned, and Joe came in.

Nothing had prepared her. Helen was right – phone calls weren't good enough. She had not had the least idea. It wasn't the long leather coat, the black hair, the dark eyes and eyebrows, the humorous lift of his mouth, the red scarf: it was no one thing. She simply had not had any notion how astonishingly beautiful he was, like a film star, one of those rare people who carry with them always an air of glamour, so you know that if you are with them, you too will be swept into the slipstream of a richer world.

Now she understood.

7

Kenneth was going to the cottage only because his mother had asked him to.

'Check he's all right,' she said.

'Make sure the place isn't falling down, she means.' His father was blunter, indicating with a nod in his wife's direction that it wasn't Gilbert who was the concern here, it was their property.

'Gilbert's perfectly capable,' she protested. When neither of them answered, she turned away. 'I'll make the tea.'

'I'll check the cottage for you,' Kenneth told his father when they were alone, 'but I'm not going out to that factory, that's his affair. Sink or swim.'

'Sink, *you* say.' Iain Sinclair got up to put another shovel of coal on the fire. The house was draughty in winter, the windows rattling in the wind that was coming down the glen from the west. 'Not making much money with his furniture and bric-a-brac?'

'Have you and Mum ever been there?'

'You know fine we haven't. As you say, it's his business.' He crossed to the sideboard and opened a door, peering in. 'A dram?'

'One, then I'll head back.'

It was Sunday afternoon, and he was growing sleepy from the heavy lunch. If he didn't make a move soon, he would be here until supper time, and he didn't want that. They still thought that when he moved in with them after Gilbert came home, he should just have stayed. They couldn't understand his spending so much money on a new house. 'Plenty of room here,' his mother had said, and, 'This will be yours anyway, one day.'

They were still in Rosemount, the big Victorian house a few miles beyond Strathpeffer, where he and Gilbert had grown up. They lived now in two or three rooms, the others empty and unheated all year round. He wondered about damp, or worse, dry rot: there was a smell that greeted him in the hall sometimes.

He and his father sat over their whisky and talked about the business, as they always did when they were together, since that was what mattered most to both. Faintly, from the kitchen, came the sounds of the lunch dishes being washed up and put away, then the singing of the kettle.

When his mother came in, they changed the subject. Work, in her view, was not for Sundays. Though they attended the Church of Scotland, that being the only church in the village, she still liked the Sabbath observed in her house.

The following Saturday, a week after New Year, he drove out to the cottage. At first he thought it was empty. There was no vehicle in the lane and the curtains were drawn untidily apart in the front windows. There was an air of stillness about the place, as if it had been abandoned. Kenneth stood in the icy air for a moment, thinking he could smell snow. Beneath his feet the path had a smooth surface he almost slipped on, and the untended vegetation was brown and stiff, frozen.

He tried the front door first, not expecting it to open, but when he turned the knob it gave way at once, opening with a creak onto the narrow hallway with the staircase leading straight up from it. The rug beneath his feet was rucked up and dusty. To his left was the living room, ahead, the kitchen. He tried that first.

At the table, red-eyed, a mug of tea in front of him, gripped in two hands, was his brother.

Gilbert looked up, unsurprised. 'Come to check up on me?'

'That's right.'

Gilbert shrugged. 'Help yourself. Look round, count the empties, see if I've cleaned the lav.'

There was a brown teapot on the stove. Kenneth nodded towards it. 'Tea in the pot?'

'Stewed, probably.'

'I like it strong.'

The pot was still hot, so he got a mug out and filled it. Then he sat at the other side of the table. Gilbert was gazing down, picking with a long fingernail at a shred of food stuck to the surface. He looked rough.

For a moment, neither said anything. The place had a smell that wasn't just Gilbert, unwashed, though it was that too. Something sweetish. He'd been smoking, and not tobacco.

The van was not in the lane. Where was it? 'You had company?' he asked.

'A friend. She's got the van.'

'She?'

'Rose.'

A woman. That might be all right. Though – 'On her own?'

'Oh yes. Tell Dad not to worry. No wild parties.'

Something though, Kenneth thought, smelling cannabis again, annoyed.

'She's getting some stuff from The Factory, to take back to sell,' Gilbert said. 'She's got a customer.'

'Well, I'm glad you're managing to sell *something*.' He had no faith in this, or in Rose. He would be getting ripped off. His London *friends*.

Kenneth rose and rinsed out his mug under the tap. The sink was full of unwashed dishes in scummy water, smears of food crusted on the plates, the mugs stained brown.

'Clear this lot up,' he said. 'Don't leave the place a tip, for Mum's sake.'

'I'm not *leaving* it. Not yet anyway.'

'You need to get a grip,' Kenneth said as he went out, turning from the look on Gilbert's face, that mocking stare.

As he drove away, he thought suddenly of Catherine. She should see him like that, he thought, she wouldn't be so keen on him then. She'd gone to her mother's, he remembered, but she might be home now. He would call her. The thought of this braced him and he was charged with energy. He put the car radio on loud, and turning onto the main road, increased his speed, driving fast back to Strathpeffer.

8

January was chilly and damp, the sky white and unchanging during the short day. It was a false winter, not to be trusted. Soon after she was home, Catherine went out to The Factory, looking forward to seeing Gilbert. 'He makes me laugh,' she had told Helen, 'and Flora loves him.'

There was a woman with Gilbert. Even Flora was inhibited by Rose being there, filling the kitchen with the smell of acetone as she sat on a chair painting her finger- and toenails purple. Later, Flora said, 'Her feet were *dirty*.' Catherine had noticed this.

'The stock upstairs is sadly diminished,' Gilbert said. 'Rose is taking a vanful of stuff to sell in London for me.'

'*Your* van?' Flora asked. They were on their favourite sofa, while Catherine hovered nearby, examining a console table.

'My van, sadly.'

'I hope she brings it back soon,' Flora said. She admired the van, red with yellow sunflowers painted on the side.

'I'll get the bus while she's away,' Gilbert said, 'or hitch lifts.'

'That doesn't sound a terribly good idea.' Catherine knew by now how few buses there were anywhere, never mind going out the Ullapool road to Gil's cottage.

He shrugged. 'She'll be back in a week or so. I can sleep here.'

Flora considered this. 'You could lie on a sofa,' she said, 'but I think it would be scary in the dark.'

Rose came out, her feet still bare while the polish dried. It was cold in The Factory, since there had been no sun for days, and her feet looked blue, not unlike the colour of the nails.

'Give me a hand to pack up the rest?' she said to Gilbert. She stared briefly at Catherine, but ignored Flora.

He jumped up with a puff of dust that immediately settled again, some on Flora. 'Righty-oh.'

Catherine would have offered to help, but there was something grim about this girl in black, with her mauve feet and her black hair with its red streak. She was like some unusual bird you rush to catch with field glasses, rare in a country garden. Her round face was heavy with make-up, a pierrot mask.

Gilbert leapt upstairs two at a time, Rose following more slowly. In a few moments Gilbert came down with a full cardboard box, gingerly, peering round the side of it, taking his time. There was a clinking noise of glass on china, with each step. Rose came after carrying a marble statuette, a nymph. She held it casually under one arm, and stopped by the kitchen, putting it down while she tugged on boots. Then she followed Gilbert out to the van.

Catherine said, 'I think we'll go home, Flora, I must call in at the fishmonger while there's still some chance they'll have salmon.'

'I don't like salmon,' Flora said. She had got up, but only to wander among the sofas, moving further away, trailing her hand along the backs, patting cushions.

'Don't – you'll be filthy.'

110

'No, I won't.'

'Gil's busy, we should get out of his way.'

Flora approached, and hissed, 'That girl's not wearing any socks.'

'It's not our business. Get your coat. You must be freezing – it's awfully cold in here today.'

Outside, she called over to Gilbert. 'We're just going.'

He left the van and came running towards them on his stork legs, skidding to a halt in front of Flora.

'Don't go! I've hardly seen you.'

'We must. Anyway, you're busy.'

'All done. *Do* come in again, I have a lovely Arnold Bennett first edition to show you. A bit foxed but nice.'

'I don't really like Arnold Bennett,' Catherine said, though this was beside the point. 'I'm sorry.'

'Oh you have to read *Clayhanger*,' he said. 'To understand fathers and sons.'

'Is it *Clayhanger*, then, your first edition?'

'Unfortunately, only something called *Buried Alive.*'

Catherine laughed. 'You're joking!'

'My dear, there is no end to Arnold Bennett.'

'So it seems.'

Flora hopped with impatience. 'Are we going home now?'

'Yes, yes, to get the fish.'

'Now you sound like an Arnold Bennett person,' Gilbert teased. He seemed to have forgotten Rose, who leaned on the van, smoking, hugging her jacket round her. The wind was picking up and it blew her red flick of hair off her forehead like a crest. Gilbert too was windblown, and Flora moaned she was cold.

'Come to supper soon,' Catherine said on impulse. 'When

Rose has gone. I'll come and pick you up, since you won't have the van.'

Gilbert glanced guiltily across at Rose, who was not looking at them. 'Soon?'

'Next Friday?'

'Sooner,' he said.

That meant a work night, and she realised there would be the difficulty of getting Flora to bed, if Gilbert was there. She sighed.

'Wednesday then.'

He grinned. 'Perfect. Can we have steamed pudding? I love steamed pudding but no one ever makes it now. *I* haven't the knack. Though I could bring some shortbread. I'm very good at shortbread.'

'I don't like shortbread,' Flora said. 'It's boring. Can you make chocolate crispies?'

'Flora!'

Flora ignored her, as indeed did Gilbert. 'I'll see what I can do,' he said. 'I too, adore chocolate crispies.'

Rose said, suddenly close, 'I'm off then, right? Get my bag out the kitchen, will you?'

When Gilbert had gone to get her bag, Catherine opened her own car so that Flora could get in, then turned back to Rose.

'Are you driving all the way to London?'

'Looks like it,' Rose said. She kicked the nearest van tyre. 'If this heap doesn't break down.'

Torn between the call of the fishmonger (what else would they have if she was too late for decent fish?) and wanting to speak to Gilbert after Rose had gone, Catherine hesitated. 'I'd better go,' she said. She waved to Gilbert, coming out with a rucksack, and got into her car.

Flora was fiddling with the car radio. 'Don't do that,' Catherine said and started the engine.

In the rear-view mirror she saw Gilbert and Rose standing by the van, apparently saying goodbye, though it did not look like that. It did not look like any kind of communication at all.

9

In the third week of January, the weather changed. Snowdrops were raising brave heads under the trees on the rough ground around Kenneth's new house, that had no garden yet, and in the corners of Catherine's small flower border. Then in a single night of blizzards, they were buried in snow. By afternoon, it looked as if the schools would be closed next day, and Catherine, anxious, called the childminder who looked after Flora till she got home from work. If the schools were closed her own older children would be at home and Tracey would have a houseful.

'I don't know what they expect parents to do.' she said to her clerical officer, Colleen, as they left the office early, the snow already heavy on the branches of the tree outside their window. The snow ploughs were out in the town, but perhaps not yet in the side streets or country roads.

'Stay at home with the kids,' Colleen shrugged. 'Anyway, I won't get out my drive tomorrow if this keeps up. I might not even manage to get *in* it tonight.' She turned up her coat collar, ready to brave the outdoors. A new shower whirled past the window, obscuring the car park.

Catherine drove home slowly in the tracks of another car, up to the new housing estate where she and Flora lived. Tracey's house was in the next street to her own.

Flora was excited. 'Our school's going to be shut,' she said, opening Tracey's front door with a flourish. 'I'll have to stay at home.'

'Looks as if I will too,' Catherine sighed. She had filled her briefcase with job applications, meaning to read through them at home.

'I could stay on my own,' Flora said, as they drove to their own house.

'Of course you couldn't.'

'Ask Gilbert to come and look after me. Nobody will be able to go to The Factory in the snow, will they?'

Remembering the chocolate crispie episode, the evening Gilbert had come to supper with all the ingredients ('The cooker in the cottage isn't absolutely *reliable*'), Catherine did not think this such a good idea.

'It would be like leaving two seven-year-olds in charge of a house,' she said.

'I'm eight now,' Flora reminded her. 'Though,' she added thoughtfully, 'I see what you mean.'

Catherine laughed. 'You're more grown-up than Gil, sometimes.'

'I would have to look after *him*!' Flora exclaimed, entranced.

Kenneth called her that night, taking her by surprise. She had not heard from him since their unsatisfactory dinner together.

'How are you – not snowed in?'

'No, the snow plough's been along our street. What about you?'

'Four-wheel drive comes in useful,' he said. 'I was going to ask you over on Friday, but I don't think your wee car would make it up the hill, unless this clears.'

'I'm not free, anyway,' she said. Hugh had asked her to go with him to the theatre, to hear the Scottish Chamber Orchestra, but she did not say this.

'That's that then,' he said cheerfully. 'Next Saturday?' When she did not at once reply, he added, 'I'll take you out for dinner – what about that? And drive you home – then you can have a drink this time.'

Are we to take turns, she thought, absurdly. 'Thank you – yes, all right, if I can arrange babysitting – I'll let you know.'

'Fine. I'll pick you up at seven. Give me your address again?'

Later, when Flora was in bed, she began to wonder why she had agreed. They glanced off each other like toy boats going down a fast stream side by side, but not together. Yet there was no question of saying no. A tiny quiver of anticipation made her impatient of the concert she had looked forward to. Cultural life, at last. There was no one but Hugh she could enjoy music with, or talk about books.

Helen called more often, airy and uncommunicative, for all she talked.

'I'm fine, not sick, just a bit tired at night. Joe says I should stop working, but—'

'Don't you have to stay longer to qualify for maternity leave?'

'Yes, but he seems to think I won't go back.'

'Why not?'

'We'll be married, so I won't have to.'

She planned to rely on Joe.

'Could you come up for a visit? When you do stop work?'

'It's a long way,' Helen said.

'You lived here once!'

'I don't know, I'm sort of rooted in London now. I can't see Joe agreeing – he's busy.'

'You could come on your own.'

'I suppose so.'

'Think about it.'

When Catherine went up to bed, she was uneasy, as if she should have said something she had not, or Helen should have been less evasive. But what could she be evading?

Kenneth was late. Catherine, always punctual, paced restlessly, invented things to do that did not need doing, avoiding conversation with the eighteen-year-old babysitter, Tracey's niece. She did not put her coat on, as that would perhaps look desperate. It was only ten minutes. Eleven. He had not even the excuse of snow, as that had cleared in a sudden thaw during the last few days. A week ago Hugh had had to come for her in deep snow, but had been prompt and ready with a rug for her knees, though of course his beautiful car was thoroughly warm. As he drove to the theatre, she glanced sideways at his patrician profile and wished she could feel for him something other than friendly fellowship and gratitude. After all, they had shared a good deal. Why was that not enough?

Hugh knew the music, Catherine only some of the Mozart. Hugh explained carefully if she asked a question she hoped was not too stupid. The evening was a success, their talking it over in the homeward car cheerful. The snow kept off and they drew up at Catherine's house under a clear sky.

'Come in for coffee,' she said. 'It's not so late.'

'I won't, if you don't mind. The gritters are out, and that suggests there's more on the way. I'll get home while it's dry.'

The light came on in the car as she opened the door,

illuminating his kind face, that she could not be in love with. He undid his seatbelt.

'I'll see you in.'

'No need.' It was only a short garden path. He got out anyway, and shut the little gate after her, watching till she had her latchkey in the lock. She turned and raised a hand. 'Thank you – it was lovely.'

He smiled, tipped an imaginary hat, and got back into his car.

He's a bit of an old woman, she told herself, with his driving gloves and his up-to-date AA atlas lying on the back seat. As if he ever needed it.

Now she stood by her bedroom window in the dark, looking out into the street, expecting – then suddenly *not* expecting – Kenneth's four-wheel drive to round the corner. She flicked the curtain back and went downstairs.

Flora followed her with a pile of books. 'I thought you were going *out*,' she said.

'I am – oh, no, Flora, that's far too many.'

'I'm giving her lots to choose from.' She swept past her mother into the living room. 'Of course Shona can't read them *all*.'

The doorbell rang long and loud. Her heart thumped.

'I'll get it!' Flora dropped the books on the floor and raced past Catherine to the front door. Now she would be impossible, and Catherine shown up as an ineffectual mother.

Flora flung the door wide. 'Hello, are you Kenneth?'

'I am,' he said, and came in.

'This is Flora,' Catherine said. 'She's just going to bed.'

'Not yet!' said Flora, retreating to the safety of the babysitter.

'Come in – sorry – I need to tell Shona I'm leaving—'

He stood patiently in the hall while she kissed Flora, said again all the things she had already said about what time she must be in bed, where they were going and that they would be back by half past ten.

In the car, Kenneth said as he started the engine, 'I feel as if I'm taking Cinderella out. All that stuff about being back in time.'

'Cinderella! I don't think so. More like the wicked stepmother tonight – I wouldn't let Flora stay up late.'

'And how are you going to prevent *that?* I just got a wee peek at your ravishing babysitter but she didn't look much of a disciplinarian to me.'

He was laughing at her, she thought, and fell silent.

He glanced at her stern profile, as she pulled on her gloves. 'Lighten up, and we'll get on a lot better.'

'*What?*'

Suddenly, he pulled over to the kerb and stopped. They were not yet on the main road, and the street was deserted. Under a street light their faces glowed pale.

'What's wrong?' For a wild moment she thought he was about to tell her to get out of the car. She was no good, she had got it all wrong. He did not even like her. What on earth was she doing? She thought of Hugh with regret.

'Catherine,' he said, 'you're a hard woman.'

'Me? You're the difficult one.' She was in despair. 'Nothing I say is right, you're making fun of me all the time—'

He leaned across and took her trembling hands. One at a time, he pulled off her leather gloves and let them fall in her lap. She bit her lip, but let her hands lie still in his warm grasp. How intimate a touch it seemed, her cool hands in his, his heat transferring to them. She found it hard to look up and meet his eyes, then did.

'I'm not making fun of you,' he said. 'I want to – I want to *know* you.'

She thought he meant to kiss her, leaning forward, but all he did was brush a tendril of hair from her cheek, and tuck it gently behind her ear. So tender was he, tears started in her eyes.

'All right?'

'Of course,' she said, turning her head away.

'Right – let's get some food.'

He released her hands and put the car in gear, driving smoothly out and onto the main road. Has something been decided, she wondered, leaning back, heavy, her hands still warm from his.

As they neared the centre of town she cleared the side window, steamed up, and said, 'I think it's raining.'

'There's an umbrella somewhere in the back, if you need it,' he answered, slowing for the entrance to the car park.

She refused the umbrella for this misty rain, but by the time he pushed open the heavy glass door of the restaurant and they went in, she felt damp and windblown.

The table was in a good corner. Their coats were taken, menus laid down, and she faced him across a candle in a glass holder and a spray of pink carnations, wondering what she looked like, and trying not to fuss with her hair.

He grinned. 'You look very nice. Did I say?'

'Thank you. The wind – my hair's probably all over the place.'

'Wine?' he asked, taking up a menu.

'White, if that's all right – something dry?'

'Here.' He handed it to her. 'I know nothing about wine. I'll just have water.'

'Right.' She glanced doubtfully at him, then at the menu.

'I'm ready for this,' he said when their first course arrived. 'Been on the hill all day – starving.'

She knew Hugh went hillwalking and had in mind that one day she might go up Ben Wyvis, whose long snow-covered back she could see in the distance when she drove through Dingwall.

This was where Kenneth had been, on the first possible day after the snow.

'In this weather? You must be very fit,' she said.

'I've been fitter. Work takes up too much time now.' Prompted, he talked about climbing with Hugh and James, ticking off Munros, and the importance of sub-tops (whatever they were, she did not quite grasp). He used a spare fork to trace the jagged peak of some hill with a Gaelic name on the white tablecloth, puckering it, moving the black pepper aside. A little careless with wine, she asked questions she did not mind were ignorant, since she could not be expected to know a thing about mountains. The restaurant was warm so he had taken off his jacket and now rolled up the sleeves of his grey shirt, neatly tucking them into cuffs just below his elbows. In its glow, as he moved the candle to serve as a cairn, the hairs on his arm gleamed. Almost, she reached out to touch them, but reined herself in, dismayed. The wine was a mistake.

'You should try it,' he said, leaning back at last, to let the waitress clear their plates and bring the dessert menu. She meant to refuse it, but when he said, 'Yes, we'll look at it,' she changed her mind.

'You think I could climb one of these hills? I would like to try Ben Wyvis.'

'Sure, why not?'

'What about equipment?'

'All you need are a few basics, like good boots and a decent waterproof.'

'I wouldn't know how to start. I'd get lost.'

He laughed. 'Not on your own, you daftie.'

She blushed. He signed to the waitress that she was to have another glass of wine.

121

'I'd take you. You need a map and compass skills before you attempt anything on your own. I assume you don't—'

'No,' she said. 'I'd be useless.' She thought, is this my second glass she's bringing, or my third?' She hoped second; they were large glasses. 'I wouldn't mind trying.'

'Once the worst of the winter's past. Maybe April.'

'We'll still be speaking to each other in April, do you think?' she could not help asking.

'We're getting on fine now,' he said, 'aren't we?' The waitress appeared. 'I'll have the chocolate thing – Catherine?'

They went on to have coffee. She did not think to look at her watch.

'I'm remembering you'll turn into a pumpkin if I don't have you home by midnight,' he said at last.

'Oh dear, what time is it?'

He held her coat, and as she slipped her arms into the sleeves, she could feel the heat of him behind her. *If I lean back, we'd be touching, but he wouldn't know I meant it.* Perhaps she did lean, perhaps he moved forward. All the length of her, the length of him, for a second welded. Then his hands were on her shoulders, turning up her collar.

'I said, didn't I?' His breath on her hair. 'You just needed to lighten up a bit.'

Was she to invite *him* in for coffee? They had had coffee, so that would not do. Blurred by wine as she was, she knew the difference: inviting Hugh in had been no risk at all.

As they reached her house, he said, 'I'm knackered, sorry, I told you I wasn't as fit. The hill's taken it out of me. I'll get home.'

'Right, yes, of course.' A pause, for her to be disappointed, and not show it. 'Well, thank you, it's been lovely, and now I feel it must be – well, if you'd like to – my turn.'

'Your turn to do what?'

'Treat you.'

'You do that anyway,' he said, and pulled her towards him. The smell of him, the dark car, the roughness of his jacket against her cheek, and then his hand, hard under her chin, raising her face to meet his.

Indoors, she leaned on the closed door, shaken. From the living room came the sound of laughter and applause, and a raucous burst of music: Shona watching television. Flora must be asleep. Good. She could not face Flora right now.

10

He had no plan. He moved rather by an instinct carved from experience of other women. There had been more than his wife: before of course – they had married at thirty – and during the marriage. He had had a brief affair with the wife of a man he knew slightly, a mistake, though fortunately she was not the sort of woman ever to talk about it. His marriage was already miserable; that was his excuse.

Catherine was new to him with her cool manner, her clear English voice, her beauty. He had not been with a woman who looked like this, fair and slender and white-skinned, her rare blush a faint pinkness on her cheekbones. The Ice Maiden, he had called her to Hugh, after he met her at that party, cosying up to his fool of a brother.

He phoned her confidently next time, sure of the response he'd get, though of course she might have taken fright, or might be the sort of woman who blew hot and cold. He wouldn't stand for that, if this was to go on. It was almost six, so she would be home from work, maybe preparing a meal, Flora there, but it suited him to call now. He was still in his office, catching up with paperwork.

He could hardly have imagined *this*.

'I have to go to away,' she said. 'Something's happened. I have to go to Gatehouse – his parents are there.'

'Whose parents?' She was making no sense, and her other life, that he knew nothing about, opened up blank in front of him.

'Alan's dead.'

For a moment he could not think who Alan was.

'My husband,' she said, 'my former husband.' She could not say 'ex' since that was what he now was.

'Was he ill? He's in Saudi, isn't he?'

'Yes, but – he was killed in a – I don't know. A fight – but someone had a knife.'

He revised his view of Alan as a smooth operator, out in Saudi to make a few bucks.

She sighed. 'He's always been the sort of person to dive in. He never can leave anything alone. He must have got between them. These men. Anyway, he was the one who died. I don't really know any more – his mother wasn't making a lot of sense and his father and brother have flown out there right away. I have to go to Gatehouse-of-Fleet, it's where they live, and there will be the funeral. And Flora. Oh God.'

'Have you told her?'

'Not yet.'

'Would you like me to come round?'

He heard the silence. Wrong thing to say.

'That's very nice of you. No, I have to deal with this. Flora will be home soon – she's at Brownies.'

'When did you find out?'

'Ten minutes ago. His mother didn't have my work number so she's only just managed to get hold of me.'

'So when—'

'They're going to bring the – bring him home, and I don't know how long that will take.'

'Longer than you think, with a death like that.'

She did not answer, as if she were thinking about this.

'Look, will I see you at the weekend, or would you rather be on your own?'

'I don't think so. I don't honestly know. I still can't take it in.'

'Call me,' he said, and gave her his telephone number at the works. 'Elsie will answer – just ask for me.'

'Who's Elsie?' she asked, distracted.

'The boss, I sometimes think. Secretary, I suppose. She's more than that now – since Dad left, she's the one who keeps me right.'

'I'll let you know what's happening.'

'Take care,' he said, and rang off.

She called him on Sunday morning.

She had more news about Alan, but it was not much. It would be at least a fortnight before they could have the funeral. She would plan her visit to Gatehouse-of-Fleet when she knew the date.

'And Flora – how did she take it?'

'I really can't tell. A lot of tears, then in the morning she seemed fine. She can be very dramatic about little things, so she has no *range* to accommodate this. Maybe she's just stunned, like me.'

'What's she doing today?'

'She's gone to her friend's house. They live at the end of the street, and the mother, Kate, has been terribly kind. She says Flora can go there any time.'

'Come over,' he said. 'Come to me.'

'I can't, in case Flora wants to come home.'

Between them, there was something that rose up like a locked door, but was just frustration. How was any of this to happen, he wondered.

Then she said, 'Let me call Kate. I'll ring you back.'

He was in the kitchen making another pot of coffee, when she called.

'I'm on my way.'

When he heard her car he went to open the front door.

'Coffee's on. I'm on my third pot this morning, so you probably need it more than I do.'

'Yes, coffee,' she said, crossing his threshold. 'What a good idea.'

On her way to the kitchen she glanced into the living room through the open door, and saw a pile of books on the floor, and the new bookcase, still unfilled.

'Oh,' she said, 'you have books.'

'What did you think – I came naked into this house?'

She laughed, unable not to. 'You said you didn't take anything.'

'I took the bloody books,' he said. 'They've been in boxes in the garage for months.'

'I didn't think you were a reader.'

'Ignorant labourer, is that it? Gets his hands dirty, goes to the football on Saturday, pub at night?'

'I didn't mean—'

They were back where they had started. Too late, he realised this, and went to get her coffee.

She was standing behind him when he turned, surprisingly close. Her eyes were bright, tears gathering. He had not thought she cried. Then, ashamed, he remembered the dead husband, the bereaved child.

'Here, you take milk, don't you?'

127

'We get off on the wrong – I mean, cross swords. I don't know why.'

'Me neither.' He picked up his own coffee mug. 'Come and see the books, then you can decide if I'm cultured enough for you.' Lightly, he touched her shoulder, as if to turn her towards the living room. More amicably, they settled there, and she knelt by the books, balancing her mug and reading titles. He sat in the armchair nearest, watching her.

'I gave Kate your phone number – in case.'

'Sure.'

'They're having a roast dinner, and Flora is happy to stay. She loves food, the kind of food they have in other people's houses.'

'I said – I'll do a roast dinner for you both.'

'Sometime,' she agreed, turning back to the books.

He wondered how they were to get from where they were to where they (how fast she had come here made this certain) wanted to be. It was a dance he had to some extent anticipated – it was how women were – but now it frustrated him. Damn her ex-husband, messing things up. He did not know the guy, and could think this unrepentant.

'Come here,' he said finally, tired of waiting.

She looked at him. 'What?'

He stood up. 'Come here.'

She rose a little unsteadily, still with the mug in her hand. He met her halfway and took it from her, setting it on top of the mantelpiece.

'What is it?'

'Enough,' he said, and pulled her towards him.

'I feel so guilty.'

'Nothing like guilt for great sex.'

Her gasp might have been disbelief or laughter but still, her hands came up on his chest and did not push him away. In a moment, they had found their way round his neck and her face was lifted to his.

Later, he said, 'How's the guilt?'

'Ah,' she admitted, on a breath of misgiving, 'I think you were right. Oh dear.' She raised herself on an elbow, her neat cap of hair tousled, pulling a sheet up over her breasts. 'There's something about death,' she said. 'It makes you want to – I don't know – do everything, be all you can. Miss nothing.'

'You've made a good start.'

'Oh God, I do have to go, I can't stay here.'

'Yes, you can. Lie down. Relax.'

She lay back, but stiffly. Still, she was here, some kind of beginning had been made, and not just a reaction to death, he certainly hoped.

There was no getting past it though. He had finally got her into bed because her ex-husband had copped it.

11

Helen had given in. She would leave the school at Easter. That was only a couple of weeks away. She was comforted by her head teacher saying music teachers were in short supply. She was surprised at Helen leaving so soon. 'You're missing out on maternity pay – and what about your continuous service?'

Helen knew all that. She could not defend her decision to this sensible woman, herself beyond having more children. 'You won't stay here either,' she dared to say.

'*I'll* move on to another job, a bigger school.'

When she went out of the playground on the day before Good Friday, with her armfuls of presents and cards and good wishes, Helen was tearful, but put that down to being pregnant. Joe's appreciation of the presents was perfunctory. 'You won't need any of that stuff. We're going up to Harrods, to kit you out.'

He was in the money. A decorator, some friend of a friend, had come in to paint the nursery. Helen had to keep shutting the door, since the smell of paint made her feel sick.

'Not that he'll be needing his own room for a while,' Joe said, his arm protective around her. He had not forgotten about Oliver. In public, he was all solicitude; in private, inclined still to expect to be run after. She had found this was what Joe liked best:

the dinner waiting, his glass of wine poured, the tea brewed and brought to his chair.

It was her mother who told Helen about Alan's death. Helen was getting used to more frequent enquiries which usually focused on her pregnancy, and favoured Joe's point of view.

'I think Joe's right, about giving up teaching. I don't know how young women these days can rush back to work when their babies are days old.'

'Not days, Mum.'

'As good as. He's able to take care of you, isn't he?'

'I do have a career—'

'Teaching,' said her mother. 'And that was always my point. You can easily pick it up again when your little one goes to school.'

This time, her solicitous, 'How are you feeling?' was perfunctory. As soon as Helen answered, 'Fine,' she said,

'You haven't spoken to Catherine, have you?'

'Last week—'

'You've not heard, then?'

'Heard what?'

'It's Alan. There's been an awful accident, out in that place, the Middle Eastern country.'

'Saudi,' Helen said. 'You *know*. What sort of accident?'

'He's – well, not to beat about the bush – ' (A first, Helen thought) 'He's been killed.'

'*What?* Are you *sure* – was it an accident at work?'

'Of course I'm sure. It's not something I'd make a mistake about. He was in a fight with some other men. Goodness knows. That's all Catherine said and I've not liked to phone the Grahams, they'll have enough to do.'

131

'Alan – in a *fight?*'

'Your father says he was always quite *pugnacious*. But it's a dreadful thing for his parents. And Flora of course, poor wee mite.' She took a deep breath, saving this for last. 'They're flying the body home next week.'

It was as if all her life, her mother had waited to say this line.

'I must call Catherine.'

Helen wondered how upset her sister was. Some things she couldn't guess about her.

'Where were you, I called last night?'

'I don't know – fetching Flora from one of her many social activities, no doubt.'

'Mum phoned – she told me about Alan. What an awful thing.'

'He got between two other men, fighting. At least, that's what his parents think, but who knows? None of it makes sense.'

'Are you all right? Is Flora?'

'I'm all right. I can't tell about Flora. She's being brave, but it's such an act with her. She might not even understand.'

I bet she does, thought Helen.

'Anyway, how are you?'

'I'm fine, never mind me. Tell me *more*, for God's sake. When's the funeral – are you going?'

'Of course. I said to Sheila we'd go down for a few days.'

'Why on earth didn't you tell me this had happened? I can't imagine you really wanted to spill to Mum first.'

'Alan's mother called her before I could. Sheila was telling everyone while she still had the courage, I suppose, while David was away seeing what needed to be done. Poor David, he must have had an awful time. He doesn't like going abroad at the best of times. Malta is all Sheila's ever been able to persuade him to.'

'Don't sound so *jolly*, for God's sake, it's awful, poor Alan, I can't believe you're not devastated.'

'Well, I'm not. Shocked. Dismayed. And sad of course, especially for his parents. But mostly numb. I'll probably feel different when I go to Gatehouse. It might be real then.'

Briskly, Catherine changed the subject. She did not think Helen should give up her job. Helen was impatient with this and then her talk about Gilbert, outrageously camp, obviously. How could she think about anything else, in the middle of this horror about Alan?

'I don't know why you go on about him,' she said. 'It's not as if there are any prospects there.'

'You want me to have a man too, so that we can compare notes.'

'So is it this Kenneth?'

'Is what him?'

Helen sighed, giving up.

Telling Joe later, Helen found him as infuriating as her sister.

'Were they divorced?'

'Yes. No. Actually, I'm not sure. They were going to be, but then he went off to Saudi Arabia so perhaps it never happened.'

'He'll have been raking it in there, tax-free. Hope for her sake they weren't. Then she gets it, not his folks or whoever.'

'I don't suppose that's even crossed Catherine's mind,' Helen said, plumping up sofa cushions with more force than necessary. 'For God's sake. That's the last thing—'

'Believe me, it's not.'

In this, though, she was sure she knew her sister best.

12

Catherine went to The Factory telling herself it was to distract Flora. It was Saturday morning, a blowy March day. On the driveway, crocuses bent to the wind, orange and purple bells bobbing. In London, the daffodils would be in full bloom, perhaps beginning to fray, but here, they were spears only a few inches out of the ground. It could still snow, people said at work.

'The van's there!' Flora exclaimed. 'Is that girl back, the one with the red bit of hair and purple toes?'

'I've no idea.'

'I hope not. Gil's funnier when she's not.'

'Flora, no more china ornaments. Perhaps a book.'

'We have to buy *something*,' Flora said, reasonably. 'Nobody's buying the sofas, are they? He won't make any money.'

'He won't make much out of selling china rabbits to you for fifty pence.'

She parked next to the van, and Flora scrambled out.

Gilbert was on his own.

'My dears, how wonderful! I thought you'd deserted me altogether.'

'I'm going upstairs,' Flora said, before Catherine changed her mind about the book.

'I'll call you down when the coffee's ready,' Gilbert said. 'Shall I? Chocolate bourbons today.'

'Is that biscuits?'

'Yes.'

'Ok.'

Catherine followed Gilbert into the kitchen. 'I'd have come before, but—'

'With my esteemed brother?'

'I've seen him once or twice, but it wasn't that.'

He shook his head sorrowfully. 'So I'm neglected for our Kenny.'

'Nonsense. *He* hasn't come to supper and wrecked my kitchen making chocolate crispies. You're privileged.'

Gilbert fussed with the coffee machine, ancient, and making, she was to discover, a disgusting brew. 'Well, you be careful, my dear. He's not such a nice fellow.'

'You don't get on, I know.' She began washing up the dingy cups. 'How on earth can you bear to drink out of these?'

He sighed. 'I need the love of a good woman. Much more than *he* does.'

'Oh, Gilbert, what nonsense.' She could not dry the cups with the screwed-up ball of dishtowel lurking in a corner, so turned them upside down to drip on the draining board and turned back to Gilbert. He was wearing a very old tweed jacket, one of the leather elbow patches reattached with large stitches of green wool. His trousers, too short by an inch, flapped at his bony ankles as he moved. She almost said, 'What a scarecrow you are,' but did not want to hurt his feelings. He laughed at himself, but he must be poor.

'Did Rose sell all the things for you in London?'

'She says. Haven't seen the money yet.'

'Oh, Gil—'

'Now, coffee. Here you are.' He handed her a cup of black liquid, smelling not quite of coffee. He picked up a carton of milk. 'Mm,' he said, sniffing. 'Off, I think.'

'I'll have it black.'

'Very wise.'

'You are so *different*,' Catherine said, as they went out into the warehouse to find a sofa. It was deserted of course, not a soul even looking round. 'You and Kenneth – I can hardly believe you're brothers.'

'Oh, but we're not. I'm a changeling.'

'That I *can* almost believe.'

'Now then,' Gilbert said, as they sat side by side. 'Tell me what's been happening. You looked so sad, coming in.'

'I'm fine now. You cheer me up. I can even forgive the awful coffee. Almost.'

'It is awful,' he said. 'But tea is my thing, really, and people want coffee in the morning. It seems more suitable somehow.' He put his cup down on a small unsteady table, next to their sofa. 'Now then, is it just Kenny, or has something happened to you?'

'Yes,' she said, 'it has.'

She told him about Alan.

'Oh, my dear.' Gilbert put his hands to his head with a gesture of despair. 'How absolutely terrible. I'm sure you can't decide *what* your feelings are. Or *should* be.'

This was so exactly the case, Catherine was taken aback. 'Yes,' she said. 'That's it.'

No one else had come close to understanding this – even Kenneth. Or Hugh, who was kind but neutral, as if it would soon not matter.

'That's *just* it. How did you know?'

'I'm good in a crisis,' he said. 'I have so many myself.'

Upstairs, Flora was sitting on the dusty floor in a patch of sunshine. It was cold, and the sun made a little oasis of warmth in a space between bookcases. She had taken several books from the shelves, but she was thinking, not reading. *Where* was her father? This existential question bothered her more, not less, as the days since his death marched past. She had of course asked her mother, but Catherine, not wanting to lie, not wanting to frighten Flora, had been uncharacteristically vague. 'Well, nowhere,' she had finally admitted, pressed to give some kind of answer. 'When people die...they just aren't there any more.'

While they had been in Gatehouse-of-Fleet, staying with her grandparents, she had asked Granny Graham, who had said firmly, 'Heaven', but she had been unable to explain Heaven in any way that made sense to Flora, who had never gone to Sunday School. Of course, sometimes in Assembly, reference was made to Heaven, but again, with no elucidation.

Flora shut her eyes and tried to picture her father. He had been away so long, this was difficult. What she conjured was a memory of him playing Happy Families, the last week she had spent with him on their own. She could see the cards, Mr and Mrs Bun the Baker, and his hand with the signet ring, but not his face, not that at all. There were things she wanted to ask him, most importantly, had he missed her? She could not picture where he was, having no image of Saudi Arabia to call on. She felt he surely had to come *home* first, before something like death could remove him. Yet that had not happened, and could not now.

'We will keep him in our hearts', the minister had said at the funeral. Flora, staring at the coffin, had come sharply to the understanding that her father was in that box. She was frozen with horror until they were out of the church and her mother took her hand firmly, saying, 'I think we'll go back to Granny's now.' They did not go to wherever the coffin was travelling in its big black car. They waited at Granny's with the sandwiches and cakes, boiling the kettle and putting out plates and knives, until everyone else also returned to the house. The frightening thoughts about her father in the box receded in the ordinariness of Granny's house and having to pass round cakes.

What she wanted to know was, was Daddy still in the box? Was it in Heaven? No, that was stupid. Heaven was – apparently – angels and sort of flying, being happy all the time.

There was no one she could ask.

She knew of course her father would not come back, but that didn't stop her wishing he would. This confusion brought tears to her eyes, and she wiped them away hastily, since it would not do for her mother to see them, or indeed Gilbert. She was like the girl in a story she had read recently, being brave, not showing her feelings to spare other people's. She *was* brave, but the book on her lap was still blurry when she bent her head to it. After a few moments she realised the sun had moved on, and she was cold. She got up and headed for the stairs, with a quick and calculating survey of the tables as she passed them, loaded with china and bric-a-brac.

'So,' Catherine was saying to Gilbert, 'we spent over a week with my parents-in-law. They want Flora to go back for a visit in her holidays – well, both of us, but it's really Flora they want. They live in an idyllic village, so pretty and neat, like something out of Enid Blyton, everything tidy and spotless. No ugly buildings, people walking their nice little dogs and the cats on weathered stone walls, washing their faces.'

'Like Agatha Christie,' Gilbert said, entering into this. 'A terrible murder at the Big House – the sinister guest suspected.'

'That sort of thing,' Catherine laughed. She looked up, hearing Flora's light footsteps. 'Did you find a book?'

'No, just this teeny weeny group of baby chickens.'

It was hideous, a huddle of yellow china chicks with blue bows round their necks, made as a single object.

'Wonderful,' Gilbert said. 'I knew you would like that!'

'Were you keeping it for me?' Flora asked, suspicious.

'I'll get you a biscuit, shall I?' her mother asked, unable to say no to the chicks, and cross with Gilbert.

When she was out of earshot, Flora put down the chicks and sat next to Gilbert.

'Are you sad?' he asked.

'A bit.' She glanced at him, cautious.

'I'd be very sad, if it was my father, and I was you. Not if it was *my* father, as we don't like each other all that much. But you did like yours, didn't you?'

'Oh yes,' Flora said. She glanced across to the kitchen doorway, but Catherine was not yet on her way back. 'Gilbert, can I ask you a question?'

'Yes.'

'Where is my Daddy now? Granny says Heaven, but she doesn't ... I don't know what she really means. I don't actually think she knows either, though she *should*.'

'Nobody knows,' Gilbert said. 'It's one of those things you don't find out till you're dead.'

'Oh.'

'So that's why it's not worth bothering about.' He leaned

139

confidentially close, his breath smelling of bitter coffee and cigarettes. 'It feels sad now, but after a bit, you won't be so sad. That's all you need to think about.'

Flora whispered, 'He's not in the box, though?'

Gilbert checked, appearing to think about this. 'No,' he said. 'That at least, I'm sure of.'

'All right.'

Catherine appeared carrying the packet of bourbons, and Gilbert said, 'She'll let you have the chicks, wait and see.'

'If it's all right, I sort of don't want them,' Flora said.

Miraculously, he understood this too. 'What is it you really want? I admire your tactics, by the way.'

'A girl with a lamb stuck to her frock, and she's holding a sort of bent-over stick.'

'The shepherdess. Her foot's chipped.'

'I know, but not much.'

'Good choice. Better, of course, than the chicks.'

'The chicks are very nice,' she said, like her mother, conscious of his feelings.

'Oh, they're not!' He made a terrible face at her and she giggled.

'You know,' Gilbert said clearly as Catherine approached, 'I don't think these chicks are tasteful enough for your mother. Isn't there *anything* else you'd like instead?'

The glance Catherine shot him was more suspicious than grateful, but Flora, playing the game, leapt up.

'Oh well, if I really *can't* have them...' She cast a longing glance at the chicks, overdoing it. 'There was one other thing, Mummy, it's not such a bright colour?'

'Oh, go on then,' Catherine sighed. 'I don't know what the two of you are up to—'

She did though, and was grateful. They would go home more cheerful than they had come.

As he walked to the door with them, a car was drawing up, and two women got out.

'There,' Catherine said. 'Customers, and it's only March.'

His expression gave nothing away. Then, as Flora got in to their car, holding the shepherdess carefully, he said, 'Be careful.'

'It's chipped already, Gil—'

'Not that. My so-called brother.'

'Nothing to worry about.' She wanted to hug him, but was afraid he would see pity where she intended goodwill.

When she looked in the rear mirror, he was talking to the two women, waving his arms like a windmill, full of enthusiasm.

13

Kenneth's mother drove up to see him at the works. This was rare enough to alarm him.

Elsie came into the store as he checked supplies, marking up on a notepad what needed replenishing before they started a new job on the Black Isle.

'Mrs Sinclair's in the office,' she said.

'My mother?' But there was no other Mrs Sinclair now.

'Yes.'

'Did she say—'

'I said I'd fetch you. I'll put the kettle on.'

He tried to finish what he was doing, but his concentration was gone.

In the office, his mother and Elsie were drinking tea, his mother in a chair, Elsie perched on the edge of the desk. When he came in she said, 'I'll get on then,' and left.

'If it wasn't for her mother, I'm sure poor Elsie would have made somebody a good wife.'

'What's up?'

'I want you to come in by and see your father. I'm not happy about him.'

'Is he ill?'

'Not ill. But not right.'

'I can't get away before half past six. The boys are over on the west, and I need to be here when they come in. After that, there's the van to unload.'

'You'll be tired by then.'

'Doesn't matter – I'll come in.'

'I'll have something for your tea, then.'

It would please her to feed him.

It was a shock to find Gilbert in the house when he got there. He was in the chair on the other side of the fire from their father's. Kenneth nodded at the two of them, then followed his mother to the kitchen.

'How long's he been here?'

'Just this minute – I wish I'd known he was coming. Never mind, I haven't put the tatties on yet, so I'll just clean a few more.'

'What does he want?'

'He's visiting, just like yourself.'

He doubted that. 'Can I do anything?'

'No, no, you have a seat. Would you like a cup of tea while you're waiting?'

'I'm fine. What about Dad?'

'He's brightened up since Gilbert arrived. He's better in company, he makes an effort. But—' She paused. Kenneth, watching her drop potatoes into a saucepan and put it on the stove, saw she was taut with anxiety.

'You're worried.'

'He's breathless. I know they put that thing in at the hospital—'

'The stent?'

'Yes, that's it. But he's slowing right down. He made some excuse when Finlay phoned about golf, and that's not like him, is it? He told me he was going to spend the morning fixing up the shed door that's been hanging off its hinges for weeks, but he hasn't done that either.'

'That's not like him, no.'

'Don't you be saying a word now, what I'm telling you. He thinks I'm fussing. It'll come better from you.'

'What will?'

'Get him to go back to the doctor.'

He went into the living room, where the two he had left, run out of conversation, were watching television. His father snatched up the remote control and switched it off.

'Ach, nothing worth watching but the news these days. And that's not likely to cheer anybody up.'

'How are you?' Kenneth asked, drawing another chair closer to the fire.

'Me? Grand. Are you started on the Fortrose job yet?'

'Next week.'

'You'll be hoping it stays dry.'

'We'll be fine.'

Gilbert stretched out in his armchair, his feet extended so far they almost met his father's. Arms crossed, eyes half-shut, he nevertheless kept his gaze on Kenneth.

'The lovely Catherine came to see me at the weekend,' he said. 'With Flora, who's turning into one of my best customers.'

'I'm glad you've got one, at least,' Kenneth said, not rising to it. 'Who's this?'

He had timed his remark for their mother coming through the door.

'A friend of Gil's.'

Gilbert, triumphant, said, 'And of our Kenny's. Haven't you told them?'

'Told me what?' she asked, looking from one to the other, smoothing down her apron, her hands restless.

'It's nothing,' Kenneth said. 'She's a friend of Hugh Guthrie's.'

'Hugh was out on the course with Tommy Macdonald and me,' their father said. 'Week past Saturday.'

'It couldn't have been that day. *You* weren't there then.' She waved away the chair Kenneth was drawing up for her. 'I'm just going to lay the table,' she said, then to their father again, 'Isn't that right, Iain?'

Grumbling, he turned back to the fire. This, Kenneth saw, was his cue. 'Mum says you've not been playing recently.'

Gilbert, attention flitting between them, unwound himself from the chair. He would go into the kitchen with his mother, not so much from tact as from reluctance to be involved.

Their voices, Gil's swooping exaggeration modified at home, his mother's soft replies, reached them along the hall. Gil had left the door wide open.

'Shut that bloody door,' Iain said. 'He thinks he's in his warehouse.' He glanced at Kenneth. 'I suppose it's keeping him out of mischief?'

'Maybe.'

His father looked up sharply. 'Eh?'

'Ach, you know what I think – it was like pouring your money down the drain.'

His father poked at the fire, not looking at him. 'Your mother—'

To forestall him, Kenneth said, 'He's had company in the cottage. Some woman. I think she's gone now.'

'What woman?'

'Not local. I never saw her myself.'

'London!' The sink of iniquity, from which they had hoped Gilbert was finally freed.

'What's this about golf anyway? Mum's worried.'

'No need. I'm fine.' The silence, too pointed, drove him to bluster. 'She fusses. I had the shed door to see to.'

'You didn't do that either.'

'It rained. Anyway, there was football on the television.'

'Since when did you watch football?'

'Now and again.'

'When you're not well enough to play golf?'

Iain Sinclair leaned back in his chair. 'That coal bucket needs filled – don't let your mother lift it.'

'I won't.' He waited, but his father said nothing, his hands rubbing along the arms of his chair, his face set. 'When's your check-up?'

'They send me a card when it's due.'

'All right, but maybe you need to go to the doctor before then.' Seeing the stubborn face, he added, 'For Mum's sake.'

'I'll think about it.'

He was glad to leave after the meal, though not to leave Gilbert with them, no doubt working up to borrowing money again. In the driveway, in the dark, he could make out the van, which he had missed coming in, parked down the lane a bit and facing downhill probably because he had difficulty starting it. Another useless thing belonging to Gilbert.

14

'Nothing like it,' Kenneth said, 'nothing so wonderful as taking a woman who's never been satisfied before, never really liked sex, and then—'

'Taking?' she said. 'What do you mean *taking*? Is that what you think of women, something to be *taken*, as if you *own* them?' Catherine sat up. 'You make too many assumptions.'

'Come on, you know that's not what I meant. My God—' as she edged away, beginning to get out of bed. 'These women who bring their feminist principles into everything – into *bed*, for Christ's sake.'

'You're impossible,' she said, hunting for her clothes, aware as she did it that this is never a dignified move, especially if you're angry. Forgotten now, the blissful hasty *undressing*.

Kenneth sat up. 'I didn't mean—' he began but she was out of earshot in the bathroom. Women, he thought, you can never get it right. He stretched and sighed again: great sex, though.

'I don't know what you want from me.' She was in the doorway, dressed except for her shoes. Her hair, usually so neat, was still tousled. 'You seem to think this is all a game and—'

'But it is,' he said. 'I notice you keep coming back for the next round.' He grinned at her, and she made a sound that was half frustrated anger, half laugh.

'Come back to bed,' he said, patting it. 'Come on, let me say sorry. You know fine I didn't mean it.'

'You meant something,' she complained, sitting on the edge of the bed.

'Aye, all right, but only that it's a pleasure having sex with you because you like it so much, and it's obvious you never liked it before.'

She turned, honesty overcoming indignation. 'Yes,' she admitted. 'Not like this.'

When she looked at him, when he touched her again, his hand running down her arm, taking her hand, pulling her close, the smell of him, the roughness of his chest hair, curly and dense, against her face, oh, it was all she could do not to give way – and then she did, she did. This was hopeless, what was she turning into?

Later, lying peacefully in the crook of his arm, her head on his chest, she listened to the change in breathing that meant he had fallen asleep, but stayed awake herself, trying to think it out, and could not, the ache of him still between her thighs, her body quieted, damp and warm, in time suspended.

April was sunny and deceptively warm. Flora was with her grand-parents in picture-postcard Gatehouse-of-Fleet, feeding ducks and helping to take Skippy the West Highland terrier for walks; making cakes with Granny and planting rows of radishes with Grandpa. The life idyllic.

Next Saturday Catherine must drive there to spend a long weekend and bring Flora home. She was having a fortnight without a child, dizzy with freedom. She and Kenneth took days off, or left early in the afternoon, to drive and then walk, or simply go to his house and to bed. Easter was late this year and they had the weather for walking. On Easter Monday he had taken her up her first hill and she had the pride that comes from doing something new and tiring. She was seduced by the strangeness of being high, seeing so far, and seeing it with someone who desired her all the time.

He was planning another hill, spreading OS maps out on the floor, crawling about, intent on finding a pull-in for the car, tracing paths to the top and back. On her knees too, following his eager finger, she breathed him in, what he was, what she was becoming.

'This is all new to you, isn't it?' he crowed, pleased to be showing her his world, and giving her so much pleasure. Ah, pleasure. She had not thought herself a puritan till now, till he went out of his way to destroy it. *Take* her – well, perhaps he had.

There were moments, during these giddy days, when she stopped caring about anything else. Dreaming at work, her mind was not on committee papers or the new computer (they were all having to get used to *this* now), nor on the meeting she was about to go to. She had not even called Helen or spoken to Hugh, or visited The Factory.

The change in her had not happened immediately. Then one night he would not let her go, content but still somehow inviolate. That wasn't good enough. It was this that made her prickle with sweat in a dull meeting, her thoughts flying off towards him, towards *herself* as she was with him. The way he had not let her go.

Helen called her, wondering at the silence. She sounded tired.

'I'm not sleeping well. Joe never sleeps much, so we're both roaming about in the middle of the night. Just as well I've

149

stopped working now. I doze off on the sofa after lunch, like an old lady.'

'You're pregnant,' Catherine laughed. 'That's how it is!'

'You sound cheerful, anyway,' Helen grumbled. 'Did Flora go to the Grahams?'

'She's there now, for a fortnight.'

'It must feel weird, being on your own. What are you doing with yourself?'

'Oh ... I climbed a hill. A Corbett, so not that high, but I'm tackling a Munro tomorrow.'

'A *what?* Oh, hills. Not on your own?' A new note crept in to her voice. 'With Hugh?'

'With Kenneth Sinclair.'

'Right. So how is that going?'

'Fine. He's—' She was in danger of saying too much. Anything at all was too much. Even at the other end of the country, Helen was onto you in a moment.

'So, is it serious?'

That, she could not say. She was still at the stage of not knowing if it was serious for *him*. She hedged and they talked of other things. Helen sounded brighter by the time they said goodbye.

She had no sooner hung up than Hugh called. She had no more time to speak now – Kenneth would be here in a few moments. Tonight, she was cooking for him, in her house. Still, it was Hugh.

'I wondered if you might like to come to a gallery preview with me on Friday night? It's only a couple of hours so we could take Flora, or if you had a babysitter we could go out to eat afterwards? The artist is a friend of mine who makes beautiful ceramics.'

'Hugh, that would be lovely, but I don't—' She could not risk taking a minute from being with Kenneth. Surely she would be with *him* next Friday night? For a wild moment, she almost said, Flora's away but I could bring Kenneth Sinclair?

'Flora's with Alan's parents, in Gatehouse. I'm going down to fetch her next weekend and I'm not sure which day. I might set off after work on the Friday, now the nights are so light.'

'You can let me know later.'

Now, she thought, having lied, she and Kenneth would have to stay in on Friday night. That was what they did most of anyway, so far. She hung up feeling guilty. Why on earth had she not told the truth? I'm seeing Kenneth Sinclair and I don't know if I'll be free? That was simple enough, surely. It was all still somehow underground, almost secret. What, after all, did *he* want?

15

No matter what time Helen woke in the night, Joe was already awake. She knew by his breathing, by the way he lay – as men often do but women rarely – on his back, hands clasped behind his head. One foot would be twitching, since he was as restless here as anywhere else.

'Sorry, did I wake you?'

She could not say yes or no to that. He might have disturbed her unconscious self, pulled her up even from sleep with the vibration of his energy, or she might simply have responded to a dream or pressure on her bladder. She had to get up twice a night now.

At any rate, there they were, alert, minds ticking, his fastest and apparently with purpose.

'What do you think—' He was off again, another scheme being hatched in night thoughts.

Early in their relationship she would say, 'Oh, Joe, it's three in the morning,' and pull him close so the thinking and talking turned to something else that was more likely to get them back to sleep. Then she became grumpy at the loss of her sleep with a teaching day ahead. Eventually, she simply turned over and tried to go back to sleep. It was his energy that had attracted her, but these days it was hard to keep up. The June nights were hot and still in the centre of London and no fresh air reached between the buildings to remind them there were fields somewhere, and rivers. The thought of taking a baby out in the fetid air of the city depressed her. She could not help but remember Hugh's garden, with Oliver on a rug in the shade of the apple tree, gazing at the dappled flicker of sun through leaves, his tiny hands reaching up, grasping air.

Not that. She shut it out, laying her hands over the bump that was enormous now. How lazy she was getting, and slow. Not long now, if the baby was on time. Joe had spent a fortune on a bassinet, a pram with a sprung carriage (kept in the tenants' storage room on the ground floor), toys, mobiles, a cot, and baby clothes in white and blue. Joe was convinced he was to have a son and conventional in this as in everything to do with men and women and family. Yet for someone so keen to be a father, he was preoccupied, fretting about his business.

'That fucking Rose Semple,' he said one morning, swallowing coffee at the kitchen worktop, biting into toast that he left half-finished on the crumby breadboard. 'She's brought another load of junk from that place in Scotland. Now and again the guy turns up a few valuables. But she's got no – what's the word – discrimination. Doesn't select. Brings the lot and the lock-ups are stuffed. We ain't got that much space. I've told her, get shot of it.'

He brushed crumbs from his T-shirt and, leaning over to give her a perfunctory kiss, patted the bump. 'Tell His Majesty in there to get a move on – you look knackered.'

'So why do you let her bring you stuff, if it's rubbish?'

'Ah, got a very nice Meissen piece – you'd hardly believe it, would you?'

'Meissen!'

'I need to find somewhere else to store stuff – outside London if possible.'

'Joe—'

'Don't worry, I'll sort something out.' He bent to kiss her again. 'You take care, sweetheart.'

Because it was too hot outside for a jacket, he rammed his wallet into the pocket of his jeans, then his new mobile phone, that he said he could not do without. She had the number and she was to call him, the minute it started.

He was at home when she had the first accelerating cramps. They had been coming and going for two or three weeks, meaning nothing except that she was being warned. They were in bed, and for once, he was asleep. Even in sleep, he seemed alert, as if at any moment he might leap to his feet. She waited, dozed, woke again to the rise of a contraction much more intense than anything so far. She stifled a cry – then … *Yes!* Closer together, the pinnacle fiercer, the fall more of a relief. Too close now—

'Joe – Joe – wake up.'

'What—' He sat up, quivering, braced. It took nothing at all to wake him. What did he think was waiting to get him, should he not be ready for it? Not the baby.

Then he was up and fussing. 'You want to go to the hospital?'

'Oh *God.*'

'We're going.' He was hauling on his jeans, dropped on the floor the previous night when he got in late, Helen already in bed. Sweating, she rose, steadying herself with one hand flat on the wall. Naked because of the heat, she felt cumbersome as an elephant. He was by her side, helping her to the bathroom, where a sudden warm trickle down her thighs told her they must go as soon as they could.

He had a taxi waiting by the time she was dressed, and he carried her little case downstairs, not letting go of her hand and helping her into the cab. She leaned back on the leather seat, sticky with heat. 'Better get a move on, pal,' Joe said to the driver. 'Unless you fancy yourself as a midwife.'

Pain seized her, paralysing. As it ebbed away, she was conscious of their dreamlike progress through streets at their emptiest at four in the morning, the early traffic just beginning.

'You ok?'

'No,' she said. 'But I will be.' She smiled at him, so tense beside her, gripping her hand, sweat on his face, his T-shirt damp under the arms.

'Yeah,' he said. 'Be three of us on the return journey, eh?'

He was right. They had a son.

'We're going to call him Matthew,' Helen told Catherine, using her new mobile phone from the hospital café. 'Joe thinks he should have a Biblical name.'

'It's lovely,' Catherine said. 'I didn't know Joe was religious.'

'He's not. He said it was something to do with – making a statement.' She did not sound sure. 'Anyway, it's a nice name, so I'm not bothered.'

'Does Joe ever think about moving back to Glasgow, now he's a family man?'

Catherine had at first hoped for that, and since Joe was not the sort of person you could live with for long – surely – Helen would be all the nearer when it fell apart. When Helen became pregnant, she could hardly wish for this. Yet she could not help hoping again, now the baby was here. You can long for someone even if you know you are better apart: long for, and long to protect. It had been like that since Oliver. All through Helen's pregnancy, he had hovered like a tiny ghost. It was up to Joe to protect her now.

'He won't move to Glasgow,' Helen said. 'He doesn't seem to have much of a family. I've never met them.'

For the baby's sake, Catherine didn't question this. 'I'll come as soon as I can – I want to see Matthew.'

'You're not interested in babies,' Helen said, amused.

'*Yours.* That's different. I want to see you, anyway.'

'So *then* will you tell me how you're getting on with Kenneth?'

A pause. 'At any rate, I understand about Joe.'

Helen would not let her off with this. 'Understand what?'

'Why you … why women end up with unsuitable men.'

'Everyone in my family thinks Joe is unsuitable – I can't think why,' Helen said crossly. 'He has money, he can provide for me and the baby, he loves me, we have fun and he's amazingly good in bed. Not that I'm thinking about that now, with stitches in my you-know-what.'

Catherine was silent. They did not talk about sex.

Helen laughed. 'Go on,' she said, 'that's why you're still seeing him.'

She sounded, even in the noisy café, a day after childbirth, herself again.

16

Hugh was in his kitchen at the back of the house, when someone tapped on the front door and he heard voices. He glanced at the hall clock as he came through (eleven, time for coffee) then Catherine pushed the door open, calling, 'Hugh?' Flora was with her. The dog, lying under the kitchen table, got up and came to greet them.

'Come in, how good to see you.'

Flora, while she petted the dog, stared at his hands, and he realised he was still wearing yellow rubber gloves.

'I was washing out the waste bin,' he said, pulling off the gloves as they followed him into the kitchen. 'Coffee?' He regarded Flora. 'Milk?'

'I like Coke.'

'She's not allowed Coke,' Catherine said.

'Oh, I might actually have that. Left over from my party.'

'That was months ago! More than a *year*.'

'Does it go off?'

'No,' said Flora.

Hugh found cans of Coke, and a variety of other unsuitable soft drinks, at the back of the sideboard. 'I've brought a selection,' he said. 'You choose, Flora, while I make coffee.'

Flora spent a long time coming to a decision.

By the way Catherine stood close to him, at a distance from Flora, he could tell there was something she wanted to say. She was always hesitant to mention Helen, and it had taken her some time even to tell him about the pregnancy. She had no need to worry, it was all too long ago. He had reached that accommodation with pain that you must, if you're to survive. It was there, but stood further off, as if on the periphery of his senses. He did not mind hearing about Helen, who was probably the most unsuitable woman he could have married.

He had told Catherine he was very glad to hear Helen would have another child. 'The best thing for her.' He was disappointed in her when she said, 'You should marry again yourself.' Women were always saying that, sometimes because they thought he should marry *them*, or their friend, waiting in the wings. He was disappointed too that she had said so little to him about Kenneth. Surely she trusted him.

He said, 'I hear Iain Sinclair's in hospital again.'

Catherine handed him the jug he was reaching for. 'Yes.'

'Any word?'

Flora held up a can. 'I want this one.'

'Not all of it.'

'Why not?'

'You know why not.'

Hugh had a sense of relief that he had to deal with Flora only infrequently. He was older than Catherine and Helen, too old to risk this kind of disruption to his life. Those matchmaking women – perhaps they saw him as a suitable father? He was better as he was.

'I think we could sit outside, if you like.'

Catherine carried the tray while he fetched garden chairs,

carefully put away last autumn, untouched by mould, the spider's web easily brushed off, though that annoyed him slightly. He set the chairs out in a sunny space, next to a wrought-iron table. Flora sat down, but wriggled. She sipped cautiously at the unfamiliar drink.

'What can *I* do?'

'Play in the garden?' her mother suggested. Beyond the lawn, kept so short only a few intrepid daisies survived, were apple and plum trees and a path winding away to obscurity. You could not tell where the wall was, from here, or the fields beyond. Surely a child's paradise.

Flora sighed. 'There's nobody to play with.' She hugged the dog. 'Just you, Bracken, eh?'

Hugh, inspired, said, 'There's a swing. I don't think you've ever been here in the summer, so you probably haven't tried it.'

Flora slipped off her seat. 'Where?'

Hugh led her down the garden between trees and out of sight, the dog trotting after them. Catherine raised her face to the sun, so that Hugh found her like that when he came back, and caught her taut, unhappy expression before she had time to change it.

'Why did she choose this one?' he asked, picking up the almost full can, 'if she doesn't like it?'

'She didn't know she doesn't like it,' Catherine said with a smile.

'Ah.'

The air prickled with what Catherine had come to say.

'You wanted to tell me something – about Kenneth?'

'Oh no.' She sounded brisk and cold. 'I haven't seen him since his father's heart attack.'

'It's about Helen, then?'

'Yes.'

159

'Baby born safely?'

'Sorry, Hugh, I should just have said.'

He wondered why she had not. Was he so fragile a soul she dared not risk his complete collapse? Yet, when she said *a son*, and told him the child's name, he did, for a few obliterating seconds, suffer what he hoped he would never feel again.

'Both well?' He poured more coffee for Catherine, his own untouched.

'Yes. She sounds fine, more like herself than for ages.'

She had been *unlike*. It was obvious that Catherine did not approve of Joe. Hugh wondered, but mildly. It was not his business.

Bracken having returned to lie at Hugh's feet, they wandered down the garden to see if Flora was still on the swing, and so that Hugh could dig up a little root of a plant he was offering Catherine for her own dull flower border.

'Wrong time of year to take it, really, but I'll put it in a polythene bag, and you must keep it nice and wet till you can get it in tonight – in shade, mind you.'

'I promise.'

He straightened, the plant in his hand, soil scattering from the root onto the swept path. 'Don't worry about Kenneth – he's got a business to run, and if his father is – well, he has to face making a few decisions.'

'Decisions about what?'

'The business. He wants to run it one way, his father another. It's always been like that. Iain doesn't believe in spending to invest and Kenneth does.'

'His father's retired, surely?'

'He's still the boss, I suspect.'

'He must want the company to do well, though?'

'It's a question of risk,' Hugh said. 'Kenneth has wanted to expand and try for bigger contracts, but Iain's always vetoed that. He knows it would mean buying new plant and taking on more men.'

Perhaps she thought the business a poor excuse for not being in touch with her. Hugh put a gentle hand on her arm, forgetting it was dirty with rooting in the earth. 'Don't you worry about his moods. That would be a mistake.'

Before she could answer, the telephone began ringing in the house. Catherine took the flower root from him, and he went back to the house to answer it.

It was a short conversation. He came out more slowly, so preoccupied he had forgotten the bag for her plant.

'That was Kenneth,' he said. 'His father's dead.'

17

'When is the funeral?'

'Next Thursday. But—'

They were standing on her garden path. Seeing his car draw up, Catherine had gone out to meet Kenneth at the gate. He looked as usual, fit and ruddy and full of energy. At the sight of him, a wave of longing and lust had overtaken her.

'Do you want to come in?' she said, pulling the gate open.

'I'd better not.' Kenneth glanced past her at the front door. 'Is Flora—'

'Yes, she's watching television.'

'I was on my way back from the site we're working at Culloden. I thought I'd just call and say sorry I've not had a chance to be in touch.'

'Obviously.' A pause. 'I'll – I'll come to the funeral of course. Just—'

'It would be better if you didn't.'

'What?'

'Aileen will be there. My parents weren't happy about the divorce.'

'What on earth has that to do with me?'

'Nothing. It's just – I've not actually said anything about you to my mother.'

She stepped back. 'I hope it goes well,' she said.

'Catherine – look—'

'Never mind. I have to go.'

She went in fast, closed the front door and leaned on it, breathing hard, her forehead against cold wood. *How dare you, how dare you?*

Catherine was glad to be at work and compelled to think about other things. At three, when the funeral was to be held, she meant to focus on the report she must write for the next Corporate Services Committee. A dull enough task, but it needed concentration. She had all the right bits of paper on her desk, her notebook open, the computer screen blank except for the title, when James Fraser stopped by her desk.

'A word, if you have time?'

'Yes, of course.'

He made for his office, so she followed, speculating. The report wasn't due till Monday.

His desk was clear of papers as always, except for a neat pile in the corner, ready for Paula, his secretary, to take away. From the next room came the clack-clack of her keyboard. He smoothed a hand over his hair and indicated the chair opposite. They both sat down.

'You know David's leaving?'

'For a job in Edinburgh.'

'That's right. I wondered—' He paused briefly, giving her a few seconds to get there before him. 'We'll need someone to fill his post until the reorganisation is through. A few months – well, probably six.' He paused. 'Or more.'

She tipped her head a little to show she was taking this in. As if she would not be!

'Would you consider it?'

She could see the possibilities beyond this: something better at the end of it. She had begun to think she might not stay in this job, even in the Highlands. Flora, she had been persuading herself all week, could adapt, as she had before.

'Yes.'

'Good. You'll have some questions, no doubt.' He glanced at his watch. 'Tomorrow, if that would be all right? Financial Services Committee in a few minutes.'

She got up. 'Thank you.'

'We'll be thanking you, believe me.' He got up too. 'Keep it to yourself meantime – still a few things to sort out.'

At her desk, staring at the blank computer screen, she thought, 'Is this it? Am I going to have a career after all?'

She became aware that Colleen was looking at her, mug raised.

'Cuppa? You're miles away.'

'Sorry.'

'What did His Nibs want?'

'Just the Committee Report. Something else he wants to put in it.'

Colleen got up, collecting mugs. 'Oh, that,' she said.

Unable to concentrate, she left at five, earlier than usual. James had gone on to a meeting away from Headquarters, and Colleen disappeared at half past four.

Catherine had driven all the way home before Iain Sinclair's funeral came into her mind. Good. Kenneth had receded in the course of the afternoon. She garaged the car, then walked back along the street to collect Flora.

'Tea?' Tracey asked. Dave was offshore, so she was in no hurry to clear the house of children and company.

'No, thanks. I seem to have been drinking the stuff all day.'

'They're in the middle of watching something on telly. It'll be finished in ten minutes – take the weight off.'

It was after six before Catherine and Flora were home. She was in the kitchen when the doorbell rang.

'I'll get it!' Flora yelled.

The radio was on so it was a moment before Catherine was aware of a muffled conversation in the hall. Then Flora burst in.

'It's *Gil*. He's a bit weird, all kind of *wobbly*. He said he had to sit down, so he's in the living room.'

'What on earth do you mean – "wobbly"?'

Flora looked anxious, and would only follow her mother, not lead the way.

'Gil?'

Through the living room window she could see the red van in the street, parked askew. He was slumped on the sofa, and he was drunk. As she went closer, she could smell drink, as if alcohol fumes rose from his skin.

'Sorry,' he said. 'Couldn't take it any more.' He grinned, sheepish. 'You don' min', eh?'

She did mind. Of course – the funeral she had blessedly forgotten.

'Flora,' she said, 'would you please fill the kettle? I'll make Gil some coffee.'

She vanished, obedient in her alarm. Catherine sat down facing him. 'What happened? Was it just – your father—'

'Fuck them,' he said. 'Why should I fucking care?'

'Ssh! Flora—'

165

'Sorry, sorry.'

Beyond strong coffee, she did not know what to do with him.

'Should I phone someone? You can't drive home on your own – you shouldn't have driven here.'

'No, no, I'm all right.'

'Mummy, the kettle's boiling.'

Flora stood in the doorway, but when Catherine got up, she followed her back to the kitchen.

'I don't like it,' she said. 'He seems different.'

'It's all right. '

'Is he drunk?'

'Yes.'

'I don't like it.'

'No, nor do I. Coffee will help. And maybe a sandwich? Is there any ham left?'

Flora opened the fridge and inspected. 'Some. I'll make the sandwich.'

'Good girl. Thank you.'

In the end, Catherine drove him back to the cottage, leaving Flora with Tracey. On the way, Gilbert fell asleep, his head lolling towards the door, face against the window. If I opened that door, she thought, he'd fall out like a rag doll. Once or twice she had to give him a sharp nudge to wake him and check she was taking the right road, since she had been to the cottage only once before.

'Gil – we're here.' He was dozing again as she bumped up the track and drew to a halt outside the croft house. As she wondered if she would have to drag him out of the car, the front door opened.

'Oh,' Rose said, 'it's you. I wondered where he'd got to.'

Gilbert was getting carefully out of the car. 'Hello, Rose, my dear,' he said with a foolish smile.

'I'm glad you're here,' Catherine said. 'I was a bit worried about leaving him on his own.' Even the surly Rose was better than no one. Gilbert went carefully up the path and Rose stood back to let him pass.

'Where's the van?' she asked.

'Outside my house.'

'You better take me back there, then,' Rose said, 'or how're we supposed to get out this bloody place?'

'What about—'

'Oh, *he's* all right.'

She shut the door and started down the path.

'Well—'

'Come on then.'

In the car, the smell of Rose's recent cigarette was overpowering. When she got a crushed packet out of the pocket of her dusty jacket, Catherine said sharply, 'Please don't smoke in my car.' With a sigh, Rose turned the pack over on her lap, end, side, end, side, and it seemed to Catherine the smell of tobacco wafted from it, repellent.

'I suppose,' Catherine said tentatively, when they had covered several miles, 'it was the funeral upset him.'

'His family upsets him. So-called family.'

'They *are* his family. I know it seems strange. He and Kenneth are not the least alike.'

'Not that surprising.'

'Why not?'

'He's adopted.'

'Kenneth?' Something rose up, a flame of astonishment and longing.

'Him! No, Gil.'

Of course. Now it made sense. She felt excluded, all over

again. Get over it, she told herself, oblivious of Rose for a few blinding miles.

Daylight had faded by the time Rose got in the van and drove off. It had not even been locked and the keys were in the ignition. Still, it was hardly surprising it was still here, untouched, in this street of four-wheel drives and smart hatchbacks. With a sigh, Catherine turned towards Tracey's house again. As she did so, Kenneth's jeep rounded the corner at surprising speed and came to a halt at her front door with the squeak of tyre against kerb. He got out and slammed the door.

'What was he doing here?' he asked.

'What?'

'I saw his van heading down the hill.'

'It was Rose,' she said, 'collecting it. That's all.' Furious, she moved away, but he was through the gate. It thudded behind him as he followed her up the path.

'He *was* here, though.'

She had forgotten she should be on her way to fetch Flora. Remembering, she stopped on the doorstep, and he almost ran into her. His closeness, familiar and heady, caught and held her.

'Are we going in?' he asked.

'I must fetch Flora from Tracey's.'

'Let's go in,' he said, and they were in the little hall.

'Gilbert *was* here,' she admitted, thinking he was annoyed about it for some reason she didn't understand. 'He'd been drinking and he was a bit – you know.'

They were in the living room, facing each other. He glanced around, as if he thought his brother concealed somewhere in this house that had no corners or secrets.

'I drove him to the cottage and Rose was there, so she came back with me for the van. It's quite simple.'

'I'm sorry you had that bother. You should have phoned me.'

'You were at your father's funeral! Actually, I thought he was too.'

'I like you angry,' he said. 'A bit of colour in your cheeks.'

This did not have the effect of lessening the colour, or the anger. 'For God's sake – I have to get Flora. You don't phone for weeks, you tell me to keep away from your family, and now you've got the nerve to turn up here and start—'

'Start what? Come here.'

She did not, so he snatched up her surprised hand and gripping it, led her to the stairs.

'Come on.'

Fury did not free her, or let her answer him except incoherently. Too late, too late, he was here and whatever she said, it was no good, would make no difference. The bedroom, pretty and tidy and unmarked by her personality or his, seemed too small for him, too small for the two of them, struggling to pull clothes off, entangled, tumbling onto the neatly made bed.

She allowed herself ten minutes of dozing afterwards, held in his arms, before she got up and went to the bathroom to wash quickly, wash him away, dress and comb her hair so that when she hurried along the road and her daughter saw her, Flora would have no suspicion something had been going on in her absence, that she must not know about, would not understand, but even so, would not approve.

'I won't be long. *Please* get up – go downstairs—'

He was smiling dazedly, saying nothing.

'Kenneth!'

'I'll get up,' he said, 'and put the kettle on. Your lovely daughter will know nothing. I do get to stay for a cup of tea?'

'You look hot,' Flora said as they walked back to the house, Catherine as slowly as she dared.

'Well, it's been a rush, getting Gil home. Then Rose came for the van.'

'Rose that was at The Factory?'

'Yes.'

'I don't like her.'

'I don't think I do either, but – ' being fair-minded – 'we don't really know her and she does seem to be looking after Gil. He needs someone to look after him.'

'I'm up very late, aren't I?' Flora said with satisfaction as they went into the house. Kenneth came out of the kitchen to meet them.

'Hello.'

Flora stared. 'What a lot of visitors tonight.'

'I beg your pardon – will I leave?'

'No, it's all right.' Flora, gracious, gave him nevertheless a searching look before she went to pour herself milk.

'Bed, Flora.'

Flora very slowly drank her milk and ate a biscuit, and with tantalising carefulness, put her glass in the sink, wiped the white moustache from her upper lip, and fetched book and cloth rabbit from the living room. She trailed upstairs with the air of someone misjudged, who is behaving impeccably.

Kenneth sat down, laughing. 'She doesn't miss much.'

'She knows *something's* going on.'

'I made the bed.'

'Thank you.' She sat down too, shaking. 'Oh God, what a

night.' She looked across at him, relaxed on the sofa. 'How did it go? The funeral.' How long ago and irrelevant that seemed now.

'My mother's exhausted. She has my cousin staying with her, so I left after everyone else had gone. It was a big funeral. He was well liked.' A spasm of grief or guilt flickered on his face.

'And Aileen?' she could not help asking.

'Oh, she was there.'

But you came here, she thought, you came to me. For sex, that urge to life that impels in the face of death. It seemed it was fiercer for him than it had been for her after Alan's death, his need more immediate. She supposed that was all it was, and felt she had been used. And yet, she used him too, didn't she? Perhaps they should start again, or abandon this altogether, having been of some use to each other.

'I'll miss the old bugger,' he said. 'But it's my mother who's going to be lost. He was her world.'

This seemed to her a terrible fate. 'What now?' she said, meaning the two of them.

'Now I can do what I like. Mum won't interfere.'

She realised he wasn't talking about her, but about his business. She glanced at the clock. 'I think you'd better go.'

He stood up. 'Give me a week or two,' he said. 'Then come out to the works – I'd like to show you round.'

What about your mother, she wanted to say, but did not. She went with him to the door. From upstairs there was silence but this did not mean Flora was asleep.

He gripped her shoulders and kissed her. 'Ok, I'm off.'

When he had gone, she stood in the hall, not knowing what to think or feel. A fool, was the only answer. I feel a fool.

I didn't ask him if what Rose said was true.

18

August came, and London seemed to slumber, the streets dusty and still in the heat, something that might have been decaying vegetation underlying the stink of diesel and fried food on the road from Archway tube station as Helen pushed her buggy with a sleeping Matthew past shops and cafés, weaving between the people coming towards them.

All summer, Joe had been promising her a holiday. So far they'd had nothing but a weekend in an expensive hotel on the south coast, nerve-racking because the baby cried so much, she was afraid people would complain. So dazed and tired had she been she couldn't remember much about the place, pretty though it was, except one walk along the cliffs, Matthew carried by Joe in a sling, leaving her with the sensation all afternoon of having left something vital behind, her arms strangely unencumbered. Joe had talked constantly to other people on his mobile phone. She began to wonder how he had done business without it. Perhaps the fashion for them would die out.

She was going to tell Joe tonight that she could not bear the heat, the dead air, any longer. She would go to Scotland and visit Catherine. She left the pushchair in the hall, chaining it to the bottom banister as usual, then heaved Matthew and her shopping upstairs to the flat. She fumbled for her key, Matthew awake and beginning to whimper, finally got the door open and stumbled in, the shopping spilling from the carrier bag at her feet as she did so. *Damn.* Now he was really crying, that thin hungry wail you could only comfort with feeding. Kicking the door shut behind her, she made straight for the sofa and sank onto it, hauling up her T-shirt, unfastening the flap of the maternity bra and latching him on.

Silence. Bliss. She thought how it used to take her twenty minutes to get settled with Oliver: glass of water, bib in case he was sick, a cushion for her back, oh, and scrub her hands first. Now she could not be bothered. 'It's too hot,' she told the peacefully sucking baby. The flat was airless and her back stuck to the stupid leather sofa, sweaty and uncomfortable. 'You're happy, at any rate,' she told him. 'I wish I was.' She traced her finger along his satiny cheek, pink-flushed. 'Happy with you,' she amended. 'Just not with anything else.'

When Joe came in and she told him she was going to Scotland, he seemed relieved.

'I'll book the flights tomorrow, right?'

A week later, he had done nothing. He'd forgotten; he was busy. She began nagging about it. Finally he said, 'For God's sake, you've got nothing else to do all day – you book it.'

She reacted badly to this, and he to her. For the first time since Matthew's birth, he went out in the evening not for business, but to the pub. She lay weeping on the bed, the baby finally asleep in his white basket.

'This is hopeless,' she said aloud, and sat up to blow her nose. At this, the baby's bluish eyelids fluttered and when she leaned over the basket he woke, gazing at her silently with his dark eyes, as if she had called him back from a distant shore and he was not quite with her yet. Her heart moved in her breast at the sight of him, and the tears fell again, but not this time for Joe.

'We'll pack a bag,' she said, 'and we can at least go down to your adoring grandparents for the weekend.'

He gazed at her. Whatever you think, he seemed to say. However, when she called her parents they were not in. She did not leave a message.

Later, as she was getting ready for bed, Joe still not home, Catherine rang.

'I'm sorry it's so late,' she said, 'but I thought I'd better check. You said you were coming here and I'm going away for a few days, so I wanted to know the dates.'

'I've not booked yet. Where are you going?'

Jealous, she wanted to know it was nowhere she herself couldn't have gone if she had the energy, and did not have a baby.

'I'm going to Skye. I know it doesn't sound exotic but everyone tells me how special it is.'

'On your own?'

'With Kenneth.'

'It is getting serious then.'

She had not been able to work out what was going on. Catherine was often secretive, but it had been particularly difficult to find out about Kenneth. Had she met him herself, when she was married to Hugh? Hugh had not had so many friends she would have forgotten, surely?

'We have to go while Flora's in Gatehouse, before term starts, so it's next week. But come any time after that.'

'Doesn't he want to take Flora?'

'Oh, no, it's not that!'

'What then?'

'What's wrong? Is Matthew—'

'He's fine. He's sleeping much better now. I was just going to feed him actually so—'

'Helen, come the week after next. Can't you just book the sleeper? That would be easier for you. I'll meet you at Inverness station.'

Tired of her own company, her dullness, she said, 'All right. I'll book it tomorrow.'

'Call me as soon as you have.'

They fixed the dates and said goodbye. Helen turned to the baby, grizzling now and hungry. 'We're going on holiday,' she said. 'Your daddy will just have to manage without us.'

She would not speculate how easy this might be for Joe.

19

Kenneth had planned to take her up Ben Dearg, but when the mist came down, he would not risk it with someone so inexperienced. Catherine was disappointed but wet already and shivering, so he was glad to get her moving fast downhill.

'Another day,' he said and she glanced at him, as if surprised. There would be other days. She had her faults, he was seeing that in the enforced closeness of a week's holiday, but she was hardy, enduring discomfort without complaint. He liked that kind of stoicism in a woman. He liked it in her. He was beginning to want to be with her, and not just for sex. That was how it worked: sex first, then if you were lucky, love. Yet something made him hold back; she was dangerous in her own way. Perhaps he was better as he was.

On the fourth evening the cloud cleared and a breeze chased ragged shreds from a sky that became in a few moments intensely blue. They sat on the bench outside the holiday cottage, leaning on the rough stone wall, a bottle of wine at their feet, and felt the sun's heat for the first time, though it was almost seven o'clock.

There was still an awkwardness in her that he found both endearing and annoying. She did not relax, even in the aftermath of sex. Something in her twitched, if not physically then in her thoughts, a flinching away from what had looked – only moments ago – like abandonment. Too soon, she gathered herself and moved away. Here, she had no excuse. There was no Flora, about to come home or having to be fetched, no critical eight-year-old gaze, seeing too much. At night she succumbed to sleep as if reluctantly, edging away from him in the darkness that was at this time of year, so far north, not complete until midnight. Then in the moonlit bedroom her fairness was silvery and she lay still, remote from him in her dreams.

The next two days were fine, but they did not attempt the hill. Instead they walked on beaches or up new paths, stopping in sunny sheltered spots to lie on heather and take their books out to read. He persuaded her to sex once or twice, convincing her no one would come upon them here: she was safe and could enjoy it. Sometimes he thought he had reached her after all. *I have you now*, he thought, then moments later realised he had not, she was cool again. Still a challenge there, he told himself, growing more determined.

At Dunvegan on their last afternoon they stopped at the bakery and bought scones.

'I'm going to make tea for you,' Kenneth said. 'We'll stop on the shore.'

In a lay-by overlooking Loch Dunvegan, he got out his camping stove and filled his little kettle with water he'd collected from a hillside burn and kept in a bottle. When it boiled, he dropped in a couple of tea bags.

'There now,' he said, 'is that not the best tea you've ever drunk?'

In the open air, with the breeze lifting her hair, the sun on her shoulders, she agreed it was. The scones were good too, crumbly and fresh.

'You're not used to this, are you?'

'What? A man making tea for me?'

He grinned. 'I meant the outdoors, the hills. Simple things.'

'How sophisticated do you think I am?'

He raised his flask cup in a toast and smiled. 'Very.'

After a moment, she said, 'My sister Helen has this theory ... the theory of one line. You can understand a person if you know one key thing about them. Everyone has a defining one line.'

'What's mine?' he asked.

'I'm not sure I know you well enough to say.'

'You've got something in mind?'

'Kenneth likes being in charge.'

He laughed. 'Not always!'

'Oh yes,' she said. 'Always.'

As they drove back to Kyleakin for the ferry on Saturday, Catherine said, 'My sister is coming to stay with her baby tomorrow. It's my last few days of holiday so I have to spend them with her and with Flora.'

'Fine,' he said, thinking of the new contract they were beginning, that he must get to grips with on Monday. He'd left Jimmy and Elsie to make sure they had enough casuals for the second and subsequent weeks, when they'd need most men on the job. He wouldn't be happy till he was on site, making the first marks in the ground, the roster done, the lorries turning up with the hard core, the cement mixers churning. Work was beginning again for him with its hard edge, something you could grasp and deal with and get the better of. He glanced at Catherine, aware she had fallen silent, but she was gazing out of the car window at the arch of the new bridge that would be open in a few months. She regretted the little ferry, still a novelty to her.

178

'It's beautiful,' she said. 'I'm going to miss it. We've had a lovely week.'

'You think so?'

'Yes, I've been happy. You've liked it too – haven't you?'

'It's been grand,' he said, satisfied at last. She put her hand on his thigh as he drove, and he covered it with his own.

20

The plan had been that the Grahams would bring Flora home, then drive west. They had a fancy for seeing Gairloch, having been there once twenty years ago. They would start early from Gatehouse, and when they reached Inverness Catherine would give them a late lunch. At one Sheila Graham called to say the traffic was much worse than they'd thought, and how busy the A9 was, they simply couldn't believe the number of caravans. Had people no consideration at all? They were near Pitlochry and would stop there for lunch, if that that all right? She hoped Catherine hadn't gone to too much trouble. Catherine, who had not, said fine, and put the salad back in the fridge. They could have dinner with her instead, and indeed they would have to stay overnight. If the A9 was a surprise they would hardly have remembered how long the road over to Gairloch would be.

By the time they arrived Flora had been sleeping for over an hour, Sheila was tired and David grumpy. Catherine, just back from Skye, was dazed from being in a state she had not experienced before, even on her honeymoon. She now realised what that week had actually been *for*. She was still full of goodwill.

Flora, thoroughly spoiled, was overtired and fractious by the time her grandparents left. She wanted to go with them.

Catherine said no, Granny said why not, and Catherine said no more firmly, making an enemy of her daughter and dispersing all traces of the blissful heights of the previous week. She was nostalgic for the cottage at Milovaig made snug by an open fire and the deep double bed with its cushiony eiderdown. She thought of the flames leaping in the fire and the heat of his body, his length the length of hers, all night long, and of the days of sunshine and lovemaking in the open air, that she was hot recalling and could not even think of in front of anyone else. She shook off her irritation, changed the bed for Helen's arrival, and fetched Flora's old crib from the loft. At last Flora lost interest in her grievances and began to imagine her new cousin, and how interesting she herself would be to this baby.

Helen came off the sleeper assisted by two young men, one pulling her suitcase on wheels, the other guiding the empty pushchair. She was encumbered only by her handbag and a sleeping Matthew.

'Goodbye, thank you *so* much!' The young men hitched up their rucksacks and walked away as Catherine took over the suitcase.

'Can I push him?' It would have been difficult to wrest the handle of the pushchair from Flora's firm grasp and Helen did not care. She had not had much sleep.

'You look exhausted,' Catherine said as they began the drive to her house, Helen in the back with Matthew and Flora.

'I look a wreck,' Helen said.

'Soon be home, and you can have a nap.'

'Is this where you live then? Deep in suburbia.'

'It's a perfectly ordinary street.'

'I bet Mum liked it.'

Catherine glanced in the rear-view mirror at her sister unbuckling her seatbelt, began to say something sharp, then changed her mind. Helen looked awful. She had not yet paid attention to the baby, taking in only a small bundle that Flora had self-importantly ferried from station to car park, but now as Helen got awkwardly out of the car with the bundle in her arms she looked across and saw him, his face peeping out, cautious, ready to pucker in indignant grief. He was beautiful, with the same heart-stopping beauty that had caught her when she first saw Joe.

'He's so like—'

'Yes,' Helen said, smoothing the blanket away from his head and showing off his black downy hair, his dark eyes, the fathomless gaze of the innocent and the corrupt.

Oliver had been fair, like Helen and Hugh. Hugh had the fairish colourless hair that becomes grey-white in middle age. This baby was a foreigner with something exotic about him. Catherine touched his face with the tip of a gentle finger. 'He's lovely,' she said.

Helen shifted him in her arms, and Catherine turned to get the suitcase from the boot. She gave her key to Flora who had capably sprung the pushchair upright and was about to wheel it up the path.

'Open the door, Flora, would you. We'll get the kettle on.'

'How good you are at dealing with this wretched buggy,' Helen said as she followed Flora indoors.

'I do Keiron's,' she said, 'at my childminder. He's two, but his is the same sort.' She glanced around. 'Where will I put it?'

It filled the tiny hallway. They would be forever banging their ankles on it, going to the front door.

'It's fine here,' said Helen, before Catherine could decide.

'I'll take Matthew,' Flora offered. 'I can hold him on my knees – in here.'

Helen followed her into the living room and when Flora was settled on the sofa, wedged firmly against the back, legs stuck out in front of her, laid the baby on her small lap. Flora held him without any of the tentativeness Catherine felt in herself, seeing how small he was, with the forgotten fragility of the recently born. The baby grizzled a little at the separation from his mother, then as Flora moved him in her arms, gently up and down, he was quiet, gazing at her.

Helen and Catherine stood in the little kitchen, while the kettle boiled.

'She's awfully good with him. I think we could just leave her to it,' Helen said.

'Showing off.'

Helen laughed. 'Maybe.'

'That's better – you look more like yourself.'

They gazed at each other for a few assessing, embarrassed seconds, then Helen ducked away. She investigated a biscuit barrel sitting on the worktop and began nibbling the edge of a digestive.

'You forget how tiring babies are.'

'Doesn't Joe help?'

'Yes, of course he does.' Helen put the rest of the biscuit in her mouth and said through crumbs, 'He's busy though.'

'Are you hungry? Have you had breakfast?'

'I didn't want the train breakfast. Matthew was asleep at last and I couldn't see the point in waking him before I had to.'

'Eggs? Bacon? What would you like?'

'I enjoyed that digestive. Ages since I've eaten one. We just have olives and pitta bread and stuff like that.'

This made no sense to Catherine. 'You must have toast.'

'Must we?'

Catherine laughed. 'Well, you can have ordinary toast and marmalade here if you want it.'

'Yes, please. I don't suppose you have cornflakes? I have a sudden desire for cornflakes. '

'No, sorry.' Catherine opened a cupboard door and gazed at it hopefully, as if cornflakes might miraculously appear. 'Rice Krispies? That's what Flora has.'

'Even better!'

They were giggling, so that Flora called from the living room, 'What's so funny?'

She was trapped by the baby, who was beginning to grizzle, so Helen went to rescue her. 'I'm having some of your cereal, is that ok?'

'I think you'd better take him back. He's a bit fed up now.'

Released, Flora shot through to the kitchen. If there was to be more breakfast, she would have some.

Companionably, they sat at the kitchen table, Helen with Matthew on her lap, her knee bouncing a little. He would not cry if she kept him moving. Catherine, dispensing breakfast, decided they would have a good week. Yet the baby unnerved her, so direct was his gaze and so unlike Helen he seemed. He was Helen's child though, and with a swelling of remembered grief, she was grateful. He was here, and he was living. Poor Hugh was her next thought, *he* won't have another son.

As soon as Flora had abandoned her half-eaten bowl of cereal and gone out to her new swing in the garden, Helen said, 'Now you can tell me all about Skye.' She shifted the baby onto her other knee and he rested on her, his thumb already familiar with the comfort of sucking, growing sleepy. 'I hope you're going to introduce me to Kenneth.'

Catherine, not committing herself, poured more tea. They sat in silence for a moment, gazing at the child, drawn by his beauty, the dark lashes as he closed his eyes, the bloom of his perfect skin.

'He is so like Joe', Catherine murmured, stroking his cheek. Something stirred, a quaver of longing for another baby, the soft weight of your own child, the tenderness of his sleep. Yet she had been glad to get all that over, as Flora grew.

'Mum was fishing when I was last there,' Helen said. '"Where did you say Joe's family is?" She meant who are his *antecedents*. "Italian?" she asked me.'

Catherine smiled. 'I thought that too. He could have Italian, Spanish or even Mexican blood, don't you think?'

'So what?' Helen said rudely. 'For goodness sake, you too.'

'Why shouldn't he? It makes him beautiful, almost exotic.'

'Foreign, was what Mum meant.'

'You said she liked Joe.'

'When he's *there*, he charms her. She sort of resents him when he's *not* there. She doesn't trust him.'

'Do you?' Catherine could not help asking.

'Do you trust Kenneth?' Helen flashed back.

There was no satisfactory answer either of them could make. Already Catherine was aware of the new loyalty that comes in with love, beyond family. She thought she was in love. She said, as she began to gather up the breakfast dishes, 'I'm afraid of my own lack of judgement. I made a mistake before.'

'Before?'

'I shouldn't have married Alan.'

'Are you going to marry Kenneth?'

Helen was imagining a ceremony, dressing up and flowers, and a party. Catherine brushed this off. 'I don't think I'll ever get married again.'

'You think that,' Helen said, 'but even now, it's the only solution for women. It means something.'

'It means you're tied.'

Their voices had lifted and the child stirred in Helen's arms. Wearily she hoisted him and he woke.

'I'll have to feed him,' she said, unbuttoning her blouse and shifting herself into a more comfortable position.

'Wouldn't the sofa or an easy chair—'

'I'm fine.'

Catherine turned away from the baby's seeking mouth and her sister's full white breast, blue-veined, the nipple starting up brown and enlarged, a drop of milk appearing. She began to wash up dishes, but beneath the sound of running water she was aware of the baby's rhythmic sucking and Helen's murmured endearments. She could not help wondering if Joe was up to this. Was he good enough? Helen might ask the same about Kenneth. She longed to speak to him and make real again the connection between them there had been on Skye.

'I'll call Kenneth, if you like,' she said, drying her hands. 'See if he'd like to come over for supper while you're here?'

Helen looked up, her gaze for a few seconds unfocused as the baby's, then her face cleared and she smiled. 'That would be nice. I hope—'

'What? That he measures up?'

'That I do.'

'Oh, for goodness' sake.'

'Well,' Helen said, moving the baby round to the other breast, 'you don't always like me, so I don't expect he will.'

'Nonsense,' Catherine said, 'of course I like you. You're my sister.'

186

In the hall, as she picked up the telephone receiver, she was nervous. He would be at work and perhaps out on site.

Elsie answered, and, yes, he was on site, on the Black Isle.

'He has a mobile phone now, though,' Elsie said. 'Do you have that number?'

She was outflanked. She'd been his lover only a few days ago; now he had a new telephone number she could easily use to reach him, and he had not told her. It was uncomfortable saying to Elsie, no, I haven't, that would be helpful. It put her at a disadvantage.

When she tried the mobile number it rang for a long time before his voice came faintly, through a buzzing noise, 'Sinclair.'

'Kenneth, it's me, Catherine.'

'Hello.'

'I wondered – we wondered if you'd like to come and meet my sister. Come for a meal?'

'When?'

'Tomorrow or Wednesday?'

'Can't do it. Too much going on here – I'll be late finishing.'

'We could eat later …' Stop, she told herself, give this up.

'Give me a call next week, ok? Should have settled down by then. We've had a few problems.' In the distance, a lorry revving, then someone calling him. 'Got to go. Sorry.'

'Another time,' she said to the empty air, the connection severed. Yet why should there be? Embarrassed and angry, she kicked the pushchair as she picked up Helen's suitcase and began to drag it upstairs. She would not say a word about Joe that might upset Helen. She had chosen him, after all, and with her child, had gone a long way ahead.

21

The weeks slipped by, featureless, after Helen went home. It was almost September. Catherine had not called Kenneth, but why did *he* not contact *her*?

Helen said, 'That's what men are like. You have to make the first move.'

'Nonsense, why should I?'

'Well, if it doesn't matter to you, that's another matter.'

It did. Helen knew that, but they did not talk about it. Instead, they discussed the miraculous baby. Helen could talk about him at length, letting Catherine's life off the hook. Eventually, she met Kenneth at Hugh's house.

If she had been five minutes later, she would not. He was on the point of leaving when she arrived with Flora to collect the last of the season's peas and raspberries from the garden. 'I have more than I know what to do with,' Hugh had said. 'Come and take some of this stuff away. I don't know why I keep growing so much, year after year.'

Flora was to do the picking. Hugh had a basket for her and she shot out through the scullery into the garden, with only a sidelong glance at Kenneth.

'I'd better be off,' he said.

Hugh said, 'You're not in a hurry, are you? I'll make more tea.'

Before he could reply, Flora reappeared. 'How do you know if the raspberries are ready? Just when they're red? They're different sorts of red.'

'An intelligent question,' Hugh said. 'Come on, I'll show you how you can tell.'

Left in the kitchen, Kenneth and Catherine looked at each other.

'How are you?' he asked.

'Fine.'

'Sorry, I meant to call.'

'You're busy, I'm sure. So am I. This new job is hectic.'

'What new job?' Then he remembered. 'Oh yes, sorry.'

A pause lengthened to uncomfortable silence. Catherine said desperately, 'So – how is the job going, the one you were starting—'

'Finished yesterday.'

'Right.'

'Look – I *was* going to call you. But my mother's been ill. She had a slight stroke.'

'I'm sorry.' Was she so unimportant he did not think of telling her?

The kettle had boiled. Kenneth said, 'Will I make you tea? What about Flora?'

'I don't want tea.' She took a deep breath. 'I'm really sorry about your mother. I hope she's getting better.'

'She is. My aunt's staying with her, so I don't need to be there as much now.'

'I wish you'd let me know. I feel—' What did it matter how she felt? He so clearly hadn't given her a thought.

'Let me make you a cup of tea,' he said. 'You look tired.'

189

'I'm fine! I don't need tea.'

'I do.'

She sat at the kitchen table in Hugh's old-fashioned kitchen, as water thrummed in the kettle. Kenneth had rolled up the sleeves of his blue shirt, and the sun lit him up as he turned to get out a clean cup and saucer for her. As she watched him, the tiredness he had noticed, and she had been fending off, seemed to go through her in a wave. She sat down.

While the kettle sang, he pulled out a chair for himself. Across the little table, she could not help but meet his gaze.

'I've had a bad few weeks,' he said. Brown with working out of doors, he seemed nevertheless washed out, at the end of some tether she'd not realised was holding him.

'I wish you'd told me about your mother. After Skye, I thought—'

'What did you think?'

'I thought we were—' Embarrassed, she gave up.

His expression was inscrutable, but in a movement so fast she did not see it coming, he leaned over and grasped her hand, raised to hook a strand of hair behind her ear. His grip, warm and hard, was not to be got out of. Her other hand came up as if in mild protest. Now he was grasping both, and they faced each other joined, elbows resting on the table.

'We get off on the wrong foot,' he said. 'Every time.'

Suffused with despair and longing, she could not answer. Neither of them heard the footsteps on the path or the voices. Hugh was at the door, Flora behind him with a basket, before they realised, and broke apart.

Hugh said, 'I've let Flora down again. No ice cream. We're going to the Spar in the village to get some.'

'I thought we were taking these rasps home,' Catherine said, hastily resuming motherhood. 'You're not supposed to eat them all now, Flora.'

Flora flashed a look at Kenneth, then her mother. She seemed to edge slightly closer to Hugh. 'I'm not *going* to eat all of them. Just some.'

In a few moments, left alone with a basket of raspberries, their scent warm in the air, Kenneth and Catherine sat down again, and Kenneth pushed the basket towards her. 'Want one?'

The fruit was warm and sweet as the late summer afternoon drifting through the open door, where a lazy bee floated, as if wondering whether to follow the raspberries indoors. Catherine took another berry, and another. Kenneth leaned forward, and with his finger brushed a stray seed in its crimson pocket from the corner of her mouth. Before his hand could move away she turned, grasped his finger between her teeth and gently, gripped. Drawing his finger back, he took her chin in red-stained fingers, and pulled her face to his.

'The table's in the way,' he said after a moment.

'They'll be back soon.' Catherine got up. 'I need some air.'

Outside, they walked slowly down the path.

'I'll come and have that dinner with you, now,' he said. The dahlias bordering the path, orange and red, were like flames.

'Helen's long gone home, so you won't meet her.'

'I don't want to meet her, I want to come and see you.'

'And Flora.'

He did not answer, but stopped with a hand on her waist, and held her again. In the heat of the kiss, she went on listening for the sound of Hugh's car on the gravel.

After a moment, they began walking again, heading for the apple trees at the foot of the garden, and the wooden bench, ash bleached grey by years of sun and rain. A white curled feather, that might have been a dove's, lay on the arm next to Catherine as she sat down. She pulled it between her fingers, straightening, then letting it spring back to its own soft comma. Kenneth, beside her, scuffed his foot amongst leaves already fallen from the nearest tree.

'Bring Flora to my house,' he said. 'Time she paid a visit. Then if you like—'

'What?'

'You'd better come and meet my mother.' He sighed. 'I know you want to.'

'Is she well enough?'

'*Well* enough,' he repeated. 'Just don't mind if—'

'What?'

'Nothing. It's fine.' He took her hand, not noticing the feather that was crushed in his grasp. 'When will you come?'

'Sunday – for lunch?'

'Fine.'

'Do you want to invite your mother as well?'

He laughed. 'Not on a Sunday!'

'I thought—'

'I don't want her to meet my mistress for the first time on a Sunday.'

'You're laughing at me. Mistress!'

'Isn't that what you are?'

Her protest was put an end to, and for a moment, she forgave. Then she heard the car on gravel, and Flora's voice.

22

On her way to have lunch with Kenneth, Catherine stopped at the supermarket in Dingwall. Flora said she would wait in the car.

'I won't be long, but you'd better come with me.'

'I don't want to. I'm reading my book.'

Catherine gave in with a sigh, and locked the car. It was only Dingwall's Tesco, not London, so she would be quite safe.

As soon as she was inside with her basket, she saw Gilbert. He was pushing a trolley. She intended to collect only wine and salad, and fish fingers for Flora who was resistant to this visit, and likely to refuse whatever food Kenneth had prepared. She glanced into Gilbert's half-full trolley and saw several bottles of wine, one of malt whisky, beer, smoked salmon, French loaves and cheese.

'Are you having a party?' she asked.

'As if I'd have a party and not invite you and Flora! Of course not. It's dinner.'

'It's nearly all alcohol. You will be absolutely sloshed.'

'I have guests.'

'*They* will be absolutely sloshed.' At least a dozen bottles.

He gave a little jump of pleasure. 'I love your English voice. *Ehbsolutely sloshed.*'

'Are you having a lot of guests?'

'A few. Select company.'

'Is Rose still with you?'

'Not still. *Back*. She was away selling stuff.'

He was in funds. She did not imagine Rose had paid for any of this. As if she had spoken aloud, he said, 'Rose was fantastically successful. I'm a wealthy man.'

'I'm so glad.'

There was a pause while Catherine wondered how to say something about the last time she had seen him, without sounding reproachful. It occurred to her that she should ask about his mother.

'Kenneth said your mother had been ill. How is she?'

He looked startled. 'My mother? I've been staying away while the Blessed Mairi is there, keeping everyone on the straight and narrow.' He turned to the shelves and with alarming carelessness threw several tins of lobster bisque on top of the bottles.

'Oh, mind the glass!'

'It's fine, a lot of wine bottles together are very strong.'

'I'd better get on,' Catherine said. 'Flora's in the car.'

He prodded the goods in his trolley. 'I think you're right, I may have bought too much. Now you'll have to come and visit, and help me drink it all up.'

'I have a new job and Flora's back at school. Life's busier.'

'Where are you off to now?'

His expression, gay and full of mischief when they met, had darkened. She thought she had better not say, 'We're off to see your brother'.

'We'll come up to The Factory soon, I promise. Flora loves it.' She's not keen on Rose, she thought, and Rose doesn't like us.

He brightened again – 'Oh, good!' – and grabbed the handles

of his trolley, wiggling it wildly to and fro. There was some consternation in the aisle as other shoppers took avoiding action.

'Oh dear, madam, I'm so sorry—' The woman stalked off, muttering, and with a slight limp from the blow to her ankle. Catherine stifled a giggle, then realising she had been too long here already and had bought nothing yet, she said, 'I *must* go. I'll come and see you – I promise.'

'Cross your heart and hope to die?'

She smiled, moving away. When she glanced back he was wheeling his trolley with abandon down the aisle, scattering the wary and startling those who did not in time see him coming.

At the till he caught up with her again as she set out her half-dozen items on the belt to be swiped through.

'How many people have you mown down?' she asked.

'Nobody important. You haven't bought much.'

'We're going to Kenneth's,' she decided, after all, to admit. 'He's cooking the dinner.'

'But in case it's not up to much—' he indicated the yellow package. 'Fish fingers?'

'For Flora. She can be fussy.'

'About Kenneth?'

'About food.' She paid, smiling at the checkout assistant, who sized her up rather than smiled back. 'I must go.'

Gilbert began rolling the bottles of wine sideways along the belt. Then the food, tossed down so that it skidded merrily after them. The goods rushed towards the checkout assistant, then huddled at the end, as if vying for her attention. She passed each thing through with methodical slowness, then took out a cardboard wine case and snapped it open, then another, and another.

'I do think it looks like a party,' Catherine said, to draw off

Gilbert's impatience. He hovered as if on tiptoe, his threadbare wallet out already.

'Yes, it does, doesn't it?'

'Well, have a nice time with your girlfriend.'

He set his hands on his hips. 'Now, you know I never have girlfriends.'

'Rose, then.'

'Or boyfriends either, sadly,' he added, with a gleam.

The woman on the checkout at last glanced their way in the midst of packing some of the food into a bag. Catherine imagined her saying to her colleague when she went for her tea break: 'I had a right pair at the checkout'.

She must go, and not provoke him further. Anxiously, she recalled Flora, waiting in the car.

'You were *ages*.'

'I'm sorry, I met Gil.'

'Where is he?'

'Still in there. He had a whole trolley full.' Of what, she had better not say.

'I wish *I'd* seen him,' Flora grumbled as they drove out of the car park. 'When are we going back to The Factory?'

'Soon. He says he's sold a lot of the furniture.'

'That's good.'

Catherine left it at that, and changed the subject. She did not want Flora to be thinking of Gilbert or The Factory as they approached Kenneth's house.

23

On Monday, Kenneth went to Rosemount on his way home from work. Here, his Aunt Mairi was keeping the place as neat as usual, if not to his mother's satisfaction. A frisson of irritation had set up between the sisters, one frustrated at being unable to manage everything herself, the other resentful that she was not adequately appreciated. It had been a sacrifice, to leave Angus on his own on the croft. Goodness knows the state the place would be in by the time she got back.

Mairi brought tea and a plate of her currant loaf, and left them to it. 'I have the dishes to get on with.' As she went out, her apron strings seemed to twitch with indignation on her tweed skirt.

'Mairi means well,' his mother said. 'Sit yourself down. I can pour the tea myself, I hope.'

He was hovering, as if to make himself useful.

'You'll be glad to get the house to yourself?' he suggested.

'Aye, well.' She handed him the fragile cup and saucer, rose patterned. 'She's used the best tea set again, though I said to her—'

'Could it not do with an airing?'

'She's a dab hand with the currant loaf, I'll give her that.' She held the plate out to him. 'But you'd think butter was going out of fashion the way she's using it up.'

He was glad of the butter, the loaf being dryer than he'd been led to believe.

'Maybe she should stay another week or so?'

'Ach, no, she's off on Wednesday. Archie's going to take her to the bus first thing and she'll get the afternoon ferry.'

'You could come to me, you know.' He made this offer secure in the knowledge that it would not be taken up.

'I'm fine where I am.'

'I just worry you're not fit yet.'

She interrupted him, as if she couldn't wait any longer to say this. 'Gilbert was in earlier. He said he'd come and stay with me for a while.'

'What? You didn't say he could?'

'He wants to, he likes to be a help. Kenneth, you're too hard on him. Your father was the same.'

What could he say? She was white-faced and tired. He cursed Gilbert, all the angrier because he could not forbid her to have his brother in the house.

'Don't give him any money.'

'He told me he was doing well. He's had a big sale of furni-ture.' She nodded towards the window. A crystal vase filled with florist's blooms, unnaturally stiff and bright, had been placed on the round table in the middle of the bay. 'He brought me these lovely flowers.'

There was nothing for it but to grind his teeth, which he only just stopped himself from doing. 'I hope he'll look after you, and not give you trouble.'

She smiled at him, her unexpectedly sweet smile. 'Don't you worry about me. I've been coping with your brother for a long time.' She held out her cup. 'You could give me a refill if there's enough in the pot.'

'Once Gilbert's away, and if you're up to it, I'd like to bring a visitor to see you.'

She narrowed her eyes. 'Who would that be?'

'A friend of mine, and her wee girl.'

His mother set her cup in its saucer and laid them aside on the low table next to her. Then she leaned back in her chair, and waited.

He was uneasy when he left her. Restless, instead of turning up the hill for home when he reached Strathpeffer, he found his car was heading on into Inverness, towards Catherine's house. Flora would be there, but the child would surely be in bed. They could talk at least. It was no good, living apart like this, with brief holidays and occasional nights. He thought of finding her a house near his, persuading her to move. But what was the point of that, in the long run? He did not want to marry again. He thought he'd made that clear, but you never knew with women – perhaps she expected it.

Intimacy had not made them close. He know nothing about her thoughts. He let his own, distracted, drift back to his mother and his brother. He would have to go there more often than even her health warranted. He would have to open the bureau and look at her cheque book. He'd done that before, discovering three days after his father's funeral, the counterfoil in her neat, legible handwriting: £100 paid to Gilbert Sinclair. Incensed, he had not been able to say anything at all.

He drew up at Catherine's gate, relieved to see her car in the driveway. Suppose she'd been out? He should have called first. He had this mobile phone, after all. No, women with young children are at home in the evenings – as they should be. Ringing the doorbell, shifting impatiently as he waited for her to answer, he had misgivings. It was already after nine o'clock and he had to be on site at seven in the morning.

Flora, in pyjamas, tugged the door open. She stared, then turned, calling for her mother. In a moment, drying her hands on a blue towel, Catherine was in the doorway.

'I thought she was making it up – I didn't realise. She's not supposed to answer the door at night.'

'It's only me,' he said. 'Can I come in – any tea on the go?'

'I told you,' Flora said.

'Bed, Flora – this is ridiculous. Upstairs.'

'I want something to eat.' She spoke to her mother, but her glance, slyly, slipped towards Kenneth.

Catherine sighed. 'You had supper ages ago.'

'I need more.'

'You can have a cracker, then clean your teeth.'

'All right.'

Having won her point, Flora ate the cracker nibble by nibble with agonising slowness. Kenneth, accepting tea, browsed the local paper, lying on the table, while Catherine got mugs out, and the kettle boiled.

Eventually Flora was ushered upstairs. Kenneth took the paper and their mugs of tea into the living room. He sat at the end of the sofa next to the only lamp lit, but he had exhausted the attractions of *the Courier* by the time Catherine appeared. It was dark outside and she was shadowy. He could not see her expression.

'You spoil her.'

'*Spoil* her? How?'

She had not moved so he had to look up at her from the low sofa. 'Give in, I meant. You give in to her all the time.'

'I do not!'

'Oh, sit down,' he said. 'Don't get on your high horse. I've had a bloody day.'

An echo, for both of them, haunted the room for a moment. It was as if they were married already. She subsided, sinking into the armchair by the window, then reached out and switched on another lamp behind her head. It lit up her hair, showing him her tired face, then her graceful movement as she leaned back, sighing.

'Did something go wrong at work?'

'Work? Nothing to do with that. I went to see my mother, to find Gilbert's planning to stay there and sponge off her. I know how it goes. She spoiled him when he was a kid and now she still spoils him. But I can't be there all the time and I can't stop him taking her money.'

'So you think Flora will sponge off me when I'm an old lady?'

He stared, astonished. 'I never said anything of the sort!'

'You implied—'

'I implied *nothing*.' He got up, restless and angry. 'For Christ's sake – she's a kid – she gets her own way too much, that's all. Gilbert is a – what was that thing they used to swop for a baby – some sort of incubus—'

'A changeling. What rubbish. He's a young man who hasn't found his way yet – but he's imaginative and he's making something of his Factory. Just because it's not the kind of business *you're* interested in, you dismiss it. You put him down.'

She had not moved, having said all this with her head resting on the back of the armchair, her eyes heavy. All the effort went into the scorn in her voice.

Anger quickened desire. 'I want to take you to bed,' he said abruptly, abandoning Gilbert, Flora – there was no way of resolving that argument tonight, whatever it had been. He found he could not think of anything but her long legs stretched out in the lamplight, her pale ringless hands clasping her mug, the loose neckline of her blouse, a button undone, the creamy skin beneath.

'Well, that's not going to happen. You're impossible.'

'What then – how are we going to fix it?'

He had not meant to say this. It was his mother's fault, giving way to his brother and leaving him impotent. Only his father had kept Gil in check; his mother, so severe in her devotion to her faith, so old-fashioned in her views, would indulge her one weakness. He did not know if he was more angry with Gilbert or with her, for loving him. He had to turn elsewhere – and where, now, could he go but into Catherine's arms? He had to have some satisfaction, some return of love.

He pulled her to her feet and she came into his arms willingly enough, but when his hands, exploring, opening her blouse further, touched warm skin, she stiffened and drew away.

'Don't. She won't be asleep yet.' She looked up at him. 'Fix what?'

'Nothing. Just – come over on Friday night, spend the whole weekend. Bring spoiled wee Flora. I'll sort her out.'

'I hope you're teasing me.'

At the back of his mind was the thought that he meant it. If they were going to be together, Flora would have to learn new ways.

'I'd better go,' he said, frustrated, since he was getting nowhere. His erection, at the thought of the child, had subsided.

'Kenneth – Rose said Gilbert was adopted. Is that true?'

He sagged, weary. 'Yes, it's true. What difference does it make?'

'It seems to make a difference to you. Why didn't you tell me?'

Before he could answer, Flora called from upstairs, and there was the sound of her feet pattering along the landing. He kissed Catherine briefly on the cheek and went out, not looking upstairs before he closed the front door behind him.

As the car wove out of Inverness and across the Kessock Bridge, he went over it again in his head: his mother, the fear Gilbert would move in with her, and Flora, her calculating gaze as she pushed a little further each time, as if daring him to oppose her. He laughed, despite himself. The wee besom. He could deal with *her*. He switched on the radio. Halfway through the 1812. He turned the sound high, the cymbals clashing, the brass thundering, drumming out thought all the rest of the way home.

24

Joe had been away for two days. Only a phone call late the night before had stopped her thinking he'd been in a terrible accident. She knew he had not; he was just *out*. He would be sleeping at a friend's place which was what happened when he did not come home. She did not think he had another woman.

Matthew could sit up unsupported. He was a contented baby, and as long as she was in sight or he could hear her, he was happy. He was so frustrated when his toys shot out of reach she thought he might crawl early, as she watched him straining after a piece of Duplo, or the plastic hippo he was particularly attached to. Joe was not as fascinated by Matthew's every new achievement as she was, or as she had expected him to be. He was proud to be the father of a son, but the son himself did not much interest him. He was affectionate, but casually, bringing presents that were usually too old for Matthew and had to be put away. Increasingly, there wasn't enough space in the flat.

This was not because of Matthew. Joe had been bringing home things he said he didn't want to leave in the lock-up garages. He kept promising it would all be moved out soon. Amongst the collection in the spare bedroom were several Chinese vases, a Royal Doulton dinner service, a set of nineteenth-century

century golf clubs, a dozen oil paintings stacked against the wall and some silverware that apparently dated from around 1750. Helen wondered if their house insurance would cover any of this, but Joe waved away her tentative question.

'Wouldn't it be better if you just sold it?' Helen had asked him, as she helped him check the contents of yet another packing case. 'Or opened a shop?'

He looked up from his admiration of a china shepherd, glossy and unchipped. 'I'm going to sell it. Not open a bloody shop, what do you take me for? I'm the middle man, I don't do overheads.'

'Clearly not,' Helen said, but the sarcasm went past him.

'There's nothing to worry about – it's not a load of video recorders off the back of a lorry.'

Until then, she had not thought there might *be* anything to worry about. Now, gathering up her child and her jacket, and the bag crammed with baby paraphernalia, she decided she had to get out for a while. From the spare bedroom a faint smell seeped out, of old stuff, musty as if from being in the houses of elderly people for years. Where did he get it all? She wondered again about Rose who still hovered on the edges of his business. She thought they saw too much of Rose.

In the street, empty during working hours, a gusty wind blew the last leaves from the thin plane trees lining the pavement. She buttoned her jacket with one hand, holding the pushchair steady with the other. Where would they go? Sometimes she took Matthew through Highgate Cemetery, where she could look at memorials to famous dead people. There was a gloomy satisfaction in that. They sometimes saw a fox slipping between trees out of sight, living his secret urban life in this illusion of countryside, his lair in the jungle of knotted vines trailing over the forgotten graves of people, she assumed, not famous at all. She turned the pushchair to face uphill and set off for the Cemetery, the wind in her face, the bag hung on the back of the pushchair bumping against her thighs. Matthew began to grizzle.

On a grey, windy day in November, when most people were at work, the cemetery was quiet and she had the paths to herself, only the man who waved his arms and berated the empty air, ahead of her. She could easily avoid him. He was harmless, just wanted to shout his sorrow aloud, and if he met anyone, doff his crushed trilby and say 'Fine afternoon', whether it was or not.

In low moments, she wondered if that was how she would end up, abandoned by Joe and the grown-up Matthew, a mad old woman wandering among graves, talking to herself. At least just now she had the excuse that she was speaking to a child, but Matthew, when she looked down at him, had fallen asleep.

She paused by George Eliot, who had defied convention and achieved greatness. *She* had not stood among the dead full of self-pity, lamenting the unreality of marriage to someone whose life was closed to her.

That was the problem: not just that she didn't know what he was doing, who he was doing it with, but that it was a world apart. She thought of Hugh, coming home from work with a pile of buff folders tied with pink tape, and going through papers quietly, a glass of whisky by his side, golden in lamplight. She hadn't understood that either, but she hadn't expected to. Who knew about the law except lawyers? How peaceful and easy a life that seemed. And yet, she'd rebelled against it.

'I'm not happy with this either,' she said aloud, startled by the sound of her own plaintive voice. Matthew stirred and she looked down at his dark head and sleeping face, his satiny skin.

She loved him beyond anything, but he was the one who trapped her. She couldn't run away this time.

The wind had dropped and raindrops began to spot the path. She turned the pushchair for home, hoping she would get there before the shower became heavy and she had to struggle with the waterproof cover for the pushchair. Matthew did not wake, and asleep he seemed impossibly heavy as she went up the stairs to their flat with aching legs. The damned stairs. Why couldn't they have a house, like other people with children? Sure, he said, in a year or so. She had no power to change a thing, she thought miserably, sorry for herself beyond sense now.

There were two men in raincoats in front of their door. Hearing her, they turned. The taller was perhaps thirty-five, his face scarred by acne. The other was older and heavier. A leap of fear made her stop. She almost turned and went back down. Should she pretend the next floor was hers and go on up? That was silly; there was nothing to be afraid of. Perhaps they were Jehovah's Witnesses, but they were not carrying those little magazines.

'Hello?' she managed finally.

'Is this your flat?' the older one asked.

'Yes.' She came slowly up the last few stairs to the landing.

'Mrs McCann?' He sounded surprised.

'Yes.'

'We'd like a word with your husband.'

'He's not here – he's at work.'

Her heart was thumping. Matthew woke, giving a cry. She would have to sit down in a minute; her legs, still aching, had weakened.

'When do you expect him home?'

'I don't know. He's often late.' She shifted Matthew up a little, taking some weight from her burning left arm, holding him against her hip. 'I'm sorry – who are you? Can I give him a message?'

The older man held up something like a wallet, then she saw the badge with the words *Metropolitan Police*.

'Detective Sergeant Bridges,' he said. 'No problem. We'll call again.'

They went past her down the stairs. 'Lovely little chap,' Bridges said, nodding at Matthew. She reddened and turned away. When she heard the front door below close behind them she got out her key and went in, still shaking. Joe was in the bedroom, a suitcase thrown on the bed, open and empty except for a couple of shirts, still in their cellophane packaging. There was another suitcase on the floor – hers.

'I didn't know you were here!'

She set Matthew down on the bed and he reached his arms out – 'Dada!' Absently, Joe picked him up. 'He's a weight, in't he?' He jiggled his son up and down, moving him through the air, farther, faster. Matthew let out a gurgle of laughter and abruptly, Joe set him on the bed again. 'Where you been?'

'Out for a walk. I was fed up here on my own.' She waved a hand over the suitcases. 'What's this for?'

'We're going on holiday.'

'What? Joe, why didn't you answer the door? There were two men outside.'

He froze. 'Two?'

'Policemen. Well, one of them showed me a card and—'

'Plain clothes or uniform?'

'Detectives – plain clothes. Why didn't you—'

'I had music on loud. Then you come in.'

He was lying. There had been no music. 'They said they'd come back later.'

'Too bad – we'll be gone by then.'

He picked up their passports from the bed, where Matthew was reaching for them. 'You put Matty on yours, didn't you?'

'You know I did.'

He flicked hers open, then his own. 'Right then, we're all ok. Get your case packed, and Matt's stuff.'

'Where are we going, and how *long*? I've got the hairdresser next week and—'

'Spain. Barcelona.'

'You've booked flights?'

This was all wrong. She wanted to go, of course she did. She wanted the sunshine and having Joe there all the time, a break from being bored and lonely. She was also frightened.

'What do you think the police wanted?' She began to get out summer things she had packed away in October. At least everything was clean.

'I don't give a fuck.' He grinned at her. 'I bet Sammy's been in trouble again.'

'Who's Sammy?'

'A guy I know. You haven't met him – or maybe you have, at Brian's. Can't remember.' He was folding a pair of jeans. He was meticulous with his clothes; they were clean and ironed. He knew where to put his hand on anything he wanted, while she cast around, opening and shutting drawers helplessly. He began taking her dresses out of the wardrobe. 'Here. What about this? Get a move on.' After a moment he added, 'Sammy's one of Rose's mates.'

'But you're not – *you* don't have anything to worry about?'

'Not a thing.' He watched her stuff clothes haphazardly into her case, and sighed. 'What about His Highness here, will I pack his stuff?'

She could scarcely believe how swiftly they were ready, a taxi waiting in the street.

'Heathrow,' he said.

He was in funds. Barcelona, the flights booked without her knowledge, a taxi all the way to Heathrow. She sat back, breathless, as they drove away, Matthew on Joe's lap, excited because he was with his father. London went on outside: the busy streets, traffic lights, tall buildings, a row of shops then offices. It was a blur to Helen. She did not know what was happening. She did not know whether to be happy or not. Panic rose at the thought of the policemen coming back, and none of them there. Too often she had suspected Joe did not tell her the truth, but had brushed it aside as unimportant. He told her the truth about what mattered – that he loved her, prized her above rubies, and loved his son. He was doing it all for them.

What was it he was doing?

He handed Matthew over and moved to the fold-down seat opposite, so that he could play pat-a-cake with him. He was also looking out of the back window of the taxi. After a while it occurred to her that he was checking they were not being followed.

25

When she pushed open the front door, Flora trailing behind in a sulk because she'd been in the middle of watching a TV programme at Tracey's when she had to leave, Catherine heard the slither of post across the floor and stooped to pick it up. There were circulars and the gas bill, and underneath, a postcard. She recognised the Sagrada Familia. She and Alan had gone to Barcelona for their short honeymoon, the one unclouded week of her marriage. At any rate, the place had been wonderful. Turning it over, surprised, she saw Helen's familiar scrawl. *We'll probably be home before you get this, but having a break – brilliant sunshine. No wonder you loved this place, can't believe I waited so long to see it myself.*

'Aunt Helen's in Barcelona,' she told Flora, fixing the card to the kitchen pinboard. It was intensely blue and white amongst the school notices and appointment cards, most of them out of date, but it contrasted nicely with Flora's most recent painting of – *something*. Yellow and red, at any rate.

Flora inspected the card. 'It's a very fancy building.'

'A church – an architect called Gaudi created it. It's famous.'

'*I* never heard of it,' Flora said. She moved on to read the rest of the notices. 'You can take down my sunset if you like. We're doing a collage now. I'll be bringing that home on Friday.'

'Was that what the egg box was for?'

Flora laughed. 'Silly. Of course not. That was for growing cress.'

Cheered by her mother's stupidity she retired to watch television, while Catherine went upstairs to change. There, struck by the strangeness of Helen's being suddenly in Barcelona without telling her about it endlessly beforehand, she sat on the bed and kicked off her shoes. *We'll probably be home before you get this.* She reached for the telephone on the bedside cabinet. If there were no Flora, she thought, I'd pour myself a glass of wine or a gin and tonic right now. Briefly, as she dialled Helen's number, she longed for this single state.

The telephone rang and rang in Helen's flat. Catherine pictured the baby grand, the leather sofas, the huge abstract painting over the mantelpiece that had no fire beneath it, just pampas grass in a large glass vase. She was imagining the flat before Matthew's arrival, since that was when she had seen it last.

Eventually, she gave up. They were not in, or not there at all. They must still be in Barcelona.

Flora called upstairs. 'Where are you? I'm hungry – can I have a biscuit?'

Later, Catherine called Kenneth. He was not there either. At ten thirty, as she was getting ready for bed, he called back.

'Sorry. Over at Rosemount.'

'I thought you might be there. How is your mother?'

'She's all right.'

She hesitated, but it was foolish to be afraid of asking. (And yet, it started such a tirade.) 'Was Gil there?'

'When is he *not*?' A gusty sigh swept along the telephone line between them. 'Bloody leech that he is. He's not even paying her for his keep.'

'He is her son.'

'Whose side are you on?'

'Side? I'm just trying to be fair. I like Gil. You're too hard on him.'

'You know nothing about it. You think because he's all sweetness and light with you, he's harmless. He's not.'

'I know he's not perfect – that night he was so drunk—'

'My father's funeral, right.'

'Let's not speak about Gil – it always ends like this.'

'Like what? You having to face up to the fact that he's a total shit.'

'Kenneth, I'm getting off the phone now. I've had a long day and I can't bear this.'

'Sorry. Don't go. Not yet – tell me what you've been doing.'

'Working,' she said. 'What do you think?' Relenting, she told him about Helen's postcard, but he didn't attach any significance to it.

'Barcelona,' he said. 'I quite fancy seeing the football stadium.'

'I doubt if that's why most people go.'

'You want a bet?' Then he said, 'Would *you* like to go? I mean, not for the football – to see the place?'

'I've seen it. That's where Alan and I went on honeymoon.'

He laughed. 'I'm not doing so well tonight. Call it a day, eh? I'll see you on Saturday.'

'There's a problem with Saturday – but we might manage over by the evening.'

She could actually feel him stiffen, miles away in his beautiful modern house, his bare, unspoiled house. She would not apologise. Why should she? Flora and she had lives apart from his. That was inevitable, as things were.

He did not like things as they were. Tense, they said goodnight.

213

Lying awake, her book laid aside, a book she had not been able to read anyway, she gazed into the shadowy dark and thought about Kenneth, Helen for the moment out of her mind. There was nothing to worry about; Helen was unpredictable.

'Why are we going to *his* house? It's boring there.'

'I said we would. Just tonight and a bit of tomorrow. We'll be home by afternoon.'

'Do I *have* to?' Flora, sitting sullen on the edge of her bed, made no move to pack her new rucksack.

'Yes,' Catherine said. 'Anyway, I'm sure there are children living near Kenneth you could play with.'

'*They're* not my friends.'

Catherine went into her own bedroom, and stood for a long moment gazing at her overnight bag. It would be easier if she kept stuff at his house too, but they had not quite reached that stage, or she had not. Flora had definitely not. With a sigh, she began to pack.

They were going in time for supper, which Catherine had cooked. She must pack the casserole pot and the pudding in a covered dish.

Kenneth had been on the hill all day and had called her from the summit at twelve. They'd started early and it was a 'wee hill' he said, only thirty miles from home. He expected to be back by five. She knew this meant he would be asleep on the sofa by nine, however 'wee' the hill. She would have liked to be with him, and his hillwalking friends. Flora's ballet class in the morning, the need to get a washing done and dried, and to shop and cook for the weekend, had made that impossible.

She thought of Helen, in Barcelona with Joe and Matthew. Joe had been working away a lot, Helen had said. At least you're living together, Catherine replied. You don't have to traipse between two houses with a reluctant nine-year-old.

'No,' Helen said, 'but neither do you. You should just get married.' How simple that sounded! It would never happen.

They were halfway to Strathpeffer when Flora yelled, 'Duffy! I forgot Duffy!'

Duffy was the rabbit she slept with, the chewed and ragged cloth rabbit cuddled since babyhood. She had begun to grow out of Duffy and once or twice had even slept over at Tracey's without him.

'You can manage without Duffy for one night.'

'I won't! I need him – I'll never get to *sleep*.'

'If I go back we'll be terribly late and goodness knows when we'll eat.' She glanced sideways at Flora's red face, threatening tears. 'All right, all right.' She glanced in the mirror and took her foot from the accelerator, looking for somewhere to turn on the dual carriageway.

From home she called Kenneth to tell him they would be late.

'For God's sake – I'm starving. I've been home since five.'

Biting her tongue – what was the use? – she said, 'I'm on my way now, so we'll be as quick as we can.'

When they finally got there, he had opened the red wine, and the bottle, she noted, was more than half-empty. In the pedal bin, when she tipped the lid open, were two crushed beer cans.

'Twenty minutes,' she said to him. He had put Disney's *Beauty and the Beast* on the video recorder for Flora and was standing with a glass in his hand, watching her.

'I'll get your drink.'

'I'll wait till we have dinner,' she said. 'Since I'm going to stick to just one.'

'Suit yourself. There's juice in the fridge.'

Flora had gone past hunger by the time they ate, and pushed the food around her plate. Catherine gave her pudding, but she scarcely touched that either.

'I want to watch the end of *Beauty and the Beast*,' she said, sliding down from her chair.

Kenneth pointed his spoon at her. 'Stay where you are. Your mother hasn't finished yet.'

Astonished, Flora stared.

'It doesn't matter,' Catherine said.

'It does. She has to learn manners.'

'What? She *has* manners – for goodness' sake, it's late, she's tired and—'

'Who's fault's that? If Madam here hadn't made such a fuss about a teddy bear—'

'It's her rabbit, she's always slept with him—'

They were raising their voices, arguing in front of Flora. Catherine felt all the rules slip from her at once. Flora burst into tears. 'I want to go home!' she sobbed, and fled.

'Now look what you've done!' Catherine cried, flinging down her spoon and rising to follow.

His arm shot out and he gripped her. 'Leave her, she'll calm down.' He pulled her back into her seat. 'You need to calm down too.'

'How dare you!' As his hand released her, she got up again. 'I think we'd better leave.'

He leaned back in his seat. 'You've had a drink. Can you drive?'

She halted. Her glass was half-full. Less than half a glass – that would be all right. They were, though, large glasses. She'd had a meal, but not a large one; she hadn't been hungry either.

'I'll make coffee first,' she decided.

216

'I'll do it.' He got up. 'You go and see to her ladyship.'

He seemed, despite what he must have had to drink, entirely sober, himself but even more so. Flora, without the benefit of alcohol, was also herself, but more so.

She was prone on a sofa and the pitch of her cries increased as Catherine came into the room. Duffy was clutched fiercely in her arms, squashed beneath her.

'I'm going to have some coffee,' Catherine said, 'then we'll go home.'

Flora stopped crying and drew in a shuddering breath. She sat up, rubbing Duffy across her face. Sitting beside her, Catherine got out a clean tissue and wiped eyes and nose. 'There. All right?'

Kenneth came in with a mug of coffee. 'Here – drink it black and take your time.' He looked down at Flora, perfectly quiet and still.

'Well, so you're abandoning Beauty to the Beast, are you?'

'I've seen it before,' Flora whispered. She would not look at him.

'Fair enough.'

He stood in the porch, watching them as Flora was buckled into the car seat. Catherine came back to say, 'Don't drink any more tonight – you've had quite a lot.'

'I don't think you should be telling me what to do.'

'It's only because—'

'What?'

She did not have an answer. 'Goodnight, then.'

He shut the door before she had turned the car.

In the morning, Flora went blithely down the street to Hannah's house and Catherine was left with a pile of ironing and her unwelcome thoughts. Eventually, she could not bear it any longer and called Kenneth.

'I'm coming over,' she said, when he answered. 'On my own, just for an hour. I want to talk to you. It was our fault, really, being so late...'

'Fine,' he said. 'I'll put the coffee on.'

She called Hannah's mother, then got in the car and drove, again, all the way to his house. She could not keep doing *this*.

He was sweeping up fallen leaves, clearing them from the porch. A cold wind blew more in as he did so, swirling them round his feet.

'A thankless task, today,' she said as she got out of her car, smiling at him. They must begin again, and not let last night matter too much. Yet her heart was in her mouth when he turned to her, stern and dark, without an answering smile.

'Come in,' he said, resting the broom against the wall.

She had got no further than the hall, and just eased off her boots when he snatched at her hand.

'Bed,' he said.

'What—'

'Come on. You know fine that's what you want too.'

'That won't solve anything—' She was halfway up the stairs behind him, letting him lead her there, the throb of anticipation, desire, blotting out rational thought.

'No, but it'll make us feel better.'

Later, drowsily, she said, 'There's no time to talk now. I have to go.' He grunted, half-asleep. Yesterday's hill walk, and the wine, had tired him after all. She slipped from the bed and went to the bathroom to wash and dress.

He started out of sleep when she came in to say she was leaving. 'What?' He sat up. 'Hang on, I'll get dressed.'

218

'I'll have coffee,' she said, 'then I must go.'

The wind was rising, spattering rain against the windows. It was suddenly so dark he had to put the light on in the kitchen. In its brightness, they faced each other.

'This is hopeless,' she said. 'All the coming and going. We can't keep doing it.'

'What do you want?' he said. 'What would satisfy you?'

They were in that halfway place again, she about to go home, he about to get on with his separate life. They were both to be alone (in this context, Flora didn't count) because they could not stay together as they were. They would be apart again for a week, and the weekend ahead no more likely to satisfy either of them than this one had done.

'I don't know.'

'You could move in here, you and Flora. Why not?'

'She'd have to change schools and I can't do that to her.'

'You'd hardly be taking her to Timbuktu.'

'It might as well be, as far as she's concerned.' She sighed. 'The disruption. I couldn't face it.'

'I'm glad you're not likely to be a refugee,' he remarked, as he followed her into the hall. 'If you think that's disruption. Off you go. Back to your nice safe life. No disruptions.'

Catherine picked up her jacket.

'I suppose you could move in with us ...' This was clearly nonsense, and she knew it. She looked around the oak-floored hallway, then at the broad staircase of his beautiful house, expensive, new and *big*. 'Only,' she hurried on, 'I don't know how Flora would take it.'

'Take what? Me sleeping in her mother's bed?'

Catherine saw this: Flora's avid curiosity and disapproval, then her disgust. Catherine had seen his curled hairs scattered in the bath and the shower tray. There would be his shaving things and toothbrush, his wet towel thrown on the floor. She imagined this in her tiny, female house. That would be disruption.

'I know, I know. That wouldn't work.'

Outside, the wind whipped her hair round her face. She got into the car but he held the edge of the door, so that she could not close it.

'I have to go.'

'You want to get married, don't you? It's what you're angling for. Would that make a difference?'

'What?'

'You heard me.' He shut the car door and banged twice on the roof. Then he turned and went into his house. Catherine drove off in cold fury.

The day after that was long and unhappy. She could not think. Eventually, lying awake in bed, she decided it had been a kind of proposal: not much of one, but for him, a huge concession. It was Monday, already Monday, she saw from the glowing hands on the alarm clock. When were they to talk again? She knew she would have to go to *his* house and talk. She had not meant to marry again either, but she found her heart beating fast when she thought of it, thought seriously for the first time, of taking Flora there and living with him. *Angling* for marriage? Did he really think so? She must not leave him thinking that.

It would be a new life for Flora too, who had no father now.

What did he mean – refugee? He thought her spoilt, making a fuss about nothing. Well, wait till he's lived with Flora for a while and he won't think so lightly of my worrying. Something bubbled up in her. She would never sleep now. The prospect of happiness – of being with him every night, of having a life where she did not have to be afraid any more of managing alone – sprang her up and out of bed. She pulled on a cardigan for warmth and went downstairs. She should make hot milk or something to persuade herself to feel sleepy. And yet she had to be up at half past six.

She did not want hot milk. Or sleep. She paced about the living room, unsatisfactory in such a small space. She thought of his long room, the big kitchen and the space around the house that could be a wonderful garden. It was as if she had been holding shut a door that was heavy, with something pushing against it on the other side, and she afraid to give way. If she stepped back and let go, the door would open and then – what then?

What We Have When We Don't Have Love

2000–1

1

The last time Catherine visited The Factory was in July, 2000, a day as rough as October. There were even leaves whirling along the ground, whipped from the verges by a blustery wind that had come and gone all day. When she stepped out of her car, the wind caught her hair and blew her thin raincoat open.

Hugh had told her Gilbert was giving up The Factory. 'I don't know how he's managed to keep it going so long,' he said. 'Anyway, he's selling off most of the stuff to dealers. You might like to look in, while he's still there.'

Catherine went through the open doors. In the entrance hall the silence was almost eerie.

'Hello?'

Gilbert appeared on the staircase, coming softly down, carrying a pile of books. When he saw her, his face lit up.

'Catherine! I've been wishing you would come.'

'Well, here I am. How are you?'

He jerked his head to indicate the upper floor behind him. 'I'm clearing out the books – there's a man going through them.'

'What?'

'He's going to take them all, but he'll only pay for the ones he wants. That's the deal.'

225

'It doesn't sound much of a deal to me. Can you trust him?'

Gilbert set down his pile of books on a table in the main warehouse. Following him in, Catherine saw there were now empty spaces, the floor marked by the feet of furniture that had been removed, and by scuffs and dusty patches left behind.

'I'm sad you've decided to leave The Factory, but I'm glad you've found buyers. At least you'll have made some money.' Yet she could tell from his slightly furtive manner that things were not going well.

'I have no money. When you have debts, I've discovered, you have negative money. It all seems to belong to someone else. Mainly the bank.'

'But surely—'

He shrugged. 'You think an overdraft means you have money, but it turns out it doesn't.'

Catherine, who had never made this mistake, sat down on one of the few remaining chairs. 'Gilbert, you have been paying your rent, haven't you?'

'Dear Catherine. No, not recently. And the bank won't listen – I asked them, what about increasing my overdraft, what about a loan for goodness' sake, till I get on my feet again, but they say not, they say I owe money with interest. Well, that's stupid, isn't it, they should let me have some more, then I'll be able to pay them back. I don't understand banks, I thought they were supposed to help businesses.'

That he did not understand banks, or indeed money, was all too clear. She thought of the weeks he had stayed with his mother after her stroke, weeks when Kenneth had become more and more angry and resentful. She had not been there when the row finally broke and Gilbert was summarily despatched back to the cottage. She had suffered the fallout, and that had been

226

enough. Since then it hadn't been easy to tell Kenneth when she saw Gilbert, but she would not lie to him. It was months since her last visit to The Factory, and she was here only because it was Saturday, and Flora was at the cinema with a friend's family, Kenneth hillwalking. 'What rain?' he had said in the morning when she queried the wisdom of this. He had been determined to go out, though that made three weekends in a row.

Gilbert sat down, exhausted. 'I'm glad I bought food last week now that I can't get any more money out of that hole in the wall.'

'You mean you haven't any money *at all*?'

He looked at her, helpless. 'No.'

She could not say, ask your family. Kenneth had made that impossible. Of course, The Factory was a foolish venture. No wonder the bank had called a halt. Yet she loved it almost as much as Flora did: the tall windows, the large dusty sunlit spaces and the eclectic contents, and loved how there was always a surprising find amongst the books (as no doubt the man upstairs was discovering), and that Flora while she was here became happy and absorbed. By now she loved Gilbert too, for all the difficulty of being his friend.

'Can you come out for a while – leave the man to get on with it?' she asked. 'I could at least buy you a nice lunch.'

'Oh, he'll be hours,' Gilbert said, rising. 'Yes, that's a good idea. Why don't we go to Ardgay House?'

Ardgay House was an expensive hotel further north, with a Michelin-starred restaurant. Catherine had had in mind soup and a sandwich or perhaps fish and chips, which Gilbert loved, but he looked so hopeful, brightening at the idea, she had not the heart to say so. At least he would be fed. She must speak to Kenneth. He surely wouldn't want his brother to starve.

Gil was pulling on one of his charity shop jackets, army

surplus khaki this time. Oh dear, she thought, the Ardgay House dining room.

'Hadn't you better tell this man—'

Gilbert flew upstairs two at a time on his stork legs, revived by the thought of a good lunch.

In the car there was a sweet smell it took her a moment to recall from student days. She had never tried it but everyone else did. It clung, she supposed, to his jacket.

'Has Rose been here lately?'

He was fiddling with a mobile phone. Catherine always called him on this as he had no other number. The Factory telephone bill had probably not been paid for some time.

'Rose?' He glanced up. 'Oh yes, but she won't stay much longer. She came with some of her friends and we had a party, but they've all gone now. I think that's what did for the last of my money.'

'You didn't spend money on Rose and her friends, surely?"

'It was a *party*. But you're right. I think they could at least have brought a few bottles of wine, don't you? They did help me get rid of stuff though, and they took away all the boxes I'd been keeping for them. Rose said she paid me everything I was owed, but it wasn't as much as I was expecting.' He peered at the phone. 'You're going to have to call *me*, Catherine, from now on,' he said. 'There's no money left in this.'

From the point where she was not going to prop him up in any way, they had already travelled. Guiltily, she determined to give him a tenner for the phone. It was dangerous for him to be without it, on his own in The Factory, or that remote cottage.

'What about the van?' she asked as they turned into the hotel drive and between dripping rhododendrons and overhanging birches approached Georgian elegance. 'Are you able to keep that going?'

'Oh yes, as long as the police don't stop me. And I've got forty quid in the glove compartment that I've been saving for diesel.'

So he did have money. 'What do you mean, the police – has the tax run out?'

'No, that's ok for months yet. It's just I'm not insured any more.'

Catherine, as she parked amongst four-wheel drives and BMWs, was speechless.

'You can't drive without insurance,' she managed at last, but Gil was already out of the car.

'Come on,' he said as she locked it. 'I'm starving.'

Perhaps there was a light lunch menu. She did not feel hungry.

At dinner, Flora was not hungry either, having eaten popcorn and ice cream throughout the afternoon. Kenneth was ravenous after six hours on the hill, so Catherine cooked, but did not eat much herself. It was not just that she'd had lunch with Gilbert: the cost of it had left her feeling uncomfortable. That and wondering whether to mention it.

Flora slid from her chair. 'I don't want any more.'

Before Catherine could say anything, Kenneth pointed his fork at Flora.

'Stay where you are. You might not want to eat, but we do. It's bad manners to leave the table before other people. I thought we'd agreed that?'

'It doesn't—' Catherine stopped. She did not feel like eating either. She was as bad as Flora, though the Ardgay House lunch had been superior to cinema food. She thought Flora ought to be allowed to lie pale in front of the television, feeling sick. How else was she to learn? Not by being nagged.

Flora had stopped defying Kenneth openly, but she sat in a mutinous silence punctuated by heavy sighs. Ignoring her, Kenneth talked about the hill, relating a story about one of his companions. All this made eating take a long time.

'You can leave the table,' Catherine said hastily, as Kenneth laid down knife and fork at last.

Too queasy by now even to enquire about pudding, Flora left.

Kenneth pushed his plate aside. 'You've not eaten much either. You weren't at the cinema with them?'

'No.' She attempted a smile. 'I've not been eating rubbish. Just…not hungry.'

'What did you do all day? You should have come with us.'

'You wouldn't have been eating that chicken casserole if I had.'

'It was great. But not a good enough reason.' He seemed to see her for the first time since coming home. 'You're not looking well.'

'I'm tired, that's all.'

'You work too hard. It's only a Council job, not worth wearing yourself out for.'

'It's *my* job,' she flared, 'and *I* happen to think it's worth doing well.'

She got up, but he caught her wrist as she reached for his plate. 'So what did you do today?'

'I went out to The Factory.'

He dropped her hand. Catherine gathered the plates and cutlery and began to stack the dishwasher. Kenneth made coffee. They moved around each other in the kitchen with the ease of habit, and for a few moments it was as if nothing was wrong. Finally, unable to endure his silence, Catherine said,

'The furniture has almost all gone, and there was a man there making an inventory of the books – valuing them or something. Anyway, soon they'll all have gone too.'

Kenneth poured coffee and she took milk out of the fridge. Still he said nothing.

'So I took him out for lunch, to cheer him up,' she said, desperate.

'I've no doubt it worked,' he said. 'As long as someone else is footing the bill, he's happy.'

'That's not fair—'

'Did he claim to have no money?'

'Well, things are difficult, so—'

'How often do I have to tell you this? He's a sponger. No sooner have I managed to stop him syphoning money from my mother's account, than he starts on you.'

'It was only lunch! For goodness' sake.'

Flora, in the doorway, looked less pale, but she was frowning.

'What are you arguing about?' Not interested in the answer, she added, 'I'm going along to Kirsty's.'

'Don't be too late. Nine o'clock.'

Flora raised her eyes heavenwards. 'It's the *holidays.*'

'Well, you've been with Kirsty's family all day, so maybe they'd like a rest from you?' Kenneth suggested. 'Come on, princess, give us a hand to clear up the dishes. We're not arguing. I'm just telling your mother off for being a sucker.'

Flora's frown deepened. She did not forgive him easily. 'Don't you dare say horrible things about my mother.'

Kenneth laughed, but Catherine said wearily, 'Oh, just go to Kirsty's.'

Flora had scarcely shut the front door behind her when Kenneth said, 'I can't deal with this. You undermine me at every turn. If I'm her father now, I'm her father, and you must let me discipline her. You give in to her all the time.'

'Would you stop!' She slammed her mug on the draining board and coffee leapt out, scalding her hand. 'Stop telling me what to do, what not to do – I'm so sick of it. Gilbert's your brother, he's in trouble and he needs your help. You ignore your own family and expect to be in control of mine. It's ridiculous.'

'If my mother hadn't spoiled Gil, he might be a better man now. But she did.'

'There's no comparison!'

'You admit that then? He's beyond it, beyond my sympathy now. You don't know the half of it. So shut up about Gilbert and concentrate on me, and your – our – daughter. We're the ones who need you.'

Catherine, enraged, flung a tea towel at him and went upstairs. Minutes later, the front door banged.

'Flora?'

When she went to the window, she saw him marching down the drive, on his way, she knew, to the bar of Mackie's Hotel.

2

The following Monday, having worked over on the west all day, Kenneth stopped in sunshine in Ullapool for fish and chips, before heading home. He ate them in the open air, leaning on his car, parked in Quay Street. He watched the Stornoway ferry coming in as gulls wheeled around the little boats in the harbour, bobbing on a glittering sea. He felt peaceful. It had been a good day. He squashed the polystyrene packaging and stuffed it in a waste bin, then wiped his greasy hands on a stray rag on the back seat of the car. As he drove, the smell of vinegar still seemed to rise from the steering wheel. But he was cheerful, confident enough (though his heart sank a little at the thought) to tackle Gilbert on his way home.

It was after nine but still full daylight when he drove up the potholed track to the cottage. The van was parked in the pull-in outside the gate, so he knew Gilbert was there. He had waited a week, partly in the hope that if the factory was being abandoned, so might the cottage be. He meant to keep calm and not lose his temper with Gilbert. Whenever that happened, it did not end well. Kenneth drew his car in behind the van and got out.

Despite the coolness of the evening, the living room window was open, the bottom sash pushed up as far as it would go. A sweetish smell drifted out along with the disconcerting gaiety of a Mozart piano quartet.

Gilbert was stretched out on the sagging sofa. The sideboard was covered with half-empty bottles of vodka and whisky, a few cans of beer and a bottle of Drambuie. He was drawing on a roll-up. He peered through a skein of smoke.

'Evening. What brings you here?' He waved the cigarette. 'Want one?'

Kenneth had intended to say his piece and go. With a sigh, he sat down on a chintz-covered armchair that had once belonged in his parents' bedroom. His mother had sat in it, dressing Gilbert as a baby. Jolted by this flash of memory, Kenneth felt sick.

'What's going on?' There was no answer to this. 'You're giving up the second-hand furniture business?'

'All sold.' Gilbert gazed at the ceiling. 'Place is empty.'

'Then what?'

'The world's my oyster.' He sat up suddenly. 'What on earth can that mean? How can an oyster be a world?'

'Stop rambling. What about money – you haven't just *given away* the stock, have you?'

Gilbert turned, putting his feet on the floor and facing Kenneth. 'Why are *you* so interested?'

'I want to be sure you're not planning to tap Catherine for money. Or Mum.'

'You could always give me some yourself, dear brother. Then I wouldn't have to ask anyone else.' He raised a hand. 'It was only lunch. A very nice lunch, and it was all her idea. A sandwich would have been fine, but she insisted – she thought I looked as if I needed a square meal.' He stubbed out his cigarette. 'There's another one. What on earth would a square meal look like?'

'For God's sake, stick to the point. Have you any money – and if not, why not?'

'I have no money. I had bills to pay – rent, electricity. You'd want me to pay my bills, wouldn't you?'

'Don't talk crap. I don't care whether you have a pot to piss in. I just want to be sure you won't bother Mum and you won't take a penny from my wife.'

As he stood up, he heard the stairs creak. He knew the sound, knew every sound in this cottage. Rose was in the doorway.

Gilbert got up. 'You know Rose, don't you, Kenny?'

'And how long is *she* likely to hang around, now you're cleaned out?'

Gilbert laughed, but Rose's blank stare followed him as he pushed past her and out of the front door. He left it open, not wanting to turn. He was climbing into his car when he realised she had followed him down the path and was at the gate.

'I hear you got married?'

'What?'

'Congratulations,' she said.

He banged the car door shut and started the engine. The radio, coming on with the turn of the ignition key, blared Mahler's sixth, but he thought he could still hear beneath it, her mocking laughter.

When he got home Catherine was in the living room, a folder at her feet and papers on her lap. She was scribbling notes in the margins and did not look up when Kenneth came in.

'Where's Flora?'

'Upstairs.'

Catherine put the papers on her lap into a folder. Now she faced him. 'Where have you been – not working all this time? Have you had dinner?'

'I had fish and chips in Ullapool.' Already, that golden half-hour of quiet seemed a week away. 'I need a drink. You want one?'

'No.'

'I stopped at the cottage.'

'Oh, you didn't—'

'What?'

'Have another row with Gilbert.'

'I told him not to touch you for money.'

She brushed a wisp of hair back from her face and he had a spasm of guilt, seeing how tired she looked.

'He didn't ask me for anything.' She picked up another stack of papers, raising them between her hands and tapping them on her knees to neaten the edges.

'Put that stuff away – it's late.'

She was packing her briefcase, lying open by her side, and did not answer. He went to fetch his whisky. By the sideboard he hesitated, then took out a second glass for her, and poured two measures.

'Here.'

She was standing by her chair, her briefcase under her arm, but she seemed unable to move, like someone in a dream. She looked up when he spoke to her again, holding out the glass.

'We both need it. Come and sit beside me.' He gestured her towards the sofa, whisky spurting up in the glass as he did so. With a sigh, she put down the briefcase.

When he woke it was dark. He lay still, listening, then he realised Catherine was also awake, lying on her back, not touching him. He pressed the button on the alarm clock that lit up the face: ten to four. Before he could turn towards her, she pushed back the duvet and got up. He closed his eyes and lay waiting for her, but she was in the bathroom for a while, water running.

'All right?' he asked.

'My eyes were sore.'

He raised his head. 'Your eyes?'

As she slid in beside him again, he pulled her close. She lay in the crook of his shoulder, but stiffly.

'I wake and they're dry and sore. Gritty. I don't know why.'

'See the optician then,' he said. 'Best to get that checked.'

'I'm sure it's nothing.'

'You spend too much time in front of a computer screen.'

She sighed, turning away. 'I don't. I'm in meetings half the time.'

'I haven't a clue really what you do all day in that job,' he said, turning to hold her, curving himself around the curl of her body. She did not answer. In a few minutes he felt himself drift towards sleep again, all the while conscious that she was not with him, was merely tolerating his touch. For all that, he did not lie awake long.

3

The house was in Archway rather than Highgate, but it was theirs, not rented, and there was a patch of grass at the back with a fence dividing it from the next houses and those behind, which had longer gardens, but were mostly converted to three floors of flats. The way the light fell, their garden was sunny all morning, but the shadows of the houses behind reached the end of it by lunchtime in winter, late afternoon in summer. There was a shady place for the baby to sleep in his pram, with the cat net firmly fixed on. Still, Helen did not leave him there for more than a few minutes without checking. The black and white cat that sat on the wall, narrow-eyed, staring at her, was not to be trusted. She was less anxious than she had been with Matthew, but there would never be, for her, the possibility of having a baby without the fear, like an electric current under conscious thought, that she might lose him.

All summer Matthew ran in and out with his friends, while Helen and their mothers sat at the back door on hot wrought-iron chairs grouped round their matching white table. The sunshade had been up all the time in June, a baking, blue-skied month. In July, it was too cool to leave Luke in the garden and Matthew was driving her mad in the house, as if he was already too big for it and had too much energy to be contained here. She was glad he was going to school in September. Sometimes, she could not believe she had got this far. They were settled, they were a normal family, she had two boys and if that black and white cat got its way, they'd have a pet too.

During the week in Barcelona, something had changed she did not understand, but when they came back, Joe set about finding them somewhere else to live as quickly as he could. Soon after that, two young men came with a van and moved all the stuff out of the spare room. When they left the flat, they had only their own things to take with them. If the police had ever managed to speak to Joe, it was not while she was there. When she asked, he touched a finger to his lips. 'Least said...'

They saw less of Brian and Gaynor now, but more, to her annoyance, of Rose Semple. Rose knew better than to smoke in their house, but she would stand at the back door with Joe. She heard them talking in low voices, and afterwards, she had to pick up the cigarette stubs and put them in the bin.

'I don't know why you bother with her. You used to say the stuff she brought you was rubbish.'

'Not all of it,' he admitted. 'She has good contacts.'

There was nothing between them apart from the supply and demand of business. Joe was fastidious and there was always something slightly unclean about Rose, a staleness when she passed too close: unwashed skin and the whiff of cannabis.

'Have you ever, you know – smoked hash, that kind of thing?' Helen had asked Joe in the early days, when some of the company he kept made her wonder.

'Not me,' he said. 'I like to be in control.'

He liked to drink too, but was never drunk, so she believed him. Not sex then, not drugs. Contacts. Helen gave it up.

During the last few months, she had not seen much of Rose. Or Joe. He was often away overnight, Brighton he said, or 'up north'. Since her contact with him was by mobile phone, he might have been anywhere. Still, there was enough money, business – he said – was good, and he was cheerful when he was home, bringing presents for the boys and working Matthew up to such a pitch of excitement it was impossible to get him to bed. It was a normal life; other husbands worked away from home.

On this July day, the London sky glaring white, the wind scuffling litter along the pavements, she was at a loose end. Her closest friends were on holiday and the afternoon stretched out bleakly in front of her. Joe was away until tomorrow night. For the moment, Matthew was content in front of a video tape of *Jungle Book*, and Luke was asleep. She could call Catherine.

Catherine would be at work. She was so important these days that she was always just about to leave for a meeting, or someone else answered her phone and said she was already in one. Still, she had a mobile phone like everyone else, so there was another number Helen could try.

The ringing stopped, but it was a few fumbled seconds before Catherine said, sounding breathless, 'Hello?'

'It's me, where are you?' In the background there was music and a loud buzzing.

'Wait a minute, I'll go somewhere quieter.'

Abruptly, the sound ceased and the line was dead. Helen waited. Then, just as she was getting up to make herself a cup of tea, her phone rang.

'Sorry, is that better? I was in a shop and somebody was digging up the pavement right outside. I'm back at the car now.'

'Shopping between meetings?'

'I was at the optician, and cutting through the shops to the car park.'

'What were you at the optician for? You don't wear glasses.'

'My eyes are terribly dry and sore, especially through the night and in the morning. I thought I might need glasses, but I don't. I've to get my doctor to refer me to a consultant, but it's probably something called—' Catherine paused. 'Where's that bit of paper? Some kind of eye inflammation.'

'Is it serious?'

'Just a nuisance. It means eye drops daily and being careful not to stare at a computer screen too long – that sort of thing.'

'Oh.' Helen didn't feel she could go on now about how bored she was.

'Are you all right – you rang me?'

'Just to chat.'

'Well, it's the middle of the working day and I do have to get back.'

'Never mind then. It was just on the off chance you were free.'

She had tried to keep the plaintive note from her voice, but no fooling her sister.

'What is it?'

'Oh, nothing.'

A sigh. 'I'll call you this evening, will that do?'

From where she stood, near the window onto the garden, Helen could see Matthew leaning into the pram. 'Yes, fine, better go.'

Outside, Luke's wail rose in the windless air. *I shouldn't have left him out here.*

'He's crying,' Matthew said. He had been trying to prise the cat net off.

'Ok, I'm here.'

Luke was heavy on her breast as she held him close, soothing. Matthew pressed against her. If she comforted the baby, she had to hold him too, even now, nearly three months after the birth. He was a baby himself again, when it was just the three of them. Mostly, it was just the three of them.

'Let me go, Matthew, let's get him inside. I think it's going to rain, anyway.'

They went up the garden, the baby wailing in the pram until she got them all indoors.

'I don't suppose you could get a job?' Catherine asked when she and Helen eventually spoke again, late that evening. The children were in bed, though Luke likely to wake any minute for a feed. There seemed no time when Helen and Catherine were both free to talk.

'A job? How could I?'

'Other women manage. They get childminders, nannies, whatever. It would do you good – I can tell you're going crazy on your own with two small children.'

'I'm not!'

'Going crazy, or on your own all the time?'

'Neither. I have loads of friends round here. It's much better than the flat that way. There are quite a few families with small children. It's just most people are on holiday this week.'

'Right.'

'It's not a job I need, it's Joe being at home more.'

How provoking Catherine was, making her say things she instantly regretted.

'He's still away a lot?' Catherine sighed. 'Seems ideal to me.'

'Are you kidding?'

For a moment, moving beyond self-pity, Helen wondered about Kenneth. Kenneth and Catherine.

Her main recollection of their wedding was of how strange and uncomfortable it was to see those three men in the same place: Joe, Kenneth and Hugh. She didn't count Gilbert, who had flitted about in a theatrical velvet suit, with a silk shirt and paisley cravat. He always looks, Catherine had said, like someone in Dickens, but that day he was too flamboyant even for that. The suit had bell-bottomed trousers and wide lapels: he must have access to a vintage clothes shop. He became very drunk in the course of the afternoon.

The wedding was celebrated in a small private hotel, miles out in the country, where most of the day Helen had felt as if she were in an Alan Ayckbourn farce. The guests drifted in and out of different rooms or onto the lawn outside through the French windows, carrying glasses of warm champagne and waylaying the waiters with their trays of canapes held high. It seemed there was always someone trying to avoid someone else, but perhaps she was too sensitive to the difficulty of seeing Hugh and Joe in the same place at the same time. Joe talked to Gilbert a lot, which astonished her, as she couldn't imagine what they had in common till she remembered Gilbert sold antiques in his factory. Hugh had been unfailingly courteous; Kenneth had ignored his brother and looked down his nose at Joe; Joe had given the impression of taunting both Hugh and Kenneth by not speaking to either of them beyond a first cool greeting when he was introduced. Catherine had given up trying to please everyone and stayed close to Flora who in turn stayed close to her best friend whose parents had also been invited. Catherine looked elegant, but slightly dazed. Helen herself had had to keep dashing to the ladies' cloakroom, a sure sign, she told herself, she was pregnant. It was because of this she suffered the whole weekend sober, when being drunk would have helped a lot. Then, annoyingly, she had turned out to be wrong and Luke did not come along for another year.

Kenneth was not her type. Aggressively male, a big guy with an aura of testosterone. You could see him on a building site, ordering people about. The back seat of his car, cleared for the wedding, was usually littered with hard hats and hi-vis jackets, stowed that day in the cloakroom of his house. In that tiny space, while the wedding party prepared to leave for the hotel, she had stared at her own face in the mirror and tried on one of those hats, bright yellow with 'SC' for Sinclair Construction on the front. Then she laughed at herself and took it off, leaving her hair ruffled. She wondered if Catherine had ever put one on, being Kenneth for a moment, in his life. Joe did not have a hard hat; he had cars and leather jackets. She had sat in the black Mercedes sport he was driving a year or so back, wearing one of his jackets, the steering wheel in her hands, trying to be Joe. She opened the glove compartment and took out a torch, several CDs and a little notebook with a black dog-eared cover. It was full of names and phone numbers, and prices scribbled opposite descriptions like 'Drum table, regentcy?' and 'Two Tiffney lamps'. His spelling was awful. Right at the back was a screwed-up bit of paper. Smoothed out, it read, 'North Circular to Edgeware, second set of lights, first right, three streets down. Rose.'

She put it back, put everything back, and got out of the car. You could not be Joe, you could not even see inside his life. Kenneth must be easier.

Now she could hear the first thin whimper from Luke.

'I have to go,' she said to Catherine. 'Luke's ready for his feed, and if I let him yell, he wakes Matthew.'

'Are you coming north soon? You ought to get out of London in August. It's a dead time.'

'I know that. I *said* everyone was on holiday.'

'I'm taking leave the first two weeks, before Flora goes back to school.'

'I'll see. Joe was saying something about Portugal.'

'It will be baking hot there – not the right time.'

Upstairs, Luke had paused, but only to prepare for a more determined effort.

'I have to go.'

'Take care.'

'You too.'

They need not be so anxious about each other, Helen thought, going quickly upstairs now that Luke's cries were crescendo. Neither listened to the other's advice. And yet, and yet – Catherine had put her finger on the sore spot again. Luke paused mid-cry, gazing up at her as she leaned into the cot to lift him. He smiled his tenuous new smile, and she gathered him up with all the tenderness of remorse.

4

The Factory was empty, the doors locked. When Kenneth walked round, trying to peer in windows, the August sunlight made it difficult to see, but he had the impression of empty space. He went on looking, his eyes adjusting to dimness. Against the far wall a broken chair slouched, and there was what appeared to be a cushion on the floor. Upstairs, of course, he could not view, but the whole place had the air of being deserted, the party over, the people gone.

He walked all the way round, but there was nothing to see. At the back, nettles and willowherb, pink spikes in full bloom, grew as high as the windows and made it impossible to get close. There was no sign of Gilbert or the red van.

Yesterday, on the way back from estimating a job on Skye, he had called again at the cottage but it was empty, the van gone, the doors locked back and front. The key was under its usual stone. This looked like a more permanent departure, since Gilbert rarely secured the place. There was a bare patch of earth where something had stood next to the stone at the front door. What had been removed? The boot-scraper. For God's sake, had he sold that with his junk? Had Rose thought it was worth something? Nothing in the cottage had any value; his grandparents' good pieces of furniture and china had been taken out after his grand-father's death. He was already late getting home, so he decided not to check indoors to see if anything was missing. All that mattered, anyway, was that they had cleared off.

Today he was seeing a client about a job in Tain, and as he set out it had occurred to him that he could look in at The Factory. He had not spoken to Catherine, but he could ask her tonight if she had heard anything about Gilbert leaving. Irritably, he wished he had seen his brother off himself. He walked slowly back to his car. It had heated up in the sunshine, and was like an oven when he got in. He turned up the air conditioning and drove back to the main road.

By the time he got home, his head was full of the day's meetings. They had finished dinner and Flora was in front of the television, when he recalled this early visit.

'I'll take the coffee through,' Catherine said, putting cups on a tray.

'We'll have it here – easier to talk. What rubbish is she watching?'

'Oh goodness knows. A quiz? Game show?'

They sat down, facing each other at the kitchen table.

'Do you want cheese?' She had begun to get up again.

'No, I'm fine. I want to talk.'

She looked wary. 'What about?'

'I was in Tain today, so I stopped off at Gilbert's place. The furniture warehouse, whatever.'

'The Factory.'

He laughed. 'Wrong name. That implies there's real work going on, which is not my impression of my brother's ventures.'

'Did you see him?'

'No. It's shut up – deserted. The place is cleaned out, as far as I could tell.'

'I thought it must be by now.'

'You've not seen him?'

'I always want to tell you – I hate secrets. You make it difficult.'

'You can see whoever you like. You don't have to tell me.'

She gave the faintest shrug. 'I've not seen him recently.'

'Anyway – he's not at the cottage either. I went by yesterday, coming back from Skye.'

'I hope—' She stopped, biting her lip.

'What?'

For a moment she delayed, topping up her coffee. He waited.

'I wouldn't like to think he'd gone away and I didn't know, hadn't said goodbye at least. But where on earth *would* he go? I'm sure he's still at the cottage, he just wasn't around when you were there.' She hesitated. 'Did you call on your mother?'

'No. I hope to God he's not *there*.'

'He's her son – he has a right to be with her.'

'Don't start.' He got up, leaving his coffee undrunk, and went out.

Upstairs, they used a small bedroom as an office, for the work they brought home. Catherine's briefcase was leaning on the desk, a file open next to the computer. Kenneth stood by the window, looking out onto the hill rising behind the house, rough ground that he had so far done nothing to tame or cultivate. At this time of year, the weeds were tall and in full flower, and he was reminded, seeing the pink spears of the willowherb, the foaming heads of giant hogweed, of the overgrown path behind the factory. That place could have been something, he realised for the first time. In other hands, with a man who had vision. Old furniture, bric-a-brac, junk – what a waste. Suppose it was a gallery, for modern art and sculpture, a space you could walk about in, and just look, peacefully look and take in, and think. There were great artists working in the Highlands – people would come. They would buy.

One day, like his father, he wouldn't be fit for the construction business. It wasn't, in any case, what he had planned for his life. Not that he had planned much. Things happened, you reacted, you did the best you could. He became aware that Catherine was standing in the doorway. As he turned, she said, 'I was going to do some work, but—'

'Come here.' He held his hands out and she came slowly towards him. 'What are we going to do with this bit of ground? We can't leave it like that. '

She had already made a difference to the land at the front and side of the house. He'd had Gavin, his apprentice, come in with a digger and turn over the earth, take away the weeds and grass, and scope out a lawn and flower beds. Catherine worked there most weekends, and gradually, a garden was appearing. He had been surprised at how willing she was to work out of doors in all weathers, to get muddy and wet, and come in with grime under her nails and damp dirty patches on the knees of her jeans. It was a different woman who worked in the garden.

At the window, they looked out together and she leaned on him. He put his arms round her so that her head rested on his shoulder.

'I must call on your mother,' she said. 'I've not been in for a week or two. I thought I'd take Monday and Tuesday off next week, to be with Flora before she goes away. I hoped Helen would come up with the children, but I don't know if she will.'

'We should have sorted out a holiday.'

'But we haven't. When Flora's in the Borders we can at least have some time to ourselves.'

'I'll take a few days off then. We'll go over to the West, take hillwalking gear and the tent. How about that?'

'What about a hotel?'

He laughed. 'Not the tent?'

After a moment, she eased away from him. 'I do have to finish some work.'

'Yes, by the way. Yes, go and see Mum.'

'It's better if I do it. If Gil *is* there, you'll only fall out with him and come home in a temper.'

He would not rise to that. He left her to her files as she switched on the computer.

Downstairs, Flora was trying to do a headstand against the wall. The television was still on. She came down with a crash, then, red-faced, saw him at the door. 'I can do it usually,' she said.

'I'm sure you can.'

She flopped onto the sofa. 'I'm bored. Kirsty's on holiday and Isla's got her cousins staying and they've gone to Skye. There's not enough people in this place. My age, anyway. Inverness was better.'

Against his will, she had had her ears pierced. The tiny diamonds winked at him as she tossed her hair back, sulking.

'Want a game of chess? Draughts? Monopoly?' She screwed up her face at each suggestion, and he laughed. 'Don't complain about being bored then.'

'All that's *boring*.'

He mimicked her. 'Bored boring Flora.'

'Shut up.' She pointed at him. 'You're boring too.'

'I'm old, as you keep reminding me. Old people are meant to be boring.'

'No, they're not. You're not old anyway, just horrible.'

They had this conversation, or a variation of it, so regularly, they hardly bothered to put any feeling into it. That she tolerated him, accepted, grudgingly, his authority, was taken for granted. 'They're all the same, at her age,' Catherine said. 'Don't worry about it.' 'I'm not worried at all,' he had told her. 'But maybe you should be. It'll be boys next, and alcohol.' Catherine had laughed. 'She's twelve, for God's sake.'

He would have liked Flora to love him, but suspected he had come too late into her life, or that he was not a lovable person. He hadn't the knack. She loved Hugh, and probably Gilbert too, but he veered away from that thought. She was still a child, despite the clothes and the music and her pre-adolescent moodiness. How could she know what Gilbert was?

At least he was off the scene. He might even have gone back to London. At this possibility, his spirits rose.

'Come on,' he said to Flora. 'Give me a game of Scrabble, at least. You always win that.'

'*Mum* wins.'

'We won't let her play. She's busy anyway.'

She regarded him for a moment, unsmiling. He could almost see the thought process that led her to the conclusion that he was here and willing, nobody else was, and she was, as he said, quite likely to win. So far, it had not occurred to her that he sometimes allowed this to happen. It would be a shock when he started trying to beat her, and did.

Kenneth usually slept first. Catherine told him that even in sleep he was possessive, arms circling, pulling her into the curve of his body, hip to groin, his hand on her breast, his breath a tiny draught on her neck. Held like this she was small, the only time she felt so, almost fragile in his grasp. During the day they were apart in their different work worlds, independent of each other.

251

At home, there was often tension: Flora, or the amount of time he was off hillwalking, leaving her on her own again. Now Flora was at secondary school, involved with the swimming club and the drama society, *her* life, despite her complaints, was not boring at all. Surely this should make them more united, he thought, a couple. Yet it had not happened.

For once, he was the one still awake. He tightened his grasp and she nestled closer to him. Folded together, turning as one during the night, they seemed united.

5

Catherine called at Rosemount on Monday, a grey afternoon. She was used to going straight in, since her mother-in-law rarely heard the doorbell. She went to the back door and through the porch with its basket chairs and smell of dead vegetation from neglected pot plants, and into the kitchen. It was empty and the house silent.

Before she reached the hall she knew something was wrong – a tiny movement, or an unnatural silence. Kenneth's mother was slumped awkwardly against the bottom treads of the staircase. At first Catherine thought she'd had a fall. Then she saw her face, the mouth pulled to one side and her eyes staring, bewildered and frightened. She tried to speak but it came out as a slur of sound, and Catherine, bending down, saying, 'What happened?' added swiftly, 'Never mind, don't worry, you'll be all right.' This, of course, she did not know. She dropped her bag from her shoulder and scrabbled for her mobile phone, pressing the emergency call button. She too was frightened.

Mary Sinclair closed her eyes. Don't die, Catherine thought, please, please don't.

The ambulance had to come out from Inverness. 'Twenty minutes,' the operator said, and, 'keep her warm, don't move her unless you have to – can you leave her where she is? And don't give her anything to eat or drink, all right?'

Catherine imagined the ambulance speeding along the dual carriageway from the hospital, lights flashing, perhaps the siren screaming. She held her mother-in-law's hand, pressing gently. 'I'm just going upstairs to get you a blanket – I won't be a minute.'

She dragged a pillow and blanket from the high-backed old-fashioned bedstead, noticing the neatness of the room, and then its coldness even in summer. A hot water bottle, emptied, was propped on the side of the washstand. She snatched it up and ran downstairs.

She tucked the blanket round Mary Sinclair as best she could and eased the pillow behind her head.

'Look, I'm just going to fill a hot bottle for you, to keep you warm. The ambulance will be here soon.' She felt the lack of a name – a name could have some tenderness in it. She had never had a name for her mother-in-law, Mary seeming impertinent, Mrs Sinclair too formal, Mother impossible.

In the kitchen, fretting while the kettle boiled, she realised she had left her phone by the foot of the stairs, or could be calling Kenneth now. She hurried back.

'Are you all right—'

Mary Sinclair opened her eyes a little and made a sound. Catherine took her phone into the kitchen as the kettle switched itself off.

She could tell he was out of doors from the noise around him, and the poor signal. Where was he working? She had lost track, ought to know but did not.

'Yes?'

'Kenneth, it's your mother. Where are you?'

'What? I'm on site, signal's awful. I'll call you back.'

'No – wait—'That might be an hour or more; it had been before. 'It's your *mother*. I think she's had another stroke – I've called the ambulance but—'

'Wait!'

The phone went dead. In a few minutes, as she sat at the foot of the cold stairway (wishing she had some idea of how to turn on the ancient central heating) closer to his mother than she had ever been, her arm round her, hearing the faint wheeze of her breathing, he called back. Indoors, in the site Portakabin probably, his voice came through clearly, and she told him what had happened.

Then she had to break off, as the ambulance arrived.

Kenneth had sat with his mother for hours, but there was no change. Catherine, who had had to go home for Flora, waited for him in empty uncertainty. Kenneth called from the hospital cafeteria to tell her the consultant thought his mother might recover, as long as there wasn't another stroke. She had not been fully conscious yet. Catherine wondered if she should let Gilbert know what had happened. She could at least try his latest mobile number. He did not hang on to phones, so she had had to delete several numbers over the years and replace them. Why did he not transfer his number as other people did? As the ringing went on, she wondered if he was deliberately cutting himself off from people he no longer wanted to contact him.

Perhaps she was one of those people now. There was no reply and no voicemail cut in. She sent a short text message instead. Tomorrow she would drive out to the cottage and see if he had reappeared.

The hospital called them at five in the morning. Kenneth had reached the phone before she was fully awake. He came back into the bedroom a few minutes later as she lay waiting, knowing before he spoke what the news would be.

'You will have to tell Gilbert,' she could not help saying.

He was up, and would not come back to bed. 'You can do that. I'm going in to the works – I'll go straight to the hospital after that.'

'Wait – you must have breakfast first.' She was half out of bed in the grey dawn light but he stopped her.

'Stay where you are. No sense both of us getting up at this hour.'

'I'm sorry,' she said. 'You'll miss her.'

He paused, as if he had not thought of this. 'Yes, yes, I will.'

He went to the bathroom for his shower and she lay down, listening to the rush of water, knowing she would not get back to sleep. There was too much to think about. He would not take holiday now.

When she came downstairs, he had made coffee and was putting bread in the toaster.

'I could cook something – we've got eggs.'

'Toast's fine.'

They sat in the silent kitchen, with the comforting smell of coffee and toast, but neither of them could eat much.

'Would you like me to come to the hospital with you?'

'No, it's all right. Are you off today?'

'Yes, remember I'm supposed to be getting Flora onto a train for Edinburgh this morning.' He looked blank, and she knew he had no recollection of her telling him this. 'Alan's parents are driving there to meet her, to take her down to Gatehouse. Should I call them and cancel?'

'Does she have to go?'

'Do you think she should stay for the funeral? '

'No, let's not subject her to that.'

'Then she should just go to Gatehouse?' She sighed. 'She's not so keen these days, but how else is she to stay in contact with them?'

'It's up to you.'

'She might be upset.' Another death for her, she was thinking, though Flora could hardly be said to have been close to Kenneth's mother.

'All the more reason for her not to be here.'

She did not answer, not wanting this discussion at five thirty on the morning his mother had died. She had not quite taken it in, and thought he had not, either.

'I'll ask Willie Mackenzie to come here his afternoon,' he said, 'to sort out the funeral arrangements.'

Catherine told Flora about Mary's death as soon as she got up.

'Am I still going to Granny's?'

'Yes, unless you'd rather stay here. The funeral is likely to happen before you get back.'

'Good,' said Flora.

'I'll tell Kenneth you're sorry, shall I?'

'Did he want me to stay?'

'No, not at all.'

'Oh, all right then.' Flora sat down and began pouring Rice Krispies into a bowl. Catherine, sitting opposite, began to go through again the arrangements for the journey. 'Don't fuss. You told me all that already.'

'I know. I just worry.'

Flora paused, spoon lifted. 'Is he upset?'

'It's his mother, of course he's – well, he's sad.'

'I just don't like being at a funeral.'

'It's fine. Kenneth agrees with you.'

As Flora began eating, Catherine stood by the kitchen window, gazing out at the garden but for once not seeing it.

The cottage was as Kenneth had found it: empty and closed up. Gilbert really had gone – and without saying goodbye. She could not help feeling hurt. Catherine had driven there straight from seeing Flora off at Inverness Station, still worrying about her taking a train journey on her own or even if she should be going at all.

Passing Rosemount on her way home, she wondered whether she should go in and check the empty house. Then, on impulse, having an hour or two before the funeral director was due to visit them, she drew in to the side of the road and called Hugh. He was home, he was sorry to hear about Kenneth's mother, and he would love to see Catherine. She should come to his office and they would go out for lunch. With a sense of relief, she drove past Strathpeffer and into Dingwall.

There were not many places to have lunch there, but the Caledonia was under new ownership and Hugh said the food was good. She had been up so early she was hungry, so when Hugh ordered steak pie, she did the same.

He did not finish his, laying the fork and knife down halfway, as if tired. He looked tired, Catherine realised, stirring herself from her own preoccupations.

'Are you all right?'

'Me? Of course. Just never as hungry as I think I am, these days.'

'Come over,' she said. 'You've not been out to see us for ages – and Kenneth said you'd not gone with them on the last few hills.'

'I'll come and see you once the funeral's over – there will

be a lot to sort out. He'll have to decide what to do about the house.'

'The house?'

'Rosemount.'

'Oh. Of course.' It would be Hugh dealing with the estate. Suddenly she thought – Kenneth might want to keep the family house and live in Rosemount. She shuddered at the thought; it was always so cold.

'I'd better get back,' Hugh said. 'Tell Kenneth to call me when he's ready.'

They parted on the High Street but as she walked away, Catherine had a moment of anxiety – something about Hugh had made her uneasy. She turned back but his thin figure disappearing through the office entrance, the inner glazed door swinging shut behind him, gave nothing away. Perhaps it was just that he was getting older.

6

Finally, in October, Catherine and Helen met again. After Mary Sinclair's death, Catherine had begun to feel guilty about her own mother, so far away in the south of England, and also living alone since their father had died a year ago.

As soon as she and Flora arrived at her parents' house, she remembered why she had left it so long to visit. Helen, with fresher memories, refused to join her.

'Come up to London,' she insisted. 'Couldn't you and Flora stay a night or two?'

Flora had been seduced by her grandmother's new neighbours. 'Noisy,' Catherine's mother complained, 'and the garden is ruined. Those boys and their football – next time it lands over the fence, I warned her, I'll hang on to it. When I think how beautifully the Fullertons kept the place I could weep.' The boys had invited Flora in to meet their puppy. 'And that dog, for goodness' sake, yap-yapping all the time, you'd think they'd have some consideration.'

The boys' mother, oblivious to this disapproval, was welcoming, the house chaotic – *we'll get it straight one day, I dare say* – with Radio 1 from the kitchen, the beep beep of a computer game from upstairs, smells of wet laundry, urine (the puppy not yet house-trained) and fried food. Flora, in love, abandoned Catherine and her grandmother, and refused to come up to London. Matthew and Luke were 'only babies' – she could see them another time.

Between the many interruptions from Matthew and his friend Thomas, and finding new ways to keep Luke amused, Helen managed to ask Catherine, at last, about her life.

Catherine said only, 'I'm fine – it's all much the same,' a lie Helen had not the time or energy to discover, though she paused when Catherine added, 'I'm a bit worried about Hugh.'

'What's wrong?'

'He doesn't seem well. He's tired all the time, and not eating properly. Everything gives him indigestion.'

'Has he been to the doctor?'

'Not yet.'

'You must make him. Keep nagging. I'm sure you are already?'

'I hope it's not nagging,' Catherine smiled.

'That's better – you looked so grim coming in. Not even all that pleased to see my boys.'

'Oh, I am, and you. I am.'

'I know. Our mother is bloody depressing.'

'It's not that. Or only that.'

'What then?'

A scream from upstairs put a stop to the conversation and Helen forgot, in the fuss of bathing a scraped knee and getting tea ready, to ask again.

To everyone's surprise, Joe came home at six and offered to keep the boys while Helen took Catherine out to eat. His looks and charm struck Catherine all over again. He had not changed, but there were faint lines round his eyes, though this might have been fatigue. He too seemed tired.

'Oh, good,' Helen said, 'there's a lovely wee Italian restaurant opened round the corner. We'll go there.'

'I booked you a table,' Joe said, bouncing Luke on his knee, the baby entranced. 'Eight. You'd better get these two settled first – make it easy for me, eh? I got phone calls to make.'

Catherine felt hackles rise, but only her own; Helen seemed to take this easily. While she got the children fed and ready for bed, Joe poured Catherine a glass of wine. 'You're staying over, right?'

'Just one night.'

'That's good, you'll give her a bit of company. She's going stir crazy with these kids. She wants a job, but I've said not yet. They need to be a bit older, right?'

'That's Helen's decision, surely?'

He laughed at this, shaking his head, as if she had said something foolish. It wasn't worth challenging. It was Helen who had to live with him, however unsatisfactory it must be.

'So,' their mother had said, 'that's both of you married again. And two more *Scotsmen*, of all things. I hope it's going to last this time.'

She seemed to believe Helen and Joe had married quietly so that the children became respectably legitimate. Catherine didn't bother to disillusion her.

The restaurant was quiet, so there had been no need to book. Certainly they were expected, the owner coming out to show them to their table, bring them the menu and claim Joe as a friend, a great guy. It flashed through Catherine's mind that Joe had booked the table while he was here anyway, negotiating some deal with Fabio. Did this cross Helen's mind? It might of course be completely innocent, legitimate business.

They made the meal last a long time. As they went through

three courses and finished the wine, the other tables filled, the place beginning to hum with voices, the waiters weaving with heaped plates through the swing doors from the kitchen at the back.

'What a treat,' Helen said. 'Out without any kids and a bagful of nappies and feeding stuff...I bet you've forgotten all that.'

'You're reminding me.' Catherine said. 'Glad I won't be going through it again.'

'So—' Expansive with wine, Helen became bold. 'How is Kenneth? You're not thinking of providing Flora with a wee brother or sister?'

Catherine laughed, dismissing this. 'You and Joe are obviously getting on well.'

'Oh yes, when he's here.'

'He's away a lot?'

'I never know when he's going to appear. Or disappear.' Helen shrugged. 'Never mind – you can't have everything.'

'What on earth does that mean?'

'You know. You've not said a word about yourself.'

Catherine repeated instead their mother's remark about her daughters' marriages. Helen laughed.

'Oh well, I suppose I let her think we meant to do it. She kept talking about second marriages and how she thought one should be discreet – not have a white dress, she probably meant.'

'She must surely have expected an invitation?'

'I told her that because Joe was a Catholic and I was divorced we had to keep it quiet. Anyway, *you* had a wedding. One more should be enough for her. You *are* happy?'

'Oh yes.' But she could not meet Helen's direct gaze and shrugged, rueful. 'We still quarrel about Flora – he thinks I'm too soft.'

'A mother's prerogative. It's not his business anyway, is it?'

'Well—'

'What about the weird Gilbert? You've not mentioned him.'

'He left the cottage at the end of July. He's probably in London, since he has friends here. The terrible thing is no one can get in touch to let him know his mother is dead. He never answers his mobile and we don't know where he's living. It's awful – I feel so bad about it.'

As she talked about Gilbert, anxiety swelled again. He ought to be found – surely Kenneth couldn't just sell his mother's house without Gilbert being involved?

'Maybe it was all left to Kenneth?'

'The business, yes, but not the house and everything.'

Catherine didn't actually know this. Kenneth's refusal to discuss it annoyed her. Hugh, when she hinted, said she must really speak to Kenneth. It was the only rebuff she had ever had from Hugh, and it had silenced her on the subject. Not with Helen of course, because how could that matter? There was no connection with Gilbert here.

Helen's mobile began to vibrate. 'Sod it. Joe.' She picked it up. 'Hi – we're just at coffee – be home soon.' A pause. 'What? Can't you deal with it? You're his father, why can't you?' She flushed, the hot colour coming up like a flame, her mouth tightening. 'Ok, ok, we'll get the bill. For God's sake.'

'What's wrong?'

'Sorry. Full nappy.'

'You're kidding?'

'Unfortunately not.'

'I thought he was so good with Matthew when he was a baby?'

They rose, Helen signalling to the waiter. 'He was. But he's done that. Joe doesn't stick with anything tedious or repetitive. As babies, of course, are.'

264

The bill was settled already. 'Joe?' Catherine asked, and Helen nodded wearily, as if all the good effect of the food and wine had vanished already. They walked the hundred yards back to the house in silence, the air colder than when they set out, a chill like winter coming.

There was a street lamp opposite the house and in its circle of light a figure moved away, someone leaving Helen's house, the gate clicking shut behind her. Helen let out a hiss of fury.

'Who's that?' A quick leap of fear made Catherine sharper than she meant to be. There had been something familiar about the figure, now nearing the corner.

'Oh, it's only bloody Rose Semple. He's not having an affair or anything, if that's what you think.'

'For goodness' sake – is that *Rose*?'

'Yeah. You could call her a business associate.' They had reached the house and Helen said as she pushed the gate open, 'I call her a fucking nuisance myself. Sorry.'

Catherine put her hand on Helen's arm. 'I know her,' she said. 'I *know* who she is.'

'Oh, never mind her – come on, I've got to see to Luke.'

'You go in – I won't be a minute.'

Catherine turned and ran up the dark street, glad she had been keeping fit, because it meant she caught up with Rose at the corner before she turned into the much busier, noisier thorough-fare with its shops and restaurants.

'Rose!'

Rose stopped, but did not turn immediately. She might have been working out who called her, before she did.

'It's you,' she said.

'Rose – hello – I think you know my sister. Helen. I'm staying with her – she said you worked with Joe?'

'What of it?' Rose was unsurprised, but that might be her manner. It was only later that Catherine realised Rose knew the connection already.

'Are you still in touch with Gil? Gilbert Sinclair, who had The Factory.'

'I know who you mean.'

'Do you see him?'

Rose carried no handbag, but her long coat, black and worn-looking, like something picked up in a jumble sale, Catherine thought, had deep pockets that bulged, as if she carried all she needed in them. She dug her hands in these pockets, and tilted her head.

'So what if I do?'

'We've been trying to get in touch with him, Kenneth – his brother – and me.'

'Oh yeah. Kenneth.'

'Could you give me his mobile number or email address?' Rose saying nothing, she went on hastily, 'Or just pass on a message?'

'Yeah, if you like.' She moved backwards a step or two. 'I got to go.'

'I haven't given you the message.'

'Go on then.'

'Tell him—' The wine was wearing off, leaving her shivery. Somehow it was hard to say this to Rose, with her indifferent manner. Catherine pulled herself together and took a deep breath. 'Tell him his mother has died, just after he left. We didn't know how to get hold of him.'

'Is that it? That's the message?'

'Yes. Please tell him.'

'Ok.' Rose began to move away, then she stopped. 'Does he need to – sign anything?'

'What? How do you mean, *sign anything*?'

'Forget it. I'll tell him.'

'Wait – is he all right? Will you pass on my best to him – tell him Catherine sends her – her love.'

Rose raised a hand in acknowledgement, or possibly just in farewell. She turned the corner and walked quickly away, the coat flapping against her short legs, the new pink streak in her hair fluorescent under the street lights.

7

There had been no question of keeping the Sinclair house. Kenneth's attachment to Rosemount had been through his mother. She had wanted to go on living in the only house she'd known in the fifty years of her marriage. House prices were rising and he thought it might sell quickly, though Hugh said you never knew with these big places, especially when they needed a lot of bringing up to date.

He and Hugh met in Hugh's office in Dingwall to begin dealing with the financial aftermath of death: arranging the sale of the few shares his father had held, which were now in his mother's name, closing bank accounts and preparing the estate for administration. Most of it was straightforward. His parents' finances had not been complex once the business had been transferred entirely to Kenneth's name on his father's death.

'Did you know they'd cut Gilbert out altogether?' Hugh asked.

'I thought they might. My father will have done that – not Mum.'

'I talked it all through with her when your father died, but I'm not sure how much she really understood. She seemed to think you would sort it out. Did you—'

'No,' Kenneth said. 'No, I let it lie.'

'He could make a claim. Adopted children are legitimate heirs, Ken, you know that.'

'I don't even know where he is.'

'Not good enough – you know that too.'

Hugh, implacable, gazed across his desk at Kenneth. For a moment, there was silence, then Hugh went on, 'You've given me all the family papers? Is there anything relevant still at Rosemount?'

He's guessed, Kenneth thought. I should just tell him. 'You've got the lot.'

'You know what I'm asking?'

'Go on.'

'I haven't found anything relating to an adoption. No certificate. No birth certificate for Gilbert either.'

'There's nothing in the house.'

'So—'

'It was thirty years ago. There wasn't the same ... rigour, you could say, when it came to taking someone else's kid to bring up. I didn't know – I didn't know until Dad had his first heart attack. He told me then. He's had enough money from us, Dad said, we've done our bit for him. Then he told me there was never any formal adoption. We've brought him up as our own, he said, we've done everything we can.'

'Do you know anything about his birth family?'

'Not a thing.' Kenneth shrugged. 'Well, they didn't come from round here. It was done through some friend in Glasgow who worked for a private adoption society. That's as much as I know, and I only got that from Dad one New Year when he'd had a couple of drams.'

'Gilbert never sought them out? He didn't try to trace his mother, for instance?'

'Not that I know of.'

Hugh tapped his pen lightly on the blotter in front of him. 'So—'

'I know it probably doesn't *seem* fair but my God, he did sponge off them for years. My mother was always so pleased when he stayed here and had a job of some kind. Then for no reason, he would bugger off without a word. It upset her. More than upset. They put the money up for his blessed Factory – paid the first year of the lease, all the legal costs – well, you would know all about that. He's had his share.'

'Ken, I'm not saying a word. As long as I have the facts – it's your business.'

'Yeah, well, it is.'

'He wasn't an easy person, certainly. Troubled, I suppose. But perhaps you should think about making some provision. I'm sure your mother expected that. When I raised it with her, she said, "Kenneth will look after him".'

'For God's sake. Look, I know you get on with him, and Catherine's as soft as Mum was. But you don't know how much of a drain he's been already.'

'I'm only thinking how you might feel later, that's all. About your mother, if not about Gilbert.'

'Well, I'll see. Though what I can do about it when he's vanished into thin air—'

'Think about it. We can deal with the estate meantime and send it to Administration so that you can get the house on the market.'

Kenneth rose. 'Is that it, for now? Catherine and Flora are due back tomorrow. She's sent me a shopping list.'

'I promised her I'd come over sometime.'

'You do that. Fix it up with her.'

270

They shook hands – Kenneth's hard grip, Hugh's softer clasp – and their eyes met.

In November, on a clear day, the skies brilliant behind the sharp outline of Ben Wyvis, Kenneth and Hugh climbed the familiar hill, but they made poor time despite good weather. Hugh was slow. There was something wrong, as Catherine had thought.

'Sorry,' Hugh said, 'I'm holding you up. Age beginning to tell, I suppose.'

Kenneth turned and saw a sudden difference in the man below him on the steep heather slope.

'Go to the bloody doctor, Hugh.'

'Yes, yes, I have.'

'What did he say?'

'Let's get as far as An Cabar,' Hugh said, 'and have a cup of tea there.'

They took a break at the cairn where they always paused on this hill, and got their flasks out. In the colder air, Hugh pulled on his fleece over his T-shirt, his face emerging cheerful, so that he seemed his usual self.

They were on their second fill of the flask cups when Kenneth said, 'Are you going to tell me then?'

So Hugh told him, making little of it, that was not little, not a slight thing. The world trembled beneath them as they perched on the hill's broad back, the land below distant, unimportant, the sun deceptively warm on their faces.

Later, coming down, they talked of other things. The estate had been signed off so the house could go on the market any time.

'Can you get that moving for me?' Kenneth asked.

'I'll ask Myra from our property department to go over and measure up. She'll do a valuation.'

'I'll have to clear it out,' Kenneth said. 'I've been putting that off.'

The sun had dipped behind the hill and it was chilly so they walked faster, Hugh seeming in better condition than when they had started.

'Catherine will help you with the house,' he said.

'Might be better to put it on the market in the spring,' Kenneth said, 'but then it'll lie empty all winter.'

'It might anyway,' Hugh pointed out.

'Ach, it's a burden. We'll just get on with it.'

Below them, the road appeared and they fell silent, the day coming to a close. For a moment, Kenneth wondered if it was the responsibility of his mother's house that made him feel heavy, a stone in his chest, then he thought of what Hugh had told him, and knew it was another kind of weight altogether, lying on him now.

8

Helen was upstairs when Joe came in. She heard the door slam. He was not good at closing doors quietly, however often she said hush, the children might be asleep.

She looked down at him from the landing as he pulled off his leather coat.

'It's freezing out there,' he said. 'Baltic. Time we went somewhere a bit warmer.'

She took this for a joke, or perhaps a hint that they might go on holiday. So she forgot her annoyance with him, that he was so late, that he had come in and banged the door.

'That would be lovely,' she said, putting her arms around him. His hands and face were icy. 'Oh, how cold you are. Come in to the warm. Have you had something to eat?'

'Yeah, yeah, I had a meal in the pub.'

'What pub?'

He did not answer but moved away to the sideboard to get a beer out. 'Want one?'

'No thanks. I was actually just going to bed.'

'What time is it?' He glanced at the clock. 'On you go then, I'll stay up a while.'

'Is something wrong?'

'I'm tired, that's all.' He sat down with his beer.

'Will I get you a glass?'

'Don't bother.'

She hesitated by the door, then came back into the room and sat next to him on the sofa. 'Where were you, Joe? I feel a fool not knowing, when people ask.'

'Who was asking?' He was alert to her now.

'Somebody rang up. He didn't leave a name, just asked where you were and when you would be back.'

'What did you say?'

'That I didn't know. I *never* know, but I didn't say that.'

'Did he leave a message?'

'No. I'm tired of it, Joe, sick of being in the dark and you being out all the time.'

'Ok, fair enough. Let's have a different life.'

'What do you mean?'

'I think we should go away for a while. Somewhere warmer. Have the rest of the winter abroad. Then we'll see.'

'But I'm working! I have two days a week now.'

'Oh, give that up. What does it matter, a few hours at that poxy school? You're always complaining about it anyway.'

'It's my *job*. I can't just let them down.'

He laughed. 'You're fed up, but you'd rather have that job than come to Spain with me.'

'Spain?'

'Or Malta. I fancy Malta. Or Tunisia, nice and hot. What do you think?'

He must be joking. She said shakily, 'You don't really mean it, do you?'

He got up and began pacing about. The living room was too

274

small for this; he seemed to fill it with his restless energy. Helen got up too. Before she could say anything more he turned to face her and grabbed her hands.

'Listen, I need to get away for a while. Can you be ready, get the kids ready, in a couple of days? You don't even need to pack in your job, just come with me. What does it matter? You won't need it anyway. We're not coming back here, whatever we do.'

He did not mean, go for a holiday, have a short break or a few winter months in the sun.

'Why do you have to get away?'

'Don't ask. It's better if you don't know about it. Trust me.'

This was the one thing she could no longer do.

All the time he was packing up and getting ready to leave, he kept asking her to come with him. He meant it, he did want her. She could not do it. There were moments when she thought she could, but those moments were as panicky and fearful as the many more when she knew she had to stay.

'The house,' she said at one point, trying to gather her wits. 'You're still going to pay for it, aren't you?'

'What? Sure. I'll put some money in the account. You deal with it, ok?'

'Deal with what?'

'All the bills and stuff. You'll be fine. If it works out, there'll be plenty money. Just – lie low for a bit. I'll be in touch.'

Then, as she cried out, unable to bear this, 'Joe – what's going on? *Please* don't leave—' he said, 'I wish you'd just come. Why can't you take a chance with me?'

'It's not just me, though, is it? It's Matthew and Luke. I can't take a chance with them.'

For the first time, he seemed to take in what she was saying. 'You're right. You got to think of them. I'm glad I never told you anything.'

'Anything about *what?*'

'Call me,' he said. 'Call me if – well, if you need to.'

'That's it, is it?' She was angry now. 'You're leaving us?'

'No, no, not leaving you, not you and the kids, just the situation. For a while.'

At the last minute, she thought he might yet change his mind. Perhaps he thought she would change hers. At any rate, they gazed at each other in silence, over the bags and suitcases he had packed, filling the little hallway of their house. It seemed his life was in those suitcases, not with her at all. The flight was a late evening one and he had a taxi waiting. It had all happened so fast she had been, she realised, in a stupid dream. This was real; they were separating. He won't come back, she thought, he's in trouble and he's getting out before it's too late.

Upstairs, Luke began to cry.

'What will I say if they – if anyone – comes looking for you?'

'Nothing. I'm away working, you're not sure where. That's all you need to say. It's true anyhow.'

'Is it?'

Suddenly he seized her, his mouth on hers, urgent and desperate, but he drew back before she could even put her arms around him. 'Say bye to the kids for me.'

'You should do that yourself,' she said. 'You should at least do that.'

'I can't.' On his dark lashes was the glitter of tears.

'Joe. Oh, my love.'

The taxi driver sounded his horn. Joe snatched up two of his bags and took them outside. It was a cold clear night, the path icy. At the gate, he almost skidded, then righted himself. As he always would.

She could not just go to bed. She settled Luke again, then went from bedroom to bathroom, downstairs, kitchen to living room, unable to settle, unable to think what she should do. She felt numb.

'I have the children,' she told herself, 'I have them.' It was all she had, perhaps, if there was no money, if he had cleared out their joint account. *He wouldn't do that.* First thing tomorrow, she must check. Or she could run up to the bank at the end of the road, on the corner of the main street, take out cash and check the balance.

Heart in mouth, she ran all the way. She had never left the children in the house on their own before. At the corner, jabbing her card in the cash machine, she began to panic. She did not like this part of the street at night, not trusting it to be safe. What if she were attacked on the way back, knocked to the ground, unconscious, nobody would know which was her house, where her children were, who she was? She snatched the money and receipt, conscious of someone behind her, waiting his turn. Or maybe waiting to take her cash?

She ran all the way back to the house and let herself in, breathless. She had not even looked at the receipt.

All was silent, the house warm and quiet. In the hall she unscrewed the square of paper and read it. Balance £621.64. Was that right? Shouldn't there be more? Now she knew the foolhardiness of the way they had lived, the rashness of allowing him to deal in cash, not querying him about money. She had her own money, her own separate savings. Thank God she had taken Catherine's advice, however reluctantly at the time. We're completely committed to each other so we should share our money, she had said, and Catherine had answered, 'You need your own. Just in case.'

In case of what? This, the unforeseen and terrible situation she now found herself in. With her children.

Later, she said to Catherine, 'I cried myself to sleep. Then I woke in the night and thought, why was I crying? Pointless.'

In a way, it was a relief. She was free.

9

'I've got something to tell you,' Helen said.

'Something nice?' Catherine knew already from her sister's voice it could not be, but hoped she was wrong.

'Joe's left.'

'What do you mean, left?'

'Left the country.'

Because Catherine said nothing, stunned, Helen began to explain, but it sounded muddled. Apparently, Joe was not to blame in any way.

'So why didn't you go with him?' Catherine asked. 'You adore him. To the point of – oh, never mind. So why not go with him?'

'I was frightened. I thought – what if I can't come back? Home. There could be years, living in God knows – Spain, Portugal, some *alien* place. I couldn't see you again, or Mum.'

'Mum?'

'Well, ok. You, Flora, Hugh.'

Catherine said. 'Is Joe in trouble? Is it serious?'

'Not really. He just said he needed to be away for a while.'

'For God's sake. It *must* be serious.'

'Oh, Cathy, I don't know.'

'Thank God you didn't go with him.'

'Please don't sound so angry with me.'

'I'm not. I'm angry with him. But as long as you and the children … Where has he gone?'

'I don't know. Spain maybe. Don't ask, there's no point now. I'm just hoping nobody turns up here to ask me.'

'Are you safe, Helen, are you and the children safe?'

'Of course we are, why wouldn't we be?' Her voice trembled, so that Catherine felt shaky too. What had Helen got herself into?

'Are *you* all right?' Helen asked at last, making an effort.

'I'm all right, but there is something I have to tell you. I've been putting it off for ages, but I can't any longer. It's about Hugh. He has cancer.'

'Oh God,' Helen cried, 'I've made such a mess of everything.'

'Helen—'

'Tell me about Hugh. Please. I can't stand this. Why does everything happen at once?'

Catherine was asking herself the same question. By the time she had explained about Hugh, the chemotherapy, and the likely way things would go, Helen was crying.

'I'm coming up,' she said. 'Joe was right about one thing – the job doesn't matter, but that's not why I couldn't go with him. It was him, I was frightened and I didn't know what he was involved in. But I'll come up and stay with you, you have that great big house now, you and Kenneth, it will be all right, just for a while. I have to see Hugh.'

'You're not making any sense,' Catherine said. 'There's nothing you can do, any of us can do. We just have to wait and see how well the chemotherapy works.'

'Oh God, he's going to die, isn't he?'

'He's going to have treatment. He might be fine. He's not going to die yet, at any rate.'

'I don't know how you can be so cool. I'm coming to see him, you're always asking me to come and stay, well, now I can.'

'I'm sorry, I know you're upset, but Hugh's going to feel awful on these high doses of chemo. Wait till the course is finished, then come and see him.'

Finally, Helen calmed down and agreed. When Catherine tentatively broached Christmas for a visit instead, Helen was clear: 'We're staying here. The kids have been invited to parties, I have friends here and Mum's on her own if I don't go there on Christmas Day.'

Impressed and faintly guilty, Catherine said, 'That's really good of you.'

'The worst thing will be telling her Joe's not here, but she'll have to know sometime.'

'Will you tell her the truth?'

'I would if I knew what it was.'

10

After Christmas, the snow came. The Sinclair house was unsold, so Kenneth kept the storage heaters on. The last thing he needed was a burst pipe.

'I'll be in Ullapool for a meeting tomorrow so I could look in on my way home,' Catherine said.

It was Sunday evening, early in January. Hugh had been with them for dinner and was getting up to go home. Outside, the sky was clear, the air frosty.

'Mind how you go,' Catherine said. 'It's icy out there.'

'At least it's not snowing.' Hugh leaned to kiss her cheek. 'Thank you. Lovely dinner.'

'I wish you could have eaten more of it.'

'Not the dinner's fault. Anyway, let's see what this treatment does.'

He spoke as if the chemotherapy beginning next week might make him feel better, and able to eat again. Catherine, anxious for him, was afraid it would not.

The road back from Ullapool was clear, though the sky was heavy and the first snowflakes were falling through the darkening afternoon as she turned into the drive at Rosemount. There was a light on upstairs. It must be Kenneth, but where was his car? She got out and went round to the back as she usually did.

The porch was not locked, and through the half-glazed kitchen door she could see the light was on there too. She hesitated. No, this was the Highlands – it wasn't a burglar or a squatter, more likely someone from Hugh's office or Sinclair Construction. Only – where was the car or van that had brought them? Perhaps it was in the lane behind the house. It must be *someone* she knew. Just go in, she told herself, and opened the door.

Gilbert was standing by the cooker, a tin in his hand. He had not heard her, and gave a cry, dropping the tin.

'Oh my God, Catherine!'

'Sorry, I gave you a fright, but you had me worried. Where on earth did you come from? Are you all right?'

He was thinner than ever, or she had forgotten how thin he was, his long legs in tight jeans, his crumpled jacket rubbed at the lapels and frayed at the ends of the sleeves, hanging loose on him. His hair was longer, straggling over his collar. As Catherine came towards him, intending an embrace, she changed her mind and smiled instead, clasping his arm. He smelled of old clothes.

'I was going to heat up some beans,' he said. 'Can you remember how to work this cooker?'

'It's as well you're here tonight,' Catherine said. 'Kenneth's going to have the system drained later this week. He's been worried about burst pipes.'

'How could I live here then? He'd have to undrain it.'

'Live here?'

'It's half my house, isn't it?'

It was not. She knew that much, though not exactly why. Kenneth would not talk about it. Good riddance, he had said about Gilbert, but here he was, back in his mother's house for the first time since her death. Rose had told him, after all.

'Nobody likes Rose,' he said when she asked, 'but she looks out for me.'

He sounded fretful, all his usual liveliness gone. It was very cold in the kitchen and the storage heater seemed to give out less warmth than ever.

'You can't stay here, it's freezing. What about the cottage – didn't you want to go back there?'

These were not the things she should be saying but in this strange meeting, in this cold unwelcoming house that nobody liked (or did Gilbert, after all?) she felt paralysed, frozen herself.

'I got the bus,' he said. At first, this wasn't any kind of answer. Then she realised he had no transport. To get to the cottage would have been impossible.

What she would have done, had he been anyone else – no, had Kenneth been anyone else – was simply take him home. He could have a bath, hot food and a bed for the night. But she did not dare face Kenneth with that.

'Actually, I don't think Kenneth has done anything about the cottage. It will be even colder,' she said, 'and I don't know if the road's passable. It's snowing again.'

'I can stay here.'

'What about tomorrow? You can't really stay here, can you?'

'Will you give me a lift to the cottage?'

She looked helplessly round the kitchen. Gilbert had dropped a rucksack on the floor and it was spilling clothes, a grubby towel and a paperback copy of a book called *The Journey to Peace*.

'I don't suppose you have anything nicer to eat with you?' he asked, frowning at the tin of beans. He looked gaunt, like someone who rarely had a decent meal.

They had cleared the house of perishable food long ago. 'I'll bring you something tomorrow. What would you like?' As soon as she said this she knew it was a mistake. He dived for his rucksack and took out a crumpled notebook.

'I'll write you a list, shall I?'

He sat at the table, and wearily, she took a chair opposite. Upside down, she saw he was beginning, in beautiful copperplate, with 'Duck liver pâté'.

'You what?'

'I said I'd take him some food tomorrow, and drive out to the cottage if the road's clear, to see if it's habitable. I didn't think you'd want him in Rosemount as it's on the market. I didn't tell him that.'

'You should have thrown him out. He has absolutely no right to be there.'

'Oh, don't be ridiculous – it's his home.'

'Not now.'

He had been on site and was still in his work clothes. The boots he was usually so careful to remove at the front door, left puddles of melting snow on the living room floor as he paced up and down in front of the stove that she had just lit. She had not put enough wood on, so it was already dying down. Distracted, she knelt to add more sticks and open the vents a little.

'Leave that! Tell me exactly what happened.'

'You want a fire, don't you?'

Flora had heard their raised voices. She hovered in the doorway. 'What's wrong?'

'Just go up and do your homework—'

'I'm hungry. When's dinner?' Her gaze followed Kenneth's footsteps. 'You've left snow all over the floor. You're always going on at me and my friends about your precious oak floor.'

Kenneth turned. Seeing his face, Flora stepped back.

'Out,' he said. 'Upstairs. You heard your mother.'

She opened her mouth to argue, then thought better of it. 'What*ever*.'

The fire had begun to burn up now. Catherine closed a vent and stood up. 'Please don't speak to her like that.'

'He was in the house?'

'Yes, when I got there. Heating up a tin of beans.'

'We'll just have to hope he doesn't wreck the place or set it on fire before I can get him out. Since you've not managed it.'

'Kenneth, it's snowing. It's freezing outside and he has no transport. What exactly do you think I should have done?'

He suddenly became aware of his wet footprints, as if Flora's rebuke had only just registered. 'For Christ's sake – look at the floor.' He hauled off his boots and, striding past her, flung them into the porch. 'Can you clear this up?'

'Me?'

'Don't get on your high horse – it won't take you a minute. I need to call Hugh.'

She could barely speak, she was so angry. She went straight to the kitchen. Flora had to be fed, at any rate, though she could not now imagine the three of them sitting down to eat together. She stopped, taking a deep breath. This was foolish: he was upset, so she must try to keep calm if he couldn't. Two of them in a temper would be disastrous. And she had to think of Flora, witnessing this, hearing too much.

After a few moments, she fetched a bucket and cleaning cloth, and went to dispose of the wet patches on the floor. Flora was playing music, loudly, but she could hear from the office upstairs the sound of Kenneth's voice on the phone.

She had gone back to the kitchen to get dinner ready when he came in.

'Hugh thinks we should let him have the cottage, for now. He'll most likely disappear soon enough when he realises there are no rich pickings.'

'Pickings?'

'He's obviously heard about Mum. You can disabuse him, by the way, when you take him his food parcel, of any notion that he inherits a thing.'

'But he *must* – he's your brother. I don't know how your parents left things, but he will have some claim. Surely Hugh told you that?'

He glanced round. 'Flora still upstairs?'

'Yes. The music?'

'Oh. Yeah.' He sat down heavily on a kitchen chair, and indicated the one opposite. Slowly, Catherine sat too.

'What is it?'

'He's not my brother.'

'Well, I know he was adopted, but what difference does that make?'

He told her what he had told Hugh. Catherine sat silent for a few minutes.

'So – do you remember him coming to the house? What happened?'

'I was a kid, so I believed what I was told.'

'What did they tell you?'

'They wanted me not to be an only child. They thought it would be good for me to have a brother or sister, so they were adopting Gilbert. They seemed to think I'd be pleased when they brought this *toddler* home.'

'But you weren't. Were you jealous?'

287

'It was far too late and I was much too old – fourteen, for God's sake. I don't know if they'd been trying to have another baby for years, or trying to adopt. Look, there's no point in raking over all that stuff now.'

'But Kenneth—' She felt she had to make the case for justice, since Gilbert could not make it for himself. 'They brought him up as their son. Surely you have a moral obligation to share your inheritance with him.'

'*Moral?*'

'I think he does have a claim,' she said. 'You're being grossly unfair. Not to say greedy. As if we haven't enough.' She stood up. 'It's because of me that he knows. I told Rose, and she must have told Gilbert.'

The minute she words were out, she was sorry. She had never seen him so furious, his face suffused with colour, his hands gripping the table edge. He stood up.

'You're not really with me, are you? Where's your fucking loyalty? Not to me. Anyone but me.'

He turned swiftly and went out. A few minutes later the front door banged and she heard the car starting up. Oh God, she thought, he's gone to Rosemount.

From the top of the stairs, Flora called, 'Mum. Can I get a pizza out the freezer? I'm actually starving.'

Kenneth came home late. Catherine was sitting by a dying fire, growing colder in the big chair beside it.

'You're still up.'

He filled the doorway in his heavy tweed coat.

'You're white – it's snowing again?'

'Just started.' He went out to the front door to shake the snow from his coat.

'Did you see him?' she asked when he came in again.

'I'm having a dram. Want one?'

She shook her head. He came to sit in the chair opposite her, his face ruddy with the cold, his reddened hands clasping a crystal glass a third full of malt whisky, winking amber in lamplight. After a moment, he said, 'I didn't go to Rosemount. If I'd gone there, I'd have killed him.'

'Where did you go?'

'Hugh's.'

'How is he?' She was weak with relief. Thank God he hadn't tried to confront Gilbert. He seemed steady now. Perhaps because of the emotion generated between them, perhaps because of Hugh, a sob rose in her throat but she swallowed it.

'He's all right. He knows it's a long business.'

They sat in silence for a few moments. Catherine began to think of going in to work tomorrow feeling as she did, but it would take her mind off this, and Kenneth, the problem with Gilbert.

'I'm going to bed.'

He drained his glass and got up to refill it. 'I'll sit up a while.'

'Don't—' *Don't have another drink*, she wanted to say. Seeing his face, she stopped, and went out, leaving him on his own.

In the morning, there was the usual rush to get Flora off to the school bus and herself out of the house and on the road to Inverness. Kenneth had left early, though there would be nothing happening on the site until daylight, if then, given the weather. Driving to work, careful on the snowy road, she felt calmer again and was able to think clearly. She could take a couple of hours off in the afternoon, get some food for Gilbert and drive over to Rosemount.

289

Colette was not in the office. Down the corridor, in the photocopying room, she could hear voices, a stir of excitement. Something must have happened. She switched on her computer and went to make a mug of tea. The small kitchen was on the floor below her office, and past the room where there was still a hubbub of speculation. Colette, seeing her, called out –

'Cath – you heard?'

Colette was the only person who called her Cath. She had not scotched this when it first happened, and was stuck with it now.

'What is it?'

Both the large machines in the room were in operation so above the wheeze and thud of their work, of papers slotting into trays with a regular swish, Colette said, 'James had a heart attack last night. Susie's been telling us.'

Susie, the Director's secretary, was one of the huddle of people in the room, but she broke away.

'How is he? Is it bad?' Catherine asked.

'He's in a high-dependency ward. They're going to see whether he needs a bypass, Paula told me.'

'I'm sorry, that's awful. What a worry for them.'

Later, at her desk, she realised there were several decisions she would have to make without James's endorsement. Perhaps she should go and see the Director. Before she could make up her mind to this, Colette put her phone down and said, 'Susie says will you go up and see Duncan.'

The Director was behind a desk as clear and tidy as it always was. He never seemed to have any papers to deal with. Perhaps as you moved up the ranks, Catherine thought, you had more and more people to take the paper from you.

'Catherine,' he said. 'Take a seat.'

So she did, and he told her that within the last half-hour he had learned that James had died in hospital.

It was almost five o'clock, and of course dark, when she remembered about Gilbert. She would have to try to see him on her way home.

Outside, it had begun snowing again, a fine powdery stuff that drifted across the car park, hazing everything in a white mist. The road worsened outside Inverness and Catherine went past Strathpeffer and home reluctantly, having stopped in Dingwall to buy groceries. She had lost Gilbert's list, but had anyway substituted it with milk, bread, bacon and other more mundane supplies.

There were no lights on at Rosemount and the house was empty. There were signs, certainly, of Gilbert's presence: a sink full of unwashed dishes, an unmade bed upstairs in the room next to his mother's, a wet towel on the bathroom floor. Where on earth had he gone? Perhaps back to London, realising there was nothing for him here. And yet, why should he? He had been convinced he was about to inherit half a house, money – something, at least.

She tidied up, washed the dishes and left, cold and anxious. Though she had no idea how he might have got there, she could not check the cottage because the snow was falling so heavily she was even unsure of the road home. At least her phone had a signal and she had recharged it at work. If she had to, she could call Kenneth for help. Her own car did not have four-wheel drive.

As she drove, she thought about James. She could not believe he was gone. He had been a good manager, giving her opportunities, responsibility and support. Now what? She wondered who would come in to take his job.

'I'm afraid this means more work for all of us for a while,' Duncan had said, 'but especially you. I know I can rely on you – James always did.'

Perhaps that was encouragement enough. Why should *she* not apply for James's job? Now she was thinking about work and the future. She could do nothing about Kenneth or Gilbert, but she could plan for herself.

11

When the roads had been cleared, and a day or two had passed without snowfall, Kenneth drove out to Rosemount. It was after eight, so he was going there in darkness, which he would have preferred not to do. But work had only just got moving again on two of his sites, after an impossible couple of weeks, and they were trying to catch up. He had been home briefly, to eat. He knew Catherine did not want him to confront Gilbert, and they had parted without a word. It was still piercingly cold and during the afternoon clouds had come in from the west, black and heavy. More snow to come.

Because Catherine had cleared up, there was no sign Gilbert had been in the house. The smell of cigarettes lingered in cold air, but in time it would vanish. He was angry about that, on his mother's behalf.

He really had gone. Yet Kenneth hesitated, as if there was a need to check again. He found himself in his mother's bedroom looking around as if there was something he must still do. Catherine had helped him clear his mother's clothes, and her small collection of jewellery was now in his own house. What else could there be? He opened the drawers of the dressing table one after another. They were all empty. Then he saw what he had not noticed before, that there was something under the bed, the corner just visible. He knelt and drew it out. It was a shortbread tin with a thick layer of dust on the surface of the lid with its photograph of Balmoral Castle. He took the lid off, heart quickening at the little heap of old photographs.

They were all of Gilbert and himself, mostly of Gilbert. Here he was as a dancing child, skinny and big-eyed, and at his side, or in the background, Kenneth, the sturdy, impassive older brother. The garden, the house at Christmas, a rare holiday with his aunt and uncle in Uist, and of course, the cottage, his grandparents on the bench at the front door, Gilbert between them. The memories blurred, but the feelings he had had then rose up, and it was as if something obstructed his lungs, making it hard to breathe.

There was nothing else in the tin. He put the lid on and shoved it under the bed, out of sight. Eventually, he supposed, when the house was sold, he would throw it out.

He shut up the house and got into his car. For several minutes he sat there without starting the engine. You could give him the cottage, Hugh had suggested. You're not using it and you don't want the hassle of letting it out so why not? Because, Kenneth had told him, then he'd be *here*, hanging round my neck for ever. Sell it then, Hugh said. Give him the money.

As he turned the key and the engine fired, Kenneth thought about this solution: the cottage sold, money in his hands, Gilbert might disappear to London for good. But there was no guarantee. He might hang on, start another useless business, the money slipping through his hands like water. Then what? Turn up on the doorstep, sponging on Catherine. Intolerable.

He took the road west, to the cottage.

The last part of the way, up the track past the farm, was difficult, but there had been a vehicle ahead of him, and he kept to its tracks. These stopped at the cottage. There was a car in the pull-in, with a mere dusting of snow on its roof and bonnet, so it had not been here long. He was surprised to see it was a black BMW, not new, but big, a top-of-the-range model. He got out and walked round it, peering inside. Gilbert's, despite what he had said to Catherine? Surely not. He never had the money for something like this. Not Rose's either, or a hire car. It must have been borrowed from someone else. Or the someone else was here.

Now he looked at the house. There was a light on downstairs in the living room. A thin spiral of smoke drifted from the chimney. Much overgrown, the path was passable because it was deep winter, vegetation rotted and died back. In several inches of snow there were footprints, coming and going.

At first neither of them moved, when he opened the living room door. The air was thick with smoke, smelling sweet like incense, but not incense. Gilbert was lying on the sofa, his eyes closed, a roll-up between his fingers, drooping over the side, the glowing tip almost touching the carpet. Rose was in the chair, that had been his mother's bedroom chair, and she was smoking too, but she was fully awake, and her dark gaze met his.

'Your car?' he asked, not having any idea what else to say. He was too taken aback to be angry, at first. And yet, what else did he expect?

'She rescued me,' Gilbert said sleepily, opening his eyes.

'You're going to set fire to the bloody carpet if you don't put that thing out.'

Gilbert did not move, but Rose leaned over and took the cigarette from him, laying it in the tiled hearth.

'Nice to see you too, dear brother.'

'What are you up to? You can't stay here.'

'Isn't this part of my inheritance?'

Give him the cottage? He would see him in hell first. Him and his sidekick. Rose might be the one he had to reckon with. He had stopped in the doorway. It was as if he could not go in and join them, could not with the slightest move or gesture, condone their presence.

'You want a cup of tea?' Rose asked. 'Just going to put the kettle on.' She passed him with a smell of patchouli. He recoiled, but something leapt in him, a flash of lust filling him with shame. She was small, ripe, grubby, and she had no beauty, but he could not ignore her animal presence. She went into the kitchen, shutting the door behind her. Disturbed, he moved into the living room and sat down, leaning towards Gilbert, his hands on his knees.

'What do you want?'

Gilbert sat up. 'I knew you'd be against me. Rose said you would. She said we'd have to get a lawyer. Where am I going to get money for a lawyer?' He made a move as if he would stand, but trembled and gave up, sinking into the indentation of his body on the sofa cushions. 'Oh God, I can't think straight.'

'No wonder. You're out of your head.' Kenneth got up. 'I'm giving you two days. I'll be back then. Make sure you've cleared out. Understand?'

Rose, in the doorway with two mugs of tea, said, 'Doesn't he have any rights? Like, half shares in his own mother's property?'

Whatever he decided, he could not speak about it while Rose was here, with the two of them goading him, blinding him with rage.

'Mind your own fucking business. It's nothing to do with you. I want the pair of you out by the weekend.'

There was no way past her in the doorway without physically handling her. At the last minute, she stepped back. Passing her, he kicked something aside that toppled over with a clang. It was the boot-scraper that had been brought inside to prop a door open. Furious, he kicked it again and strode out of the house.

He had driven all the way to the main road before he calmed down. He should have told Gilbert that if he got out now, he would let him have the cottage, or at least the money from the sale. That would be the bargain. Why give them till the weekend? He should get them out now, then it would be settled. Rose could drive: she seemed compos mentis, even if he wasn't.

He turned the car and drove back up the track. The strange glow in the living room window meant nothing at first, was just firelight or a lamp flickering. Then he realised it was something else. In the seven or eight minutes he had been gone, they had set fire to – to what he did not know. But there was fire.

13

The fire was less than he feared, though the smoke was terrible, billowing through the open doorway, choking. Rose was flapping at it with a tea towel, as if fanning the flames was all she could think of to do.

'What the hell happened here?'

'It was only a fag end – he dropped it by *mistake* – then the whole bloody thing went up—'

He shoved her roughly out of the way and dived for the rug. It was an old rag rug his grandmother had made – he had a second's sentimental pang before he flung it on the armchair, smothering, heavy and smelling of coal dust and smoke. That was what you got for having ancient furniture, a danger, going up in flames at the touch of a live spark. If that was all it had been.

There were no flames now, just smoke thick as smog making him cough and gasp. Rose leaned in the doorway, white-faced with shock. Where was his brother?

When the smouldering had subsided, he took the rug away and threw onto it the contents of a bottle of mineral water left on the sideboard. Then he stood back and brushed his black hands down his jeans and smeared his arm across his face, clearing his eyes.

'Where is he?'

She said nothing but there came from above them an eerie high-pitched giggle. He pushed past her to the tiny hallway, and at the top of the stairs, gleeful and unsteady, Gilbert hopped from one giddy foot to the other. Rage took over and he would have been up there in a flash, grabbing him – the bastard, high as a kite, heedless, *stupid*. Gilbert, seeing his brother come for him, sidestepped, caught his foot in a loose ripple of carpet, swayed, teetered, overbalanced.

If it had been anyone else Kenneth would have stayed where he was, caught him, breaking the fall. He was so much bigger and bulkier he could easily have done it.

But did not.

Gilbert came crashing down in a silence more frightening than any cry. It was Rose who shrieked. She was crouched over him, sobbing. 'Gil, Gil, you wanker, get up, get *up!*' She shook his shoulder and tried to raise his head, but Gilbert, eyes half-closed, did not answer. She turned to Kenneth. He was stone; he could not speak. 'What's *wrong* with him?' she begged.

What he meant to say was don't move him, we'll get a doctor. He heard the words in his head but he could not speak. Gilbert was very still; he must be unconscious. In a moment, he would come round. Still he could not speak.

'Christ, Kenneth – *do* something!'

When she turned back to Gilbert, there was blood on her hands, the hands that had held him. A little trickle of blood seeped from his head where it lay, awkward, on the floor. The iron boot-scraper lay on its side next to him. She stared at her hands, then in disgust wiped them on the rug, over and over. 'He's bleeding, he's hurt his head – oh *fuck*, look at all the *blood!*'

'For God's sake,' Kenneth said, his voice coming free at last, 'stop that wailing. Shut *up*.' He knelt down, but did not touch either of them. Then he forced his hand to Gilbert's warm neck and felt for the pulse. Something moved there, faintly. He stood up.

'I'm going for a doctor. Don't move him, just stay here.'

Her whole body was quivering as if seized by palsy. Kenneth put a hand firmly on her shoulder for a second and gripped it. 'You don't have to do anything. If he comes round, don't give him alcohol. *Anything*.'

He moved towards the door. She was still shaking. Jesus, they were a pair – how had he got into this? It was all unreal and he moved as through a dream, not believing any of it was happening. He got into the car and drove on to the turning place. There was a widening of the lane where the strip of woodland began, of alder, rowan and silver birch, the bare bones of the trees coated with white.

As he drove back towards the main road, it began to snow again.

He had a few seconds of hesitation, passing the Foresters' farm. He could stop there and use the landline to call an ambulance. No, quicker to get John, a doctor. He had decided to go for John Heslop who lived in Garve and was not so far away. He need never tell Jim and Maureen Forrester and no one else need be involved. He would get John to come and take a look. Maybe it was nothing, maybe Gilbert would come round in a few minutes. He should phone John – that might be quicker. Now and again he checked his phone for a signal. There was none at the cottage and you had to reach the main road before it was strong enough for a call. Then he gave up. He would tell John when he got there, and take him back with him.

In the snow it was difficult to see the turning for John's drive and he almost went past it. Concentrating, focusing only on this, he changed down gears, unable to risk braking, and got himself up the short drive. When he put his lights off, he saw the house was in darkness and there was no sign of a vehicle in the car port. He had lost track of time – how late was it? He got out and, plunging through snow that was deeper here in this sheltered place, he reached the front door. He hesitated then rapped hard, making his knuckles sting. No bell – didn't he have a fucking bell? He couldn't see one.

No light came on; no one answered. In the unearthly silence, snow falling steadily on his shoulders, on the doorstep in front of him, he waited, growing colder, all the heat of what had happened, the fear and drama, draining out of him. Slowly he turned and walked back to his car. A good deal of snow came in with him as he got into the driver's seat.

He sat there, not moving, growing colder still. Around him snow whirled, settling on the windscreen in seconds, whiteness against blackness, the empty world outside. He laid his head on his arms on the steering wheel, breathing deeply. He should just have called an ambulance. Indeed, he should do that now, as soon as he got a signal. Then he decided to go back first, to check there was no change, to look again, know for certain his brother was breathing. In the end, it would be quicker to get him in the car and take him to Raigmore, than wait for the ambulance to come to them. His rational mind told him this. Perhaps it made sense, perhaps not. He no longer knew.

For it was in his mind now, the thought he had pushed aside, that Rose had not been able to articulate, that the fall might have killed Gilbert. He allowed himself to think that might have happened. Whether it had or not, he should go back. He should turn the car again before the snow was any worse. Yet he went on sitting with his head on his arms, breathing in his own sweat, the day's exhaustion and grime, smoke and coal dust. How much easier his life would be if Gilbert were dead.

Perhaps he sat there for two minutes, perhaps longer. Five, ten. Afterwards, he told himself he had been in shock and time meant something different when you were stunned like that. Eventually he heaved himself up and turned the key in the ignition, edged the car round and headed back to the cottage. The snow was thick on the road and he engaged four-wheel drive, to make sure he did not skid on the bends. There was no possibility he could go at any speed. His own tracks, he realised, would have filled by the time he reached the lane. His heart was beating so fast and hard it seemed audible, but he must keep steady, he must get there in one piece.

The tracks, after all, were still there for his wheels on the lane, but the headlights showed only whirling snow against the darkness, and it was familiarity with the way that kept him straight, though the wheels threatened to lose purchase on the last steep part. Once he thought he might have to get out and walk. Then he saw the lights of the cottage. He took his car to the turning place and moved it round, since later it might be more difficult to do that.

There was still, of course, an overpowering smell of smoke, but the fog itself had cleared inside the house, so he could see the hall as he opened the door. Fear leapt up – what was he coming back to?

They were not here. Gilbert was no longer lying on the floor; Rose was no longer kneeling beside him. Relief turned him to water, so that it was all he could do not to sink to his knees. He gripped the door, then slowly, closed it behind him.

'Rose?' His voice echoed in silence. There was no reply. He

went into the ruined living room where the charred armchair stood askew by the fire, the rug beside it. The smell of smoke was overpowering.

Empty.

Cursorily, he checked the other rooms, then ran upstairs. They would be in a bedroom, Gilbert resting.

Nothing.

Nothing of theirs remained, only the detritus they always left: empty crisp packets and cigarette cartons, beer cans, plastic carrier bags and dirty food containers.

They had disappeared.

He bounded downstairs and outside. In the dark and snow he had not noticed that the BMW had also gone. He leaned against the front door, weak with relief. Gilbert was all right and they had legged it. He was angry they'd gone like that – what if he had come back with John Heslop? Such a fool he would have looked. That would please his brother.

He checked that there was no fire smouldering anywhere, even in the grate, before he shut up the cottage and got into the car. He could come back later in daylight, assess the damage and clear up properly. Then, as if all will to action had simply drained out of him, he sat there without moving, his mind blank.

Of course Gilbert was not fine. Of course he was not sitting merrily in the passenger seat of Rose's car (*Rose's car?*) while they mocked him as they drove away.

Gilbert had been dying when he left him. He knew that, as surely as he knew himself.

When he got home his own house was in darkness. Catherine and Flora would be in bed and asleep. Thank God. He took his boots off and left them at the front door, then crept up to the main bathroom, not the shower room off their bedroom. He did not want to wake anyone. He stripped and stuffed his clothes in the laundry basket, then went into the shower, the shock of cold water stunning him, then turning to hot as he stood there. He let it run as long as he dared, scrubbed himself, got the smell of smoke from his hair and skin, from under his fingernails.

At last he got out to towel himself dry. Still the smoke seemed to cling. It must be coming from his clothes. His skin smelled of that shower gel stuff Catherine bought. He used the towel to wipe steam from the mirror. His own face looked back at him, eyes reddened by smoke, skin pale in the white bathroom light.

He went silently along the hall to the bedroom where Catherine, he hoped, was asleep. She turned as he slipped into bed. 'Where have you been all this time – oh—' Her hand on his skin. 'You're damp.'

'Had a shower,' he mumbled. 'Go back to sleep.' He heaved over and away from her, pulling the duvet round his shoulders. After a moment, he felt her do the same, and they lay back to back, apart and in silence. She sighed, but soon her breathing grew faint and he thought she was asleep.

In the morning Gilbert would be all right and he would have been worrying for nothing. Worry! That was not the word. He knew, his eyes opening in darkness, that he both wanted Gilbert to be dead and feared it. *I should have called an ambulance.* He could not think why he had not. He lay awake, listening to the thud of his heart, pounding in his ears.

The snow stayed on the high ground until the beginning of March. Then there were storms, washing melting snow downhill, swelling the burns and raising the rivers to the lip of their banks. On Ben Macdui the body of a lost climber was revealed, a man for whom the mountain rescue team had searched for nearly two weeks at the end of January.

Everything comes to the surface in the end, Kenneth thought, reading the report in Elsie's *Press & Journal*. All you can do is wait.

Getting to the Other Side
2004–5

1

'I shouldn't complain,' Hugh said. 'I've had much more time than they thought. Than I expected.'

'It's so unfair.'

'Oh – fair.' He smiled. 'You're old enough to know nothing's *fair.*'

It was a cool September afternoon, a Sunday, and Catherine was making tea. She moved easily around his kitchen, familiar and content. She liked to have something to do and someone to look after. It was a pity about the marriage.

Soon Flora would be going away to university in Edinburgh. After that, Catherine had said, she could be here whenever Hugh needed her.

'We'll see how this lot of chemo goes,' he said. 'I'm sure I can manage.'

'If you don't want me—'

'Catherine.' He clasped her arm, the most he would ever do, that and a peck on the cheek when they said goodbye. 'I like you being here. Hazel Macallum treats me like a halfwit, George doesn't know what to say, and Ronald is just embarrassed. Cancer *is* embarrassing. But you are good company as ever, and restful.'

'This sounds awful,' she said, 'but I like being here much

better than that little house in Inverness. I thought going back to it, when my tenants left, would be the ideal solution. But Flora has hated it. She actually misses Strathpeffer, and for a time she missed Kenneth too, I think, though she'd never admit that. And moving schools again wasn't the best thing for her, at that stage.'

'It's all in the past now, and Flora is doing fine. Stop worrying. But you should leave that wee house if you don't like it.'

'Where would I go? I work in Inverness, and I have good friends there. It makes sense.'

'It's such a pity,' he said sadly.

'What? Oh that, let's not talk about it. You know why I left. He was impossible. After Gilbert set fire to the cottage and then disappeared again he seemed to go mad. I think we were *both* mad for a while.'

'Have some of this nice gingerbread,' Hugh said. 'Beata brought it.'

'How is that working out? She seems nice.'

'These Polish lassies are hard workers,' he said, taking a piece of gingerbread himself, but not eating it. 'Chrissie used to talk all the time, but Beata just gets on with it. She does my ironing too. I've never had such nicely folded shirts.'

Catherine laughed. 'She sounds perfect!'

'Anyway,' he said, 'you know you're welcome here any time.'

'Eat up that gingerbread,' Catherine said. 'You need to put on a bit of weight to cope with the treatment and stay strong.'

He pushed the plate away, overtaken by a wave of exhaustion.

'I have to go to bed for a while,' he said. 'Sorry. You stay as long as you like.'

'*Hugh*. You should have said!'

'It's fine. Stay a while. I like to think of you here.'

'All right. I can do a bit of weeding.'

'One thing,' he said, when he reached the door. Best to say it like this, when she could not argue or comment. 'I've been seeing to my will. Typical lawyer – I'd never made one though I'm always telling other people to make theirs.'

'Oh.' She did not want him to talk about this; nobody did. It was like admitting death was not so far away.

'I have no family now so I'm leaving you the house, you and Helen jointly, now that fellow of hers seems to be off the scene. But he's not to get his hands on it, should he ever turn up.'

Catherine had frozen with shock, but he did not give her a chance to recover. He raised a hand in temporary farewell, and made his way slowly upstairs.

When he rested like this, several times a week, he felt guilty for falling asleep during the day. He had gone on working, mainly from home, but it had not been possible this time to maintain his usual level of commitment.

Despite the reassurance of his consultant that the tumour had responded last time, and might again, the need for this second course of treatment had convinced him he had had his reprieve. He had no faith that he would have another. The imminence of death, and what would happen afterwards, when he was not here to see it, occupied his mind. In quiet moments, he thought of nothing else. He feared he'd become morbid, and with Catherine was determinedly cheerful, lest she should be made miserable too.

His will was a small thing, easy to accomplish once he had made up his mind about the house. The rest was harder. Somehow, he must put his affairs in order: throw out anything he did not want others to see or have; rationalise his investments or sell them; decide which charities were to benefit from the money he would leave. He had once thought of leaving Helen money for her boys, but she had someone to look after her. Except now she had not. Then he had thought of the house. If Catherine was included, he felt the place was safe in their hands. He could trust Catherine. He had not told Kenneth yet.

Kenneth often came to keep him company in the evenings, now they could no longer go on the hill together. He was a changed man; Catherine was right about that. Not mad, perhaps, or not now, but he worked non-stop. His business was his life.

The fire was a long way in the past, but even when it happened, it had taken Kenneth over a week to tell Hugh.

'That's the end of it – the pair of them have gone, thank God. He won't be back.'

'You thought that before,' Hugh said, smiling, but Kenneth's face was grim.

'He deliberately set fire to the cottage.'

'You said he was high on something—'

'Not so high he didn't know what he was doing.'

'But surely they would only endanger themselves – it doesn't make sense.'

'I know what I know,' Kenneth said, and Hugh, with a cold lick of fear, realised there was more, that he would probably never learn. But they had gone; they were out of the way of Kenneth's anger. That could only be a good thing. Yet he was sorry not to have seen Gilbert one last time. He was such a character; he brought to life any room he was in. That Factory – what a place.

Hugh closed his eyes, but as soon as he decided to sleep, he felt more wakeful. Oddly, what came into his mind, as he went over the provisions of his will, was the thought that at least he had no dog to worry about. Bracken had died four years ago, his last Labrador, and he had not replaced her, having had enough experience of the broken-hearted aftermath of losing an animal.

The bedroom was chilly, but he had switched on his electric blanket, so beneath the duvet he was starting to feel warm. How comforting bed was, what a refuge. He knew every inch of his bedroom, knew which books lay on the floor by the bed, read or waiting to be read, knew how the curtains looked when drawn across the windows, the deep velvet folds reaching to the floor, cutting out almost all light. The mahogany dressing table, once his mother's, was too big for any modern house, the mirror spotted now, reflecting a pale green room, a faded carpet, a satin quilted eiderdown. He hardly saw the detail of it, so long had he absorbed this house into his consciousness.

Did Catherine really mean to go on living in that mean little semi in Inverness? Surely not. Perhaps she would want to live here, afterwards. For a moment he resented her, resented the fact that she would go on living beyond his life. That was stupid, a selfish impulse. We do not all die together, friends and relatives. Some must go ahead and plunge into that unknown he had once felt so sure of, growing up with his devout and cheerful parents. How certain they had been that Heaven was there, that life would continue, different and yet recognisable. It had seemed, in his mother's description, like a garden, peaceful and rambling, and always summer.

The garden. In bleaker moments he knew might not see the spring, and divide the clumps of primroses in the shady part next to the shed, or discover how well the new cherry tree fruited. Heaven's garden seemed far less attractive to him than his own, as he went along its paths in his mind, inspecting borders, tying up straggling stems, pruning the forsythia that had grown too high by the wall. He was glad he'd worked so hard in it last summer, but you could never finish all the work of a garden.

He had done what he could. The rest was just waiting.

2

Helen sometimes wondered about Joe's car. In the confusion and misery of his departure, it had not occurred to her to ask him. It was possible he'd got rid of it, though a key for the BMW was in the little bowl on the kitchen windowsill, where he had always dropped it when he came in. The problem was, she did not know where he had kept the car. Sometimes it had been parked in the street, but he had garaged it when it wasn't needed. Not in the Camden lock-up he had had when she first met him: that would be too far away. Perhaps it was stowed where he kept the rest of the goods that were always in transit, just bought or about to be sold. There must be keys for those lock-ups.

She had searched the house, but even when she found a bunch of keys in a drawer in the bedroom, one of which might well have opened a garage, she still didn't know where it was. Joe had not of course taken everything with him. The house was scattered with his possessions: an old leather jacket, cracked and worn smooth at the elbows; rolled up pairs of socks; discarded mobile phones without their SIM cards; CDs, even a couple of ties, one black for funerals, one striped that she had never seen him wear. There were T-shirts in the wash he had forgotten, several of his notebooks in the sideboard, and a watch that no longer worked.

For about a week she searched, trying to find evidence, not just of where the car might be, but of where he might have gone, or of what had precipitated his going. There was nothing that could conceivably be a clue and abruptly she gave up. In the end someone would tell her, or he would come back. In the night, she ached for him and wept, and now and again wondered in which mews or back lane, an expensive car waited for release.

It didn't matter anyway; she still couldn't drive. Living in London meant it had never been necessary, and living with Joe meant she was not encouraged to learn, and after the children were born, had no opportunity. Meanwhile, there *were* her children, and there was work, as much work as she could get. In time, she trained herself not to think about Joe or to encourage Matthew to think of him. One day she cleared out all his possessions, filling the dustbin. By the time Matthew came home from school, there was nothing of Joe left.

Now, more than three and a half years later, she had a full-time teaching job, Luke was at nursery and she had stopped expecting that Joe would come back. She had no idea where he was. Somewhere abroad? Perhaps not even that. He had not been in touch after the first few weeks, when an occasional text message appeared on her phone, making her heart leap with fear and hope. She had tried to get messages to him, but the phone number became unobtainable, and if he had another – of course he did – he had not used it to contact her. Catherine said how strange it was, that Gilbert had disappeared like that too. How could people do that – just change their phone and not give you their address?

'I don't know about Gilbert,' Helen said. 'He was always a bit weird, and once his mother was dead, what was there to keep him? It was different with Joe. He has children, he had *me*.'

315

'Do you think he's all right?' Catherine asked.

They had this conversation, or a variant of it, even now, if rarely. Perhaps they didn't like the unfinishedness of such departures. Helen still wanted an answer, still wanted, when she lay awake, a message telling her not that he was all right – she had stopped caring about that – but that he had *loved* her, that it had been hard for him to go. The tears glittering on the night he left might well have come from fear and pity for himself.

These last few weeks, since Catherine had broken the news that Hugh was to have more chemotherapy, she had thought as much about him and their early marriage, as about Joe. At half-term she planned to leave the boys with her mother, so that she could go alone to the Highlands and see Hugh. Her mother had finally stopped asking when Joe was coming back. 'I never thought I'd have a daughter who was one of those single mothers,' she had remarked recently, 'and now I have two.'

Next, Helen thought furiously, as she packed the children's things, she'll be telling us we made our beds so we just have to lie on them. At this, her knees went weak and she sank onto the bed amid boys' shorts and jumpers, and lay there laughing, then in tears. How ridiculous it all was, love and marriage and crying over men. It all came to the same in the end.

She sat up, shivering. Oh, poor Hugh.

Under a heap of clothes, her mobile started ringing. She dug it out. It was Gaynor; she never gave up. With a sigh, Helen switched her phone to silent. Now and again, Gaynor still called to ask after Joe. They were never going to get their money back. The first call had been a few weeks after he left, a freezing February day, sleet falling so heavily she could not get her phone from her bag and stop in the street to answer it.

When she called back, Gaynor said, 'Hi, Helen, how's tricks?'

'I think you rang earlier?'

'Oh yes.' Casually, she asked after Joe, but not as if it mattered. She laughed, bright and shrill. 'You've disappeared lately, the pair of you. Off the face of the earth, I said to Bri. How about coming to a party on Saturday – we're still in the same place—'

'I can't. Joe's away.'

Silence. Then the bright tone again, 'Well, when he's back would you ask him to give Bri a call? Just … he'd like to chat … Nothing important.'

She learned, when Gaynor's calls became less friendly and more urgent, that Joe owed them money. There was nothing she could do about that. They would have no receipt, no IOU. Joe never liked paperwork. She stopped taking the calls, and Gaynor seemed to have given up. To get another call now, after months, years of nothing, was unnerving. She should do what Joe always did, when things got too difficult: buy a new phone and change the number. What a nuisance that would be when it was only Gaynor she didn't want to hear from. It was a pity, since she had liked her once.

What if Gaynor or Brian had heard from Joe?

Downstairs, the doorbell rang and Sara called, 'Yoohoo! Here we are,' as she came in with Luke and her own little girl.

Helen made tea and she and Sara sat in the kitchen talking about their children. In the living room the television blared with laughter and hysterical children's presenters.

She would delete the voicemail and she wouldn't call Gaynor back. Better not to know, whatever the message.

3

In the last few weeks, with Hugh as the amused intermediary, Kenneth and Catherine had agreed which days each would keep him company. Having slept in the afternoon, he was wakeful and ready for talk in the evenings. Sometimes Kenneth caught sight of Catherine in Dingwall High Street, but if she had not seen him, he did not cross the street to speak to her. All that ever passed between them now was a cool nod and a turning away.

Aileen had married again, the son of Willie Mackenzie, the undertaker. Young Will had become a roads engineer, so they met now and again, working on the same contract. He was a nice fellow, and quiet. Aileen would have it all her own way there. Perhaps Catherine would one day want a divorce, so that she could marry again. She must meet plenty of men, in her job.

Hugh had kept out of it, saying only, 'You're as stubborn as each other. But it's not my business.'

Whatever Hugh said to him now, he would take it. There was no arguing with a dying man. He was even thinner, and had lost all his hair. The chemotherapy, Kenneth told himself, but it was cancer too, hollowing him out. They talked about the hills they'd climbed, the days they'd shared. They talked about music and politics and whatever was in the news. They sometimes talked about Kenneth's parents, but never about Gilbert. They played draughts and dominoes, but no longer chess.

'My brain doesn't work well enough for that,' Hugh said.

They sat in the piano room on either side of the fire, the coal settled to a red furnace that reflected its gleam in the whisky in their crystal tumblers. Kenneth, the heat burning on his trouser leg, drew back a little. Hugh had won the draughts three times in a row.

'I think we should try chess,' Kenneth said, disgruntled.

Hugh laughed. 'Bide your time,' he said. 'You'll soon be winning every game.'

'Ach.'

'It's true. Better face it.'

'You'll revive once this bloody treatment's finished. You did last time.'

'Tell me what you've been up to.'

Kenneth had been working long hours and so not here for more than a week, but what was there to say about the sewage works at Inchvannie or the rerouting of the power lines near Kyle? It was just what he did all day and of no possible interest to Hugh.

Hugh, taking pity, said, 'I'm having another visitor tomorrow.'

'Who's that?'

It was the fire making Hugh's fair skin a little pink over the cheekbones; he was not an emotional man.

'Catherine's bringing Helen with her.'

'Helen! Well.' Kenneth thought of Catherine, then Aileen. 'How do you feel about seeing her? I'm not keen myself on keeping up with ex-wives.'

Hugh smiled. 'I've had a card at Christmas from Helen every year, and for my birthday too.'

'So is she angling to come back, do you think?' Even to Hugh he couldn't say, for the spoils, now they're in sight. Perhaps Hugh guessed.

'Not for a minute.' Hugh leaned forward and took up the fire tongs.

'Here – let me do that.'

As Kenneth added coal to keep the fire going, Hugh said, 'A funny thing – he always had a big car, that fellow. Joe. Catherine says Helen has no idea what happened to it.'

'He'll have taken it with him,' Kenneth said as he sat down, rubbing his hands to get rid of the coal dust. 'When he scarpered.'

'He was supposed to have gone abroad, but I have my doubts about that. Anyway, Helen found the keys of the car, but she's never found the lock-up where he kept it. She had no idea where that was. A man of secrets, Joe.'

'A thug.'

'I don't think so. But on the shady side of the law.'

'He'll have had another set of keys.'

'I dare say. But Catherine says Helen is sorry for the car on its own, never claimed.'

'It's a car, not a bloody dog.'

Hugh laughed. 'Helen always believed objects had feelings. An animist, is that it?'

Kenneth, dismissing this, said without interest, 'What kind of car was it anyway?'

'Mercedes? Audi? Something like that. No, a BMW – a black BMW. That was the last one, anyway. He was always changing them apparently.'

Kenneth's foot shot out, an unwilled reflex, hitting the tongs so that they clattered across the grate. Hugh looked at him, but said nothing. After a moment, he suggested, 'You could put the kettle on. I can't manage the whisky, I'm sorry to say. But a cup of tea.'

Kenneth, as he got up, said, 'For somebody who hasn't seen his ex in years, you know a lot.'

'Catherine keeps me up to date. I think she feels she ought to. I find it quite – amusing.'

Something in his smile reminded Kenneth of – what? In the kitchen, waiting for the kettle to boil, he realised it was Gilbert. That same mischief. He gripped the tea caddy so tightly the tin buckled in his fist. When he put it down it fell over and loose tea spilled out on the work surface, a scattering of black ashes.

Joe had been in the cottage that night.

This disturbing thought was still in his mind next morning as he drove to Aviemore. Before submitting his tender for work on a new development he wanted to inspect the site and speak to the local councillor who had objected to the planning permission that was now granted, despite protests. As well to know what the locals thought the problems were, though he had a good idea.

It began to snow while he was still on the dual carriageway going south out of Inverness, a barely visible floating of dry distant specks, never landing on the windscreen. Ahead was the Slochd, the highest point on the A9, where the road would be bleakest.

For years, he had schooled himself not to think about this road when he was on it. From being merely a too-familiar part of his life, since the night of the fire at the cottage the journey had taken on the quality of a nightmare, the memory of a nightmare. In daylight, he had for a long time after that night been unable to stop himself looking from side to side beyond the road, where the ditches plunged deeply and invisibly, or there were thick belts of trees. He could not help but imagine that somewhere, buried or simply hidden, Gilbert lay. What remained of him. The first time he slowed to a crawl, so violently was he shuddering, to retain control of the car. He finally stopped in a lay-by and waited for common sense, or merely self-preservation, to be reasserted.

Now he did not look to either side, he just drove the road. It was never again so bad as the first time, but he did not lose that consciousness of what might have happened: Rose and Joe, driving back south with Gilbert's body, stopping to get rid of it, dump it in snowy darkness, hoping it would never surface or be found, or traced to them if it were. Joe must have had a lot to lose, not to risk an ambulance or take the opportunity to land Kenneth with full responsibility.

In easier, saner moments, he thought this a ludicrous idea, and as the years went by, it became an impossible one. Everything in the hills comes to light in the end. Or so he told himself.

4

What Helen had intended to do was leave the boys in Hertfordshire and take the train to Luton, from where she could fly direct to Inverness, but her mother decided to come and spend the week in London. She wanted to shop in town, and Helen, afraid the whole arrangement might fall through, did not bother querying how this was to be done with two small children. This meant she flew from Gatwick. Later, she thought how strange it was she had her mother to thank for this.

Because she left as soon as her mother had arrived, she was far too early, even for all the palaver of checking in a bag and going through security. It was strange being without the children: she had constantly the feeling of having forgotten something, laid it down or left it behind. Her suitcase checked in, the feeling grew. She was light as a feather, unencumbered. She sat with a cup of coffee and a newspaper, having forgotten to bring a book. Idly, she checked her phone. Gaynor had called again. Another voicemail. Perhaps she should listen to it. She felt safe here in the airport, huge and anonymous, full of other people aimlessly filling in time as she was. There was a constant low hum of noise you could easily not hear, so it felt quiet. She got up and wandered through the duty-free shops, trying on scent. There was no longer Joe to come home with a surprise bottle of Chanel or Dior (and now she wondered where he had got them), so she did not wear it.

The voicemail nagged. Perhaps she should try to find a quiet corner and listen. She made for the bookshop first, to get something to read on the plane. At the far end she browsed the older stock, and as she did, dialled and listened to her messages. A lot of buzzing. Perhaps she would hear nothing anyway.

Look, you don't want to speak to me, fair enough, and he probably never left you with nothing, but Brian's not looking for the money now. No point. Give me a ring though.
To hear this message again, press 1. To save this message, press 2. To delete this message, press 3.

She pressed 3.

Message 2: *You should call me. I don't want to give you a heart attack, leaving a message. Brian says I should tell you. Right.*
To hear this message again –

Helen pressed 3, impatient and annoyed.

Message 3: *It's me again. I'm not trying to frighten you or nothing, but Joe's – well, maybe you don't want to know? But for your kids' sake, Helen, if he turns up – don't have him back, that's all I'm saying.*

She pressed 1, and growing faint with disbelief, listened to this again. Gaynor had probably been drinking when she left this message, going by her voice, slurred and emphatic. Gaynor was only like that when she'd had a few.

Joe's what? Dead. No, not dead. *If he turns up ...*

She had lost all sense of where she was and slid down, her back to the bookshelves, till she was sitting on the floor, legs out in front of her, phone and bag on her lap. A woman on her way to the till tripped over her feet and tutted, giving her the kind of look people give street beggars when they have no pity. Helen drew her legs up, but like a reflex, barely conscious. The awful thing was this phone call had made her start hoping. Gaynor wouldn't have said all that if she didn't think Joe was likely to appear, might be at the house even now, his key in the lock, her mother surprised there with the children and Matthew leaping up – *Daddy!*

Helen began to search for Gaynor's number: callback, that was quickest. Someone almost kicked her, then checked, and stepped carefully over her legs. She came sharply back to herself, saw charcoal-grey trousers at her eye level and looking up, a young man in a suit, his briefcase placed beside his shiny black shoes. He leaned down.

'Sorry,' he said. 'Are you all right?'

Helen, flushing, tried to get up, but it was awkward, he was in the way and her legs seemed stuck. How had she got like this – so stupid, making a show of herself, her mother would have said.

'Let me give you a hand.'

He had her on her feet, she was not sure how, and he picked up her bag, discarded on the floor.

'Here you are.' He grinned at her. 'I wondered if all the best books were on the bottom shelf.'

'Sorry – oh dear, thank you.' He was a little taller but not much, a slight young man, a boy, his suit charcoal grey, his lovely shirt palest pink, his tie pink and grey stripes, and a glimpse of pink and white spotted braces. She was dishevelled, a woman without even a child by her to justify being so crumpled and foolish.

He went on gazing at her. 'What blue eyes you've got,' he said.

'So have you.'

'Mine are lighter.'

'Are they?'

'When is your plane?'

'Not for ages, I'm too early. I'm usually late, so it feels strange. I keep looking at the board in case I've made a terrible mistake.'

'Oh,' he said carelessly, 'there's always another plane. I wouldn't worry.'

'Not to Inverness.'

He laughed. 'Is that where you're going?'

'What about you?'

'I have three-quarters of an hour. Then I'm getting on a plane to Paris.'

'Oh,' she sighed. 'Paris.'

For a moment they looked at each other with a wild imagining of something impossible. He would say, come with me, and she would go. Then Helen remembered who she was, and what she was supposed to be doing.

'I'd better get a book,' she said. 'That's what I came in for.'

'Me too.'

'Well—'

'Let's have coffee first.'

'All right.'

After half an hour of talking about the books Helen had read and he had not (he made a list on his phone), and the books he had read and she had never heard of (she didn't make a list) they left the café and he prepared to walk to his departure gate.

'I don't even know your name,' she said, as they shook hands, decorous and smiling. 'Not that it matters, I suppose.'

'Patrick,' he said.

'Helen.'

'Well,' he said, 'if I'd known – Helen! Of course.'

Then he turned and walked quickly away.

In Inverness, Helen told Catherine about this encounter. 'What did he mean – *Helen, if I'd known?*'

'Perhaps he's a classics scholar and he thought you were Helen of Troy,' Catherine said.

They were driving to Evanton, going straight from the airport to see Hugh since he was too tired by evening for the strangeness of a meeting with Helen. But this precipitate visit frightened her – was he likely to die so soon she had to see him immediately?

'Well, I think he was a city trader or something,' Helen said, bringing her mind back to Patrick. 'He had braces on.'

Catherine laughed. 'Did he ask for your phone number?'

'Oh no. He was too young.'

'Too young to have a phone?'

'Too young for me.' What was wrong with Catherine, being so flippant when they had only just met again, and such tragedy lay between them and before them? On the flight, Helen had grown sober and sad, ashamed of herself falling for Gaynor's tricks, embarrassed she had made such an exhibition of herself and become the source no doubt of Patrick's mirth when he relayed their meeting to his metropolitan friends, young and successful like himself.

Tears filled her eyes as she turned away, looking out of the car window. The narrow road to Evanton was lined with trees, the leaves drifting down brown and gold, the sun dappled through branches growing bare, the firth below shining with the blue of reflected sky, calm as a pond. Overhead, a skein of geese flew in towards the water, calling raucously their messages of reassurance as they arrived. Were they exhausted, reaching this familiar shore? Did they *recognise* it? Here she was, arriving for the first time for years, going to Hugh's house, barely remembering the road.

'Oh, Cathy,' she said, 'I can't believe all that's happened. And there's so much we don't even know.'

She was thinking of Joe, but from Catherine's swift glance, she thought her sister might not realise that, and be assuming it was the gap between them, the little they told each other. She did not bother to explain. She talked too much, and some things were best kept to yourself.

5

In the icy dark of a January night, Kenneth drove to Evanton when he had shut up the works, stopping at the supermarket in Dingwall for a pie to be heated in Hugh's oven. Hugh was hardly eating now. He had been given drinks he took with a straw, strawberry and vanilla flavour, apparently containing all the vitamins and minerals he needed. Kenneth picked up the repeat prescription for him when the supply ran low. The smell, when Hugh peeled open the plastic lid, was chemical and sweet.

Beata cleaned the house, laid the fire in the piano room every morning, and made soup that had to be liquidised for Hugh to swallow it. Catherine came in after work on the nights when Kenneth was not there. She was with him most of the weekend too. He was alone only in the day when there was neither Beata nor the community nurse with him. Then, he said, he listened to music and slept.

Kenneth had begun seeing a woman he'd known slightly when he was married to Aileen. Coming across her at the theatre, where she'd gone on her own because the friend she should have been with was ill, they had a drink together before going in for the performance. Kenneth couldn't recall why he'd bought tickets to see a popular comedian he did not much like, but it was a way of filling Saturday night. Fiona was divorced but he remembered her husband as a football fan, a fanatical County supporter who worked for the Council, something in building maintenance.

On impulse, he asked her out. She was a pretty woman, dark and plump with neat ankles. She said yes. Several outings, drinks, dinners later, he was wondering how soon he could get her into bed. Not long, he thought. He missed the sex. That was what he told himself: not Catherine, not marriage. Just sex.

He pulled into Hugh's drive, the car skidding on paving slabs. Black ice – he would have to watch for that, going home.

Hugh was in the piano room, the fire blazing up. A bottle of Glenmorangie was on the low bookcase. Hugh did not drink now, having lost the taste for it. Kenneth heated up his pie and ate it, and Hugh had one of his awful flavoured drinks.

They had gone beyond board games, but a Chopin nocturne was playing, and they could still talk. He had not so far told Hugh about Fiona. There was no reason not to, and no reason Hugh shouldn't in turn tell Catherine. Yet he'd said nothing.

'Cold out there,' Hugh said. He looked alert, a good sign.

'There's black ice on your drive. Don't you go out.'

'What would I do that for?' Hugh grinned. He nodded at the whisky bottle on the bureau. 'Help yourself.'

'A wee one,' Kenneth said, as he always did, and covered the bottom of the glass only, since he would have to drive home and you didn't take those sort of risks any more, even when it wasn't icy. The pleasure wasn't the same anyway, without Hugh.

They sat listening to music, content with silence, then Hugh cleared his throat.

'I have something to say.'

'Oh yes?'

'You know Catherine's been very good to me.'

Kenneth put down his glass, filled with misgiving – but why? 'Sure.'

'You both have. Between you and Beata, I'm well looked after.'

'If you're thinking we can't manage, you're wrong.'

'No, no, it's not that.' He straightened in the armchair, moving to ease the discomfort escalating to pain, despite the tablets they gave him. 'Catherine is on her own, and though I wish the two of you would sort out your differences – well, it's not my business.'

'No, it's not.'

'Ach, come off it, Ken, I'm not doing any marriage counselling.'

'It sounds a bit like it.'

'Too late for that, eh?'

Kenneth thought of Fiona, warm in his arms, and her soft giggle of pleasure when he flattered her. 'Much too late.'

'Well then, I was thinking what I might do.'

For a crazy moment, Kenneth thought Hugh meant to marry Catherine himself. 'We've never divorced.'

'I hadn't thought of that, I admit,' Hugh said. 'But it's up to Catherine to deal with it. She'd want it to go to Flora eventually, and Helen's boys, I dare say.'

'What? You've lost me.'

'I'm leaving the house to Catherine. This house. In fact, to both of them. Catherine tells me Helen was never married to that fellow Joe, and he's off the scene altogether now. I've no one else, nobody who needs it. *You're* all right. You can have my CDs and my books and whatever else you fancy. The Peploe will go to my cousins – I suppose I should leave them something. They'll probably sell it, but if they don't, well, a fragment of Scottish culture will make its way to Queensland.' He drew in a harsh breath, as if talking had tired him, but before Kenneth could speak, added, 'George Macallum is executor, by the way.'

331

'Oh, for God's sake,' Kenneth burst out, 'you're not dead yet, man!' He did not know whether this protest was horror or relief. That Joe McCann should ever get his hands on anything of Hugh's – this place! No, he trusted Catherine for that. It would never happen.

'You have to think of these things,' Hugh said mildly. 'It's a pity you can't have another dram – you look as if you need it. Was it such a shock? I didn't think you'd mind.'

'I don't. You're doing the right thing.'

They sat in silence for a moment looking at the fire, the flames licking up, gold and red and blue. They were held there, gazing, the only sound the tick of the carriage clock and the soft collapse of a burning coal.

'I wish her only the best, you know,' Kenneth said. 'It was my fault we parted.'

'She can be stubborn, I suppose.'

'She could only deal with what she knew about. I wasn't straight with her.'

'Weren't you?' Hugh still gazed at the fire, but he was listening. 'What about?'

'Gilbert.'

'Ah. I thought that might be it.' When Kenneth did not speak, he added, 'Are you going to tell me?'

There was a long pause. How tempted he was to speak to Hugh, who would never repeat it, and whose opinion of him would not waver. If it did, how could that matter now? Yet as he thought it over, it seemed a selfish act to confide in a dying man. There was nothing he could do to shift the responsibility from himself, or the guilt.

'I won't burden you with it,' he said at last.

'That's up to you. But don't keep blaming yourself for a

332

relationship that was always flawed. Your mother spoiled him, no wonder you resented—'

'It's not that. Not now.' He wanted that whisky! 'Never mind, forget it.'

Hugh said, 'There's no need for you to worry now. It's been more than three years since Gilbert left. He'll have made a life for himself somewhere else – in London no doubt.'

Abruptly, Kenneth stood up. 'Will I put the kettle on?'

If Hugh was surprised, he did not say so. 'Fine. I think Beata got some chocolate biscuits – they'll be in the blue tin.'

'Do you want one?'

'No, just tea.'

As he stood in the kitchen waiting for the kettle to boil, absently eating two biscuits as he did so, Kenneth turned his mind resolutely from Gilbert, and the conversation. He must never think about it. He would just go mad.

When he took the tea through, Hugh had fallen asleep. He drank his own, washed up both mugs, and putting the tartan rug that lay folded on the piano stool across Hugh's knees, he put the guard on the fire and left.

The temperature had dropped further and the slabs beneath his feet were slippery. He would take his time, going home. The car radio came on with the engine as it always did, but it was opera on Radio 3, a litany of despair from a wailing soprano. He jabbed buttons to find something else to listen to, but the road needed his attention. After a moment he realised he'd inadvertently let loose the opening chords of a country and western song. As he turned onto the main road, he thought he'd put on a CD instead. Then the voice soared, and the words filled the car.

I shot a man in Reno, just to watch him die.

He had had that line in his head for years and had always

thought it belonged in a film. It wasn't a film at all, it was a song: it was Johnny Cash. He remembered now. He'd got the line wrong anyway. Shot, not killed. And no 'once' at the end. *I killed a man in Reno, once.* He had been so sure it was from a film with Steve McQueen. One day, he thought, I'll forget the things that actually happened to me, or maybe the past will be a blur of half-remembered impressions, and I'll get it wrong.

That would not be a bad thing.

He told this little story to Hugh the next time they met. It wasn't one of his usual days, but Catherine was in Edinburgh for a meeting and wanted to stay overnight so that she could see Flora. He told the story because Hugh was grey and ill, and he wanted to amuse him, to take his mind from whatever was distressing him – pain, he supposed. Catherine had said when she asked if he could take her place, 'He doesn't eat at all now, just has liquids. Beata said he struggled with the soup she'd made, and it was pureed lentil.'

They did not meet, but they communicated occasionally by phone, always about Hugh, though now and again he asked for Flora. He was conscious that Fiona's daughter and Flora were good friends. This time, the anxiety in Catherine's voice was unmistakeable. She loves him, Kenneth realised. I wish she loved me. The thought was fleeting and soon suppressed; all that was over and he didn't want it back.

'A friend of mine has this theory,' he told Hugh as they settled by the fire, 'that everybody has a line that defines them. The line tells you something vital – it's factual, not opinion or feeling. If you know what their line is, you'll understand them.'

'And forgive? Is that the idea?' Hugh smiled.

'That would depend on the line, wouldn't it?'

'What's mine, I wonder,' Hugh mused. He thought about it. 'Give me an example.'

'Well...' Put on the spot like this, the only person he could think of was Gilbert. *I'm a victim*, he thought was his brother's line. No, that was a feeling, not a definition. *I was adopted.* Yes, that was it. He had a sense of entitlement and grievance and it all came from that. Unless of course he knew he never had been. A whole other level of grievance there.

'I know Beata's,' Hugh said suddenly, cutting off this disturbing line of thought. '*I am the oldest of eight children.*'

'My God,' Kenneth said, diverted. 'Is she?'

'Yes. Maybe you could add, *and my mother died when I was twelve.* She had to grow up fast and become an adult when she was only a teenager. It's why she works so hard, I think, why she has such a profound sense of responsibility.'

Kenneth realised Hugh had understood the theory of one line better than he had himself.

Then Hugh said, 'So, the friend whose theory this is, would that be Catherine?'

'Rumbled.'

'Why won't you say her name?'

The name was as powerful as the line. He could not say it. 'I will – I do!'

'Hm. Anyway,' Hugh added, looking momentarily better, brightened with mischief, 'it's not her theory, it's Helen's. She was always looking to find that core truth about people. *She* thought it made her able to judge better. So that's where Catherine got it.'

Kenneth was silenced. He had thought at the time it was a fanciful theory for someone like Catherine, but now he had adopted it himself, he thought he could understand why she had. Had she said she'd thought of it herself? He couldn't remember.

He was shaken, uneasy. Through his head ran the line about Reno. The real line. *Just to watch him die.*

'Mine,' Hugh said, 'is, *he never wanted to be a lawyer.*'

'I think you're joking now,' Kenneth said and Hugh smiled.

They had a quiet evening, not talking much. Kenneth had a book about the Munros with him, while Hugh was reading, slowly as he always did, a history of the Second World War and a gardening book alternately, depending on how he felt. He did not seem to have made much progress with either in the last week or so. *The Herald* lay on the floor beside his chair, still folded. He is drifting now, Kenneth realised. He has moved beyond caring about the outside world. He was reluctant to go, though Hugh had fallen asleep as usual. He would rouse himself later and go up to bed, but still, it was hard to leave him.

Outside in the blowy February night, he stood breathing fresh air, and it came to him that Hugh's house, that had smelled of polished wood and roses from the garden and smoke from the open fire, now smelled of sickness, a fetid human smell that met you in the houses of very old people, with windows never opened and clothes never aired.

It was not late. He pulled out his mobile phone and called Fiona. Yes, she was at home, and it was fine to come and see her. Relieved, he drove away.

6

Hugh died in the spring. He saw the snowdrops under the trees and the primroses in hidden corners by the wall, but they withered where they were, undivided, because he could not go out and take care of his garden. Catherine promised she would let the daffodils die down before the grass was cut, and she would prune the forsythia immediately it had finished flowering. His instructions and advice grew fainter by the day.

She lived at Rowanbank in the last weeks. Kenneth sent some of his men to move the piano to the living room, so that a hospital bed could be brought in and put by the French windows, the fireside chairs set beside it, and she could sit with him there during the day, or by his bed at night. In his last week at home the lilac blossomed. With the window open a little for fresh air, the heavy scent came in, and he drowsed, breathing in its sweetness.

They were reaching a point where he needed more medical care than could easily be provided at home, so when a place became available in the hospice he was taken there. A few days later, at four in the morning when no one was with him, he died. Catherine took the call, and before she could feel anything about it, phoned Kenneth and then Helen. If she wondered whether Hugh had made his will as he had said he would, it was only because she had grown to love being in his house. Perhaps she could buy it? She had not told Helen about the will.

At the funeral, George Macallum spoke to her as they came out of the church. 'You were a good friend to him.'

'He was such a good friend to *me*.'

'Come and see me next week,' George said, 'when you can. No hurry. No surprises either – he said he'd spoken to you.'

Helen had cried all the way through the service, silent tears falling onto her breast. She had no black, just an old navy raincoat she wore to go to work. Catherine and Flora were in black, elegant and slender. Flora had cried too, her eyes pink, mascara smudged beneath.

'Where are all his relatives?' Helen asked, when they reached the hotel by the crematorium, where they were to have soup and sandwiches. 'He had cousins in Australia.'

'Too far for them, I expect,' Catherine said.

'We are his family, aren't we? And Kenneth?'

Catherine and Kenneth had been stiffly polite, avoiding each other. This was the time when they should have come together, but it would not happen. Hugh had said, why don't you see if he feels the same?

'The same as what?' Catherine could not be angry with Hugh when he was so weak, those last days before he had the hospice place, but she could not let him think all would be well with Kenneth, just because they both loved him.

'You're as bad as each other,' Hugh had said, giving them up.

Kenneth, in an unaccustomed suit and black tie, stood out from the other men, big and stately, a handsome man. When anger and frustration did not get in the way, she could see that. Flora spoke to him as the sherry and whisky were handed round.

Afterwards she said, 'He was asking for you, Mum.' She added, casual, 'I thought his new girlfriend might be here, but she's not.'

A little cold trickle ran down Catherine's spine. Ah.

'What girlfriend?' Helen asked, since Catherine would not.

'My friend Eilidh's mum. She's divorced.'

Flora sped back to Edinburgh next day, and her new life.

'You know,' Helen said as they drove away from seeing her off at the station, 'you never did take me to that factory place of Gilbert's. Is someone else running it now?'

'It was never a viable business. It's empty – all the stuff was cleared out. I think your friend Rose found buyers.'

'Not *my* friend.'

'Gil's then.' They had stopped at traffic lights. 'Would you like to see it – I mean, where it was?'

'Sure. We're not doing anything else, are we?'

When they got there, the long approach to the factory was heavily overgrown and many more of the window panes were broken. The place was derelict. A fence had been erected, extending the one that bordered the other half of the factory, secured with padlocked gates. An enormous *For Sale* board had been erected in front.

'It's for sale! Gil didn't own it, did he?'

'No, he had a lease.'

Catherine stopped the car and they got out. The April wind blew dead leaves into the air, but the trees were hazy with green buds. When they had shut the car doors, all was silence.

'What an amazing building.' Helen stood gazing up at the first floor windows, blank and toothless, the sun not reaching them yet.

'I'm sorry I can't show it to you,' Catherine said. 'They've made sure nobody can get in now, I suppose because of vandalism. It's a pity about the windows.'

'Let's look,' Helen said. 'There might be a way in.'

Catherine did not think so, but she followed Helen around the perimeter. At the back, where the new fence was supposed to join the old, long grass grew thick, but there was a narrow gap.

'Hey, look, come on.'

'There's probably a burglar alarm,' Catherine warned. 'We'd better not.'

Helen ignored her, pushing through the grass. The nettles were low, easily climbed over so early in the year. Pulling her sleeves down to cover her hands, she hauled brambles out of the way until she could step through. She was on the other side.

'Come on.'

More carefully, trying to protect her clothes, Catherine followed.

When they had made their way to the front of Gil's half of the factory, it was easier, the grass not so long or the weeds so thick and tangled. Outside the gate their car waited, but there was no sign of anyone else and when they paused, all they could hear was birdsong, and the wind making little swoops through the trees. The doors were padlocked and chained, but they could reach the ground floor windows. They stood on tiptoe, peering in with hands cupped either side of their faces, to cut the outdoor light.

'It's empty,' Helen said. 'It's enormous – did he fill it?'

The floor stretched dusty all the way across the great hall where the sofas and tables and wardrobes had stood crowded together, leaving narrow paths where Gilbert had led Flora, dancing towards the little wicker sofa. Something caught in Catherine's throat – loss or grief, or just the cheap nostalgia that means nothing.

'I wish we could get in,' Helen said.

340

'The books were all upstairs, and the bric-a-brac. The little things. Occasionally he had stuff I think might actually have been antique. Not that I would know.'

Joe would, Helen thought. She was walking round the building, growing excitement convincing her they would find a way in. Then she found a door: not the double delivery doors, also fiercely padlocked, but a door overgrown with grass and brambles, which would be hidden by the summer. They took turns trying the doorknob, stiff and creaky. It turned, so something else prevented the door from opening.

'It must be bolted on the other side,' Catherine said.

Helen leaned against it and shoved with all her weight. The door shifted, reluctantly scraping over the concrete floor.

'You coming?'

There was no stopping them now. In a moment, they had negotiated a dark corridor and were in The Factory. The vast space where Gilbert had housed his furniture lay before them. As if it had been waiting for them, the sun reached the far windows and gleamed through, lighting up pale dusty floorboards. None of the internal doors was locked, so they could walk through, glance into the dirty kitchen – empty, Gil's packets of tea long gone – and then climb the broad stairway to the upper floor. Here, there were only bookcases with a few scattered books lying on their sides, and a cardboard box full of broken china on the remaining long table. Catherine went to examine the books while Helen poked around in the box.

'It would be nice to have a souvenir, wouldn't it?'

Catherine had found, incredibly, the copy of *High Wind in Jamaica* she had pointed out to Hugh on her first visit. She had a much cleaner one at home, but tucked it into her fleece pocket anyway.

Behind a teapot with a broken spout was an intact plate that might, Helen thought, be Coalport. Something was wedged between them making the plate stick. She pushed her fingers in to free it, and brought out, small and buckled, a black notebook.

Catherine was still turning over books. Helen opened the notebook, and saw a short list in his spiky, unmistakeable handwriting:

Stafordshire choclate cup

2 Coleport plates

Spode serving dish

His haphazard spelling. Helen breathed deeply, steadying herself, and slipped the notebook into her pocket.

'I'll have this plate,' she said. 'I think it's Coalport.'

'Do you want to look downstairs again?' Catherine asked. 'There's a little office, near the back. Though I doubt if there's anything there now.'

Helen said, 'If you like.'

'What's wrong – are you ok?'

'Yes. Let's go, eh? In case anybody comes.'

'You weren't bothered about that five minutes ago!'

More quickly now, they made their way downstairs and out again, through the dark corridor to the light at the end, and the thicket of brambles.

7

While George was dealing with Hugh's estate, and because she could not settle in her house in Inverness, Catherine took a week's leave at the end of May. She went south to stay with Helen and visit her mother. She felt changed by the experience of being with Hugh, and still slightly unreal, a faint film between her and the rest of the world. She wanted to talk to someone about what she had learned: that it was a privilege to be with the dying. She would have liked to think she might carry out the same loving care for her mother one day, but that would never happen. Her mother would not even want it. At present, the favourite daughter was Helen, because of the boys, though Mrs Harrigan had told Catherine they were very spoiled and she had had to instil some much-needed discipline while she was looking after them.

'I hope you didn't say that to Helen.'

'I always speak my mind, as you know,' her mother said.

Catherine longed to make the obvious retort to this, but she contented herself with, 'I'll see you soon,' and went to pack her case.

In London it was five or six degrees warmer than the Highlands, and Catherine was grateful for it. She had forgotten the different seasons of the south and the heat of the city.

The boys were noisy and lively and fought all the time with astonishing ferocity, but remembering the younger Flora, she tried not to judge Helen for Matthew's rudeness, or Luke's yells when he didn't get his own way. Still, it was something when she was quite glad to take the train into Hertfordshire and have a day with her mother, looking forward to how quiet that would be.

Back with Helen, she was newly thankful for someone she could speak to without evoking disapproval or discontent. She had given up the idea that she could ever feel about her mother's dying, as she had about Hugh's.

'I've got a babysitter for tonight,' Helen said. 'You remember that Italian restaurant up the road? Well, there's a new owner and I think the food's better. More *authentic*.'

Since neither of them had ever been in Italy for more than a week, Catherine wondered how Helen could know. Still, it was a night out, and there were things to talk about they had been keeping aside: in particular, Hugh's house. Helen had stopped being astonished and guilty and tearful, thank goodness. Now perhaps they could have a sensible discussion about what to do next.

Catherine began tentatively, when the waiter had taken their order and left them with a bottle of wine and a bowl of olives. 'I feel it's your house in a way, that you have a sort of right to it, since you were married to Hugh.'

'He left it to both of us. It's yours too,' Helen said with an air of being generous.

Catherine had been steeling herself for this. 'Do you *want* it?'

Helen sat back, an olive halfway to her mouth, nonplussed. 'How do you mean, want it? You mean let it out or something?'

'Live in it.'

'But it's miles away – I live in London.'

'I thought it would be a chance for you to move.'

'Oh no.' She was definite about this. 'It's a lovely house, but the time for being in it ... that went, years ago. My home is London. I couldn't move the boys.'

'I moved Flora when she was about the age Matthew is now.'

'No, no, I don't want to leave London. There's no question of that.'

How certain she was, almost defiant. Puzzled, Catherine said, 'What do you want to do with it then?'

'Sell it, I suppose. It seems a shame after it was in Hugh's family for generations, but he didn't grow up there, so – yeah, let's sell it and then we'll both have some money. Did you ask George what he thought it was worth?'

Catherine's heart was beating so fast and hard she could not swallow. She put her wine glass down.

'I've been thinking.'

'What?'

'Would you mind if *I* lived at Rowanbank?'

Helen was silent. Is she angry, Catherine wondered, but Helen was never angry.

'Oh,' Helen said. 'I never thought.'

'What, that I might like to live there? I hate that house in Inverness and I love Rowanbank. I love the garden and it's so peaceful. Well, it was peaceful with Hugh in it, so I hope I could hang on to that.'

'I used to be the one who liked houses, not you,' Helen marvelled. 'How strange.' She picked up her fork and traced a pattern on the white tablecloth, making grooves first one way, then the other. She looked up. 'So, I wouldn't get any money then?'

Catherine laughed, which was better than crying. 'You idiot. I'll pay you your share. Most of the money from the sale of Alan's house in London is in trust for Flora, but I could take out a mortgage. I'd have to sell the Inverness house first but I think I could manage. I have a decent salary and despite Flora being an expensive sort of daughter, I've saved quite a bit.'

Helen, who had not saved, was impressed and jealous. 'Oh dear, you do think of everything, I wish *I* had. I'm useless.'

'What's brought that on? You're doing very well with your boys and a full-time job – I admire you for that. Joe left you in an impossible situation.'

Helen flushed. 'You're not usually so nice to me.'

'Hugh's good influence,' Catherine said, but the little joke went awry, for they both began to cry, Helen more obviously, wiping her eyes on the edge of the tablecloth.

Appearing with their seafood risotto the waiter hovered warily. Then he decided not to notice the tears and put the plates down with a flourish.

'Black pepper?' he asked, producing a pepper mill the size of a wine bottle. 'Parmesan?'

'Yes,' said Helen, and 'no,' said Catherine and they smiled at each other, a little tremulous.

They ate steadily for a few minutes, then Helen said, 'It's a brilliant idea. You're very clever. I get to visit Rowanbank, you get to live in it, and I get some money. Perfect.'

Her expression was faintly discontented, however, as if she had been outmanoeuvred. There was something about her manner this evening that was making Catherine uneasy. Sounding this out, she said, 'You'll be able to get a bigger house when the money comes through.'

'Oh no,' Helen said. 'Matthew loves his school and Luke is going there in September. I can't move away.'

'Well, a better house in the area?'

Helen flushed. 'I'll see.'

Catherine laid her fork down. 'Has something happened?'

Helen concentrated on her last mouthfuls of food. Eventually, she pushed the plate away and picked up her glass. 'Here's to Rowanbank,' she said, 'and dear Hugh.'

'What is it?' Catherine said, ignoring this. Her heart skipped. 'It's not Joe, is it? Have you heard from him?'

'No, of course not, but I found something of his. I don't think he's abroad. In fact, I don't think he ever went to Spain or any other foreign country.'

The little black notebook, tucked in her dressing table drawer, taunted Helen.

'I don't see it proves anything,' Catherine said when she told her about it, 'except possibly that Joe was Gilbert's buyer. I suppose it confirms that Rose was the go-between, but we've known that for ages.'

For Helen, there was nothing reassuring about this.

8

Helen was still on Frankie's mailing list for the gallery in Highgate, and occasionally, when she could arrange a babysitter for early on the Friday evenings when these events happened, she went along to a preview of his latest exhibition. She didn't know anyone else likely to be there, and Brian and Gaynor thankfully never appeared. She could not help looking for Joe in the crowd. How little it took to rekindle that hope. Frankie did not know where he was. She had asked him and Frankie was brutally direct.

'You're better off, sweetheart,' he told her, the first time she saw him after Joe had left. Still desperate then, she had asked, 'Do *you* know, Frankie, where he is?'

'Don't know, don't care,' Frankie said with a grin, so that she was cheered up.

He greeted her like an old friend every time she called in at the gallery or went to a preview, but never mentioned Joe – and rarely Rose. Rose did not appear either. In earlier days it had crossed Helen's mind she might be with Joe, but she had long ago discounted this as impossible, since Rose was clearly still around, even if she hadn't seen her.

A couple of weeks after Catherine went home, she had a free Saturday afternoon while her children were playing at friends' houses, so she walked up to the gallery. It was beginning to rain so she turned up the collar of her old navy mac. It was, so far, a fine misty rain, hovering in the air. The pavement was greasy rather than wet. She was glad to be out on such a depressing afternoon, if only to see Frankie.

The gallery was empty even of the girl who sat in the reception area, with her languid air of doing a favour for the customers with her presence, since her real life was obviously lived elsewhere. Helen went to the door at the far end and finding it ajar, pushed it open. 'Frankie?'

He appeared from the back office, mug in hand. 'Hiya! How you doing? Just made coffee – you want one?'

The gallery was unusually empty for a Saturday, but it was a bleak November afternoon. She took off her wet raincoat and hung it over a chair. 'Thanks, yes.'

'Come out to the front,' he said. 'Sally doesn't do Saturdays now. Hard times. I'll need to get rid of her altogether if I don't sell something soon.'

He did not seem downhearted about this, but then, he never did. He took out his cigarettes and offered Helen one. She shook her head.

'Frankie, you know I don't smoke.'

He stood by the front door, held ajar, so that the smoke would blow into the street. In the windless air, it hovered, then evaporated suddenly in the rain that was becoming heavy. 'People don't like the place smelling of fags these days.'

Helen put her cup of undrinkable coffee down on the reception desk amid leaflets for artists whose work (still awful, in her opinion) lined the walls.

'Frankie, do you still see Rose Semple?'

Frankie flicked his cigarette stub onto the wet pavement and closed the door. 'She's been in, yeah, tried to flog me a Fergusson a few weeks back.'

'What – a *real* Fergusson? The colourist?' Helen knew about the colourists, since they had been so much liked by Hugh. *I learned something in that marriage,* she thought, wondering what had happened to the little Peploe hung at the top of the stairs in Rowanbank.

'Might have been real, might not. Either way, I wasn't touching it. She must think I was born yesterday.' He gave his hoarse smoker's laugh, then spluttered, coughing and trying to catch his breath. 'Jesus, I should give up the fags.'

Helen sat down on Sally's chair. 'Rose was trying to sell you a stolen painting?'

'I wouldn't go that far,' Frankie said, cautious.

'Well, what then?' It was what she'd been afraid of all along, with Joe. Might as well face it, she thought. *Better off without him.* Everyone thought so. She thought so herself, only she could not *feel* it; she still wanted him to come back. She knew how mad that was, but there were moments when she could conjure a sense of him close by, his energy making the very air vibrate, and she longed for him as painfully as ever. She wanted to believe it had all been Rose's fault.

'Look, hen,' Frankie said, almost fatherly, perching one fat hip on the side of the desk, 'your Joe was getting his fingers burned, so he hopped it. Shot the craw. Got the hell out. Wise move. You're a nice lassie, you find yourself another man.' He tapped the desk and moved away. 'Now then, what d'you think of this wee picture?' He peered at it, a canvas six inches square, mainly black with some red marks like drips of blood near the bottom.

'It's horrible,' Helen said, getting up. The conversation was over; Frankie had said his piece.

He laughed. 'Ach, you're right, but the punters like this stuff.'

'You've not sold it yet,' Helen pointed out as she collected her coat. 'I'd better go.'

'I'll tell Rose you was asking for her,' Frankie said, winking.

'Don't bother.'

At the door, she turned back to say *see you then*, for she was almost fond of Frankie, the only link with Joe, and the past that belonged to Joe, the good times at the start. Because she turned in the middle of opening the door, she nearly collided with two men coming in, and moved back apologising. She tried to go sideways past them through the now open door, into the grey street.

'Hello — *Helen?*'

Surprised, she paused, holding onto the wet door with slippery hands, the rain so heavy it was already in her hair and trickling down her face. For a few seconds, because he looked different, wearing jeans and a jerkin, his hair soaked dark and flat on his shapely skull, she was puzzled, then she remembered the suit and the unlikely braces.

'Hello!'

A Message from the Other Side
2014

1

Kenneth's first sight of Rose, when she came back to the cottage and found him waiting for her, was a shock: it was as if time had slipped backwards to show him the same young woman, all in black with a cap of inky hair. The small stocky figure getting out of the red hatchback disappeared from his view out of the front window as she went round the side of the house to the back door. Appearing in the kitchen, in colder light, she hardened into someone thirteen years older, made up not for style but to give her the appearance of a girl. That did not survive the first glance.

For a few seconds she was frozen. Then, 'I thought you might turn up,' she said.

'I didn't think *you* would.'

'Well, here I am. Sorry to disappoint you.'

'You've got a nerve, walking in here. Who's with you?'

Surely she did not have the money for the car drawn up outside, gleaming and new, even if it was hired? He did not want to be caught again, with Joe making an appearance this time.

'Just me.'

Though neglected, the cottage had the air of being at least temporarily lived in. Through the smell of damp filtered wood smoke, cigarettes and fried food. There was grease burned around one of the rings of the electric cooker; she had been here more than a day or two.

'I'll put the kettle on,' she said. 'You want a cup of tea?'

'What's the game?'

'I thought you might want to know how I was. What happened to me.'

'You're wrong there.'

Water drummed in the kettle. 'Nice of you not to turn the electricity off – I was a bit worried about that.'

'I'll see to it tomorrow.'

Why had he done nothing about the cottage, leaving it to rot? Now that he was here, standing in the bare kitchen watching Rose put tea bags in mugs while the kettle boiled, he realised he'd been a fool not to deal with it. All he'd done, in cowardice and revulsion, was leave himself open to exactly this: Rose turning up and holding him to ransom.

'Milk?' she asked.

He left soon after, nothing resolved, but determined to have the electricity cut off, then to go back to drain the water system. It was a miracle none of the pipes had burst one winter, the place flooding. His father's obsession with insulation had saved the place from that, he supposed.

At least he had been *able* to go back. There was no atmosphere of terror, of that night, and only the charred furniture and rug to show where the fire had been. But he still could not bear to be in the same room as her. She would have to go. Did she want money, was that it?

'Money? I won't turn it down if you're offering, but I didn't come for money.'

'What then?'

She smiled, tilting her head. 'You'll find out.'

It was at that point, enraged, he turned and left.

Outside, he noted the name of the hire company in the back window of the car. Perhaps she was on her own. Perhaps she didn't need money. What *did* she want?

Driving back, he called in at the Forresters'. He should have sold them the cottage when Jim wanted it. Too late now: Maureen was on her own with the son and his wife, Jim taken by cancer three years ago. Maureen wouldn't want the cottage and Kenneth suspected the son hadn't got his heart in the farm. The place looked run-down, the yard that Jim had kept immaculate, littered with unused machinery, a feed bin kicked over and empty oil drums. A few hens pecked about, but the rope for the dog was loose on the ground, its kennel empty, the roof broken in.

Hearing his car, Maureen came to the back door, wiping her hands on a towel. 'It's yourself – we've not seen you for a while.'

'Just looking in at the cottage.'

'You've a visitor then?'

Nothing got past her – though what had taken her further up the lane to see the car, and note Rose's arrival?

'Not for much longer.'

'Passing through then.' She gestured with the towel. 'You coming in for a cuppa?'

'Thanks, I won't stay.'

'We've had our dinner – do you want something to eat?'

In the kitchen, an infant in a high chair gazed at him, small hand halfway to his mouth, about to cram in a piece of the cake that was in crumbs on the tray.

'The young ones have gone up to Inverness,' Maureen said, as she filled the kettle. 'I'm babysitting.'

'A cup of tea will do fine.'

'Sit yourself down.'

The infant's stare was unnerving. He pulled his chair round, so that he wasn't directly opposite. *Passing through*. Maureen's words suddenly registered.

'How long is it since you noticed there was someone in the cottage?'

She looked at him, surprised. 'A few days.'

So Rose hadn't been here much longer than he knew. He was grateful the place was so remote, so difficult for her to live in. That, surely, would drive her away soon enough.

He sat with Maureen for half an hour. She was lonely, her life focused on the grandchild now Jim was gone. They talked about Jim, about Kenneth's parents: the old days. The kitchen was warm and the child, growing sleepy, lay with his thumb in his mouth, nestled on Maureen's lap. He found it hard to leave.

As he did, he said, 'If you notice anything – anything at all – up at the cottage – give me a call. The woman staying there was a friend of Gilbert's. She needs a place to stay for a few days.'

'Ah, I thought there was something familiar about her. She was here, oh, must have been the last time I remember seeing your brother. My goodness, that's years ago now.'

His heart thudded. He got up to go, afraid she might ask about Gilbert. At the door, the late afternoon sun slanting across the yard, showing it up in all its untidy neglect, Maureen said, 'I didn't think she was a friend of *yours*. Strange looking lassie.'

'You can say that again.' He paused by his car. 'Nice to see you.'

'Aye. Take care, Kenny.'

The next day he called Helen. When, later, he saw he had missed a call from her, he did not bother ringing back. What could she tell him, anyway? Now he was glad he had let that go. He had never got on with Helen, a woman who could leave Hugh Guthrie and then get involved with a charlatan, a waste of space, like Joe McCann.

2

Helen loved a day at home on her own, a day when there was nothing particular to do, just a series of unimportant tasks that might easily be left till another time. If she completed even some of them she felt virtuous. There was also the little luxury of taking longer over lunch, even of having walked to the village in the morning to buy herself a cake along with the newspaper. She could eat her silly cake slowly as she read at the kitchen table, sunshine lying across the plate, pink icing dissolving in her mouth, the leftover crumbs of sponge picked up by a licked forefinger.

She liked the empty spaces in the house, its quietness, only the discreet murmur of Radio 4 in the background or a spatter of rain on the window, welcome because she need not pull on boots and go out to weed. Instead she could read for longer, or tidy the dresser drawer that was so hard to close now, the leg of a pair of sunglasses or a matchbox catching every time. She could listen to the Afternoon Play in peace as she scrabbled around among the collection of unused but obviously useful objects, this sifting yielding some surprises: a lost key, a cat's worming tablet (a pang of loss, while she mourned the poor cat), a ball of twine, a couple of pound coins nestling in the corner at the back. For weeks to come, each time she opened the newly gliding drawer and admired its neatness, she would think of the radio play and remember the couple searching for their daughter, or the old man reminiscing, these fictional characters linked with the ball of string, the plastic dish full of brass screws and carpet tacks.

Patrick being at home got in the way of these pleasures, and changed the whole day. Soup would have to be made early in the morning, the village shop driven to because there was no time to walk, cold meat and rolls bought for a more substantial lunch. He also commandeered the radio, as if it were the only one in the house, which was far from the case. Goodness knows where the others were. One might still be in the garden shed or lying abandoned, ruined, by the rhubarb patch. Later in the day, when she switched it on again herself, beginning to prepare supper, it was annoying to find her station replaced by a jangle of harsh music and loud excited voices. With a floury finger, she tried to re-tune it.

She loved to have him there of course. Everything brightened as they talked, ideas sparking, until they both believed all their plans were possible. She also liked to think of herself as a woman so desirable she was still taken to bed in the afternoon, but that (or the dozing afterwards) did use up a lot of the day.

Sometimes he was busy himself, having jobs to do he had left too long ignored or postponed, so that he went at them in a great rush. She was included in this urgency, since her presence was necessary to steady the ladder, hold the tool he happened not to be using at that moment and hand him nails one at a time. After he had finished, flushed with success and off to put the kettle on, she swept up and put the tools away or washed out the paint brushes. The day was gone and she had done nothing, nothing she had meant to do. She loved him, and reminded herself how awful it would be if he were not there to annoy and hold her up, and get in the way, and of course make love to her. She did not think about the past at all, if she could help it.

Of course, this foolishly adolescent marriage would scarcely be possible if Luke was at home, but he was not. Matthew came home sporadically, and for longer stretches between university terms, but being a student had made him so suddenly independent she was still, in his second year, surprised by his being an adult. Luke was away because he was at school.

She and Catherine had suffered boarding school too, and though Catherine had thrived, becoming Head Girl, a model pupil, Helen had not. Still, Luke seemed happy, and who could turn down such a prestigious music scholarship? From their quite different perspectives, Patrick and Catherine had persuaded her it should be celebrated and accepted. Still, she missed him. She missed both her boys, and perhaps allowed Patrick *his* boyishness in the face of middle age, because she did. Oh, my loves, she thought sometimes, caught in the middle of a dull day by the force of their absence. Of course, when they were home, she had three male people filling the house, leaving trainers in the hall for her to trip over, filling the laundry basket and emptying the fridge. You love it, Patrick said. Admit it.

In a fortnight, Matthew would be home, then Luke two weeks after, the summer officially begun. Patrick was in London for two days to see someone about a possible bit of work. Not that she believed in that – he was off to have good lunches and dinners, to reminisce with someone still working in the City, then come home saying, *thank Christ I'm out of that.* She was alone, her last solitary days till September and the new term.

It was raining. She was a fair-weather gardener, admittedly, but it had been raining most days for all of June and she had got

361

out of the habit, since that afternoon of the phone call. She stood looking out of the kitchen window for a long time, a mug of tea cooling on the worktop next to her. The phone call, troubling and mysterious, from the stranger murmuring 'It's me' and claiming to be Gilbert, had gone on disturbing her for days. It brought back too much unhappiness from those years with Joe, then without him. Now it nagged again, slipping too easily into the empty space of her day.

She had resisted the dog Patrick wanted to get after the cat died, but now she thought a dog would be undemanding company, and she would have to go out, to walk it. She had just decided she would walk to the village anyway and buy a few things from the little store that doubled as Post Office, to give her afternoon purpose. Somehow, she could not bring herself to enjoy being alone today.

She was in the porch putting on her waterproof when the telephone rang, not the house phone but her mobile, left on the hall table. It might be Patrick, having a moment on his own, or the Education office, wanting her for relief teaching. Damn. She would not answer it. If it was Patrick, he would call again.

When she got back to the house there were two missed calls and a voicemail, all from the same, unrecognised mobile number. Selling something, she thought, going back to the front door to shake her waterproof. It was of course possible Patrick was using someone else's smartphone, having run out of charge on his own.

In the end, having made tea and opened a packet of chocolate biscuits, she sat down and called her voicemail. At first there was only a buzzing noise, then, crackly, a voice at first unfamiliar. *Helen, Kenneth Sinclair here. Sorry to bother you, but I wondered if you'd heard from somebody I think you used*

*to know. Don't suppose you're still in touch. Maybe you'd give me
a ring? Rose Semple. Have you heard anything of Rose Semple
lately?*

Her heart was beating hard and fast. She stood up breathless,
the chair scraping on the flagstones. Oh God, not *now*, it was all
so long ago. Fumbling, she pressed call back and waited.

Kenneth Sinclair. Leave a message.

She took a deep breath, waited a moment, and tried again.

Kenneth Sinclair. Leave a message.

Well, it was him. That was as much as she could say. Catherine's
ex-husband was phoning her about Rose. The link was Gilbert of
course, so perhaps it *was* Gilbert who had called. It was nothing
to do with Joe, calm down, you're being ridiculous. She called
Catherine, expecting (since her sister still had usefully filled, fully
employed days) another voicemail.

'Helen?'

'Oh good, you're there, I thought I'd have to leave a message.'

'All's quiet – school holidays have begun up here. Are you all
right?'

'Yes. No. I'm not sure. Kenneth called me.'

'What?'

'Your husband. Ex.'

'I know who he is,' Catherine said. 'What on earth did he
want?'

'He left a message about Rose.'

'Who?'

How slow and irritating Catherine was, her mind on meetings, school budgets, God knows what. Helen didn't even know
what her job *was* any more. Something boring in education.

'Catherine, you must remember Rose Semple. Gilbert knew
her. And Gilbert – or somebody pretending to be Gilbert

– phoned both of us. Has he phoned Kenneth too – or Rose has maybe? It doesn't make any sense to me.'

'Or me,' Catherine said, still steady, but perhaps not quite as cool as usual. 'I told Kenneth about the phone call. He didn't seem bothered.' She paused, then hesitant, said, 'Are you going to call him back?'

'I tried, but I didn't get through.'

'Let me know.'

'I wondered if I would come up for a few days. It's a couple of weeks till term ends here and Patrick is dotting back and forth to London, seeing people about jobs.'

'He's getting a *job?*'

'We're not running out of money if that's what you think.'

'It's not my business. You said he had enough from that city job for—'

'Anyway, I have a bit of time and they keep ringing me up to do teaching, and I don't want to, so I thought—'

'Fine, I'm taking next week off anyway. Come. Help me decide about the garden.'

Hugh's garden. Now theirs. Well, Catherine's. Sometimes Helen said that strange thing to herself, or to other people, *she bought me out*. I sold my bit of Hugh's house, because I needed to, I needed the money, I needed to manage after Joe left. I sold all my stake in the house and the grand piano and the garden and the past. The past. I sold my marriage to Hugh.

She had once said something like this to Catherine, but that had been a mistake. No sympathy there. Only Patrick allowed these flights of morbid self-indulgence; she would not have dared air them in front of her sons. No wonder I love Patrick so much, she thought, missing him.

Later, lying on the sofa eating chocolate biscuits and reading a novel about a love affair gone wrong, a novel with a pink cover showing a long-legged girl with stiletto heels and a champagne flute, she decided it was all right. Everything was all right. Patrick would be home tomorrow and all the things she was so afraid of were in the past. Extinct. The word was crisp in her mind; it seemed to slam shut a door that had been creaking open. She would like travelling north, seeing Catherine and being in Hugh's house. It was peaceful there.

Later, the only phone calls were from Patrick, and cosily, his mother. Liz liked to chat and had probably been on the phone to several other people already. She talked much longer to Liz than to Patrick, who was in a noisy pub.

She forgot she had not tried to call Kenneth again.

3

What Catherine wanted to ask Helen was, 'What would make you suspect someone was actually dead, when you've not seen them for years and there's been no contact?'

She could not, of course, ask this, for Helen's thoughts would leap to Joe. Catherine was thinking about Gilbert. She was now almost sure it had not been his voice on the phone. She suspected Rose, whose voice was husky and had the same London twang Gil had adopted, despite being brought up in the Highlands. He was a chameleon; he could take on the colour of his surroundings. How well he had suited The Factory, though. That was his place.

It was a Country Store now, selling everything from animal feed to shortbread, garden tools to Barbour jackets. The restaurant was popular and she sometimes met friends there for coffee or lunch, though she was never the one who suggested it. It was not that the place in any way resembled The Factory as she remembered it, or that it even reminded her of Gilbert now, but she felt uncomfortable being there.

She had not thought Gilbert might be dead, until she spoke again to Kenneth. They met by chance at the bank in Dingwall; she was coming out as he reached the door. She might simply have nodded and gone past, since even now that was all they seemed able to cope with. Yet Helen's arrival tomorrow, Helen's call, meant she could not.

'How are you?'

He seemed glad to stop. They stood aside from the door, letting other people go past. 'Fine. You?'

'Did you speak to Helen?' she asked. 'She told me you'd been trying to get hold of her.'

'No.' He shrugged. 'It doesn't matter – it was a passing thought.'

'She'll be here tomorrow, if you want to—'

'Here? What for?'

'To visit me.'

'Right.'

An awkward pause followed, but before Catherine could move away or risk asking more, he said,

'I wondered if she'd had a phone call too.'

'From—'

'Anyone. Anyone to do with my brother.' He flushed, as if unable now to say the name.

'It wasn't him, I know that. It was someone trying to make us think—'

'Think what?'

'That he's around, maybe coming back. I don't know – you asked Helen about Rose. Do you think it was her—'

'I know it was.' He took her elbow, then dropped it fast, stepping back. 'Sorry, look, have you time for coffee or something?'

'Yes. I'm on leave this week.'

They walked together to the café by the station, busy at lunchtime but half-empty in the afternoon.

'I'll have tea,' Catherine said as he went to the counter.

'I'll get a pot. You want a scone? Cake?'

'No, just tea.'

'I'll get scones,' he said. 'You look as if you could do with one.'

What did that mean? Annoyed, she sat down.

'They're bringing it,' he said when he came back. 'Scones included. Butter, jam.'

'Yes, fine.' *You look as if you could do with one.* She would not ask him what he meant, not wanting to have that sort of conversation. They should stick to Gilbert, to Rose, to whatever he wanted to tell her. He had put *on* weight. *He* did not need the scone.

'I see you more often in Dingwall,' he said.

'Oh—' She dismissed this. 'They moved the whole Staffing Unit in the last reorganisation, so I have a base here now. I'm still in Inverness a lot of the time.'

'Is this another new job?'

'I'm in charge of – never mind that. How do you know it was Rose, phoning Helen and me? How on earth did she get the phone numbers anyway? Helen has a new name and a new life. A new husband.'

'I'm sure she has her ways. Anyway, she's here.'

Oh Helen, Catherine thought, I'm glad you don't know that. '*Rose?*'

'She's staying in the cottage. I went there after you called me, and there she was.'

'Did you think Gil was there, that *he'd* come back?'

He did not meet her eyes. 'No,' he said. 'I knew it wasn't him.'

The waitress came with their tray and began the business of putting out cups and saucers, teapot and scones. They sat back, silent, as she did this with extraordinary slowness. When she went away at last they sat for a moment saying nothing, then Kenneth picked up the teapot. 'You like it weak, don't you? I remember that.'

Catherine put out a hand, not quite touching his arm. 'It can sit a minute,' she said. 'Tell me what happened. How did she get in?'

'How do you think? Key was in the usual place. It's the bloody Highlands. Nobody breaks into a cottage in the back end of nowhere. Nobody normal.'

'So—' She was imagining this strange prowling of Kenneth around the cottage, then going in and coming face to face with Rose. 'Gilbert's not with her?'

'*No!* For God's sake – I knew *he* wasn't coming back.'

'He might. It seems likely, he always seemed sort of dependent on Rose.'

Ignoring this, he poured tea, then split his scone in two. 'Eat,' he said. 'You're too thin.'

Icy, she withdrew. 'If you want to tell me about Rose, so that I can at least reassure my sister, that's fine. But you have no right to make personal remarks to me. About anything.'

'Oh for God's sake, woman, loosen up. I thought I'd had *some* effect on you. Obviously it's worn off.'

To still her trembling hands, to stop herself rising and walking out, she took up a scone and put her knife through it, then began slowly to spread each half with butter. Not that she had any intention of eating it.

'What do you mean, reassure your sister?' he asked. 'Why would she be bothered about Rose?'

'Because of Joe, her links with Joe. I did tell you, but it was years ago, you probably don't remember.'

'I remember all right. But he's another one who's not coming back.'

'I'm sure that's true.' She sighed. 'I actually think he's in prison, and Helen either doesn't know or doesn't want to.'

'But Rose *is* here.'

'Are you going to throw her out?'

The place had been empty for years, so it did no harm to have someone in it, lighting a fire. He admitted that. In June, it had struck cold, so long uninhabited, with mould on the kitchen ceiling and a smell of damp. For all that, he wanted rid of her.

'You should have sold it,' Catherine said in answer to all this. 'Then you wouldn't have the problem on your hands.'

He laughed. 'You could say that.'

After a moment, Catherine absent-mindedly began to eat her scone. Kenneth, who had finished, wiped his hands. There was a crumb at the side of his mouth. A wife would put up her hand and gently brush it away, she thought, and did nothing. Then, unable to bear it, she touched the side of her own mouth. 'You've got a crumb—'

He took his hand roughly across his mouth. 'Ok?'

'Yes.'

'Glad to see you eating,' he said. 'How have you been?'

'Fine. Changed my job again last year, as I said, but even so, I've been thinking about reducing my hours.'

'Nice to have the chance.'

She saw, as she might not, had they still been together, that this was not an attempt to needle her about her job, but his own frustration. The business, she could not help but know, seeing Sinclair Construction vehicles all over the place, was thriving.

'Would you like to retire?'

'Oh. Retirement. I'd like not to have the responsibility. Some days.' He glanced at his watch. 'I'd better go – I should get back to the office.'

'Do you still have Elsie to look after you?'

'No. Elsie went to live with her sister in Oban, after the sister was widowed.' He grinned, and his face was transformed. She saw it light up, saw *him* light up, as he must sometimes. 'I have Kelly, who has every man in the place at her feet.'

The throb she felt was not of course jealousy. 'My goodness,' she said.

'You don't have to worry – she's twenty-two. I'm not a cradle-snatcher.'

'*Worry?*'

'Never mind me.'

They were about to part. In a moment she might not have the chance to speak to him again. 'Are you still with—' It was not Fiona, that had come to an end, but there was another woman – what was her name?

'Carol,' he supplied with a faint grimace. 'No, she got fed up with me too. Usual complaint – no – what's the word?'

'Commitment?' she suggested, smiling.

He grinned. 'Yeah, that's it. Amongst other things.'

'So—'

'I'm single again. You?'

'Oh yes.' She didn't want to tell him, though once she had longed to, there are other men who want to be with me you know, who don't find me difficult, who take me out to dinner, who *like* me. All that was a sideshow, anyway. Her life was Flora, and work, and the house, with Hugh's garden.

She shouldered her bag and got up. 'Thank you for the tea.'

'It's been good to see you. Don't worry about Rose – Helen won't come across her. She'll be out of that cottage and back to where she belongs. Wherever the hell that is, these days.'

'It's strange Gil's not with her. Do you think *she* knows where he is?'

He stopped, his face darkening, the grim look back. 'Oh, she knows all right.'

'Then—' His expression was so forbidding, she could not go on.

'If I could tell you,' he said, 'believe me, I would. I owe you that.'

He turned away before she could reply, and walked swiftly towards his Land Rover that was parked by the station. He had driven off with a wave by the time she moved.

4

What had thrown Kenneth into confusion was how he had felt. Not when he saw her, as he did from time to time, not even talking to her, but that stupid gesture, touching her elbow as if to draw her aside. Just that touch and he was, for a few hot seconds, on fire again. It had wakened the terrible longing of the first days after they parted, when he had burned for her, a physical presence in his house, in his bed. Most of all, in his bed. You're over sixty, he told himself, driving away, you're a fool.

What he was most a fool about, of course, was that he had let her go: because of Gilbert, because of Rose, and what had happened. The shutter came down, as it must. He blinked, cursing the sun in his eyes, hauling the visor down. But that was not the shutter: it was his own will, that had to cut off whatever thoughts he might have about the past, and that terrible night. He had become an expert in denial. *Fuck* Rose. That she had come back was bad enough, that she intended to get something from him, was worse. That if he gave her what she wanted – and he did not know what that was – she might still not go. She ought to be more afraid of me, he thought angrily. He swung into the yard and brought his vehicle to a halt. For a few minutes he sat there gripping the steering wheel. Then Andy was rapping on the side window, saying something. He opened the door and got out.

'What?'

'Are you coming up to Alness today? They'll be finishing in an hour.'

'No. You go. Tell them—' He halted, gathering his wits. 'Tell Doug I'll be up tomorrow, and make sure the guys know we'll need them another week.'

'They know. I was up this morning.'

'Then leave it. I'll see Doug tomorrow first thing.'

'Right, you're the boss.'

He was beginning to doubt that. Andy was more than competent. It had been a good move to bring him in, with his shiny degree and five years in the oil industry. Now that jobs were vanishing in oil and gas, he had been delighted to get this one. Andy believed, given Kenneth's age, that there were prospects.

Kenneth did not want to sell or even hand over management. If you stop, there is too much space. The grind of writing tenders, getting contracts, making decisions, planning jobs, executing them, bringing it all together; the weight of twenty men full-time and all the casuals they brought in, plus Kelly and Susan who did his books, and all the other people whose livelihoods were affected one way or another by Sinclair Construction: these things constituted his life and were what got him out of bed in the morning. He could not give all that up. Yet it weighed on him more heavily each year.

He still missed Hugh. There was no one he could talk to as he had talked to Hugh. There were other people he could go on the hill with, but he let the weeks go by without getting in touch, and was so tired at the weekend he slept when he wasn't catching up with paperwork.

Kelly left swiftly at five. Unlike Elsie, she had a social life and it was Friday. She drove off fast in her little silver hatchback. Her real life was in Inverness, he supposed, drinking in Johnnie Foxes, or wherever they went now. He shut down the computer and plucked his jacket from the back of the chair. He locked up carefully as he always did, checking the garages and goods shed and putting the padlocks on the front gate.

Home, and the whisky bottle, and falling asleep in front of the television: his weekend. Tonight, something in him rebelled as he drove down the lane to the main road. At the junction he hesitated, as if he had a choice about where he might go. Into his mind came a picture of Catherine at the café table, her long-fingered hands halving the scone, the nails short and unpolished, clean and pale pink. She still wore her wedding ring. She had chosen the thinnest band they could find, something she could forget about, she said, *I'm not good with rings*, but for all that, still there. In one direction the cottage and Rose; in the other Evanton, Hugh's house, still in his mind Hugh's, and Catherine.

He called up his phone book on the car screen; she was no longer in his favourites of course: these were now limited to work contacts. He found her home number, still under Hugh's name, and pressed the button. She might save him yet.

'Have you plans tonight?'

'Well—'

'Let me take you out for a drink.' He glanced at his watch. 'I'll be with you by seven, half past?'

A tiny pause, then, 'All right. I'll see you then.'

His spirits lifted, he turned left, heading for Strathpeffer. He would go home to change, then head straight back to Evanton to pick her up.

It was as if the car had its own momentum, going straight

on, ignoring the turning for his house, out onto the Ullapool road, Garve, the cottage, spurred on by the promise of talking to Catherine later, the salvation he had glimpsed. He could face Rose, face her down. Get rid of her, once and for all. If not – Catherine would help. He told himself he could tell her some of the truth. If Rose tried to tell her more, who would she believe? Not Rose.

The hire car was sitting outside the cottage. The front door, long shut and always stiff, was standing open. From indoors came the sound of music, Radio 1, he guessed. It had been a blowy, dull day, but as he'd been driving here, the skies had cleared and now the wind had dropped it was warm. There was a scent of clover, like honey, as he went up the path, and the more delicate warmth of the pink rose that still bloomed by the gate, despite the competition from cow parsley and brambles. At the open door he could smell frying bacon, and her cigarette.

She met him in the narrow hall. 'Well, look who's here. You want a beer?' She held up a bottle.

'No. I'm not staying.'

'You could have one with me.' She disappeared into the kitchen and returned with another bottle, the cap snapped off.

They stood at the front door. He held the beer, not meaning to drink, wrong-footed, blinded by the low evening sun. Rose was clearing the bench in front of the living room window. She dragged away the long grass and the climber trailing over it.

'Here,' she said. 'We can sit on this.'

Reluctantly, he joined her, setting the bottle on the space of bench between them. After his grandfather's death, his parents went on coming out here on occasional weekends, to tidy the garden. He remembered playing here while they sat on this bench, with mugs of tea and his mother's fruit cake, in a rare hour of leisure. He had come as a teenager with his friends, drinking illicit cans of export after a day at Silver Bridge, swimming all afternoon, diving off the rocks into the deep pools. Then, while he was away from home, first as a student in Aberdeen, then working in the south, Gilbert had laid claim. Gilbert. The black cloud came over him again and he shivered in the sunshine.

'We should have a chat,' she said, lighting up, the smoke hovering in the still air in front of them.

'About?'

'Why'd you never sell this place?'

'Didn't get round to it.'

'Needs a bit of work now.'

He let this lie. Rose blew a smoke ring. He was conscious of her physical presence, of a force she still had. She wore no make-up for once, and her skin, though lined around the eyes, was clear and pale. Her hair was damp at the back of her neck as if she had just washed it. Where it was dry, it looked softer, as if the dead black dye were wearing off, and it gleamed reddish in the sun. She smelled of something that was not tobacco, something chemical he supposed, shampoo or shower stuff, but it was like fruit, sweet and wholesome. Her feet were bare, white beneath the black leggings, the polish on her toe nails dark red but chipped. Her feet looked vulnerable.

'What do you want?' he said. 'You can't stay here. How much is that hire car costing you? It's ridiculous. This isn't a place for anyone to stay in for weeks on end. I told you, I'm going to get the electricity cut off and the system drained. I should have done that years ago.'

'You never came back, did you?' she said.

'What?'

'I don't think you've been back since – since that time.'

It was this, her slight hesitation, gave her away. She too was afraid of that night, of her memories and what had happened. Even Rose, coarse and sly though she was, could not say aloud the words that had gone round and round in his head for days, weeks, years. Then because she could not say them, suddenly he could.

'He was dead, wasn't he?'

In the silence he heard her swallow. 'We drove till it was empty – the road. Still snowing. I was more scared of the snow than anything. What if the van got stuck? So I kept driving and I kept thinking, he'll wake up, he'll be ok, he'll not be well, of course not, we might have to get him to hospital.'

'Don't – I don't want to know.'

'You shouldn't ask then.'

They had both stood up, and so much taller, he looked down at her. He saw a middle-aged woman who could not change, someone stuck in the past, someone who had to do what she could to carve out her place.

'Jesus,' he said. 'I need to get out of here.'

She threw down the cigarette stub and stood on it, forgetting her feet were bare. With a yelp she hopped sideways, losing her balance. 'Fuck!'

He caught and held her. Now between them there was only the terror of what they had done. He pulled her nearer, rougher than he meant to be, but what he was mad enough to do to her he could not, for dizzying seconds, tell. Angrily, he thrust her away.

She laughed. 'Fuck off — that's not what I come for.'

Sickened, he said, 'Joe McCann. Were you always in with him, fleecing Gil, taking that stuff from his factory place – stuff he didn't know the value of?'

'Gil got his cut, he did all right out of it.'

We drove till the road was empty.

Joe *had* been here, all the time. He conjured the firelight, the conversation with Hugh, all those years ago: a black BMW. She couldn't have got Gilbert into the car without help. Joe was tough with hard muscled shoulders and powerful arms. It would have been nothing to Joe. *Joe had been here all the time.* A thrill of anger, or fear, went through him.

'Where is he now?'

To his surprise, she reared away from him, flushing. 'Shut up. You said you didn't want to know.'

'Joe,' he said. 'Joe, I meant.'

'Don't know. Don't care. Not where Helen thinks, at any rate.'

In prison, Catherine had said. Abroad, Helen believed. Exiled. Neither, he thought, he's still around somewhere, looking out for number one.

Catherine. Oh God. Impossible now to see her. He cursed himself for his stupidity in being here, even talking to Rose. That was mad, if anything was.

'You have to leave,' he said. Cash, he thought, ashamed, cash can't be traced. I could give her cash. He wanted no link with her to appear on the tracery of his life. Too late for that, but at least he could keep the money out of it.

She sat down on the bench again and lit another cigarette. 'Not sure why I came really. Thought I might see you, give you a fright, didn't see why you should get away with it. You got right away with it.'

'So did you.'

'It didn't mean nothing to you. *He* wasn't nothing to you.'

Stilled, he looked down at her. 'He was, God save me, my brother.'

She looked up at him, cheeks drawn in as she inhaled. 'That's what you think.'

What did she know? Something about Gilbert only Hugh had been told? What had Gilbert said to her?

'I'm going,' he said. 'And I want you out of here by the time I come back tomorrow.'

She said, 'He was *my* brother, if that makes you feel any better. Till he got adopted and I got fostered. My little brother. He was the cute one everybody wanted and I was the one got shoved pillar to post.'

'You're making this up,' he said.

'Not me. My social worker helped me trace my family.' She grimaced – it was hardly a smile. 'I don't give up easy when I get started on something. So I start by finding out where my little brother went, then after that I keep on at it, on and on, till I know where he is, and it turns out he's in London too.'

'You don't seriously expect me to believe this stuff?'

'Believe what you like.'

Kenneth thought of Gilbert's birth certificate, that he had seen just after Gilbert's arrival. His mother had explained this little boy was being adopted, and would be his brother. *So you'll have to be nice to him. Look after him.* He shook off the memory. The name on the certificate had not been Semple, whatever it was. Murphy, he thought, something Irish-sounding. He would know it if he heard it. Maguire. Mahoney. At the time, as an adolescent, he hadn't been willing to show any interest.

'His name wasn't Semple.'

'Neither was mine. That was thanks to *Mr* Semple.' She glanced sideways at him. 'I was married once. Long time ago – didn't last.'

'What was your name before that?' He would recognise it, if she said it.

'Monaghan.'

He went cold. Then reason rose up and told him it proved nothing, Gilbert could have told her this. He wouldn't give her the satisfaction of letting her see he was shaken.

'Why d'you think I kept looking out for him?' Rose said. 'It was all Joe's idea, but I made sure Gil never got in any trouble.'

He seemed to have shifted from one nightmare to another. 'What was Joe's idea?'

'Using The Factory.'

Now he understood. His mind leapt to it as if for years some rubbish had lain between suspicion and understanding, and a hot wind had just blown it away.

'Was it *all* stolen goods?'

'Jesus, no. Them sofas! Hot stuff he had to get out of London. Nothing too big – nothing that wouldn't fit in the van.'

'How long was it going on – all the time he had The Factory?'

'No, it was all totally legit at the start. Gil found some nice bits and pieces and I got a few sales through Joe. He sold them on. *Almost* totally legit, at any rate.'

'So what happened?'

'Joe needed a safe place well away from London. Who would think of looking in the fucking mountains, for God's sake? He would probably never have thought of it, but then he met Gilbert and bingo.'

'Did Gil know the stuff was stolen?'

She shrugged. 'He knew and he didn't. But Joe must have spun him some story. He could be very persuasive, Joe McCann.'

'But they met in London through you – it was because of you—'

'No.' She grinned. 'That's the laugh. They knew about each other because of me, me knowing Helen and her sister. Then they met here – at your wedding.'

Nausea rose in his throat with such suddenness it was all he could do not to vomit at her feet. He swallowed, his heart heaving, as rage took over.

Seeing his face she edged away. 'Hey – it was all Joe's idea.'

He was just sane enough to realise that was true. He saw them again, Joe with his film star looks, his cocky grin, his hand on Gilbert's arm as he drew him aside: not just to wind him up or annoy Hugh, not just to be provocative. It had all had a purpose.

Now there was someone else to blame. His mind veered away from the wedding to the cottage, that night, the fall, and the snow whirling past his windscreen as he drove away, his life destroyed.

'So it was all because of Joe you were here that night, that you were with Gil. Joe was here too, wasn't he? Where the fuck was he? Upstairs, listening?'

She shrugged. Dropping her cigarette stub, this time she put it out carefully with a small stone. 'He was keeping out of your way.'

He said grimly, 'He was right to do that.' Before he could ask another question, she said,

'It was an accident.'

'That's what we've been telling ourselves. All this time.'

'The thing is,' she said, looking straight at him, 'Joe always knew what to do.'

'What?' He felt sick again.

'When you'd gone he – he took care of everything.'

'*Jesus.* What does that mean?'

'You know,' she said. 'You know what it means.'

5

Catherine gave him until seven forty-five, which she thought generous. Then she called Kenneth's mobile number. It went to voicemail, but she did not leave a message. Restless, she had not eaten, but she was hungry now, or angry – she could not tell which. Irritable, at any rate. She opened the fridge door and stared helplessly at almost empty shelves.

She was eating scrambled eggs and toast when a text came in from Flora. *Skype, Mum? Ten mins?* She answered: *Fine.* She put her dishes in the sink and ran hot water over them. Then she went upstairs to get her laptop and turn it on. In the bedroom she could prop it on the dressing table and if she sat on the end of the bed, she was the right height for Flora to see her, and for her to see her daughter, half the world away in Toronto. Flora had been there doing research, but now her work was done she was staying on for the rest of the summer, travelling and seeing friends. She would be home by September, to complete her PhD.

In the big bedroom at the front of the house, which had not been Hugh's, Catherine waited for Flora's call to come through. The sun came into this room late in the afternoon leaving it warm, and it was still, at midsummer, light outside. Birds were singing in the rowan tree whose branches almost touched the window, their day not done.

Why had he wanted to see her, and why had he changed his mind? Disturbed, she thought, I have been *fine* without him. Those last weeks they had spent together before she left had been impossible; *he* had been impossible.

There was Flora now. She leaned forward and pressed the video symbol. Flora appeared, a little blurry, but her voice was as distinct as if she were in the next room. She wore a vest top and her fair hair was loosely tied up.

'Hi!'

'Hi. How are you?'

'Boiling – it's so hot here. We're having a barbecue tonight. What are you doing?'

'Nothing much. Helen's arriving tomorrow, so I've been making up her bed and getting the room ready.'

'Patrick too? The boys?'

'It's still term-time, with them. Patrick seems to be looking for another job.'

'Wow. His millions haven't lasted after all. Is he getting his red braces on again, do you think?'

Catherine laughed. 'I can't imagine it. He seems much too laid-back for that sort of job.'

'You know what, Mum?'

'What?'

'I had a dream about The Factory – Gilbert's place, that you used to take me to when I was little?'

'Yes.'

'It was incredibly *real*, the dream, so I told Matt and Sophie about it, about The Factory, and they said what was he doing now, Gilbert? I said I didn't know, he just left, and nobody knew where he'd gone. That's right, isn't it?'

'I wonder what made you dream about it,' Catherine said, uneasy.

'You've never heard from him?'

'No, never.'

'Sophie said why not try Facebook – you know, do a search, what do you think?' When Catherine did not reply she said, 'Mum? Can you still hear me?'

'Yes. Yes, I hear you. I don't think Gil would use Facebook. He might, but he wouldn't keep it up. He was more concerned to be out of touch than *in* touch.'

'That's a shame.'

From downstairs, there was the sound of her mobile ringing. She kicked the bedroom door shut with a stretched-out foot so that she would not hear it. Flora had begun talking about something else.

Later, she went down to check. Missed call, Kenneth Sinclair.

'Don't you ever want to give up work?' Helen asked. It's so lovely here and you'd have all the time you wanted for the garden.'

She was lying back in a garden chair, her glass of wine in the hand resting on its wide arm, eyes closed. Catherine, leaning forward for the bottle that stood on the wrought-iron table with the remains of a Victoria sponge, paused. Was this what she should do? Stop work, focus on the garden, have lunch with friends who had retired, bump into Kenneth now and again in Dingwall, and have nothing else in her life, plenty of time left over for thinking about the past?

'Four days a week would be perfect,' she said. 'But it's not possible yet.' She topped up their glasses. '*You're* still working.'

'Just part-time.'

The garden was full of birdsong and the scent of roses. Beyond where they sat by the back door, the lawn with its borders blooming with peonies and geraniums, gave way to the apple and plum trees, the shady part where you could not see the crumbling wall at the end. On the right were the fruit cages and vegetable beds, all neatly weeded and mulched, with rows of thriving peas, beans, cabbages and the feathery tops of carrots. Helen opened her eyes and gazed.

'You're so productive,' she murmured. 'All I have are weeds choking a few ancient perennials, and rhubarb that keeps coming up whether I do anything with it or not. I do try,' she added, defending herself. 'I'm just not so dedicated, and anyway, I have Pat and the boys.'

'The boys who are away at school and university, you mean, and Patrick who doesn't have a job?'

'Oh, shut up,' Helen said, but amiably.

They fell into easy silence, then Helen said, 'Have you heard anything more from the person you thought might be Rose?'

Catherine hated to lie, but perhaps she need not. Her sister, plumper now, and despite her fairness, brown already after years in the warmer south, her pretty polished shoulders and fair hair tumbling as usual from its loosely gathered knot, was not the nervous, unhappy woman of the years with Joe, or the anxious period after his disappearance. A meanness in Catherine she could not quite crush, made her want to startle her sister into realising it wasn't so easy here on her own, unsupported, with no happy ending. She had the house of course, Hugh's house, but it was not enough.

'Was that the doorbell?' Helen asked, sitting upright.

There was the crunch of feet on gravel and round the side of the house came Kenneth, looking to see if anyone was at home.

Catherine got up, brushing cake crumbs from her skirt.

'Very civilised,' he said. 'Wine and cake in the garden.'

'Hello, Kenneth.' Helen got up too and Kenneth went to shake her hand, but she hugged him. 'How are you?'

'Fine. I did ring the doorbell—'

'Sorry – Helen thought she heard it—'

Awkwardly, they stood as if they were all waiting to be told what to do next.

'Wine?' Helen asked. 'I'll get you a glass.'

'No – no, I'm driving back. A cup of tea would be good, though.'

On her own with him, Catherine said, 'Have a seat.'

They sat in silence, then Catherine, to fill the minutes till Helen came back, cut another slice of cake. 'It's fresh today – Helen made it. She seems to want to feed me up or something.'

'Look—' He put the cake aside. 'I'm sorry. Sorry about the other night. I made the mistake of going to the cottage—'

Nervously aware of Helen, she said, 'What happened? Is Rose still there?'

'Yes. I hope not *now*, but she was and – anyway, I was later back than I meant to be. I need to speak to you, but not with Helen—'

Helen was behind them, a tray in her hands, with flowered cups and a silver teapot that had been Hugh's mother's. 'I thought I'd make tea for all of us.'

She heard, thought Catherine.

Kenneth asked about the boys, and Helen, apparently unsuspicious, talked.

'Proud mother,' Kenneth said, teasing. 'And so you should be.'

He's trying hard, Catherine realised, not just hurrying the conversation on, in case Helen asks what it is she's not to know. She could not help but warm to him, the sun gleaming on his summer-brown skin, his profile strong and firm, still without a double chin, despite the extra weight he carried. She must not love him now; it would only end in misery again. Yet she itched, momentarily, for Helen to be gone. She would certainly not leave the two of them alone, since without her to intervene, Helen might question, and he might say something about – what?

Joe. It had to be Joe McCann. He must be at the cottage too. She went cold, thinking of how long it had taken Helen to get free. If he hadn't left her, she would still be in thrall. Women, she thought, we can be such fools.

'What was all that about?' Helen asked as soon as Kenneth had driven away.

'What?'

'You know.'

'He seems to want to see me again.'

Helen gazed at her for a moment, sceptical, then gave it up. 'Well, if that's it ... do you want to see him?'

Catherine, flushing (but that was only because of wine in the middle of the day) said, 'Nothing will come of it, anyway.'

'Do you still see dead people?'

This abrupt change made Catherine laugh. 'For goodness' sake, that sounds like somebody in a horror film!'

'You know what I mean. You said you saw Hugh.'

The back of his head, the narrow shoulders, the way he walked with a slight lift at each step: she had seen him in Debenhams when she was shopping last week, but that was ludicrous, and she could not tell Helen.

'It's a strange feeling,' she admitted. 'I even see Dad sometimes, except it's just another old man with a bit of a stoop, like he had, the last few years.'

'But not our mother,' Helen sighed.

'Helen, that's awful – don't!'

'I saw her a couple of weeks ago. She doesn't really know me now, though maybe she does, and actually hates me. I get this frightful *scowl*.'

'Oh dear. There's nothing we can do, and she's at least safe in the nursing home.'

'All the money from the sale of the house is going towards that very nice nursing home,' Helen said. 'We inherit nothing. Only from Hugh, who has always taken care of us.'

'You do say the most terrible things.'

'If you *say* them,' Helen pointed out, 'you don't think anything worse. I don't mean it. Or not much.'

The sun had dipped behind the apple trees and the terrace where they sat was growing cooler.

'Let's go in,' Catherine said, rising and gathering up cups and plates.

As she followed with the teapot, Helen said, 'You've never seen Gilbert, though.'

'What?' Catherine paused, the tray heavy in her hands, as if weighting her to the spot. 'No, I've never seen Gil. I keep expecting him to come back. But Kenneth said it was only Rose at the cottage.'

'*Rose?*'

'Sorry. I shouldn't have said anything.'

Helen was white. 'For God's sake. When was this?'

Catherine crossed the threshold of the back door and laid the tray on the kitchen table. Following her, Helen thumped the teapot down beside it.

'Tell me!'

'I don't know more than that. He found her there and told her to get out, but it seems she was still there when he went back the other night. Just Rose,' she added, trying to reassure, 'on her own.'

'Right. *You've* not seen her?'

'Let's go through—' Catherine went into the piano room, where the curtains were no longer drawn to protect the grand that Helen had once played. It was covered and that was enough, Catherine thought. She liked the way the afternoon sun slanted across the room that was so much warmer than the living room. They sat down on the chairs at either side of the empty grate. Catherine had a flash of memory, of Hugh and Gilbert sitting here, the fire in a glow of settled logs, the night of Hugh's party for her. She had met Kenneth then, and it had been the beginning of something. Something that was now over, she told herself, not believing it.

'Well?'

Helen would not let this go. What had possessed her to mention Rose?

'She seems to have been there for a few days – she obviously knew where to find the key, to get in. Kenneth hasn't been back there in years, as far as I know. He took against it after that awful night when Gil set it on fire.'

'What's she doing here after all this time?'

'He doesn't know. Probably she just wants money. She made her money sourcing stuff for Joe, didn't she? And with him out of the way—'

390

Helen's voice rose. 'But he's been gone for *years*.'

Catherine could understand why Rose was linked to Joe, but what was she to Gilbert, or he to her? This had always puzzled her. It seemed an odd friendship and even the business side did not convince. Rose took advantage of him, but Catherine could not fathom why Gilbert, naïve though he was, kept up with her. Certainly, once the business was done, The Factory gone, there seemed no reason for *her* to have anything to do with *him*. Besides, in London, surely there were better contacts she could make. The whole arrangement was inconvenient, at least. Yet the connection had clearly not been broken, and if anyone knew where Gilbert was, Rose did.

'Anyway, it's only Rose in the cottage, and she may have gone by now,' Catherine said. 'So there's no sense in worrying about it. I wish I'd known – I think I might have gone to see her myself. She's the only person who can tell us about Gilbert.'

'Or about Joe.'

'But—'

'I still want to know,' Helen said.

Catherine hoped Rose really had gone. 'There's no sense digging all that up again. You're happy now – let it be.'

'He's the boys' father. I can't.'

That was not why.

'Look, I'm sure Rose was never – Joe's not *with* her.'

'I never thought she was,' Helen said sharply. 'Not like *that*. She was useful to him, that's all.'

Catherine thought about Joe, his flashy, irresistible good looks, his mesmerising presence. It must have gone the *other* way, she thought, realising this for the first time. It would explain a lot, if Rose had fallen for Joe. Now she had thought of this, it seemed obvious, but she did not think she would say so to Helen.

They sat on, as the sun ebbed from the room. How Catherine wished she had said nothing. The last thing Helen needed was information about Joe. Anything to *do* with him.

Then Helen said, breaking the anxious silence, 'Let's go and see. I want to drive out there, and ask her.'

6

When Kenneth reached the works the yard was empty, the men still out. Kelly had spotted him from the office window and he was no sooner out of his car than she was running unsteadily towards him in her foolish high heels.

'I've been calling your mobile – did you not hear it?'

He took the phone from his pocket. 'Sorry – it's out of charge. My fault. What is it?'

'It's Donny – he fell off a ladder at the site and they had to get an ambulance – he's in Raigmore.'

'What? What ladder?'

'He was going up the scaffolding but—'

She was breathless and anxious, knowing it was bad, but not really why it was such a terrible thing that had happened, beyond Donny's broken leg. Elsie would have known; Elsie would have understood at once.

'Had he been drinking?'

She bit her lip, wide-eyed at his grim face and growing frightened. 'I don't know.'

'Fuck.' He strode towards the office. 'Get Andy.'

'He's gone to the hospital – I think he's still there.'

'How bad's Donny?'

'He's got a broken leg, but—'

'He's alive then?'

She giggled, on the edge of hysteria. 'Oh my God, yes, he's not *dead*, but Andy said—'

'Has he reported it?'

'Reported?'

'Never mind, call his mobile. Fuck this phone – get it charged, would you?'

She scurried after him into the office.

'I'm sure he'll be all right,' she said, as she waited for Andy to answer his phone.

'Let me spell this out. Donny's had an accident. We don't know if he was drinking. I've told Andy again and again he's to be sent home if there's any doubt. Health and Safety are going to be all over us. Jesus.'

'I'm sorry,' she said, sobbing, tears blurring mascara under her eyes. 'I'm really sorry—'

'It's not your fault. Here.' He took the phone from her. Andy's number had gone to voicemail. He left a curt message and hung up.

'I'm going to the site, to find out what happened. If Andy phones, get him to call me – damn, the phone. Give it to me, I'll charge it in the car.'

'You could take mine,' she said, her breath coming in little panicky gasps. She held out a pink smartphone with a sparkly cover.

Despite himself, he smiled. 'Never mind, Kelly, we'll sort it out. Will you stay here till I call you?'

'Yes, I don't mind, I'll easily stay late, Mr Sinclair.'

'It won't be too late, I hope.' He patted her shoulder. 'Dry up. It'll be all right.'

At the site, work had stopped and the men stood around talking and smoking. The job was almost finished and they were due to take the scaffolding down next day.

Derek, his clerk of works, came to meet him as he got out of the car.

'We've been trying to get hold of you.'

'I know. What happened?'

'Donny got here late, as usual. I said to him to go home, he shouldn't be on site. He says he needs the work. I tell him, if you need the work, keep off the drink.'

'Had he been drinking?'

'When's he not? Last night, I suppose. I've been sending him home, but he keeps turning up.'

'You shouldn't have let him near the place.'

'I thought he'd gone, but the minute my back's turned, he's up that fucking ladder—'

'Kit on?'

'Hard hat, hi-vis, the lot, thank Christ. He wasn't drunk – just—'

'I know.' Kenneth walked over to the scaffolding. 'Show me. Then we'd better get the forms filled out.'

From the site, his call made to the Health & Safety Executive, he drove to Inverness, and Raigmore Hospital. Andy called while he was still on the road.

'Broken pelvis, broken leg. It could be worse.'

'I dare say that's not much comfort to him right now.'

'They've moved him to Ward 10 from A&E. I was just going home, but I'll stay till you get here.'

'Don't bother. I'll see you in the office tomorrow – eight o'clock.'

'Ok, fine, see you then.'

Andy was subdued, as well he might be; it was his first experience of a serious accident.

In the ward, Donny was dozing, probably doped with painkillers. The cotton bedcover was raised above him on a cage, his pelvis and leg both in plaster. They expected the bones to knit, but it was going to take some time, the staff nurse told him.

'Does he have a relative we should call?' she asked. 'Your colleague didn't know, and Donny's not been making a lot of sense.'

'He's on his own,' Kenneth said. 'No close relatives.' He dug out a business card and handed it to her. 'Anything you need – call me.'

When she had gone, he sat on a grey plastic chair by Donny's bed. He was for the time being in a single room, dimly lit, the window looking out onto acres of car park. The subdued sounds of hospital business, of the world beyond, were just audible: a trolley rattling, voices, a telephone ringing briefly, and very faintly, traffic outside.

Donny turned his head, eyes bleary. 'Sorry, boss.'

'Aye, well.'

What could he say? Donny was never going to work for him again – work for anyone, probably.

At least I'm not in *his* state, he thought with absurd relief. It had occurred to him that he had no idea who would be contacted if *he* had an accident, and was taken to hospital. His parents both dead, his first wife remarried and his second wife estranged. No children, and his only brother— He scraped his chair back and

Donny stirred. 'I'm leaving now,' he said, 'but I'll look in again later. Just you get well.'

What was the point in saying anything else? In due course, someone would question him about the accident, as they would question everyone who had been there, and Andy and Kenneth who had not. It was probably going to be all right, if Derek was telling the truth and he had in fact told Donny to go home. Fairly all right, perhaps.

Still, it was only just beginning.

Driving home, he had a desperate and stupid longing to keep going on to Evanton, and Catherine. If Helen had not been there, he might even have done it.

7

It was after seven by the time they reached the cottage; Catherine refused to go until she was sure the effect of the lunchtime glass of wine had worn off. All the way there, she kept saying, 'I really don't think this is a good idea,' but when Helen said crossly, 'You didn't need to come,' her answer was always, 'You don't even know where it is.'

Beyond the farm the track was much more overgrown and rutted than when she'd come here last, taking Gilbert on one of many lifts home. She had offered to help Kenneth clear up after the fire but he had forbidden her to. He had been so angry and bitter she had not dared disobey, or question his decision to shut the place up altogether.

She hoped Rose had simply gone back to wherever she came from. Her heart sank when she saw the hire car, and the front door of the house standing open.

'Someone's here, at any rate,' Helen said. She was tense – with anticipation? Surely she didn't think Joe would be here? Why on earth would he? *Let him not be*, Catherine prayed.

It was only Rose, coming to the door when she heard the car. She was in leggings and a long black jumper, bare feet her only concession to the heat of the day. For a few seconds, she looked unchanged to both sisters as they got out of Catherine's car and walked up the path, pushing past the tangles of willowherb and wild raspberry encroaching from the derelict garden.

'We thought you might have left already,' Catherine said, since Helen seemed struck dumb, and stood behind her as if unable to move further.

Rose gazed at them, for a moment inscrutable. Then she waved them in. 'You want a beer? Cup of tea? It's all I got left.'

'You are leaving then?'

'In my own time.'

They followed her into the cottage, then wished they had stayed outside in the sunshine. Here, the air was stale and smelled of fried food and smoke, with an undertow of what might, Catherine thought, be mice. The place was dirty and unkempt, Rose's presence something on the surface of this neglect, not touching it. And yet, she seemed to belong far more than they did, with their clean hair and fresh clothes, their air of comfortable prosperity. You could not say Rose looked prosperous. For the first time, Catherine was unintimidated by her. She almost felt pity.

Helen had still said nothing. Then, as Rose filled the kettle (pointlessly – they were never going to drink or eat *here*) she asked, 'Are you on your own?'

Rose set the kettle down and stared at Helen, as if seeing her for the first time. 'What do you think?'

To stop Helen mentioning Joe, Catherine said, 'I wondered if Gilbert might be joining you – if he thought of coming home.'

Rose's face was blank, giving nothing away, but there was something contemptuous in her demeanour. She came closer, and they could smell cigarette smoke. Helen, before she could stop herself, recoiled. Catherine stood firm, waiting.

'You don't know, do you? Well, ask your husband. Ask *him* if Gil's coming back. He's the one who knows what happened to him.'

Catherine felt sick; there was something he had not told her. Now she wanted only to leave, to get out of the place for good. Damn Helen.

'He wants you out, I do know that,' she managed to say.

'I'll go in my own good time,' Rose said. 'He doesn't have any say in it. I got nothing to lose now, I can do what I like. Tell the whole story if I want to. Then me being in his fucking cottage will be the least of his worries.'

'I've no idea what you're talking about,' Catherine said coldly. 'Come on, Helen, let's go home.'

Rose, moving swiftly, snatched up a bottle of beer and raised it. Helen backed away, clutching Catherine's arm, and Rose laughed.

'Don't worry, I'm only a danger to myself these days.' She took up a bottle opener from the table and snapped off the lid. 'Cheers,' she said. 'Sure you don't want one?'

'Tell Gil when you see him,' Catherine said, 'that I miss him, and I wish him well. Tell him that, at least.'

'I would,' Rose said, 'if there was any fucking point.'

She watched them from the door as they got into the car, Helen scrambling in, as if in panic. Catherine drove on up the lane to the turning place that was still there, though also overgrown and difficult to negotiate, the ditch invisible. Holding her breath, she willed herself to manage it and get them swiftly out of here. As they drove past the cottage again, Rose waved the bottle in the air, then smashed it down on the front step, where it shattered round her bare feet, beer splashing up in huge beads of foam.

'She's mad,' Helen cried, 'she's absolutely crazy. Kenneth should get the police, he should have her *evicted*.'

They were both shaking.

'I'll call him,' Catherine promised.

'Oh, I wish we hadn't gone there,' Helen moaned. 'As soon as I saw her I felt threatened. Do you think she knows *anything* about Joe? But she wouldn't have told me if I'd asked her. Would she?'

Catherine, filled with foreboding, did not reply.

When they were home and Helen was comforting herself with a large glass of wine, Catherine called Kenneth: first his home number, then his mobile. But Kenneth was at Raigmore, sitting beside Donny's bed, and the phone was in his car.

8

The next day, when she could still get no answer from his mobile number, Catherine tried the Sinclair Construction office. A girl answered, sounding young: Kelly, she remembered.

'He's not available, I'm afraid. Who shall I say called?'

'It's his – it's Catherine. Catherine Sinclair.'

A little gasp as this registered. 'Oh, Mrs Sinclair, sorry, he's got the Health and Safety people in, so he'll be tied up all day.'

'Is something wrong?' She had lived with him long enough to know this could be serious. 'Sorry, none of my business. Would you just tell him I called about the cottage? He'll know. But don't interrupt him if he's busy.'

'The cottage. Right, I'll tell him.'

Catherine went upstairs. Helen was still in bed, but awake, her iPad propped against her bent legs. 'Hi, just reading the news. How are you going to vote?'

'Vote? In what?'

Helen sighed. 'The referendum, of course. You're not going to vote for independence for Scotland?'

'Why shouldn't I?'

'Because then we'd be in different countries and I'd need a passport to come and visit you.'

Catherine sighed. 'Don't be so silly. Anyway, that's the last thing on my mind right now.' She sat on the side of the bed.

'Have you spoken to Kenneth?' Helen asked.

'Not yet.'

'She's not safe, is she? What if she sets fire to the place again? I bet it was her fault the last time. I honestly think she's gone off her head. She was always a bit strange.'

'Helen.'

'What?'

'You don't seriously want to find Joe, do you?'

Helen's gaze slid away. 'Oh,' she said, plucking at the duvet, 'I don't know.'

'You're happy with Patrick. Don't risk that.'

Helen's eyes filled with tears. She tried to blink them away, but more came. 'I don't want to. Patrick's so sweet to me.'

'Well then. I was relieved when I met him, and happy to see how kind he is, how good for you.'

Helen dashed away the tears. 'You thought he was far too young.'

'No, I didn't. Not really. That's not important.'

'You seemed to think it was. And you thought it wouldn't last.'

'I was wrong then. I'm glad I was wrong. I worry about you, that's all.'

'Do you?' This seemed a new idea to Helen. 'Don't. I'm fine. I'm happy now.'

'You won't be if you let Joe back in.'

Helen sighed and closed the iPad, laying it on the floor beside the bed. 'I never told you – Gaynor called me again.'

'Who's Gaynor?'

'Her husband Brian worked with Joe. They were both in antiques.'

'What did she say?'

'Years ago, before I met Patrick, she called me several times leaving messages. I never called her back.'

'Then don't.'

'That's what I'm saying – I was scared, so I didn't. I realised I didn't want to find out about Joe, if she knew where he was or something like that. Anyway, that was years ago, and I think actually she was just trying to give me a friendly warning. Then a couple of weeks ago there was another call. This time she didn't leave a message, so maybe it was a mistake, she didn't even mean to call my number. But it frightened me, the thought that Joe – that he might – well, just the thought of maybe going back to…that life.'

'Yet you were determined to see Rose.'

The sun had crept round to the bedroom window and a shaft of yellow lit up the bed, striking across the pale blue duvet and Helen's hands, restlessly moving, the gold ring Patrick had given her winking with diamonds.

'I don't know what got into me,' she said. 'Just – I thought – if he's here I could challenge him, face him, make him tell me—'

'What?'

But Helen did not know, or could not tell her sister. After a moment she said, 'Let's do something nice today, since it's my last.'

'The sun's coming out.' Catherine got up, straightening the duvet. 'I'll make us a picnic and we'll go – oh, to the sea. Rosemarkie, or up to Cromarty. What about that?'

'Lovely,' Helen said, leaning back on her pillows and closing her eyes. How anxious she looks, Catherine thought. Rose's fault. Joe's fault.

Helen had flown home by the time Catherine managed to speak to Kenneth.

'I'm sorry you've not been able to get hold of me,' he said. 'I realise you've phoned several times, but we had an accident.'

'At work?'

'On site. I don't think there will be too many repercussions. I hope not.'

'Surely not,' she said. 'You're always so careful.'

'Not careful enough, it seems.'

'Are *you* all right?'

A pause. Had she said the wrong thing?

'I'm fine. Is Helen still with you?'

'No, she flew home yesterday.'

'Then would you like to go ... I mean, meet me? Coffee or something? Lunch?'

'Yes,' she said, almost as he finished speaking. 'Yes, I'd like to.'

'What did you want to speak to me about – will it keep till we meet?'

She thought of Rose smashing the bottle, that look on her face. 'Yes ... yes, of course.'

'What are you doing tonight?'

'Nothing.'

'I'll book somewhere.'

'Come round, if you'd like to. I can cook.'

He did not hesitate either. 'Seven thirty? I'll be here till gone six, and I need to go home and change.'

Catherine had been sitting at the bottom of the stairs while she spoke to Kenneth. Now she leaned against the banisters, the phone slipping from her hand. The telephone in Hugh's house had always been in the hall, with a bedroom extension, and she had never had that changed. It was handy to be able to sit here, a neutral temporary place, and she went on doing it, though she could have taken the handset elsewhere.

Weariness swept through her. I can't be bothered getting up, she thought. Around her the house was silent, then the hum of the fridge started and she became conscious that from here she could also hear the carriage clock in the piano room. If she got up and went in there, Hugh might be in one of the fireside chairs and she could sit opposite, and ask him what to do.

No need. She knew what he would say. So she would be pleasing Hugh, and that was a good thing. A pulse quickened that had been dormant a long time. You might call it excitement, she thought, but she knew it was something else. What a fool – you're over fifty. You should know better. Sitting perfectly still on the stairs, admiring with one tiny part of consciousness the look of her new pale blue loafers against the crimson hall carpet, she felt something momentous happen, her whole body alert and quivering and yielding to it, so that she could do nothing but cling to the newel post with one hand, balance herself on the stair with the other, and wait, wait, for this to pass. When it did, she would be a different woman, all over again.

9

Kenneth was telling himself this might, after all, be another chance. Don't kid yourself, his inner voice tormented, but he ignored that. Take it easy and see how it goes, he decided.

He could not wait to get everyone off the premises. Andy had offered to lock up, but all this week he had taken responsibility for that himself, as if there was no one else he could trust. He could see how Andy was taking this. Too bad, he shrugged, driving home fast to Strathpeffer. He stopped on his way to pick up a bottle of wine, and found himself hesitating at the banks of flower bouquets at the front of the supermarket. Don't be a fool, he told himself finally, and must have said it aloud, since a woman standing nearby gave him a startled look and moved away.

His own house smelled musty when he went in to get changed. No wonder – it was barely lived in. All he did here was watch TV, eat easily heated-up meals, and sleep. It was no longer his refuge and pleasure. When had it altered? Ah, he knew that.

He locked the door behind him and set off, the bottle of wine rolling on the passenger seat next to him. This time, he turned left without a thought of the cottage, and was well on his way to Evanton when he began to ponder going out there to check Rose had really gone. What was there here for her now? It did *her* no good to rake up the past, any more than it did him. He wouldn't think about it. Not now. He had other plans.

Catherine was taking good care of Rowanbank. The lawns were mowed close, the flower beds kept tidy, and she had had the external paintwork renewed. Tubs of red pelargonium stood on either side of the entrance, jewel-bright in the low evening sunshine. The gravel crunched beneath his wheels as he came up the drive, and for a bewildering giddy moment he was back fifteen years, calling on Hugh, expecting to see a black Labrador on the doorstep, the sound of the Goldberg Variations filtering out into the open air.

Catherine appeared at the door in a striped apron over her jeans and white top, her hair caught behind her ears, the sparkle of earrings catching the light as she came out to meet him at his parked car. As he held out his bottle of wine, he remembered suddenly that this was where they had first met.

Indoors, the rich smell of tomato and garlic gave him a yank of hunger.

'It's nearly ready. Would you like a drink – orange or something? Since you're driving?'

The journey here had taken him a long way in his imagination. It was like spinning a new web to catch her in, that this time she must not even sense until it wound about her, about both of them. He had even begun to assume he would not be driving home. Seeing her, friendly but still cool, he relinquished this fantasy. Wait, he told himself. This could all go wrong – it did before.

'Orange is fine,' he said. 'Have you any ice?'

In the kitchen she poured two tall glasses of orange juice, putting a sprig of mint in each, and chunks of ice. He watched her long fingers, delicately snipping mint. They were chilled when they touched his, handing him his glass.

'I've put up the little gate-legged table in the piano room,' she said. 'I thought we'd feel silly looking at each other from either end of the big dining table. And the kitchen is a bit small.' He followed her through the hall. 'It's my only complaint about this house,' she went on. 'Oh well, not a complaint, that would be ridiculous.'

They settled in the fireside chairs. In the grate, on this warm evening, was a white and gold vase filled with pink roses from the garden. For a moment they sat in silence but he had the feeling there was something Catherine wanted to say. He waited.

'I never got the chance to ask you,' she said, 'or I didn't take the opportunity—'

'What?'

'Whether you ever minded about the house, about Hugh leaving it to Helen and me.'

'It wasn't up to me to mind or not,' he said brusquely. 'Not my business.'

It was as if the years had gone, and they were back where they had started, at cross purposes already. He needed to say something that would sound less – what? Abrupt, maybe. She was trying to apologise when no apology was needed, but he wasn't helping matters. He tried again.

'Hugh told me about his will. I really didn't mind. After all, *I* didn't need a house and—'

'I did?'

'You never suited that miserable place in Inverness.'

'That was my home!'

He had done it again. 'Sorry. Sorry, I didn't mean—' He started to laugh.

'What on earth is so funny?'

She had not thawed a bit; he had offended her.

'Oh, damn you, Catherine, you get my back up every time, and I annoy the hell out of you. Sorry.' He sobered. 'I shouldn't have come. Do you want me to leave?'

'Leave?' She flushed. 'I spent ages making the lasagne!'

'In that case, since I'm starving and it smells wonderful, I'll stay and eat it. Then I'll go.'

They stared at each other, astonished at what had happened already. Then she smiled, and he gave way. 'Sorry. Sorry, sorry.'

'Stop saying that! There's nothing – well, never mind. Let's start again.'

'We keep doing that.' He finished the orange juice, the mint catching in his teeth. 'For God's sake, get me a real drink.'

She got up. 'We'll have a glass of wine. By the time you've eaten half of that lasagne you'll be fine to drive home. I made a lot.'

He rose too and stood facing her. 'That's what I made for you,' he said.

'What?'

'Lasagne. The first time you came to my house.'

'Oh dear,' she said. 'That wasn't such a success.'

'We'll have to see if we can do better this time,' he said, meaning it to sound like a joke, but he could not go on.

'I'd better check the oven—'

He should eat the meal and go home. He was finished with women, such a failure as the whole thing had turned out to be, and now his business threatened, and the cottage probably wrecked for good by that bloody woman. He should eat the food and go.

Instead, before she was beyond reach, he moved close and

took her hands, her cold hands, and held them. After a moment, she moved as if to pull away, but he gripped harder. 'Food first, eh, and drink. Then … then we'll see.'

'Yes,' she said. 'We will.'

He followed her to the kitchen, so that she could pour wine and he could help her carry the dishes to the other room.

The food was good and the wine, despite his hasty choosing, was all right. She relaxed, and so did he.

'By the way,' he said, 'you never said what you wanted me for – Kelly said you rang up last week.'

So she told him.

When he heard what had happened, and what Rose had said, he decided he would talk too. Softened by the hit of wine after a day without food, fooled by her newly tender consideration, and her beauty, and his own folly, his own hopes, he thought he could at last tell her the truth.

10

'I've even thought of leaving altogether, not that that would help. But if I left the area, it would mean selling Rowanbank, and I don't think I can bear that. I have to do *something*, though, I can't just pretend nothing's happened.'

'But what *has* happened?' Helen asked again. She had never heard Catherine sound like this.

'I'll tell you when I see you.'

A pause, while Helen wondered what to say, and Catherine's tight voice was replaced by the echoing noises of the airport where she waited for her flight to Gatwick.

'So how long do you think you'll stay with us? I mean, it's lovely, I'm very glad you're coming but—'

'A few days. I'm back at work next week and I have to be there. I'm speaking at a conference in Glasgow. Oh God, I can't imagine that right now. But work's a relief so perhaps I'll be glad of it. Only – just now I can't—' To Helen's horror, her sister's voice cracked and she could not speak. Catherine, who never cried, was breaking down.

'Oh, you must stay as long as you like! We'll sort out the space, don't worry, the boys won't be home all that long, Matt's going to France and Luke—'

'It's all right. A few days is all I need.' Catherine was in control again. 'I have to go now. I'll call when I'm on the train to Victoria.'

Helen rushed through to where Patrick and Luke were watching Wimbledon.

'Something's terribly wrong with Catherine,' she said. 'I'm so worried.'

Patrick reached out his arm to enclose her as she sank onto the long sofa between them. 'Here, come and have a cuddle. It's two sets all.' On her other side, Luke patted her thigh.

'You all right, Mum?'

Catherine laid out her case on the conveyor belt and put her iPad, jacket and polythene bag containing cleanser, moisturiser, scent and toothpaste on a tray. She was not wearing a belt and her shoes were light flats, so she did not have to take them off. She waited to be waved through the scanner. She felt as if a bubble of some kind enclosed her so that everything was muffled, and unable to touch her. She moved carefully inside the bubble, silent and holding herself straight.

There was a crowd in Departures; the holiday season had begun. She began to look for a seat where she could wait in peace without being jostled by tourists. At the far end, a figure sat reading, stooped a little, his head bent over a paperback, his hair thin on top, fairish grey hair. *Oh, Hugh, if only it could be you.* For a moment it was, and she glided towards him with her little suitcase following her on its smooth wheels. When the man looked up he was a stranger, not as old as Hugh had been, nor as kindly in his expression.

What if they are all here, she wondered, in a sort of cosmic ante-room? What if I spot someone else? Then she did. James, who had been so good to her, wearing a pale green jersey over an open-necked shirt, sitting close to a woman in a beige jacket. James looking as if he might be ready to play golf, except that he too had to wait here, his dark head bent towards his wife, while she examined their boarding passes. She was quite close before she could be sure it was not James. Oh, for goodness' sake, her common sense cried, of course it can't be him! Yet she went on looking to see who else might be there.

Seated in the café, hands clasping a takeaway coffee, was a young man with a broad nose and thick brush of hair whom she could not fail to recognise. He would still *be* this age, he would be no older than when she had left him in London all those years ago, taking Flora with her, and leaving him to have his dream of making money in another country. She felt giddy, as if it was no longer a silly game, as if it might indeed be Alan drinking coffee at Inverness Airport, and perhaps waiting for her to come and give an account of herself, of what she had done in all the years granted to her that he had not had.

I'm going crazy, Catherine thought, I should get a cup of tea to steady myself.

Just the act of asking for the tea and paying for it, helped. She felt better, and could even sit near the young man who was of course not Alan, nothing like him when you got closer.

The trouble with allowing the bubble to vanish was that she began to think again, to go over and over what Kenneth had said, and how they had parted. If she had ever been so stupid as to think they could start again – well, that was over. How could she ever trust him? All those years of lying couldn't just be forgotten, even if what he'd told her didn't matter. He was so broken though: it was not as if it had made no difference to him. He had paid for it. Her mind darted between two extremes, each for a few seconds seeming the only one that counted. There was Helen too – what should she tell her? She could not decide. She sat stirring the tea bag in the mug, watching the milk dissolve.

'Wait,' he said. 'You have to wait, and let me tell you all of it.'

'There's *more?*'

'There's who Rose is, *was*, and what Joe was up to. His connection to them both. There's more.'

'It makes no difference,' she said, 'no difference now, since Gil is dead. I don't care about them, I only cared about him. He was so vulnerable, he was such a *kind* person. And you left him, you left him to die, you did nothing, you left him with Rose. Who *didn't care.*'

'She did,' he said. 'She cared because he was her brother.'

'*What?* No.'

'That's what she said. It's possible I suppose. He was never formally adopted, and I know nothing about his real family or his background. My parents never spoke about it, and they left no papers, no evidence, you might say. My mother always wanted to believe he was their own son. But he wasn't. He never was.'

'He could have been – if *you'd* accepted him.'

'It was nothing to do with that,' he said, and anger rose, blinding, for a moment. No, if he lost his temper, it would be over; she would make him go. 'Look, I didn't believe her, I think she's a liar who makes things up to suit herself. But ... this time, when she came back, I wondered. She's in a bad way. What you said about her – when you and Helen saw her. She's wrecked.'

She was silent for so long he did not dare speak again or even move. If I move, he thought, it's over. Then she said, 'Did Hugh know?'

415

'No. He was the only person apart from you that I *could* have told. But I didn't. Then he was too ill.'

'All right, tell me. Tell me the rest.'

So he did.

He even told her how for years he had been haunted by the landscape on either side of the A9, how he had thought of searching every belt of trees, then realised it would make no difference, or make it worse, because if he ever found Gilbert he could no longer pretend he might still be alive.

'All my adult life, I was glad when I didn't have to see him, have anything to do with him. But after that there were times when I would have given anything to see him. Ironic, eh? It would have been such a relief. Then the months went on. Nothing. And I began to be glad I'd never have to see him again.'

'Had you *no* sense of responsibility? Of guilt?'

'You don't know me at all,' he said, 'if you think I don't feel guilty.'

'You *should* feel guilty. You left him when he was dying.'

'I didn't know that,' he said, and it was as if he believed this now. 'He wasn't moving, but he could just have been unconscious. I went for help.'

'You didn't bring any.'

'I was going to take him to Raigmore – I'd have done that. But I told you – they had gone.'

'Didn't you think maybe *Rose* had taken him to hospital?'

'She was terrified. She didn't want anybody asking her awkward questions. Neither did Joe. And whatever Joe said, she would go along with it.'

'So why did Rose come back? Now.'

'I wondered if she wanted to punish me, if she blamed me, but if it was that, she'd have come sooner. In the last day or two it's occurred to me they might have left something behind and she thought, after all this time, nobody else would be looking for it. So she could come and get it.'

'What sort of thing?'

'I don't know,' he said. 'Something small, that Joe forgot to put in the car, or somehow missed. Part of their stash, whatever you call it. God knows, it's not something I've any experience of, stolen goods.'

'So if she's gone, it means she's found it and she's left.'

'Perhaps.' He sighed. 'I'll go out tomorrow and see if she's still there.'

'I don't think that's why,' Catherine said, after a moment. 'Too many years have gone past. I think she came because she has nothing and no one else. She seemed, I don't know, a lost soul.'

He snorted at that; he had no pity.

'I also think,' Catherine went on, 'that she was in love with Joe. Not that it was requited, I'm sure. I doubt if he ever cared for anyone but himself.'

'That I do agree with.'

'None of us liked Rose. We didn't give her a chance, maybe,' Catherine said. 'I think we underestimated her intelligence. And maybe...maybe her *need*.'

Still scornful, but not wanting to argue, he could not answer that. They fell into silence, Catherine rolling her full wine glass between her hands, unable to drink. He could read nothing from her face, so remote and pinched.

'You wouldn't burden Hugh with it, but now you've burdened me,' she said, with a faint sigh.

'I'm sorry.' The spasm of guilt was as bad as any he'd had, but it couldn't remove the relief he felt that he *had* told her.

'It's over, though, and there's nothing you or I can do.'

She looked at him, her face unreadable and sad – perhaps also disbelieving.

'What can I say to Helen?' she asked at last. 'All those things we've not told each other over the years, the things I kept from her about myself, about you, about my feelings. Maybe this is just one more thing I shouldn't tell her. I didn't want to talk to her about Joe ever again. She's not really over him – he still has a kind of hold on her.'

'Maybe if you tell her the truth, that will finish it. She'll see him for what he was.' As soon as he said this, he knew he had laid himself open. 'And now you know all about *me*.'

'It's different,' she said, though she did not look at him. 'Joe was – is I suppose – a criminal. He didn't care. You do.'

'Yes,' he said, then driven beyond common sense to be honest, added, 'but not always.'

At last she looked up and straight at him. Dismayed, he saw there were tears in her eyes. 'I've never once seen him,' she said. 'I thought that meant he was still alive, somewhere in the world, poor Gilbert.'

'I don't understand.'

She dabbed the tears away, and tried to explain.

'I know it's stupid and I'm not a fanciful person, so I don't know why this happens to me.'

'It's common,' he said. 'It's a normal thing, to think you see someone who's just died, it's part of grief, not being able to believe it.'

'No,' she said, 'I know about that. This goes on happening years after and there's no pattern to it.'

For a moment he did not speak, but he topped up the wine in his glass. 'You've never seen him,' he said at last.

'No, but you can't read anything into that. You can't take a single bit of comfort from it. I won't let you. You *should* feel guilty.'

'It put me on the other side,' he said.

'The other side of what?'

'That's what I ask myself. The other side of some sort of divide. The guilty and the not guilty. There was no way of crossing it – of reaching over. Reaching you. It sounds crazy, but I *was* crazy. I was like a fly on a windowpane, I knew there must be a way out, but I just kept bashing myself against the glass. And then you left. Of course you did.'

They stared at each other, and it was as if, despite all their misunderstandings and crossed wires in the past, that gulf of incomprehension between them had vanished. Then she turned away, as if to say, too late.

'I'm sorry,' he said again.

'So am I. Oh, so am I. This is the worst thing that could have happened. For all of us.'

He put his glass down on the table. 'I'd better go.' He didn't want her to see how close he was to giving way altogether. 'I'll call a taxi. I'd better not drive, though I feel stone cold sober. I wish I didn't.'

'Wait,' she said as he got to his feet, the chair squeaking as it scraped over the polished floor. 'I'll make up a bed. There's no reason you can't stay. Just for tonight.'

He thought of lying in a room that was not her room, sleepless. He couldn't do it.

'I'll call a taxi.'

But she got up too and moved round the table, agitated, her hands raised in protest. 'I can see you're upset. Please don't leave when—'

He held his breath. 'Only if I stay with you,' he said. 'Only with you.'

He moved towards her and helplessly her hands fluttered away. Then he realised, she's trembling, I've frightened her. But whether she was afraid of what he had told her, or of the state he was in, he did not know. It wasn't true that he felt sober. His head was throbbing and he knew he was no longer thinking like a sane man. What did he hope? That in the morning she would no longer be afraid, that she would even forgive him?

No. What he hoped was that in the morning, it would seem, as it so often had before, like a terrible dream you must try to forget.

Catherine left the half-drunk tea on the café table and wheeled her suitcase towards Gate 1. She entered that state of suspended animation you must adopt in a long queue that moves like a sluggish raindrop down a dry window. Since she had felt like this all day, it was easy to slide into a dream and think of nothing. Indeed, she had to think of nothing; to think at all was too painful. No wonder she was seeing things.

Then, as she finally reached the uniformed girl checking boarding passes, and went beyond her to the exit, she half turned back to the Departure Lounge, one quick glance, for no reason, just a last look.

That was when she saw him.

Only Gilbert moved like that, on his long stork legs, only Gilbert made that swooping pounce on a chair when he had decided where to sit, just as he and Flora had all those times, diving between sofas across the breadth of the factory floor, choosing a new seat to try out.

She was pressed forward by the people behind her and in a

second was out of the building. She looked back, straining to see through the windows, but it was too difficult, the place too distant, the crowd too dense.

He had gone. She had lost him.

Moira Forsyth writes with warmth and sensitivity. THE TIMES

Tell Me Where You Are

The Douglas family is full of secrets. Now there's another secret, and a new crisis is looming.

'Sensitively written. contains keen characterisation and a strong awareness of the problems facing women today.'
Scottish Review of Books

Paperback ISBN: 9781905297350
RRP: £7.99
Also available in eBook